Dear John

Happy reading
in 1990

from

a 7 q

WITCHCRAFT
Nigel Williams

faber and faber
LONDON · BOSTON

First published in 1987 by
Faber and Faber Limited
3 Queen Square London WC1N 3AU

Photoset by Parker Typesetting
Service Leicester
Printed in Great Britain by
Mackays of Chatham Kent

British Library Cataloguing in Publication Data

Williams, Nigel, *1948–*
Witchcraft.
I. Title
823'.914 [F]   PR6073.I4327

ISBN 0-571-14823-9

'Rebellion is as the sin of witchcraft.'

from
The Book of the Prophet Ezekiel.

PART ONE

THE WITCHFINDER

1

Lambourne Hospital,
Gloucestershire

July

I saw life differently then. Lying here, on my clean white bed, as the ward trolley begins its afternoon rounds, laden with drugs, I try to picture myself on that day in February when I went into the Museum for the first time. All the images are of someone hopelessly young. Even when I try to describe it, the voice I reach for is one that was mine before he took over my life, its tone one of mild self-deprecation, its promise that old English one of decency and restraint. But this is not that kind of story. It's a story of wilful cruelty, of decay and betrayal, and, listening to my voice now, as it tries to tell it Jamie's way, I hear the irony shade into bitter cynicism, and the hovering giggle slide up the scale until it is a hyena crow of self-satisfaction.

'And what,' said the young man behind the desk, 'is your interest in the seventeenth century?'

He asked this question in the tone of a hotel desk clerk, checking in a couple who have just announced they have no luggage, no means of identification, and that their married name is Smith. It was as if the British Museum was bombarded with requests from suspicious individuals eager to try any excuse or stratagem just as long as they could get in out of the cold and wrap their fingers round a juicy slice of pornography.

'I am a writer,' I said, pausing as I always do after this description of myself.

The young man sneered visibly. 'They all say that', his expression seemed to say.

'And an honours graduate in history from the University of Oxford,' I went on.

This had absolutely no effect on him whatsoever.

'Yes?' he said.

3

From the pocket of my anorak I got out the crumpled letter which Gottlieb had written on my behalf.

'This is a letter telling you who I am,' I said.

TO WHOM IT MAY CONCERN

Jamie Matheson is one of the most astonishingly talented young novelists and screenwriters to have emerged in Britain during the last five years. Witty, ferocious and intellectually rigorous, he has been translated into both Finnish and Norwegian.

He is at present working on a project for this company that requires historical research and I would ask that you give him access to the facilities of the British Library,

Yours sincerely,
Nat Gottlieb
Executive Producer – '*Cavaliers*'.

The young man looked up quizzically.

'*Cavaliers* eh?' he said.

'It's a working title.'

'Mmm.'

He pouted again and glanced over my left shoulder like an orchestral player wearily registering the eccentricities of yet another conductor. I marvelled once again at Gottlieb's ability to splash about adverbs of degree such as 'astonishingly' or 'uniquely', especially when yoked to adjectives such as 'brilliant', 'talented' or 'powerful', on occasions when these adjectives were to be applied to writers to whom Gottlieb had paid money. Words mean nothing to Gottlieb, except as a way of getting what he wants.

I didn't like the Finnish and Norwegian bit either. Just because my books aren't of world import, i.e. long. Finns are very discriminating. I don't want to be of world import anyway. It's too late. I no longer have the urge to write sentences that wind gloriously upward like a mountain road, snaking through mists, along the edge of ravines, skirting pine forests, vertical

4

clumps of rock and dizzying drops to dried out riverbeds, to come out on level ground, nothing below them, nothing beside, behind or before them, nothing, in fact, in view, but a magnificent prospect of absolutely fuck all. On my passport it says 'Screenwriter'. I'm proud of that.

'And how long,' said the young man, 'will . . . *this* . . .' (here he tapped Gottlieb's letter contemptuously) '. . . take?'

This was obviously a trick question.

'Clearly,' I said, 'it's not a question of years.'

I should bleeding well cocoa said the expression on the young man's face.

'But,' I went on,' it's not something I could do in . . . weeks.'

Christ, there were several million books in there. What did the guy want? For me to break down and admit that I lacked the intellectual equipment to know which were the right ones for me to read? The young man squirmed forward on his seat and sighed elaborately. On the other side of the room a young woman was talking her way quietly, earnestly into possession of a reader's ticket. What was she offering? Money? Sexual favours? A combination of the two?

'Six months?' I said, trying to keep the pleading tone out of my voice. But he was ready for this show of reasonableness.

'Do you have any identification?'

'I'm sorry?'

'A driving licence?'

I looked blank. He became patient.

'You see I have no proof that you are . . .' – he tapped the letter again – 'Jamie Matheson.'

He said this is a tone of rank disbelief, as if to suggest that not only was it unlikely that I bore the names in question but that 'Jamie Matheson' itself was such an improbable construct that the chances were heavily against anyone anywhere actually being him.

To reassure myself as much as anyone else, I groped in the saddle-bag that lay at my feet. The young man peered over at me as my hands scrabbled blindly for that rare thing, a copy of my last novel. As I fished it out and thrust the back of the jacket at him, I felt, once again, a stab of doubt about the title. *Say*

Goodnight to Alfie Barnacle. No. No no no no no.

'There,' I said, pointing at the black and white photograph on the back, 'that's me. Author. Picture of me. OK?'

He pursed his lips. Even the studio portrait made me look like something that crawled out from under a stone in a Scandinavian fairy story. Meg always said that I looked like a troll. Jake Bolewski's picture just made me look like a carefully lit troll.

'Jamie Matheson,' said the young man, in tones that hovered just on the edge of a giggle, 'is already widely known as a screenwriter, author of the thirteen part series *Dust Ashes* . . .' He widened his eyes and drew his chin into his neck like a chicken on the move. I suppressed the urge to discuss the work in question.

'Me,' I said thickly, 'I wrote it.'

Even as I said it I wished, once again, that it were not true.

The young man did a lot of squinting between studio portrait and subject. He reminded me of an East German customs official, or the keen young Cuban who kept me for three hours at Havana Airport. Finally he said, wearily:

'Do you know which papers you'll be looking at?'

'If I knew that,' I said between clenched teeth, 'I wouldn't need to go in in the fucking first place would I?'

'Will you need to go to the North Library?'

'I will need,' I said, 'to go to the South Hall, the West wing, the North Transept, the East Tower and the South East Corridor. I want to go all over the British Library. Please.'

'Very well,' said the young man, 'we can probably issue you with a ticket for six months.'

He started to recite the rules governing the conduct of those lucky enough to get into the British Library but the life had gone out of him. I could tell he was already gearing himself up for the next encounter – some charlatan calling himself Graham Greene perhaps, or a Nobel prizewinner in search of a quiet kip. I was photographed, presented with a plastic ID card and sent on my way.

I was in. I was a historian once again. A serious person.

The first thing that struck me as I stepped into that great, echoing dome, was that my friend was not doing his job thoroughly enough. It was abundantly clear to me from one

6

glance at the figures bowed over volumes, each eerily still in a private pool of light, yellow as parchment, that the British Museum Reading Room contained the largest collection ever of madmen, freaks, timewasters, and tramps in search of low-cost daytime accommodation.

There also didn't seem to be many books there.

Fearing that, if I remained standing too long without apparent purpose, uniformed men would appear out of the ground and hurl me back into the foyer, I started out at a brisk walking pace for the centre of the circle.

Between me and the central desk lay a circular block, divided into segments marked with enigmatic inscriptions. HUL said one of them, another simply ING. Each segment of the circle was packed with tall, brown volumes. They were the closest thing to books I could see. I veered off from my confident progress and, seizing the nearest to me, yanked it out of the shelves in a manner intended to suggest I had better things to do with my time. I had no idea what it might contain. From my limited experience of the British Library, I guessed it might be the by-laws, or a 7,000 page curse on all users of the place.

It seemed to be some kind of catalogue. But it was only when I had turned over several of the stiff cream pages, studded with pasted slips, that I realized quite how much of a catalogue it was. The low wooden block filled a circular space of upwards of fifty yards. There must be well over a thousand of the brown volumes and each volume was well over a thousand two-foot square pages and on each two-foot square page were hundreds of the pasted slips and my Christ there were absolutely fucking millions of books in here (wherever they were hiding them) and where oh where was I going to start?

It was clear to me that this catalogue was a work of reference encompassing all the known world – except possibly the bit of it recognized by jerks like me – and that my best hope of progress lay in studying, as minutely as possible, that which it was pleased to present me. This volume appeared to go from TRO to TRU. Very well. I was leafing through TRU. Truth was in TRU. Trunck: *Social Mobility in Thirteenth-Century Milan*, I read, and then *Trunk – Elephant*'s cf. Oliphant.

7

It was obviously the sort of catalogue that told you what to do rather than the other way round. I set off anti-clockwise around the circle, in search of O. For some reason I felt feverishly excited at the thought that I had been asked to cf. Oliphant. Was this some black joke of the catalogue's? *Oliphant – Elephant, geddit*? Was there any such person as Oliphant? What were the chances of there being an entry under O for Oliphant, and if there were, of it being anything to do with *Trunk – elephant's*.

Ockrent, Charles: *Some Elements of Photography* (1928). *Oil*: a novel by Marjorie Beamish, 1932. Okar, Jan: *Hungary in Turmoil*. Oliphant Oliphant Oliphant – come on, I know I'm only a screenwriter with a second in Modern History but don't think you can get round me this easily . . .

Next volume.

Glancing round to see if anyone else was as impressed as I was by my high pressure scholarship, I pulled out the next volume and discovered that someone called Elspeth Oliphant had, in 1952, written a children's book entitled *The Elephant's Trunk*, a book that, as far as I could see from the catalogue, had not been reprinted, had had as little impact on the world as a chance remark at a cocktail party and only served to underline the purposelessness and vanity of all the books listed here, mine included.

Directly underneath her entry – neat as a tombstone – I read Oliphant, Ezekiel: *A Cursèd Lie Maintained and put aboutt by the Government and a Shorthand Taker Thoroughly Rebutted* Printed and Bound by the Author, Northampton 1650. And, if I hadn't been so impressed by that title and the three hundred-year-old smell of its urgent capitals, I would not have made it my first object of study, and perhaps if I had come to it later I would not have read it with quite so much thoroughness, and if I had not read it with quite so much fucking thoroughness I would not be here now, on a hospital bed, with the green lawns and the cedar tree outside, no hope left in me at all, either for the future or for our idea of the past.

Future ages may Judge mee, nott from my Deedes & Thoughtes, but by that which I leave of Mine owne selfe in that *Black Ink* that outshines and outweares oure mortall Courses. And yet, what I have left hath been nott Spoken Plainlie, as wee were wont in oure Assemblies, but put down *slantwise* for Feare of those same Courtes and Majesticall showes of Lawe, wherein I have been most abused. Yea are nott all Courtes butt a snare of the Devill & a hollowe Sorcerie, that hath made mee *a brother to Dragons and a Companion to Owles yea was my skinne black upon mee therein and my bones burned with Heate.*

It was for this, when I writ my *Cursed Lie Maintained and put aboutt by the Government* I writ those Wordes in Feare, which caused mee to walk in the waie of Vanitie. It was a Terroure of those same Rotten Courtes and Assemblies that hasted my Hearte unto Deceit, & bid mee Cloake my Opiniones in Wordes that were not mine but those of mine Enemies. But now I dwell in the clifts of the valleys, in caves of the Earthe & in the Rocks, now may I spoeake plain the Wordes of my Hearte & I pray that when this, my last and True Confession be finished, it may lie where some may chance to Reade it, for I feare of the Accounte that shall bee made of mee by them that sit in Judgemente upon mee, synce they are of the Abominable and Hellish Compact with the Poweres of Darknesse that hath now all of this oure *Englande* in its grasp.

It is They that ask mee, now I am close Confined by them, aboute my Association with Master Sexby, but I answere them nott, knowing they purpose to entrap mee & when they say hee is put to the Deathe in the Towere, at the nexte turne *a Man for oure Times & what is a Killing when it is noe Murder*, I stand fast, knowing that their Fleshe shall bee laid upon the Mountaines. For in truth, they knowe little of my historie, nor does anie man save by his Fellowe's confession. And synce that the Historie of this oure present Age is given over to the Devill's servants I trust nott anie to know the Truth of my Case unless hee read this my Confession, for Hell hath a waie to Charm its Path into the Utmost Secret parts of Government & into the Innermost parte of the temple, by which this present Evill hath come upon us, as the sword, judgment, pestilence or famine & wee stand before Thee in this Howse (for Thy name is in this Howse) & cry unto Thee in this oure affliction that Thou wilt Heare and Help.

Softlie now, for I heare the Souldiers in the outer room. Softlie. That they may nott Heare mee.

2

As well as Ezekiel's *Cursèd Lie* I ordered three other books but was told they were all at Woolwich. I didn't dare ask what they were doing there. The small African behind the desk told me that one of them had been damaged by bombs. But Oliphant was, within twenty minutes, waiting for me in a silent chamber at the other end of the dome – the North Library. The attitude of the staff towards me, though courteous, recalled that of an El Al stewardess to a young man with a Moroccan passport. As I carried the pamphlet to my chosen seat the elderly librarian who had handed it to me watched with careful watery eyes.

> Say then Masters, if this Inlet to Liberty and Freedom is not all a cozening by the great Lords of the Army? And if their great baggs of money be not the coverall and sole prop of such fig-leaved clothing as the doctrines of For-mes, Worships or the particular claims of Land? Look to the great Lie, Master Sectary Secretary, and consider well how but your version of the late Events be nothing but the false and Perjured Testament of one who would change the Hands of a Clock and think he has cheated Our Lord of what is His Commodity – Time its very self.

I felt it entirely likely that I was the first person to have looked at Ezekiel Oliphant's little effort for three hundred and thirty-six years. Indeed, it struck me as entirely probable that no one – apart, perhaps, from Mrs Oliphant and the little Oliphants – had ever, at any time, bothered to wade through its fifty-odd pages.

The fact of the matter was – in spite of my bold words about seventeenth-century prose style – Ezekiel did not have it as far as authorship was concerned. Printed and Bound by the Author, I muttered, and Comprehensible only to Hee! Then I thought of Gottlieb and my five-storey house in Putney, of

Meg, Juliet, Thomasina, Gwendoline and Emma. I thought too about the National Westminster Bank and of the steady blue eyes of the person in charge of the Putney branch. And I started to read.

> Necessity dissolves all laws and government and hunger will break through stone walls, but the Wickednesse I uncover will make ye weep for the misery that is to some as well as the Woe that is past. Weep and Howl for the Wretchednesse that is almost upon you even though Loftinesse is laid low, yet, whirling in from the Parliament, come all sorts and Manners of Abuse, yet even these are as a Cloak to the greater Evil of which I speak, perforce in a soft voice as a Schoolboy that fears his Master . . .

Ezekiel's major problem, apart from a tendency to fire off capital letters without system or design, was that his writing method tended to resemble my own. He seemed possessed of an atavistic desire to fill up a page without too much regard to what, if anything, he might be saying. 'Ezekiel,' I mouthed aloud, 'Wherefore this Furious and Disjoint Address, and to what end or purpose this Mad Yoking of Abstract Nouns? Do Thou Us a Favour Master Oliphant – and convey ye the Point and Purpose of this Discourse so that Wee May adjourn to the Museum Taverne!'

I looked up. The librarian was watching me. Already I was on the way to becoming a British Library Nutter, first class. On on on.

The point Ezekiel seemed to be making – apart from the general observation that Woe, Pity, Terror and Human Iniquity were about to descend on everyone in the London area – was that somebody somewhere had lied about something, or covered something up, and whatever it was they had lied about was serious. So serious or dangerous or frightening, in fact, that it could not be referred to directly. Not that Ezekiel was a man given to the direct statement where the Roundabout Threat would stand in its stead.

> Shame shame for Shame Master Secretary of the Council –
> that He whose task was to report the words of Great Ones

should be himself so cunning in the tongues of Belial and Ashtaroth! Strong after your sort for the Law and Liberty of England yet are you part of the Greater Falsehood, hidden only by the late Death of the Man of Blood. Nay but call you to mind his words – 'Wee have laboured to please a Kinge and I thinke, except we goe about to cut all our throates we shall not please him; and wee have gone to support an house wh. will prove rotten studdes, I meane the Parliament.' For shame Master Secretary fie for shame!

That was the point at which I stopped. Not only because Ezekiel was beginning to make me feel dizzy, but also because I thought I recognized the remark in quotation marks. I could not have said where it came from but something about it – not only the spelling, which was even more risk-taking than Oliphant's – *something* smelt, well, significant. It recalled to me Professor Dewes' study at Oxford, and him leaning across and tapping me on the knee:

'You're very bright, Matheson. You care passionately about politics. You have an idealism and a strength of will which is rare. I think you could do something very remarkable indeed in time. But unless you care about the truth, about scholarly truth, you will waste your life. Not because you have to be a natural scholar, I don't think you are a natural scholar. But whatever you are engaged in must be engaged with responsibility . . .' Here that famous, creaky grin. 'And if you are engaged in the study of history your first regard must be for accuracy, the dull and scrupulous pursuit of truth. That pursuit is crucial to each of the arts. You tell me you want to be a writer. Isn't your task as a writer simply to tell the truth?'

'It might be to lie entertainingly, Professor.'

The grin faded.

'Is a mountaineer afraid of heights? A diver of the sea water? A writer who is frightened of the truth is in the wrong element.'

'He might not know what the truth is, Professor. Don't you think?'

Dewes leaned forward in his chair. 'That,' he said, 'is why the Lord God gave you intelligence.'

Of course the quotation recalled Dewes because Dewes had

taught me the seventeenth century. And Dewes had fought for me when they were trying to sling me out. It was Dewes who had introduced me to Lilburne, Winstanley, Overton, Walwyn – to the Diggers and Seekers and Ranters and Anabaptists, all those curious millenarian groups that surfaced in the 1650s preaching destruction and change, building the City of God in the ruins of England's revolution. And I had rewarded him by reading to him, over the period of a year, the neatly typed essays of a bloke in Balliol called Hughes-Carpenter. I even read one of them twice, remarking to my tutorial partner as we left 'He likes that one.'

To this day I don't know whether Dewes knew I was cheating him. In the room with me at my tutorials were Harrington, white-faced and passionate, a copy of *Oceana* under his arm, Cromwell and Ireton, faces set in judgement; and not only the men and women of the middle years of the seventeenth century but their later interpreters – Firth, the great Victorian scholar, Bernstein the social democrat – there was a room full of voices at Merton, looking out at the sweep of Christ Church meadow, studded with poplars, and none of the voices spoke of the here and now. I recalled that shaky, greying head, those big bulbous hands twitching at the beautiful china. Where was I when Dewes was in trouble? Where was I when –

I didn't want to think about Dewes. Ezekiel Oliphant, I decided, was getting to me. I would return to him tomorrow, after rinsing my mouth out with the twentieth century. 'It's style you want,' I told myself, 'you're reading this stuff for *how* it's written, not for what it is or isn't saying. You are not and never will be a historian. The writing of history is only another department of fiction anyway. You are in a rather junior department of the fiction trade. Because what Gottlieb wants is a soap opera in fancy dress. Give Gottlieb what he wants. There are plenty of people dying to do just that.'

I pushed back my chair and stretched. Everyone else seemed to have gone. In here, quieter than in the main library, dry, hot and timeless, like some unvisited desert, the past was present, but ushered in neutrally like an exhibit in a trial. It was not a country to be explored – it was coming upon me like a virus, numbing my contact with the wooden desk, the yellow light, the thick, bumpy paper of the pamphlet.

I realized there was one reader left, a girl of about twenty-five, with a bright, untidy mass of red curls. She was looking at me. Or had I been looking at her? Suddenly embarrassed, I got to my feet and carried Ezekiel back to the man at the desk. He didn't look too pleased to have him back.

'By Our Lady,' I said, 'the Troublesome Discourse of This Our Fanatick Friend baffles the spirit into a most melancholy and Disaffected Humour.'

'You what?' he said, suspiciously.

'I've had enough for today,' I said.

'You have indeed,' he said. 'It sounds like you're losing your marbles.' Here, he leaned over the counter. He cackled rather madly to himself, and as I went towards the door that led back to the dome I thought I heard him muttering to himself 'Too many books. Too many books.'

I stopped at the door and looked back at where I had been sitting, trying to look like a man who had forgotten something. The red-headed girl was still looking at me.

A thin drizzle was blowing against the colonnades of the museum as I unlocked my bicycle. Four o'clock on a February afternoon – already the lights were on in the bookshops in Great Russell Street. In the street, black and silver, choked with cars, an old man in a coat that stretched to the ground pushed a pram piled high with rubbish towards Tottenham Court Road. His shoes were tied with string, and his hands and face, chapped, bleak, were discoloured with travel and tobacco.

'Nay my masters. You see the Pitiful condition of this our Yet Monarchicall Countrie! Ask not of me the Law or Justice that ensures that man a Beggar – the other one divinely appointed to the Velvet Couch or the free gratis maintenance from Treasury or Great Corporation. Mark this ye horseleech lawyers and still apostate men of the Parliament – there is Levelling yet to be done in England and when that the New Levelling comes in so far will ye fall yea as far as ye have dared to rise!'

I addressed this last remark to a taxi that cut ahead of me to the left, half-way down towards Tottenham Court Road. Cyclists are the tramps of the road. All motorists have to fear from us is our anger, the justified rage of the oppressed. No language, therefore, better in which to curse Juggernaut or Hired Conveyance of the Wealthy (are not taxicabs the Sole and Entire Privilege of the Commercial and Professional Classes?) than the prophetic tongue of the 1650s, the apocalyptic speech of Praise God Barebones, Clarkson, the Ranter, and, of course, Ezekiel Bore-the-Arse-off-You Oliphant?

I pulled out in front of an estate car decorated with endless baubles of rain, and, rising high in the saddle, did some fancy foot and buttock work in the glare of his headlights. For the first time in months I felt good.

3

I felt good all the way down Oxford Street, down the Bayswater Road, the length of the favourable incline of Holland
Park Avenue and through into the roundabout at Shepherd's
Bush, where cars and lorries, stalled mulishly in the drizzle,
were overtaken and forgotten. I felt good down the Fulham
Palace Road, where yet more cars and lorries waited in the rain
behind yet more lorries and cars, all, in their turn, forgotten
and overtaken by Jamie Matheson, cyclist, historian and
author.

It wasn't until I was puffing up Putney Hill that I realized
that I had been thinking about the girl with the red hair. Not
thinking consciously. I simply became aware that she had been
present in my thoughts without my permission. I didn't think I
liked this. I like to keep my thoughts under fairly strict control.
I don't wish them to go the way of my dress sense, budgetary
skill, or children.

What worried me even more than any of this was the
thought that this was why I was feeling so good. I rejected that
thought sternly, pushed the bike up our front path (which for
some reason known only to her, my mother-in-law has painted
green) and rang the front door bell. I never, as a matter of
principle, own a key to any house in which I live. Meg says
this is not a matter of principle but simply of ensuring A that I
will always be living with someone, and B that they will always
be in the house when I return. But then Meg has a very low
opinion of people.

'Hullo, dear.'

Perhaps Meg installed her mother in the basement so that
someone else was available to answer the door to me.

'Hi!'

At one point I think I thought I could control my mother-in-
law, and it was, perhaps, with this in mind that I agreed to her
decamping from her bungalow outside Portsmouth. I think I

also felt, at the time, that wherever a mother-in-law happens to be is not relevant, since mothers-in-law are capable of action at a distance.

'Meg has taken the little girls to the swimming pool.'

'Ah,' I said, marvelling at the sinister implications Juliet manages to impart to the most neutral information.

She winced and backed into the hall, taking the door with her. This housekeeper-like gesture seemed designed to confirm my legal right to the property, as well as suggesting that, as a grown man, a monstrous, seething mass of violence and appetite, I needed at least four foot clearance on either side when going through a door.

'I think the little one had the squits.'

'Really?'

I put the bicycle against the wall and, pulling off the yellow visibility band, began the difficult journey to the stairs. Would she speak? If she did, would I answer?

I hung my anorak over the radiator. A hot feeling in the small of my back told me that she had not descended to her basement flat. When I turned I saw she was still standing by the door, her arms at her sides, poised improbably for action, like a tailor's dummy or a wax statue in Madame Tussaud's. Something about the angle of her neck warned me that she was about to speak.

'It's raining,' I said quickly.

This threw her.

'Yes,' she said, in her deep throaty voice.

Seizing my advantage I started up the stairs. 'Nothing but rain,' I went on, 'filthy, endless rain.'

'Yes,' she said, and reached up one hand to pat at her immaculate, steel grey coiffure. There was nothing vain about this gesture. Its function seemed to be, rather, to reassure her that her head was still there. She made a game bid for recovery as I reached the first landing but her heart was not in it.

'It's rainy,' she said, 'even for February.'

I stopped and peered through the balustrade at her, marvelling at her ability to speak without moving her lips. I was safe now. In a minute I would be in the bathroom, taking off all my clothes. She has not yet felt the urge to watch me defecate or take a shower, although there are times when I think this moment is not far away. I took in her green cardigan, her gigantic black glasses, her tweed three-piece suit, her enormous hands, her uncanny resemblance to Mikhail Gorbachev.

'Yes,' I said with real feeling, 'even for February it's appalling.'

There was no way she could follow that. In the five years she has lived with us, I have developed a line in untrumpable banality that staggers even me. As I pulled off my sweat-stained shirt I heard the door clang and her heavy brogues begin the climb down to her flat.

I would telephone Rick Mason tonight. Rick would be able to place that quote. He might even have heard of Oliphant. Knowing Rick, he had probably written a two-thousand-page book about Oliphant, Oliphant's views, Oliphant's social status, Oliphant's mother-in-law . . . The thought of Oliphant's mother-in-law halted me, and I tiptoed on to the landing to check that she had not effected re-entry. Then, still on tiptoe, I went down the stairs and bolted the door that connects our house to her flat, a place that looks as if it had been decorated by a group of very drunk elderly women.

As I pushed the bolt home, I thought again of Ezekiel. 'Nay Mistress, for your Mother hath a right to a place on the earth and yet in so large a District is it Right and Reasonable, I ask you, that she should pitch her Tents in So Close a Proximity to our Dwelling Place? Is there not room enough in England yet? Hath the Crone not heard of Norfolk? Of the unsettled Zones of Cumbria and the far North of Scotland? Are not these, Wife, fair and comely and, in sum, *distant* enough places for her to find accommodation?'

He sounded, from the pamphlet, like a man with a mother-in-law problem. His style had a peeved, desperate quality to it. Most probably, in pursuing some vague and ill-defined notion of equality and holding things in common, Ezekiel had moved his mother-in-law into his gable, or turret, or whatever they *called* granny flats in 1650. Like me, lacking the nerve to go the whole way and set up an Anabaptistical family of love, in which superannuated hippies would share each other's bodies and devise complicated rotas for washing up (note to self – did they have washing up in 1650?), Ezekiel had probably opted for the mildly extended family, and, surrounded by aunts, mothers-in-law, female children, wife, mistress and female cousins, had sought to assert his threatened masculinity by writing pamphlets such as the one that was starting to obsess me.

The thought of my mother, aunts, cousins and lack of a mistress of any kind, drove me to the telephone. Rick Mason was in. His small, cautious, Northern voice summoned him up before me – his wire glasses, his pug fresh face, his lovable blink that no woman had found quite lovable enough.

'Jamie – hi!'

'Hi!'

'How are you?'

I answered the question, as I always do, carefully.

'I'm very well indeed actually, working on a new novel and a new stage play and very well indeed.'

I hoped that the sub text of this, *I am a major talent on the world stage*, was clear but Rick's subsequent remark made it obvious that I would have to improve my track record or my public account of it, probably both.

'But still churning out the old soaps . . .'

All my life I have wanted to be a serious writer. To say one small true thing about the times I live in, the person I seem to be, the view from my window across to the square flats at the top of Putney Hill. I don't want to bore the arse off the public with tall stories about men who grow breasts or giant lizards who symbolize our unconscious fears of women. I don't wish to lecture my fellow countrymen about the evils of colonialism or the perils of racism. I don't write to strike attitudes, I write to tell the truth as I see it. But that is not enough, it seems, for me. And so here am I – condemned to the soap mines – endless reams of paper, and endless whitened strip feeding into Gottlieb's mouth, who comments, as he swallows episode after episode – 'I don't like the taste of this.'

'What can I do you for Jamie?' said Rick mistaking my despairing silence for a desire to get on to the matter in hand.

'Look,' I said, 'it's in connection with something I am writing. There's a quote I feel I know, but I'd like you to see if you can trace it.'

'Is it seventeenth century?'

'It is.'

A silence. Then –

'Pity old Dewes –'

'Yes.'

Neither of us wanted to talk about what happened to Dewes. Well, even if Rick did, I didn't. I pulled the creased fragment of paper from my pocket and read my transcription of Oliphant's quotation.

'Wee have laboured to please a Kinge and I thinke, except we goe about to cutt all our throates we shall not please him; and wee have gone to support an house wh. will prove rotten studdes, I meane the Parliament.'

'Is that it?'

'Yes.'

'Sounds familiar.'

I was beginning to sound like a quizmaster in some dizzyingly obscure TV game show.

'And it's seventeenth century, you say?'

'You have two minutes, Dr Mason. You are two minutes away from the Ford Granada.'

'I *know* it.'

I did my Hughie Green voice: 'Dr Rick Mason lecturer in History at Lancaster University, specializing in Witchcraft. Going for the Ford Granada . . .'

'I know it, Jamie.'

I had expected him to say – as most historians do, when asked any question – 'It isn't my period.' What always irritated me about the study of history was its absurd search for exactness. How can one be exact or precise about something as intangible as the relations between people and people, people and nations, or even, God help us, nations and nations? The narrowing of focus historians seek – *Everything You Always Wanted to Know About June 1563* by a Pulitzer Prizewinner – is nothing more than a cry for help from people who, in respect of their chosen disipline, are rather in the position of a surgeon with a blunt pen-knife or an anaesthetist with a wooden mallet.

'You have one minute Dr Mason. This is Jamie Matheson for Putney Television and –'

'That's it.'

'What's it?'

'It's the Putney Debates.'

I had heard of the Putney Debates. In a church at the bottom of the hill, on the South side of Putney Bridge, now fenced in like some freakshow for a Godless age, is the rebuilt tower of the church where, in 1647, the Council of Cromwell's New Model Army debated the constitutional future of this country. Were we to have a democracy, a constitutional monarchy? If we were to have a parliament who should elect it? What were an ordinary Englishman's rights? These questions were debated by Cromwell, Ireton and the 'agitators', the elected officers of an army of the people whose nearest modern equivalent would be the Red Army of the Soviet Revolution. For a moment I saw the faces of the soldiers – the fleshy, unyielding features of Cromwell, the thin, aristocratic profile of his son-in-law Ireton. And then, just as I realized I had no basis whatsoever for assuming that Ireton's profile was thin or aristocratic, that I had conjured this picture out of the air and the sound of the word 'Ireton', I realized that Rick was talking, eager, excited.

'Yes yes yes it's bloody Sexby.'

'Sorry?'

'Edward Sexby, an agitator in the army and a friend of John Lilburne's – Lilburne the Leveller. Sexby was tortured to death in 1658. A great English radical. Tried to slip out of the country in disguise. Grew a beard. But nicked.'

I was interested in Sexby. He sounded a lot more interesting than Ezekiel Oliphant. 'Why was he tortured to death?'

'Cromwell. Sexby is thought to be the author of a pamphlet called *Killing No Murder*, a work which justified any assassination of the Protector. He'd been negotiating with Charles II, although as I recall, Sexby said he'd only talk to him if he didn't have to bend his knee.' Rick laughed gloomily. 'Great English Radicals. Could do with a few of them now, eh? Bloody Miners' Strike. Bloody Thatcher. No bloody bollocks anywhere. What are you these days Jamie – SDP?'

'I'm a Tory Anarchist,' I said, 'with Liberal tendencies.'

'I *thought* you'd end up SDP,' said Rick, in his bitten-off Yorkshire accent, teasing me out of my corner as it had done all those years ago at Oxford. Ten? No, fifteen. My generation is fifteen years away from Marx and optimism. It is fifteen years since I stood behind Rick at Grosvenor Square and two huge policemen lifted him like a child high in the air, up, up up up until he broke free of their unparental hands and landed on the floor of the green meat wagon like a sack of coal hitting the cellar floor. He teaches revolution now, and, from time to time, I try to write about it. Neither of us preaches it, or, as Meg would say, *does* it.

I thought about the Miners' Strike. About the images on the television of the massed ranks of blue police, about those huge men on the piazza at Covent Garden, holding out their buckets for cash, lost among the shoppers, searching for such essential items of equipment as electric carving knives or lamp stands in the form of the human torso (£175). I remembered the face of one of them, as Meg tipped in her fiver – stone, unyielding; and how he'd said 'She can afford it' to her friend. And how Meg had said 'I can. I know.' But that hadn't made it any better because then he had become friendly, and the point had become lost, as so often in England, in politeness. The incident had not prevented Meg from buying a pair of leather boots that cost four times an unemployed person's weekly wage.

The silence between us, across the miles of telephone wire, lengthened; there was simply nothing to say about any of that.

'Why are you interested in Sexby?'

I felt suddenly, violently jealous of Rick. Alone in his study, a licensed time-traveller, his constant companions the great figures of the past, always *right* about things, in the way academics are. And me, struggling hopelessly with the present, even when writing about the past, with the rain on my window, the creak of the stairs outside, the placards in the newsagents' up the road, always trying to make sense of the unassimilable moment, always wrong, cheap or over-violent or sentimental or crude.

'Er—'

I still don't know why I didn't tell him about Oliphant. Had Ezekiel started to work on me even then? Was he protecting his reputation from the prying eyes of the professional historian? Whatever it was, I stammered what I knew to be a

23

deleberate lie. 'It really isn't at all important.'

Rick sounded surprised. If it wasn't important why was I asking him about it?

'It would be nice to meet. I have to come down to London any day now. Meg and the kids OK?'

'Fine.'

I didn't ask him over. For some reason, now I had the information I needed I wanted to get rid of him as quickly as possible.

'I'll see you, Rick.'

'See you.'

I put the phone down and stared down into the garden below, the climbing frame, the shed, the three stunted fruit trees.

Down below in the hall I heard the front door bang. Then the scuffling run of small feet, the sawn-off treble dialogue of children. 'Thomasee-eena . . .' 'Gwendoline's got *my pencil* . . .' I went out on to the landing and prepared to meet my family.

When those same Souldiers asked mee questions concerning Master Sexby, at first, I *am* assured, my Countenance told the Honeste Truth, when I said to them *I have NO THOUGHTE of hee of whom ye Speake.* At which they asked mee divers questions concerning the Business at Putney, to which I answered, as I do most earnestly believe, that Matters of State bee none other than the Arguments of Sorcerers & Witches, synce their pacte bee with the Devill to Cozen this most Unhappie countrie & those who dwell in her. And agaynste them I set the Wordes of that same *Ezekiel* for whom I am named *'Woe bee to the shepherdes of Israel that doe feed themselves! Shoulde nott the Shepherde feed the Flockes? Ye eat the fat and ye clothe you with the Woole and ye kill them that are fed; butt ye feed nott the flocke.'* Thus doe I make it plaine I know their sorceries and howe they Purpose to deceive mee.

'Nay Master Oliphant,' says one of them to mee, 'wee know of youre *Cursed Lie* which you lay at Oure Doore, but is maintained and put about by None but you.' Whereat I knew what I had written told hard with mee. But what I write now is no Meer

Vanitie, as I do now do count that Worke, nor yett the reckoning of a Daie Book where *Tom* or *Jack* purpose to give an account of howe this journey was taken or what Meate was Dressed at Supper, but an Honest & Humble version of the details and Circumstances of my Unhappy life, writ in the eie of the Lorde who knoweth *the Idolaters who speake Vanitie and the Dreame who hath seen a false Dawne yea the Diviner that proffereth false comfort and goeth his Waie as a Flocke with those that are Sinners.*

And soe I must speak plain. And yet am troubled that the Faces and Formes of those that were the Traffick of my life are no longer Cleer as once they were, as it was when the souldiers asked mee of *Master Sexby*. For synce they spake to mee of him, sometimes Master Sexby wears the Countenance of the Devill yea even of that Cromwell who is become an idol of the Heathen. And their Questions made my tongue cleave to the Roof of my Mouthe for shame. In truth I have no cleer recollection of Him or of those Times now past. How then shall I write plainlie for the eie of the Lorde that sees my Unperfection, when my memorie bee so clouded by Time and Pain and the present Feare of Deathe? Yet must I to the taske I sett myselfe, and now with the souldiers quiet in the Room without, take up the pen agayn, to say 'Having been given pen and ink by Sir William Devenish . . .' For hee alone of the partie took pitie of my condition. And yet I cannot write. And yet I muste, lest some, somewhere, when I and all this present Showe bee Duste should chance to Reade. Synce Truth in the eie of the Lorde shall abide. And I begin agayne. *'Having been given pen and inke by Sir William Devenish . . .' Courage, for my Master's sake & for those that are fallen in the fight.' Courage. Begin agayne . . .*

4

Why should Ezekiel have it in for Sexby? They sounded as if they ought to have had a great deal in common. Insofar as I had a mental image of either of them, Oliphant and his Agitator were a perfect match. I could see – like those cut-out clothes for dolls my sisters used to have – a leather jerkin, a black stovepipe hat, and, somewhere or other, a voluminous pair of breeches. They had no smell as yet – were merely images. I could not smell the body to which they belonged, but then the flesh and smell of the past is always imagined falsely. How can we know that, back in the Civil War, the sweat or the breath of another were precisely what they are for us now?

And yet, so shameless is the imagination, that as I went down the brown, carpeted stairs to meet my children, I realized I had already given Oliphant a beard. A different one from Ireton's – a silky, effeminate version of the goatee, that he tugged nervously whenever Mrs Oliphant or any of the little Oliphants asked him what he had been doing that day.

'What have you been doing today?' said Thomasina.

She put her pale face on one side as she said this, and shook her pony tail at me. Although she is only nine you could not call Thomasina a girl. She has a disturbing, womanly quality to her. She wears the perpetual half-smile of one amused by young men's antics, and her big eyes slide away from me in what could be modesty but could equally well be deception. It amuses her to humour me.

'I've been to the year 1650,' I said.

'Was it interesting?'

'It was very interesting,' I said. 'They had chopped off the King's head and so they were a bit excited but on the whole it was extremely interesting.'

Meg moved through to the kitchen, extending by her silence what I took to be a remarkable tolerance to this conversation. I heard the thump of groceries hitting the floor.

'Why did they chop off his head?'

'Because they had rebelled against him and won.'

'But why had they rebelled aginst him?'

'Because they didn't like him and he was the King and in charge of them.'

'Like you're in charge of me?'

My eldest daughter, as so often, had gone to the heart of the matter. Better historians than I had tried and failed to explain the deep causes of the English revolution. Perhaps its origins were in hatred of the all powerful father. After he had destroyed Charles what did Cromwell do? Invent a father title for himself. I went through to the kitchen – pine and tiles and lights in places where you would least expect them. It looked, as usual, as if it was about to celebrate some vaguely pagan feast.

I sat at the table and watched Meg, her neat shoulders, her shoulder-length black hair.

'How was it?' she said.

'OK,' I said.

She grabbed an onion, roughly, and began to slash at it with a carving knife. Thomasina and Emma (four) watched her with respect. Gwendoline (seven) settled herself in the corner with a biro and a sheet of paper, her large, plate-like face set with concentration. I watched Gwendoline.

'Am I forgiven?' I said.

'Oh sure,' said Meg, 'sure sure sure.' She held her hands under running water, her face slightly away, her eyes smarting from the onion. I could tell from the way she checked her image in the darkened glass of the window that she was feeling better. It was the briefest of vanities; but without vanity we are nothing.

'You're feeling better?'

She stopped on her way from sink to sideboard, her black hair bouncing, her thin face suddenly alive with worry. 'Shouldn't I be?'

'No no no,' I said, 'not at all.'

In order to improve the atmosphere I decided to talk about myself. 'I had an extraordinary day,' I went on, 'with an extraordinary man called Oliphant. It's rather strange but I have stumbled on this man and I rather feel no one has ever heard of

27

him before, he's a nonentity I suppose, just any man anywhere but I heard him talk to me, speaking across three hundred years, cutting through history like –'

As I talked Meg moved swiftly along the row of kitchen units, chopping, slashing, tasting and crushing; like a judo black belt she suddenly pounced on the fridge, as if it had been trying to jump her, and threw herself at the door. I knew she wasn't listening to me. I paused.

'Yes,' she said, 'disturbed by the silence,' I expect it was.'

I decided to continue. 'And I had this extraordinary feeling that I was actually *there*, that I was back in 1650 when something was happening in England, when the revolution we droned about was in progress, when people had finally taken that risk, stepped out of the roles assigned to them and *dared*. You know?'

I stopped. She stopped slashing and chopping and tasting and hurling herself at things, and was standing very still and quiet, her face away from me.

'Look, I'm sorry about last night. I was drunk.' I could feel the remains of a headache at the edge of my eyes. 'What were we arguing about anyway?'

'You said,' she replied, 'that I was a crazy woman.' Her arms hung limp at her sides, the knife dangling downwards like a grotesque steel finger. I went over to her and put my arms round her.

'Well I was drunk,' I said. 'You're not crazy.'

She looked up at me – her large blue eyes trapped, close to my jersey. 'I am,' she said, 'I'm a nutter.'

'Well yes,' I said, 'you are a bit . . .'

'What?'

'Odd.'

She dug me in the ribs and went back to the sideboard.

I watched her pale, thin face for a while and tried to remember what it had been like when she was crazy. It was very clear to me. Her screaming at the top of the stairs in someone else's house. Her digging her nails into her face. Her grabbing one of the children and shaking her again and again. What I couldn't remember was what it was like the other side of that. When we had walked together, hand in hand, down some street in a provincial town, or held each other close in some cheap hotel

28

bedroom, listening to the noise of the street outside. I started to sweep the crayons and rubbers from the table. 'I spoke to Rick Mason today.'

'Oh did you?' She was brightening at the thought of Rick and of Rick's often-expressed fondness for her. The children had disappeared upstairs. Outside the rain had stopped and the wind was up, pulling at the leaves of the trees on Putney Heath, soughing round the house, sobbing its way up to Tibbett's Corner.

'Isn't it an extraordinary thing to study for a living. Witchcraft.'

'I've always been fascinated by it,' said Meg, slightly edgily.

'Wouldn't it be wonderful,' I said, 'if they found a witch who wasn't an example of the oppression of women or the durability of outmoded belief systems in rural areas but actually *was* a witch.'

Meg had now resumed slashing, chopping, tasting, leaping and hurling in a style even more bravura than before. As I paced across the sanded, stencilled floor she leapt on a packet of frozen peas and disembowelled it, swiftly, expertly. Somehow her left hand introduced a saucepan below the cascade of frosted green nuggets, but her right hand had already moved on to other things. The two halves of a turnip were jumping in opposite directions, surprised by her steel blade. I went to the fridge and groped for the wine as, above me, she beheaded a leek.

'I mean a real witch with a black hat and a cat and a broomstick, who had it off with the devil and turned the milk sour and capered around a cauldron with other witches.'

'You mean,' said Meg, 'like my mother.'

'That sort of thing.'

Down below in Juliet's flat I heard the bass rumble of her smoker's cough. A thud. What did she do down there? I had a sudden vision of her, arms folded on her chest, performing the kind of dance usually done by the Red Army – a Cossack number among the crochet-covered armchairs and sofas. 'Ca-arlinka – Ca-arlinka . . .'

I held up a bottle of milk. It had the consistency of old yoghurt. 'People like Rick,' I went on, pulling out a bottle of

Côtes de Provence from under the tomatoes, 'are determined to prove that reality is as grey and unchanging as they are. I didn't dare tell him what I was doing. He would have condemned it as unhistorical. But I don't see why my vision of the seventeenth century is any less valid than his lists and statistics and fragments of court reports, all off which are there simply to bolster up a theory derived from a nineteenth-century German Jew.'

'And what,' said Meg in a frankly satirical voice, 'is your vision of the seventeenth century?'

With one hand she held a saucepan under the cold tap, with the other she cracked an egg into a small mound of flour. Slowly and laboriously, like one of those elderly and not very interesting primates in the London Zoo, holding up a wisp of straw for close examination, I brought the bottle and the corkscrew together. 'Well basically,' I said, 'it's men in long curly wigs and cloaks, versus blokes in leather jerkins with coal scuttles on their heads.'

'I really look forward to the series,' said Meg.

I addressed myself to the task of unscrewing the cork. 'I am making a serious point,' I said. 'Our images of history are fundamentally ahistorical. They're a mess, made of our reading, our experience and our essentially *narrative* way of understanding the world. The seventeenth century is, basically, a soap opera.'

'Or it will be when you've finished with it,' said Meg.

The cork popped. Meg lit three gas rings simultaneously, snarled open a can of tomatoes and allowed them to flow in a graceful semi-circle from her extended arm into an orange tureen.

'Where are the glasses?' I said, moving arthritically past her.

Meg thinks I am intellectually lazy. Meg thinks that the seventeenth century is just the seventeenth century and nothing else. Meg thinks we should not speculate about facts. But what does she know? She had the breakdown, not me. I always tried to protect her from the memory of that. I was silly in order to amuse her, to help her forget the dark side of things. Perhaps that was how I wasted my reputation.

When later we were sitting at the table, the children in bed, the candles lit, and the wind at last quiet on the hill, I swear I was not thinking of myself when she turned to me and said, 'I'd like to study witchcraft. Like Rick.' I was thinking of her. I was thinking of what had happened before, of how she cried jerkily and quietly into me, that night on the hills above Lewes. I was thinking of the dreadful pallor of her face that night when we brought her to the hospital. I laid my hand over hers, and feeling the hard ridge of our wedding ring against my palm, said 'No more study, darling. And not *that* . . .'

'Why?'

'Because my love – you would go –'

A pause.

'Odd.'

But this time she did not laugh or dig me in the ribs. She looked at me across the unstable, vertical crescent of the candle flame, her big eyes dark with worry. Neither of us spoke.

Having been granted Pen and Inke by Sir William Devenish, at whose House hard by *Whipps Cross* I now do find myselfe, I determine to sett down this Night, while I still have Libertie, the Details and Circumstances of my most unhappy Life. Not onlie that it may cause mee once agayne to reflect on the Chances that brought mee to the Case in which I now find myself, but also that it may Instructe those who come after mee. Are not oure lives worth more than oure passage through them? Synce they are Examples and Lessones to those Unhappy Creatures who are destined to follow in the same Unhappy Courses as wee, in the years to come after; who must nott, as the *Calvinistes* believe, merely follow their Trackes, as Marbles in a boy's game of Finde-the-Hollowe, but, by long and earnest contemplation and attention to the voyce of Hee who is above us all, take up the Burthen of their lives in glad Heart, and walk in the Paths of Righteousness and Truth, so that their Briefe Mortalitie appear a verie Texte for Future Generations.

I was born Ezekiel Oliphant, the son of Thomas Oliphant the Printer, in the village of Stavely, near Essenden, in the Countie of Hertfordshire, in the yeare of oure Lord sixteen hundred and twentie, and was called by my father, who had been Master of a

Print Presse in London, *Runt*, since I was, from birth, a sicklie and infirm Creature. And though I now would wish to Bless and nott Abuse him, and come to understand his Cholerique Dispositionne – for though hee was a Printer, yett hee *hath no presse to call his owne*, being come from the Citie of London, where hee practised this Trade, in the pursuitt of my mother's Fortune (which, it fell out, was no fortune but a few Meane Fieldes). Hee worked for a Master Stanley in the Town, and was Vexed extreamly to *Labour in Anothere's Vineyardes. For*, saith hee, *a man must master his owne selfe before he ever seek to master others*. Which I could nott argue for the Truth of, yet know hee sought Masterie over all, and so quarrelled with this same Stanley and gained no Emploiement for himselfe except the possessioun of a few Cold Printe Letters, with which he was wont to play, running them through his fingers as a Child a prettie String of Beades, or a Catholique his rosarie. Wee lived most miserablie upon my mother's *Estate*, as hee styled it with Contempt and Disfavour, and trulie to say in my tenderest yeares did *the tongue of the sucking child cleave to the roof of its mouth for thirst and did the children ask bread and yet no man gave it to them.*

My Father was a great man of above six foot in height, Bearded, as were the Pyrattes in Matthew van Leeming's book, which I had by mee when the Soldiers took mee – and, as I remember it, a Laugh that would shatter the verie Glasse in the Church Windowes and a Curse that would Cracke both Doores and Pewe. His Curse was more Often Used than was his Laugh, and, if hee cursed anie it was the Priest that was Appoynted to that same Churche who favoured such Robes and Vestments and *Arminian foolerie* as were commanded by the Archbishop Laud, for though my Father took Delighte in Bigotry of his Making, yet he was farre, in his reckoning, from this *Poyson of the Commonwealth*. Whereat his Religion was but to rail at this same Priest and nott to seeke the Lorde's Face as he went aboutt. For in those daies were oure eies dim and oure heartes most faint, neither sought wee Godd, where Hee might make his face to shine upon Us, and was the Mountain of Zion desolate yea foxes walked Upon it.

It may bee that in some other Place, my Father would been

served Ille by the Justices or at the same *courts ecclesiasticall* where hee would have been more than warmed a littel in the hand, but in oure village were Fewe who would dare speak agaynst the Parliament and Presbyterie, which manie took to bee the Opinion and Argument of my Father, although in Truth hee spake more of Foulnesse than Godly Reason and thought *anie Churchman worth the Roastinge*, and mee his weakest son, the more to be pitied the more I affected the Deep and sincere studie of Religion. Thus were his Curses at the abominable, Romish practices of the Archbishop meer Straw Opiniounes, and I would dare swear there were manie who spake agaynste the King and the Archbishop with no thought to the Vertues of Reason and Contemplation, wherefore *the young and old lie on the ground in the streets: my virgins and young men are fallen by the sword; thou hast slain them in the day of thine anger; thou hast killed and nott pitied.*

Of my five Brothers, but two survived Infancie, and of those two but one staied with mee in oure House at Stavely. For there were Fewe of anie close to him, who had anie Stomache to his Rage and Excess or who did not feare his Hand when it was raysed agaynst Us. Of those two, one was the eldest, that hee styled Thomas the Younger and Thomas the Younger took Himself to Hertford, to a Brewer there named Toller, which caused my Father the most Distress I had seen in Him, which Caused mee to wonder for I had not Thought him to love anie Mortall Thing save his Owne Selfe. Yet did hee love this Thomas, the *elder of us* and *the Younger Modell of himself*, most sorely and went after to him at Hertford. Thus is it written in the Book of Lamentations that *Hee hath led mee and brought mee into darkness, but not into light. I am the man that hath seen affliction by the rod of his wrath.* For the Lord Punisheth oure sinnes yea when oure love is born of Sinne, doth he Chastise us even with that same Love whereby wee thought to be Saved. For this Young Thomas would not goe with him but spake harshly to him and so my Father came Home empty handed and beat myselfe and my brotheres Adam for the Offense of Another.

Agaynst mee, from my earliest Youth, hee had a particular Enmitie. For I loved nott the Sports and Pastimes which hee enjoyed – Toss Penny and Catch at Molly (which were oure Countrie Diversions) and neither would I take Relish in Quarreling, Fighting or the Swearinge of Oathes, but, from my earliest yeares, my Mother having taught mee my Letters, found Solace and Recreation in the Studie of Anie book which came to hand. Hee was wont to say of mee *that even small beer would curdle on his tongue.* And, as I grew in yeares, add yet fouler insultes to my name, styling mee Shitt Breeches and, before my school-fellowes, the Finicall Hogg, my face being plump and square, and my being, from earliest Youth, Particular as to Appearance and Costume.

And soe it was, when I was ten years of age, and Young Thomas was gone from us, my owne brother Adam, which was loved by mee as much as my owne life, took sick and died of a Fever in the Space of Three Daies, not knowing Myself or my Mother, though wee called him by Name, and I was left alone with the *Black Beare* as Adam and I were wont to call my Father. At which time, as hee feared never to regayne my brother Thomas the Younger, hee was debauched with bothe Wine and Beer, and spake us littel sense after Noonday, after which Houre I was frightened to go to him, for I could nott Grasp upon what Matter his mind ran – and likewise feared his Hande upon mee.

One afternoon he comes upon mee at my Booke in the Chamber that lay betwixt the Printe Press as hee termed it – though there was but Littel there save what hee had apportioned to himself from this same *Stanley* – and bids me take from the Boxe in the Chimney corner a Letter. 'For,' says hee, 'synce you are the Scholar of the familie I would be sure you knowe youre *letteres*,' And I did as hee bid mee, taking unto myself the S from the box of *cold print.* Though there be those who would Conteste that all is meer Chance and no Providence guide oure Actions – I have heard the wilder sort argue such Propositions when I was with the *New Modelle* – yet is it clear to mee that Hee who is above All shapes each Minute according to His Design and Purpose. For that same S which I tooke unto myself is patterned after that *serpent* that was more subtil than any beast of the field which the Lord God had made, which said unto Eve 'Yea hath God said Ye shall not eat of every tree of the garden?' And

34

neither could I with any Ease or Comfort shape my mouth to say it without a Lisp to shame One less advanced in Yeares than mee, which well my Father knewe, for hee loved to Mock mee. 'Speake Ezekiel,' says hee, 'as I have commanded thee! But I, from Terroure of Him and his Hande stood there like a Mourner at a Funeralle, dumb to any Showe or Sign save the beginnings of Teares, which affected mee when anie spoke harshly to mee, for I was, then, *so much in my Bookes as to be Scarce there at all.* Whereat hee seizes mee by mine Eare and catches at my Cheeke with his great Hande, saying *hee would learn mee to speak like a Christian synce I made such pretense of Godlinesse.*

O Almighty God who hath shewed his Grace to mee and yet in Whose Wisdome are all my Transgressions seen and accounted, was nott this same lettere S even as the subtil Beast that hath perswaded Man to his Falle? And was it nott my Lot to suffer and Accept meeklie as did Hee who suffered for us upon the Cross, laying aside my Heade in Submission to the Yoke it hath pleased God to lay upon mee? For it is written in Booke of the prophet Ezekiel that *Rebellion is as the Sinne of Witchcraft*, and that same Satan who was cast out from Heaven, likewise raysed up his Heade agaynste Ordered Governmente, which when some of the Armie argued for the Justice of Oure Cause, as if anie and everie taking up of Armes agaynst Authoritie were to be counted Just and Reasonable, I disputed. For was it nott the King who raysed his Standarde agaynst us at NOTTINGHAM? And there are, I dare swear, Authorities that Declare agaynst the People. But of my Fathere, though I may plead I was Maddened by the Usages to which I had been Subject, yet was hee still my Fathere to whom I owned Obedience.

And so it was, when his Hands comes again for my Cheeke I catch at his Thumbe with my Teeth, and, though hee swore and Cursed mee I would nott let him goe, but Hanged there, like a Dog that hath a Pheasant for his Master and is fain nott to Lose it.

At which hee rained bothe Blowes and Curses on mee until at last he seizes a Pole agaynst the Chamber Wall that hee was wont to carry about with him, when living, to kill Moles withal, and Smote mee upon my back and at last I loosed my Teethe from out his hande and ran to the Yarde and from the Yarde to the Greene for there was a Madnesse on mee that Daie and I would not submit to him in anie wise but thought onlie of my Misfortunes and of the hard Usage to which I was subject. And hee comes out the Chamber Doore and calls to mee that my Nexte Welcome shall be a Whipping, but I made Promise I should have no more Welcomes of him be they Whippings or Kisses.

My Mother had neare to an Acre of land about the house, thick with Trees and through the Shade of this I took my waie, while, from the House the *Black Beare* keeps up his Rushing Torrent of Abuses to which I made no Answere, synce from my youth hee, by his Example had taught mee the Worth of Silence, whence in the New Modelle I was termed *Close-Mouth* Oliphant. For though I evere loved Plainness of Religion I had a Terroure of the *Captaines of the Rant*, as much as if they been Arminian or Papist, fearing in all things the Abominable Vice of Excess, to which oure Age is most Subject. And so it was *I heard nott his cry and went upon my waie seeking the Lord.*

The sorrow of Children cannot bee mended except by Kisses and Favoures; yet None were granted mee either by the Black Beare or my Mother, who was so in feare of him she durst not showe me the Caresses naturall to a mothere, and had, by her owne Example grown less Fond of me, for Man is an Animall that will seeke a Patterne, even in his Owne Behaviour, synce his substance is hid from his owne self for God hath made us in Secret, curiously wrought in the Lowest Parts of the Earth. Which usage had accustomed mee to Solitude which ever calmed my Spirit and in a little space was the Hurt and Injury hee had done mee, mended. The waie I took was hard by the Church, where the Flowers and Grasses were as a balm to mee for as it is written *the Lord GOD planted a garden eastward in Eden; and there hee put the Man hee had formed and out of the ground made the Lord to grow every tree that is pleasant to the sight.* And when I came to the Church there I sate mee down by the Wall, neare to the Doores but I entered nott, for my Fathere had so spoken agaynste our Priest and his Priestcraft, beinge wont to say *oure man did the Archibishop's work for him*, I was grown fearful of the place. And is nott such Feare and bigotry the source of so manie of our Present Ills? Synce, though the Kinge's Waie was in Erroure to manie of us, yet is oure task and Dutie to seek the Kingdom of God and His Righteousness, and nott to Abuse his Temples synce Pollution and Uncleanlinesse are naught but Shadowes on the Soul and to Think Eville is to Perform the same, as I was taught by the *Cooperites*.

There sate I about the space of an Halfe Houre, when into my Viewe comes a Ragged and Infirm Horse, that scarce seemed able to carry his Carcase for himselfe, yet was between the Shafts of a Cart, and upon the Cart a Man, behind him a pile of Barrelles as you may see at a *cooper's* or the Yard of a Taverne. Which, whether they were full or emptie were such a Burthen to the Creature he scarce seemed like to take his Waie past the church, whence hee and his Master were bound. The least of his Burthens was this same Driver, who sate in a broadcloth coat and dun-grey Britches, over his face a broadbrimmed Hat of the kinde I have seen the Spaniards weare. For hee was as Thinne and *Stringed-out* as the stem of a clay pipe, and his Nose was sharper than anie Pen, and yet the Sweetnesse of his Visage and the Gentle and Godly carriage he gave himselfe made mee doubt hee could be a Cruell or Fearsome Master. And hee calls out to mee as the Cart drew close to where I Rested 'All alone?', to which I gave him the answer that I had Fled my Father synce I feared a Whipping and hee gazed on mee with such a Sensible and Kindlie Eie I was like to begin afresh thinking of my Troubles and nott to Rail or Abuse my Fathere but to weep for the Pitie of my Circumstances, which indeed I did, though I was much Ashamed thereby. 'How then?' says the stranger, 'What's the matter now?', and in a space has all the Matter of my Storie out of mee, for this same *Nehemiah* as I found his name to bee, was ever skilled at seeking out the Matter of another's troubles, synce hee thought so little of his owne. And as I talked hee made to Nod, gravely and quietly as I gave him to understand the Feare in which I Held my Fathere, and the Unhappinesse of oure Householde, so that I hardlie found myself in my perfect Senses, and wept as I spoke, at which hee nodded the more and *kept Plain Counsel* as the *Cooperites* are wont to say.

Now as I called upon my Fathere's name agayne hee holds up

37

one Thin Hande and bids me Cease. 'For,' says hee, 'if such an one as hee may be can Abuse and Grievously Trouble thee in such a mannere then hee is no Fathere. For what,' says hee, 'is the fathere of my bodie, *my bodie fathere is no fathere, neither shall I take mee a Wife nor have anie to Share my Fleshe synce I have yet a Fathere in Heaven so take no thought for your life what ye shall Eat or what ye shall Drinke; nor yet for youre bodie what ye shall put on. Is not the Life more than Meat, and the bodie than Raiment and is nott God's Righteousness more than anie of these, than Life or Bodie. So I say unto you, take no thought for the Fathere of thy Bodie but for the Fathere of thy Soule that is in Heavene.'* Which, though I took but littel account of it then, is the doctrine of the *Cooperites*, who hold no Covenant with the Loves of the Flesh, nor loyaltie to Those who Engender Us, save onlie God the Fathere in whose Infinite Wisdome and Mercie wee may trust as in no Othere. But when hee spake these things to mee I was amazed and knew not what to say, onlie that hee spake softlie where *The Black Beare* used a voyce that Roared like anie Cannon – and so hee asks mee my Name and I tell him how I am Christened, at the which he starts up, with 'Son of Man I will send thee to a Rebellious Nation that hath rebelled agaynst mee; they and their Fatheres have Transgressed agaynst mee, even unto this Verie Daie. For they are Impudent Children and thou Son of Man bee not afrayde of them, though Briars and Thorns bee with thee and Thou dost Dwell among Scorpions.' By which I was given to Understand – for hee emploied a Most Wondering and Astonished voyce and raysed up his hands to Heaven – that in Discovering mee, was hee Blessed, for the Wordes hee spake were of the booke of the Prophet EZEKIEL for whom I had been named when my *Bodie Fathere* was indeed a Godlie and Righteous Individual and rayled not at Babylon upon his owne account but sought oure Fathere which Dwells in Heaven and for whom is all our Endeavour and Laboure. Which Booke, indeed, I had almost, having then a meer ten yeares of Age, by Hearte and answered him straight with 'Son of Man I have made Thee a Room in the House of Israel . . .' and gave him Chapter and Verse from the booke of that Prophet, at which hee was much Amazed, my being, as I have related, not much Above ten yeares and my Stature and Manner giving mee the

Appearance of one even less Advanced in Yeares. And at the conclusion of our Talk hee says to mee that his Name is Nehemiah, who was the King's cup Bearer that was the Builder of the Temple. And have wee nott laboured to Build a Temple here in this England these Fifteen Yeares or more? And how have wee been Served as wee laboured at the Breadth of it and the Height and thought to Add Cubitts to the Stature of its Strength? For as much as wee laboured to Build there were otheres who sought our Destruction and the Destruction of the Temple, whereat wee were nott amazed but Suffered meeklie as oure Lorde did, Answering not Wrath with Wrath and *turning awaie our cheeks from the Blowe* as the *Cooperites* teach. For was nott the Manner of the Kinge's death a great betrayal synce wee *answered Blood with Blood? And were nott the late councils of the Armie but Shadowes to trick us by oure New Master?*

And yet then, as I heard Nehemiah the Cooper talke and denie all thought of Duty and Obligation to hee I termed then my *Bodie Fathere*, I bethought mee I had come home indeed, and when hee says to mee I am to goe with him, and Goe not back to my House, and that I should bee his *Cup-Bearer* and come up on the Cart, I thought nott once of my Fathere and Mothere but went as hee commanded mee and Denied hee who had the Engendering of mee. For what is a Familie but the Mutual Exchange of Kindnesse and Love and if there bee not anie Love, where then, is that same Familie? Or is it merely A Band who Gather together in Erroure and Feare of the Darknesse without, taking no Thought for the Lord God who shall bee the onlie Health of oure Countenance. And so it was that I went with him, and hee raysed me up to sit by him and I looked nott back at that place but Journeyed in Good heart nott knowing what I Might Finde with my Newe Master but Trusting I might fare better than I had, which proved nott the Case, for as much as wee flie Eville yet Eville findes us out and in my Heart was still Wickednesse and Rebellion, so that *I knew nott myselfe* as the Cooperites say, *and had opened a doore to Satan and granted him Possession of my Soule.*

5

From Putney through Wandsworth to Battersea (which was the route I cycled to the Museum the following morning) one seems to pass from one country to another. In one region the big, graceful houses stand at a decent distance from each other, like guests who know themselves to be at a distinguished party; in the other, gigantic featureless blocks, whose windows resemble the formal wilderness of graph paper, glare down at their occupants as they scurry from pub to fish shop, like angry, uncomprehending parents. Scrawled-on bus shelters, boarded-up shopfronts and huge, gloomy pubs stare out at the visitor from more prosperous suburbs, and the careworn faces in the street seem to say 'It won't be long. It won't be long.'

I thought about the tower blocks (NO BALL GAMES ALLOWED) and the doomed landscape of the inner city as I checked into the Museum and picked up yesterday's book at yesterday's paragraph, like a miner cutting on from the next shift. Ezekiel's voice boomed over the dirty, windblown February streets like a commentary on a film:

Truly it may be proved that any of their nests are feathered with what is rightfully the Republique's, and not of their own for which the wealthy and well assured will surely do penance. Yea as the father shall be unseated by the son, the husband by the Wife and the shepherd by the Flock he tends, so shall the Nation rise against itself and –

He was in a particularly barmy mood this morning. I looked up and found I was staring at the girl with the red hair. She pulled her shoulders in and cocked her head at me. Her eyes seemed to glisten. I dropped mine to Ezekiel.

Yea Master Sectary – ye have set about most falsely and sought to hide what should not be hidden from the People and Army. A great Evil, hath, by your offices been concealed!'

I looked back at the girl. She was still looking in my direction. 'This,' I mouthed at her, 'is boring.' She leaned her head forward and her hair fell across her face. I mouthed again: 'Boring.' She grinned and nodded. The nod seemed to involve the whole of the upper part of her body. Her arms, I noted, were plump and tanned. Strange for February. She was wearing a loose, grey sweater, and round her neck was a brass chain. Had she been skiing? She didn't look like the kind of girl who went skiing. She looked like a postgraduate student. She looked, too, as if she belonged to someone, although I could not quite imagine who that someone might be.

'Coffee?' I mouthed. She did some more of the nod, which now seemed to involve quite a lot of waist and buttock movement as well. I pushed back my chair and got to my feet. The man behind the desk watched us as we went out through the swing doors, his eyes as blank and watchful as those of a Parisian concierge.

In the forecourt of the Museum, a group of Japanese tourists were huddled together, dividing their attention between guide and rainwashed building. The girl and I walked, a few yards apart. 'Or maybe,' I said, 'a drink?'

She looked up at me. 'Why not?' She had a slight London accent. I felt hectic and light headed. As we reached the gateway I thought 'I'll have a large gin and tonic.'

'What are you working on?' I asked.

'Seventeenth century,' said the girl.

'Snap,' I said.

She looked away from me. Out through the gates. We dodged a taxi and reached the opposite pavement. The world smelt fresh and vulgar after the Museum, and as we pushed open the pub door I caught a whiff of the girl's perfume. It was strong, with a cloying sweetness to it.

'I'm into handwriting and manuscripts,' she said, 'no interpretation. I just tell you whether the evidence is genuine. My speciality is dating things.'

'What would you like to drink?'

41

'Pint.'

This was, I felt, a somewhat strenuously interesting choice of drink. I watched her figure as she made her way to a table at the back of the pub, and noted that she had a slight waist but the beginnings of a stomach pouting over the edge of her jeans. I sought the eye of the barman.

'Nay Master Matheson, hast thou become a seeker after harlotry? A dabbler in women of the town and a haunter of carnal taverns and unreligious ale houses? What of thy Wife – yea and thy three children? And thy mother-in-law? Thou hast, Master Matheson, responsibilities.'

'Too right, Ezekiel,' I muttered. 'Why do you think I'm in the pub at a quarter to twelve, drinking large gin and tonics?'

When I joined her with the drinks she pushed back her ragged sweater to her elbows, with the air of one about to get down to business of some kind. I found myself gazing at her forearms, the plump curve into the crook of her arm, the throwaway delicacy of the wrist.

'Where did you get your tan?'

'I'm always tanned,' she said, and grinned; 'touch of the tar-brush.'

I drank deeply. She studied her pint morosely. 'So the fraud squad call you in, do they?' I said. 'To check that *Leviathan* wasn't really written by a nineteenth-century antiquary?'

'There aren't many fakes and frauds in the field of scholarship,' said the girl, 'apart from the contemporary humans involved.'

I didn't want to talk about fakes and frauds. At the table next to us an American in a duffel coat was discussing Ronald Reagan. 'Reagan,' he was saying slowly, 'has gone *beyond* ignorance.' I felt that lightness again.

'I'm not so much into evidence,' I said, 'as character. At the moment I'm interested in writing about Sexby.'

'Ah yes,' she said, sipping at her pint in a ladylike fashion. Was she a historian? 'And what else do you know about him?'

I realized that she thought of *me* as a historian. One of the charms of new acquaintance is the freedom it gives us to act out a new personality for ourselves. As I spoke my words seemed to animate her, she dropped her listlessness and I heard myself

42

talking about Cromwell, about Sexby's flight from England, about his shameful death (I described it as shameful) in the tones of authority. I was a teacher, a storyteller, and she listened as my children listen, glistening with belief.

'And what else do you know about him?' she said when I had finished. I could have been giving news of a killer virus that affected only Goths or Vandals to a late Roman Emperor. She wanted to hear all that I knew about Sexby. And so I made up other things that Sexby had done. His friendship with Hobbes. His wife who had betrayed him with a foot soldier in the Royalist Army. His struggles with gout and scurvy. His ability to extemporize rude verses about prominent members of the Rump Parliament. His fondness for animals. His clothes – wild and disordered – which caused him to be called Slop Sunday Sexby by the well known pamphleteer Nehemiah Woldpoke. Had she heard of Nehemiah?

'You're making this up,' she said. 'What are you *doing* in the Museum?'

'Actually,' I said, 'I only came across him because some loony quoted him in a pamphlet and accused him of being a liar.'

'How do you mean?'

Actually Ezekiel hadn't said that Sexby was a liar, had he? He had quoted a remark of Sexby's, made during the debates of the Army Council at Putney in 1647, and then gone on to accuse some nameless person – Master Sectary Secretary – of being involved in some nameless and unspeakable evil. The redhaired girl was looking at me curiously. 'Are you OK?'

'Fine.' But I wasn't fine. If we were being serious about it, why should Ezekiel, an enraged radical (that did at least emerge from his otherwise impenetrable prose), attack the Army? Wasn't the Army the true voice of the English Revolution? Not exactly. As I recalled it, the leaders of the Army were violently opposed to men like Sexby. And why that quotation, while we were at it? And who or what was this mysterious secretary?

'I didn't realize they had secretaries in 1650,' said the girl. I had spoken aloud.

'Oh they did,' I said, addressing myself to the present with some pleasure, 'they had Temp Agencies and Typing Pools . . .'

'Ye Typing Pool,' she said, and she laughed again. It seemed

43

easy to amuse her. Unlike Meg, of course, she had not yet heard all my jokes.

'They advertised for smart clean girls on Ye Local Radio,' I continued, 'and ye smart clean girls went around and perched on men's knees.' She was skipping from side to side on her seat now. 'Did they,' she asked in that sharp London accent, 'do shorthand?'

I stopped.

Shorthand. Something about shorthand. What about shorthand. Imp you check this. Wht abt shthand? Shorthand. I stared at the girl as if she were a revelation. My hand seemed to have found hers. She did not move away. 'What —' The Putney Debates had been transcribed in shorthand. By the Secretary of the Army, William Clarke. Master Sectary Secretary. Ezekiel had managed to gain access to the 1650s equivalent of a War Office memo on the subject of the storing of Cruise missiles. Which suggested to me that there might be more in his vague apocalyptic threats and rambling talk of evils and great conspiracies than might at first appear.

'Look,' I said, 'I think I may have happened on something rather important. Do you mind if I get back to the Library?'

'Not at all,' she said, 'what —'

I was getting to my feet. 'Tell you later,' I said. 'Let's meet here at five thirty.'

She looked at me sharply. 'Haven't you a home to go to?' she said.

'Nay. I am a wencher and a stopper out and one most stubbornly addicted to Pleasure in All its Formes.'

The sharpness was still there as she said, 'You look married to me.'

I shrugged and grinned.

'I always fall for married blokes,' she said. 'Always.'

We finished our drinks and went back out into the street, across the formal courtyard, cluttered with cars and tourists. Up the steps and through into the Library's remorseless silence. Ezekiel's voice was calling me – 'Nay Master Matheson for shame for shame! What lies before thy very eyes and very nearly lost and not spoken of. A wicked and foul conspiracy, my Lord. A suppression to outstalin Stalin! A maggot at the heart of this most cherished and protected Rebellion, taught as the corner-stone of our present liberties that yet ye know to be no liberties but yet more cunning bonds than were put about us by the Old King or the New Protector! A canker in the body of this your boasted Jewelle, your much talked of Parliamente!'

And why not? I thought. There have been conspiracies and suppressions before in England. Yes, and evil too – not always of the nameless variety. The past is still with us and only by understanding it can we exorcise it. I ran up the steps of the façade and pushed my way into the Reading Room, alive with what I thought of as the honest hunger for knowledge.

6

There were no further clues, however, in Ezekiel's pamphlet. The tone of the piece grew more imprecise with each paragraph. Its central section was a confused and confusing meditation of the nature of evil, and the last three or four pages a threatening vision of the future of England – '. . . this distressed and Unregenerated Rotten Carcase of Soules condemned in the Sight of God . . .' – that managed to combine the wilder excesses of the Book of Revelations with the fanatic zeal of a Workers' Revolutionary Party manifesto. After a while I didn't enjoy reading the tortuous sentences. I had caught a glimpse of the personality behind them, and did not like what I had seen. He was sick in the head, my Ezekiel; the pages of his book gave off the smell of mental disorder, sour, implacable, frightening. I pushed them away from me and went out into the Museum.

I wasn't here to investigate historical truth, I told myself. No one was paying me to investigate historical truth. What I needed, before I got too involved with Oliphant, was a few credible characters and the beginnings of a plot. Would Ezekiel be any help to me as far as Gottlieb's project was concerned? I didn't think, somehow, that Gottlieb would go for Ezekiel. I could hear him now, pacing his richly carpeted office, pulling at the remains of his hair:

'I *mean*, Jamie, I just don't believe the audience will go for someone called Ezekiel. And I don't go for him. I don't see where he's coming from, what he represents in our terms. He has no pazzazz, no charisma. He doesn't speak to me.'

'But Nat, I want to show Ezekiel as a rounded character. We see him at home eating a simple meal, then we track with him as he gets up and walks through the bustling seventeenth century streets to the simple Puritan church where –'

'Church! *Church*! You write a six-part series for me and you kick off with a guy called Ezekiel going to church! We are *dead* we try anything like this, Jamie, dead – you hear me?'

46

I looked up at an Assyrian figure. Apart from the wings and the claws it looked rather like Gottlieb. I shrugged at it defensively. I had set myself a hopeless task. And made it even more hopeless by embarking on research. Why should a tired old hack of nearly forty, with no ideals left to him, not a kosher ism to his name, suddenly acquire an interest in historical truth? Truth of any kind is not what I deal in. I was a socialist for a while in the 1960s, when such things were fashionable. Now it is fashionable to be self-reliant I rely on no one but myself. My interest in Ezekiel would get in the way of the job in hand. 'You hold a mirror up to nature if you like, Jamie,' I told myself, 'but please remember: it is someone else's mirror and they tell you which way to point it. Get *on* with it.'

'Get on with what?' said a second voice. 'Remember your only real talent is for using what is front of you. Experience is experience. Even in a library. Why not a six-part series about a vital historical document that proves that the Putney Debates were not transcribed accurately? That Cromwell and Ireton didn't actually say any of the things that were ascribed to them by the secretary of the Council of the Army?'

I wasn't too sure about this. It would probably take nine episodes to explain to the great British public what the Putney Debates were. And when they had been told, they wouldn't give a stuff if the whole lot had been faked by an agent of the Spanish Inquisition. If we were going to make it a forgery story we needed a cash element. I could hear Gottlieb – 'OK Jamie, it's a forgery story. There is only one forgery story, and it involves a *very valuable painting*. All other forgery stories – apart from the one about a large quantity of bank notes – are dullsville. Who cares about – a forged poem, for example? And a forged fucking *debate* – my God, what are we doing here? Look, I'll tell you what – I'm only thinking aloud here – a forged picture of Cromwell. What do you think? I'm only thinking aloud of course but –'

I was going off the forgery story.

OK. What did I care about? Right now – what actually mattered to me? What, deep down in my heart, was the concern that really counted? What was my central passion?

I was silent with myself for some time.

My bicycle?
No.
My wife?
Er. . .
Children?
Well of course, but –
The girl in the Library?
Come off it.

And then into my consciousness came a voice. Not the voice of someone inside my head, but that of a separate character. A most peculiar illusion, and one I have had, on occasions, when in the act of composition. It was a wheedling, thin sort of voice. Old maidish but with a hint of threat. And I was not in control of it. It was speaking to me.

'It is,' said the voice, 'no great matter, and one that needs not a great enquiry or setting forth of this or that Supposition, to find the Concern that now agitates your troubled and long imprisoned conscience Master Matheson! Seek no further for the Cause or Person who stands at the very centre of all you have ever fought or wished for, but know it to be that Distressed and Malignant creature to whom I was yoked by matrimony, and yet who, as I will solemnly swear before the justices, was a most perjured and false Witch, in league with Satan himself!'

Historical research or not, I had a character. I could always change the bastard's name. Henry Oliphant perhaps. An evil, sanctimonious Puritan, obsessed, in rather an unpleasant way, with conspiracy theories. The sort of man who came home in the evening, got out his prayer book, kicked the cat and abused his wife. Whose idea of a good time was a five-hour chat about where to put the altar rail. A man with no friends but a good deal of influence. A coward and a bigot. Probably a hypocrite too. Not averse to a crafty glass of sack with his lifelong friend Mend Thy Britches Mowbray. The kind of man whose doublet was always stained with gravy and whose ruff looked as if it could do with a wash. I liked the idea of his being married to a witch. I could see Gottlieb going for a witchcraft element.

'Aye,' said Ezekiel, with a Puritan businessman's relish for a deal, 'and mayhap Yonder Israelite would hire Meryl Streep to play her.'

'Shut up, Ezekiel,' I said. He was getting silly. And I don't think people actually said things like 'mayhap' even in 1650. He was getting silly and low on capital letters. I would have to demote him. Put him on the back burner. Leave him stewing in my imagination for a few days. He might emerge – such is the power of fantasy – as a troubled, serene and intelligent spokesman for liberal values in the eighties. On the other hand he might very well turn out to be a one-liner.

  But I liked the idea of a witch wife. I liked it very much. I got up and went back into the library. The redheaded girl was still bent over her books, her curls falling across her face. She looked up when I came in, her eyes bright, and gave me the smile. Then she mouthed 'five thirty' at me. For no good reason I felt suddenly, violently happy – the way one is when a child, offered some simple pleasure that seems as if it may only be the first in a long line of gratification, from the here and now into the unimaginable future.

  'Beware of the woman,' croaked Ezekiel, 'of her Lasciviousness and Unruly Nature, and of her Eie, Bright and Hard with lechery and Falseness! A witch, Master Matheson! By my hand – a Witch!'

  'Aye, berkfeatures,' I replied, 'but a good looking witch, no?'
  I pulled a blank sheet of paper towards me. At the top I wrote

1. 1647. A tavern. We see a group of apprentices at a trestle table, wearing leather aprons, and drinking and eating and talking. The table is piled high with bread, salt beef and gherkins (CHECK THIS) and the young men discuss the state of the nation in bawdy voices. 'The King is Mightily Incensed Against the Commons . . .' 'Aye, and Great men still make sport of the Humble.' Etc. Slowly the camera pans off them ,snf,st the back of the tavern, alone, in a black doublet and hose we see Ezekiel Oliphant, a hard-faced man of thirty-nine. He seems troubled. One of the apprentices gets to

his feet, tankard in hand, and ambles over. Ezekiel looks up quizzically.

APPRENTICE: And how fares thy wife – old sourmilk? How fares Anna the witch?

The camera tracks in on Ezekiel's face, expressing grief and bitterness. Cut to –

2. Int. The Oliphant home – a modest half-timbered affair in Cheapside. Anna Oliphant, a beautiful, red haired woman in her early thirties, is standing at the mullions (CHECK THIS) of the windows and looking out over the courtyard where a group of soldiers in the uniform of the King's army are rolling a large barrel towards a wooden cart. They are talking about the war, and the news of it. 'Upstart Rebellion hath a grip of the City I am told' – 'Aye, like a whore that serves her Clients Backwards, exposing the least Part of Herself' etc. Anna seems troubled by this. Her red hair is ragged and wild and her

Her what? Her knickers are in a twist? Her three year old daughter Edwina is playing with a bladder or whatever they played with in 1647? Her fingers are restlessly intertwined? Her broomstick is lying on the table, greased and ready for the Sabbat? And, more importantly, how old is Meryl Streep? Would Meryl Streep want to play this part? Why have I given the Meryl Streep character red hair? Should I give her some dialogue, fast?

I was through for the day. These are the kind of tough decisions that send your average screenwriter to the bottle well before lunch. I was worried too about these apprentices; did they work for Ezekiel? Or was he just a guy who hung around taverns, nursing a bottle of sack, waiting for someone to buy him a drink? Actually, if he was a Puritan, what was he doing in the tavern anyway?

Well, doing what I had been doing in the tavern presumably –

consoling himself for the fact that his wife was a witch.

Hang on, hang on. Who said anything about my wife being a witch? My wife is a graduate of Oxford University, a cordon bleu cook, a mother of three. And a fully paid up witch too, I imagine.

'Actually,' said Ezekiel in a whining, creepy voice, 'your wife is sick in the head.'

I wanted him to talk the way he wrote, but he wouldn't. His voice buzzed in my ear like a mosquito. 'Remember,' he said, 'three weeks ago? When she said she heard voices? Remember that, Jamie? There were two men in the room with her all of a sudden, and they were talking about her. You must remember that, Jamie.'

I did remember. I remembered it well. Barnes Common in the snow. The two of us walking with the children. 'I've got everything,' she had said. 'I've got money, I've got children I love, I'm married to someone I love, I've got everything. And yet I hear these voices. All the time. These voices.'

'And what do they say to you?' I asked. 'Get up? Clean the kitchen? Or do they advise you to send your children to public school?'

Ahead of us the three girls ran into the snowdrift, piled high on one side of the path. The sky was the colour of a new bruise. I remembered other walks like this, in Sussex, in Barnet, near to my mother's cottage. Walks with no children, walks with one, walks with two, neither of them able to even stagger a few paces, and now a royal progress with three walking, talking, self-sufficient young women. And suddenly these walks, taken over so many years together, seemed utterly and completely pointless. Where were we walking to? What were we walking away from?

We were walking away from something, of course. We were walking away from a shadow, always at our backs, that grew longer and longer with each year until there were no lit spaces offering escape. And I wanted to walk faster. I wanted to break into a run, to hurl myself forward, over by the pond, left into Barnes High Street, left at the river, on on on, anywhere that wasn't here, anywhere that was a little further away from my life, my pointless, endlessly repetitive, desperate re-enactment of the right suburban rituals, walking children or dogs (they could be dogs for all the notice they take of us) on ugly little bits of open ground in the city where my father did much the same thing for sixty pointless years.

It didn't do him much good, all that walking, did it? He walked himself right into a brown wooden box and a slab in Hendon cemetery that reads ARTHUR MATHESON, PRIEST AND POET. My mother chose the description 'priest' but my father wasn't a priest: he was a vicar. One of the new vicars, who don't believe in God or evil or any of that rubbish. Who think RESURRECTION is the title of a novel by Tolstoy.

'They say awful things to me,' Meg was saying, 'awful, awful things.'

'Tell me what though.'

'You wouldn't mind, would you? You'd tell me what to do. You'd probably be able to use them. You use everything. You use me and the children. You use me up until there isn't any of me left. But these voices . . .'

'What did they *say*?'

Or was it in Barnes? Did this conversation happen in Lewes? In the other house? In the narrow kitchen with the drab blue table? I know at some time over the last three or four years – maybe then, or maybe only now, in my hospital bed, staring at the green, featureless wall opposite to me – I turned to her and said 'But what did they say? You say I won't help. It's because you don't want me to help. You love your misery and your sense of failure and your idea of yourself as a bad person, as an evil person so bloody much, don't you? Well don't blame me for it. I'm falling out of love with you, Meg. I'm simply out of love for you. How can I give you anything when I don't want to be here in this cosy, walleyed suburb walking away from the same shadow that swallowed my father. If you're crazy go and see a fucking doctor.'

She did go and see the doctor. He wasn't worried. He'd seen crazy people before. He'd seen people a lot crazier than her. So she got halfway through a sentence and was unable to complete it? So she slept thirteen hours on the trot? So she locked herself in the bedroom and cried for hours? So she spent two hours naked in front of the mirror examining every part of her body, in case she had cancer – cancer of the feet, the ears, the legs, the eyes, the nose . . . My God there was nothing crazy about that; she was just being cautious.

He was about as much use as me, that doctor. If she'd gone to him and told him she thought she was a witch, he would probably have told her to work through the experience. To buy a cat. Ask a few sympathetic women round. Maybe light a fire, who knows? Dance a bit.

I feel bitter now, at the thought of all those women who were supposed to help her. The sisters. Some sisters they turned out to be. Susan Tomlinson sitting in the kitchen, her long, blonde hair combed carefully enough to qualify her for Crufts. She looked as pleased as a prize dog as she talked endlessly, coherently, of her problems, to my unhappy, tongue-tied wife: 'You see Norman doesn't really help me insofar as I feel that he is the sort of person who fails to grasp my needs . . .'. There was Sarah Jackson who could speak of nothing but her hysterectomy. There was Daisy French who could talk for hours on the admirable nature of the preparatory school she had chosen for her gifted son. There was Norma Lewis, Manny Fitzwater and Juliet Dromgoole, all of whom wanted to write; and there were, besides, Emma Latham, Marjorie Beamish, Annie Williams and Suzie Mackenzie, all of whom had marital problems of one sort or another. There were sisters a-plenty. Meg's problem interested them as sisters, and as sisters they spoke about it, wistfully, briefly before embarking on the all important business of discussing their children, husbands, lumps, phobias, dreams, queries and dinner party menus. They appropriated her helplessness to themselves and passed on. They didn't want to help but managed to make it look as if they did.

It was the other way with me. I wanted to – oh how I wanted to, but had no words or gestures that would make things right for her. I watched her go further and further into herself. It is a terrible thing to love someone who cannot love themselves, and to love that very quality in them most particularly makes it even harder to bear. I looked across at the redhead. She was deep in her books now, those square shoulders firmly set against intruders, her chin cupped in her right hand. I noticed the fingers, short, stubby, the nails chewed to the quick. What was

53

she reading? Some seventeenth-century laundry list perhaps? We were both of us, her and me, hovering between now and the Great Rebellion . . .

It was, I realized with a start, nearly five o'clock. At that distant trestle table Ezekiel put on his stove pipe hat and prepared to trudge back through the miry streets to his cottage, thrown into a pile of crazy, black and white buildings in some overgrown street where the light hardly reached. He turned to the camera and addressed me directly: 'All's fair in a world ripe for dissolution,' he said. 'This England is Ripe for a New Cleansing Fire which will Burne out your Old Appearances and Judgements. Take Take Take and Savour. The only Just Rebellion is the Rebellion against the Law that condemns us to One Woman in the Licensed Harlotry of the Marriage Bed. Both are Whores. And this one seems, at least –' I tried to answer him but found I could not. He winked coarsely in the direction of the redhead. 'The Old Wife is stale,' he said, 'I can see by your smiling. And synce Ye be bound to the Lecherous Course, take it at a Runne and Jumpe, as the Spaniards do, for wee knowe nothinge after this Our Beinge is Dissolved!'

He winked again and I rose to my feet. The redhead turned to look at me and this time, when I mouthed that we should, perhaps, leave the library now, there was complicity in both our eyes. That, I think, was the moment when I was first unfaithful to Meg, and the only witchcraft used, whatever happened later, was my own self-will. Even my fictional characters are there simply to justify my urges. Perhaps that's why I'll always be a hack.

As we left the Museum for the second time, just as we passed through the front gates, quite naturally, we linked arms, as if we had known each other for a long time. It was only then that I asked her name.

'Anna,' she said, looking up at me. 'Do you think it's a nice name?'

'I couldn't have made up a better one,' I replied.

54

7

'Why,' she said as we turned up towards Bedford Square, 'don't
we go back to my place?'

I had a mental image of a lengthy tube ride to somewhere like
Dulwich or Cockfosters. The tube is a great passion-killer, and
there was something almost alarmingly immediate about this
girl's smile. I recalled an early erotic encounter with a girl called
Jane Foat, who, seconds before I was about swoop down on her
and place a hawk-like, thirteen-year-old kiss on her lips, stuffed
no fewer than eight egg sandwiches into her mouth. Timing was
the thing.

'Where is your place?'

'Here,' said the girl whose name was Anna. Her voice seemed
to have lost that London twang. Indeed, I was finding less and
less to connect her with the person I had met at lunchtime.
There was something rather proper about her now, as she
turned into a house that faced the east side of the Museum, her
shoulder bag bouncing against her thighs. On the other side of
the street, a group of African students dressed like businessmen
chattered their way up towards Dillons. Behind us a group of
upwardly mobile businessmen who looked like students
mooched south towards Covent Garden.

As she went down the stairs ahead of me, I saw that her hips
were narrower than Meg's. If her legs hadn't been so short,
from the back anyway, she would have been beautiful. That
small, precise bottom waggled busily as she pulled out a huge
bunch of keys and began to sort through them.

This was all going rather fast for me. 'Well,' I said, in what
was intended to be a light, casual tone, 'I suppose this is where
you show me your etchings.' My voice seemed to have a frightened, hysterical quality to it. I was, I realized, staring greedily at
her behind as she preceded me into the dark hall of the flat. It
was trying to tell me something as it bounced perkily this way
and that, inside the denim of her jeans. Something like 'Do not

do this, Matheson. Turn back while there is still time'. Something like 'This girl is desperate'.

But they never come on desperate, do they? Not the first time. The first time they are cool and self-possessed and amused and glad to be single. It's only later they start looking moodily into the distance and telling you how lonely they are. How you, unlike other men, can talk to them, are sensitive and understand their needs. So how come you didn't ring them at the weekend, you insensitive bastard?

I'm a big expert at all of this. You can tell, can't you? Jamie Matheson: cyclist, author, historian, stud.

I was now actually licking my lips. Had she seen me? I tried to put my tongue away tidily, behind my teeth, as she moved about the room, putting records back in their sleeves, adjusting lights, and, from time to time, shaking those red curls so that you could see the elegant neck, tanned, hold still for a moment and then sail back into motion. I could not rid myself of the impression that all her actions were designed to display herself to me, and, although I could find no rational reason for this assumption (I look like a troll, I hardly know her) I could tell that my expression, indeed my whole physical attitude, was coming to resemble that of a man in the front row of a Soho strip joint. My eyes were glazed over with the effort of expressing lack of interest, my tongue had escaped from my teeth and was lolling over my parted lips like the tongue of the wolf in the fairy story. Everything about me, as I sprawled tensely in her battered sofa, seemed, if you will excuse the expression, cocked.

And as I watched, Anna scuttled from bachelor girl's washing to bachelor girl's paperbacks (*Studies in Contemporary Radical Politics*, *French Provincial Cooking*, *Crochet Made Easy*, and next to that, *Women to Women: A Study of Nineteenth-Century Feminism*) and I looked furtively around to see where she kept Virginia Woolf and *The Women's Room* by Marilyn French. But as she scuttled I watched her more and more. She looked more and more like one of those female pigeons in Trafalgar Square, waddling out of range of a male pigeon which is waddling, even more determinedly, towards it.

When the floor was clear, she knelt in the middle of the carpet, and looked up at me, helplessly. 'Drink?' she said. 'In a minute,' I replied thickly, falling forward on to my knees and shuffling towards her like a communicant seeking the wafer. My hands seemed to be outstretched. For one brief moment I thought she might skip to her feet and trip lightly to the kitchen, that it was all some terrible mistake. And then I realized that it was a terrible mistake but not *that* kind of terrible mistake because her head was on one side, her arms were reaching for mine, her mouth was open and limp, and the two of us appeared to be kissing, gripping each other like two swimmers out of breath, supporting each other towards the shallows.

With a thump she fell back on the floor and I rolled on top of her. The kiss seemed to be lasting a long time. Did I kiss Meg for this long? Did I kiss Meg at all these days? The answer to this was almost certainly 'no' or 'not enough'. But in spite of that Meg was certainly in the room with us, talking me through this one, advising me on points of technique. Somehow the fact that I wasn't kissing *her* made it easier to be gentle, sensitive, tactile, and all those other things she was constantly accusing me of not being. 'Stroke,' she was saying, 'just stroke me. Gently.' 'Of course, Meg. Of course.' It's easier to stroke you now you're five foot eight instead of five foot six. Now you have red hair instead of black. Now you have brown skin not white. Now you are lying in my arms making small gurgling noises, instead of frightened on our bed, scene of so much history, as inert as a bag of groceries. Now your big blue eyes aren't watching me, criticizing me.

This girl, who did not yet know I was supposed to be cold, vain, voyeuristic and fundamentally anti-women, appeared to be fooled by my performance, even muttering, as I slipped my hand down from her neck to her shoulder, 'Oh', and then again 'Oh Oh Oh . . .' It was as if I was chipping away at her piece by piece, thawing her reserve, and each little whimper seemed like a victory, the capture of valuable territory. 'Oh', she mewed again, and then 'You're so sensual.'

I wondered whether I had heard this right. No. Hang on. This could not be right. What had she actually said? 'You're so sensible,' perhaps. 'You're so *cynical*.' Possibly. 'You're –'

Despite these reflections, and despite the fact that, as I helped her off with her tartan man's shirt, Meg's face was above me, now amused, mocking, everything seemed to have a quality notably lacking from lovemaking with my lawfully wedded wife – pace. The slow controlled ferocity with which I kept my mouth clamped to hers as I moved my right hand down to the top button of her jeans, would have done credit to one of the more celebrated of Hitchcock's tracking shots. She wriggled out of her trousers with the natural, larky spontaneity of the French Nouvelle Vague, and when I slipped my fingers between her panties and her buttocks, digging my nails into her flesh like a housewife testing fruit, as my tongue fenced with hers, saliva went from mouth to mouth and still those little animal cries continued 'Oh Oh Oh . . .', the moment had a self-absorbed rightness, a vulgar, massive certainty that made *Gone With The Wind* look like the early work of Robert Bresson.

This was a wide screen, Hollywood fuck. At least it was until the doorbell rang.

She went as rigid as a rabbit at the sound of gunfire. 'Oh my God,' she said, 'it's Derwent.' I slid her panties over the firm globe of her buttocks. 'Can't Derwent wait?' I asked, with a certain amount of lazy charm. The doorbell rang again. 'You don't know Derwent,' she said.

I didn't know Derwent, but I had a horrible feeling I was about to be introduced to him. I felt somehow that it was going to be difficult to like Derwent. She was zipping up the front of her jeans, the fawn tan of her thighs and buttocks, once more shrouded in denim. Fort Knox. Oh shit shit shit shit.

As I got to my feet I saw myself in the full length mirror on the other side of the room. My face was scarlet and my hair, never my best feature, gave me the appearance of a threatened hedgehog. There was steam on my glasses. I looked uniquely like a man interrupted in the act of intercourse.

'Hullo there,' said a voice from the door, 'I'm Derwent, mate.'

I looked up into a large, square face, preceded by a large, square hand. Derwent Mate was wearing a long, black gabardine, a rather arty scarf, and a haircut that looked as if it had cost too much money. He didn't have the kind of face that can be improved by something as trivial as a haircut. The nose, the moist eyes, and above all the skin – or at least the bits of it not covered by beard – all needed fairly major surgical work. Had he got prickly heat? I wondered. Some form of psoriasis? Or had he just had a damned good lunch? As he came towards me a fireball of garlic snaked across at me. He was smiling with almost obsessive frankness. 'Who are you, Mate?' he said. 'I'm Jamie,' I said. But I was not looking at him: I was looking over his shoulder. There in the light from Anna's hall, still in his black outfit, stovepipe hat in hand, was Ezekiel. He was, like Derwent Mate, dripping with rainwater, but unlike Derwent Mate he was not smiling. He seemed depressed.

'Well, mate,' said Derwent Mate, 'cold old night rain started again February filldike I ask you nice place to be nice flat nice girl mate, eh mate?'

'Yes,' I said.

Anna raised her eyes as she went past me to the kitchen. I watched Ezekiel. 'Oh Pitifull Condition of Humanitie,' said Ezekiel, 'oh world of Drudges and Whores! Is this what wee of the New Modelle fought and died for?' He seemed to have something against Derwent Mate. I too thought I might have something against him. So far I had physical appearance, dress sense and dialogue (content and delivery of) against this character. I sat back on the sofa and waited for more evidence. It was not slow in coming. He advanced into the room, rubbing his hands. 'Actually mate,' said Derwent Mate, 'thing is basically, mate great girl don't you think basically, mate?'

'Yes, mate,' I said. Ezekiel was looking curiously between the two of us, as if we were a couple of fish in a tank and he was attempting to sex us. Anna re-entered the room. 'Derwent's in advertising,' she said.

'What Manner of Thynge,' said Ezekiel, 'is Advertising?'

I tried looking away from him at the light bulb, and then switched my gaze back in his direction. He refused to vanish. He just stood there, fingering his stovepipe hat, waiting for me to explain what advertising was. I decided against this and instead, leaning forward with the kind of false *naïveté* I had seen Gottlieb employ with the very famous, said, 'It's funny, I've never heard a really good definition of advertising.'

Ezekiel narrowed his eyes.

'What *is* it exactly?'

Both Anna and Derwent Mate looked rather startled by this

question. But Derwent Mate, as I thought he would, rose to it. 'Advertising,' he said, 'is the dissemination of product image and product factual detail in order to enhance consumer awareness of such image and essence of product or brand as the advertisers, in consultation with the manufacturers, may wish to establish.'

I wondered whether he had got this from a book. Anna looked at me sideways and winked clearly under the illusion that I was doing this for her and not for Ezekiel's benefit.

It didn't help Ezekiel at all. He turned his mouth down and screwed his head into his neck, as if someone had just offered him a dud consignment of salt cod at well above the asking price.

'Certayne Master Matheson,' he said, 'the very Tongue wee of the Army of God spake, hath been most notoriously abused and Perverted in this your Wicked and Abominable Age. Nott one worde of his is to mee any other than Shadowe and Speculative Ignorance!' It was remarkably true, I thought, that the development (if such it could be called) of the English language seemed to have been achieved at the expense of both richness and clarity. I might find Ezekiel's language hard to follow – but in the seventeenth century there was much less of a sense that language was granted to conceal, rather than illuminate, thoughts and intentions. Languages, like empires, have their cycles, and we are in a period of decline.

Certainly, I reflected, if Derwent Mate was anything to go by, we were all absolutely fucking finished and might as well go around on all fours barking like dogs, instead of continuing to pretend to talk to each other. Outside an ambulance, or some other official vehicle on a mission of vengeance or mercy, screamed up the street. Derwent Mate got up and helped himself to a drink from the home-made looking table in the corner of the room. He was clearly under the illusion that I genuinely wished to hear about the advertising trade. 'Basically, mate,' he went on, 'we are in the business of clarifying or exposing the heart or centre of what the individual *wants* from a product. For instance – an umbrella. Why does the average consumer require an umbrella?' I knew the answer to this question was not 'to keep dry'. I sat on my hands and watched Ezekiel to see if he was going to ask me what an umbrella was. But he was no longer listening to the conversation. He had hitched up his black coat and was scratching at his belly with one long, blackened finger. I watched his nail dig into the white flesh, scarred with an ugly looking rash. As he scratched the blemish, it went from dull red to furious crimson. I thought 'In 1650 you scratched an itch as you do now. Nothing whatsoever changes. It is history that is the illusion. The past is with us now, in the texture of meat, the feel of silk against your hand – in weather, stone, or any of the unchanging things.'

The siren passed on. I heard the rain drive against the window. I did not share these profound thoughts with anyone. Derwent was in the middle of answering his own question: 'An umbrella, mate, is first and foremost a fashion accessory, mate . . .' I looked sideways at Anna. She was holding her glass up to chin, but not drinking from it. Her head was to one side, like a sparrow's, and her brown eyes stayed on his face. On the wall behind her was a poster that said NO CUTS IN JOBS AND SERVICES. Next to it another one said something in Spanish about Nicaragua. We were going to win, or they were going to win if we weren't careful, or someone was going to stop someone else winning.

I liked this girl and I liked her flat. I liked the simple, primary certainties of her posters, the consistency of her reading matter. It reminded me of the days of certainty, of the night Nick was busted by the Special Branch in that flat in Acton, oh of too many things, but above all of the feeling that progress was not an ugly or impossible word, that there was still something to fight for, even here in rainy, dark, unimportant Britain.

Ezekiel was mouthing something at me. He was speaking now in the voice I might have used, had I been addressing him. 'Time to go,' he said. 'She'll keep. And he is *really* boring.' 'Time to go,' I said. 'Time to go?' said Anna. 'Time to go,' said Derwent Mate.

She came with me to the door and said she was sorry and we would meet again. He was, she said, wincing, a *very* old friend. I laughed at the way she said this because then I didn't know her enough to be jealous; in fact, I thought jealousy was something that happened to other people. She looked up at me and touched the collar of my coat. She looked like one of my little girls so I kissed her lightly on the forehead and walked out into the rain.

I looked back into the room as I went, but Ezekiel had gone. I didn't blame him. I was, I felt, much the most entertaining person in the room. What else was there to stay for?

8

They ask me a lot about Ezekiel in the hospital, which is fair enough, as my continued insistence on his appearances is probably the most important single piece of evidence that I am off my trolley. But, as I tell Dr Masters, I don't feel particularly crazy before or after he appears to me, although it can get fairly embarrassing when he is actually around. The trouble, as I tell Dr Masters, is not his cropping up and then vanishing in the way he does. A hallucination is not, I insist, proof of insanity. Writers spend their days inventing imaginary people, and I seem to remember Gustave Flaubert shouting at someone 'I am Madame Bovary.' They didn't lock him up, did they? Although, re-reading *Bouvard et Pécuchet*, I think it might not have been a bad idea.

No (I turn from my hospital bed and look out at the lawn, the trees, and the Cotswold stone wall that separates us from the outside world). Ezekiel's showing up is fine; I can handle it. It is Ezekiel himself who is the problem. It is who he is and what he is and what he has managed to make me do. He was always that way. From the beginning he was sly, treacherous, double-thinking and double-talking. From the very first he talked about witches. From well before Professor Rick Mason got in on the act.

In fact, looking back at what I have written, I feel rather pleased with myself. I don't think I show any traces of mental instability. My prose style may be a little effortful here and there but I don't come over as a screwball. Mind you, I haven't got very far yet, have I? I mean I'm fine when telling you what I had for lunch, or how it all started. No problem. I come over in these pages as a quizzical, amused Englishman, don't I? A perfect advertisement for our national character and our famously incomprehensible humour. It would only take me five minutes, though, on the subject of witchcraft, for me to create a less favourable impression. I might strike you as ill, as distressed, as lonely, angry, cruel, and frightened of dying. But these too are English characteristics.

Perhaps I can sound so big and bold because here, in this antiseptic ward, with only MacDonald and O'Flaherty for company, the harsh sounds and smells of the Rebellion seem no longer real. O'Flaherty keeps telling me that in Ireland they forget nothing (he also shows me pictures of a woman of about fifty, in pebble glasses, nearly circular in shape, who, he tells me, is the most beautiful thing in all of Clonakilty; when he gets out he's going to marry her). I, like the polite Englishman, smile as if to say 'Sure, England's finished. England has not only no future, we have no past. We never fought with each other over land and money and liberty, or if we did it was only an accident. On the hills near here, three hundred years ago, a group of horsemen did not chase a tired, sick man across the fields, as he screamed for help, as he howled that he was the victim of a foul conspiracy. There were never any witches in England. Dr Martin of Edinburgh was not "put to the torture of the boots, which is a most exquisite torment in which the legs are crushed in steel, and it was ordered to be applied by King James that he might admit his compact with the Devil, but so obdurate was he in wickedness that the blood and marrow spurted forth and he did cry out exceedingly.' 'Nothing of importance ever happened or will happen here. It happened abroad or round the corner or under the cover of darkness.'

What I don't say to O'Flaherty is that I know our history, the history of England, to be more fantastic and cruel than even he dreams of. That what was done to Ezekiel and his like in the name of good government, beats women and children crawling along the high roads of Ireland tugging grass out in handfuls and cramming it into their starvation-ravaged faces. Why don't I tell him what I know? Because he wouldn't believe me. He'd say I was crazy. He doesn't share my delusion. O'Flaherty thinks the whole of the British Isles' electricity system is controlled from a stopcock in the main drain of the German Hospital (the last loony bin he was in). *Christ* – you can see this in O'Flaherty's face as he tells you this – *you didn't know that?*

For much the same reason, dearest reader, I do not tell you what I know. I take care to present myself as a reasonable, sceptical person. I don't want to be like one of those unhappy Jews who came out of Eastern Europe in the last war and tried to tell right little, tight little Englishmen what was going on in the camps. They weren't believed. Why not? They weren't telling it right, were they? And so I tell you my story as a novelist does, with all the tricks of perspective, scenery . . . I shade in characters, take it day by day, until (I hope) you will come to understand why I came to feel as I did, way back in February.

Who knows how far the witch business reaches anyway? We have no way of knowing. No way of checking. The newspaper I am allowed tells me that unemployment is down and exports are up, that there hasn't been a riot in months. Northern Ireland was noisy but is quiet. The Prime Minister is in control. But how in God's name am I supposed to believe the newspaper any more than I believe O'Flaherty, knowing what I know? How can I assume that anything, any of them, from the fluent Dr Masters to my apparently honestly tongue-tied wife, is true? For this country is so founded on lies, so wound about with hypocrisy and double-dealing that nothing can be credited. The Queen's librarian worked for the Russians. British democracy works. We won the war. Spot the deliberate mistake.

I can see Meg clearly. She comes into this hospital. She knows all about mental disturbance, knows how to talk to the nurses, and she comes in at her pleasure. She stands by the door of the ward in that white nightdress of hers, her painfully thin arms raised in supplication. Across her white neck is a thin trail of blood. Where did you go Meg? In what attic or miserable street are you hiding? How can someone disappear so completely?

Anna comes too. Passes me on my walk, from cedar tree to library. She puts her head on one side, the chirpy schoolgirl, and she mouths 'I love you' the way she mouthed at me when I left her flat, the night after I got back from Oxford, when –

Go away. Go away and haunt some other fucker, the pair of you. Soon the trolley will be round with the pills. Then the roar of one of the planes from the American base nearby, and the quiet three hours till bedtime, the dust dancing in the diagonal rays of the sun. Where was I? Back in February. Well get back to it. Go on.

I walked back from Anna's flat to the Museum. Yes. It had not

65

stopped raining. There was a couple outside the Museum Tavern, kissing in the downpour, arranged romantically against the lighted glass of the pub window. I unchained my bicycle, looking carefully round for Ezekiel as I did so. I rather relished the idea of explaining the mechanics of my Holdsworth Whirlwind to him. But he was nowhere to be seen. Perhaps he was collecting a group of figures from the history of the English Revolution who he thought might interest me: 'And this, Master Matheson, is the Captaine Generalle of our New Modelle, Noll Cromwell . . .' I could have wished that Ezekiel displayed a little more consistency, a criticism levelled at many of the characters in *Alfie Barnacle*. My fictional characters, as I think I said, tend to be there to explain or justify the whim of the moment. It was chilling to find that when they did what fictional characters are supposed to do – i.e. got off up the page and walked away – they remained as unconvincing off the page as on it. Ezekiel reminded me – at this stage anyway – of a not very efficient robot; he was very much first draft material.

It amuses me now, after all that has happened, to think that I wished a character on him. My God, he was consistent all right. So consistent that I wonder sometimes whether his early appearances were all a bluff, a careful simulation of the kind of rubbish I usually write, an acting out of the character he knew I would want him to be. Just as scientists talk of our 'picture' of the atom, or the 'templates' for some twisting segment of poly-peptide that makes up our genetic pattern, so too we 'picture' other characters before we know them, blending fragments of morality, sexual desire – or lack of it – and half-remembered words our parents spoke about people long since dead, until, with 'he's a bit like . . .' or 'she's the sort of person who . . .', we arrive at a wholly invented character to whom another human being is expected to conform.

I don't want him to come back. He hasn't got into the hospital. But I am terrified he may return. I address myself to the page again, going back to when I was a nasty/nice, humorous Englishman, living out the cosy world of my own fiction.

It was after eight. I decided to cycle back along Oxford Street, down through Bayswater, Shepherd's Bush, and from there to Hammersmith. From Hammersmith I would cycle across Barnes

Common to Putney. I needed time to think. I cycled, as I do when in meditative mood, like those old men on their solid black machines who hug the edges of roads like wrinkled, soon-to-be-extinct birds. From time to time I looked up at the illuminated shop windows, crammed with after-hours' wealth, then Hyde Park to my left, locked up for the night like the tired exhibits in the shops; Notting Hill Gate, still managing to be raffish after all these years; Holland Park, as quiet as only the rich can be quiet; and, last outpost of the smart, Shepherd's Bush.

In Ezekiel's day, of course, all this was open country. The army camped at Putney, in open fields. London, now, could be any city. It has given up the search for a style and recommends itself, like a boxer on the ropes, simply by the fact of its still being there. The lights are on all the time but the town is never quite alive. Half awake, like someone keeping going on cigarettes or coffee or dope, its immigrants and natives alike avoid your eyes. Out into Hammersmith roundabout. Drive into me you bastard, kill an innocent cyclist. Make your day. I'll come back and haunt you.

How was I going to look when Meg opened the door to me? I would look different. She would know the difference. She would, she *must* know that I had been with another woman. What else was our intimacy worth?

Perhaps her mother would open the door to me. Her mother always looks at me as if I had climbed straight off another woman anyway. Or rather as if I had been bothering one somewhere. I don't think Juliet thinks I am capable of normal, healthy sexual activity. I am for her a fatal blend of wimp and wild rapist, an incarnation of all that is least attractive in males, at once grotesquely macho and unspeakably effeminate. The moment that sums it all up happened when I passed her naked on the stairs. I mean I was naked: she had clothes on. As I recall, she raised her left forearm, and blocked out the light from her eyes. Turning her head as she passed me she cried 'It's all right!'

Well. Maybe it was all right for her.

The gutter was strewn with huge, irregular diamonds of black water as I pumped my legs the length of the Fulham Palace Road. Up on to Putney Bridge; ahead of me, floodlit, the church where Sexby and Cromwell and Ireton and the rest of them argued. In the middle lane. To my right and left the threatening noise of engines, coming close in, like enemy planes, and then safely away in front of me, tail lights glowing like exotic insects . . . They're warning you, Jamie. Play it safe, Jamie. You're in trouble, Jamie.

It wasn't Juliet or her daughter who opened the door to me. It was Rick Mason. 'Hullo, Jamie,' he said. 'I've been trying to seduce your wife.'

'Did you succeed?' I said.

'It's you she wants,' he said, 'for some reason.'

I parked my bike in the hall and followed him through to the kitchen. Meg was sitting at the table, a bottle of wine in front of her. The room smelt of meat and bread and pepper. She looked up and smiled at me, and for a moment I could not understand what I had been doing with a stranger in some basement opposite the Museum. The stranger and the stranger's friends were nothing to do with me.

Then I saw the quality of the smile. It was stretched across her face with all the *élan* of an inadequate rope bridge. Her big blue eyes went from me to Rick and back to me, again and again, in search of reassurance that I knew not even an embrace would provide. Her face had that walled-in look. She was down and staying down. It would get worse later.

Rick could not know this. He was now seated in what I have come to think of as my chair, hunched over his glass of wine, looking in need of a rather different kind of reassurance – the kind solicited by professional northerners. 'Say you're sorry,' his tiny shoulders seemed to be demanding. 'Sorry for the empty woollen mills, the dole queues, the deserted Rugby League grounds. Apologize, publicly, for the demise of the steel industry. Get down on your knees and grovel and lick and plead for mercy for the populations of Rotherham and Leeds. Say "I am a Southerner and I smell." Now.'

I moved to the table and insinuated myself with Home Counties sneakiness, on to one of the wooden pews that, ten years ago, when we were young, Meg and I thought fashionable. I looked out at our balcony, the neat garden below it, and beyond, the lights of the luxury flats on Putney Hill, and thought how much this lush and inessential landscape would displease Dr Mason.

'Where've you been?' said Meg.

'Pub,' I said. 'I met Norman Tomlinson in the Museum.' What was I saying? My God what was I saying. First principle of falsehood: *a lie should be as close to the truth as possible.* In certain circumstances it may be possible to tell the truth so long as it looks like a lie. For example: 'I've been fucking a girl I met in the Museum. Ha ha ha let's have a drink.'

Oh God. Oh God oh God.

'How's Norman?'

'Fine.' Phone Norman. Square Norman. Phone Norman now and convince him we were in the pub – 'Norman old man, do us a favour, man to man. I was getting my leg over a bit of crumpet and . . .' *I am not cut out for this.*

'How's his glossy load of rubbish on the Baroque?' said Rick.

'He's having trouble with it,' I said, gathering confidence in the whole Norman episode. I had a clear picture now of me and Norm sitting up at the bar swigging a pint and chatting. In many ways, I reflected, it would have been an easier, more rewarding way of spending the evening. It would not also have induced in me my current sensation which was that of being interrogated by senior members of the Gestapo, who were so high up and secretive they obstinately refused to admit they had anything to do with the secret police whatsoever.

I sneaked a look at Meg. She didn't look any different. *She believes me*, I thought; *she can't tell the difference.* This is how people lie to each other. It's easier this way. Who needs trouble? She need never know. I sneaked another look at her. She did look different, I found. Scareder, smaller, greyer . . . This frightened me, so I looked away and began to talk about Norman. 'He's been having terrible trouble,' I said, 'with his editor. He's really been giving him a hard time. It was nice to see him actually. We talked about history and about how difficult it is to establish the truth of anything, we –' What had he drunk? What was he wearing? Why did I mention him? Shouldn't I have said I passed out at my desk? My God, suppose he's here! Suppose he dropped in and is in the lavatory or out on the balcony admiring the paintwork? Do I know another Norman Tomlinson who also

69

wrote a three volume, lavishly illustrated load of rubbish called *Tendencies in the Baroque*? Must head the conversation off Norman. 'We didn't say much it was pretty boring there's not much to say about Norman is there?'

'You seem to be managing fairly well,' said Rick. He smiled, sourly. 'And while we're about it – the truth is very easy to discover. It's the only thing that matters.'

I did not like the way he said this. 'Not,' I said quickly, 'when you're dealing with evidence. How do you know when people are lying? You don't. You just decide to trust certain people. Which is a completely arbitrary, self-interested and absurd decision, which invokes all the meaningless words like love and social justice – Meg was looking at me oddly. She knows, I thought, she knows. And then *she doesn't know. Nobody knows anything about anyone or anything.* Rick warmed to the argument. 'Listen Jamie,' he said, 'the things you talk about are not just words. They are tested by behaviour. By the will and desire to work for a country that is no longer divided along the lines of race and class, and too by the search for truth in the discipline one has chosen, whether it is the exact sciences or, as in my case, the detailed examination of a particular period of history or –'

'Or,' I said, 'as in my case, the provision of tired old story lines to satisfy the fifty million moronic racists who make up the population. On whom you and your like are going to inflict all those tired old ideals that they don't want to think about, or at least not in the way you want to think about them.'

Meg looked up at me piteously. 'Please,' she said, 'please don't say things you don't mean.'

At least we weren't talking about Norman Tomlinson. I went to the table and sat down. The Tomlinson problem could wait. Had my outburst sounded odd? Very probably. Odd enough to make her suspect? No. But the curious thing was, I found that already, so early in the game of deception, I had come to believe the hateful things I was saying. And would not have said them to the red-haired girl. Oh no. To her I would have talked airily about Nicaragua, about unemployment, my radical past, perhaps even my hope for the future. To Anna my cheap optimism – to Meg my even cheaper despair.

Meg was smiling. It cost her a lot but she was smiling. I could see Rick thought it was just another smile. 'What brings you to London?' I said to Rick.

'Oh you know . . .'

'Witches?'

'Not witches,' said Rick, 'a witch-hunter I'm after.'

I relaxed. No one seemed interested in whether I really had had a drink with Norman Tomlinson. 'Who is this witch-hunter then?'

Rick smiled; his small face glowed with peace and satisfaction. 'Ezekiel Oliphant. The so-called Bloomsbury Witchfinder.' He leaned over the table towards me. 'I'm on his tracks,' he said.

I was with my Master NEHEMIAH in the town of Hertford, hard by the Fountaine, for a space of ten Yeares, during which time my Habits and Opinions were formed, and Never Once did I return to that House where I had been so notoriously Abused, nor did anie seek mee where I was, for as it is written *Ye have cast aside the Children in the Daies of Thy Iniquity and asked nott where are the Fruits of Thy Loins.* And indeed it is fit I now say some fewe Wordes concerning the Politiques and Religion of those Yeares, in which the King Charles Stuart, did most grievouslie Harass and Trouble his People. The which I cannot doe well unless I also RELATE the Manneres and Opinions of those godlie and Gentle People (for wee ever spurned the name of Sect or RELIGION) to whom my MASTER Nehmiah belonged. For while it may bee the Case that Governments, whether of King or Parliament, concern themselves with the Form and Manner of Worshippe, how then shall the people Choose their God, unless it bee on sufferance from the Government? And how shall they Seek the Lorde's Face, unless they *seek it in the Mouth of the Cannon and on the Sharpe Edge of the Sworde*? Wherefore it was, though I hold it Sinne, as the *Cooperites* do, for anie to take up Armes agaynst his Brothere, and hold with them, *that there is no Killing nott Murder*, yet, as I will Relate, I went for the Armie, thinking onlie Thus to Preserve my Soule agaynst Corruption. And yet *in all Action is sinning*, as the *Cooperites* say, and neither was the Manner of my Coming to them in Meekness and Love, as they Teach us it must bee, but in my Possession by the Spirits of Pride and Rebellion. But oh Lord God teach mee how in this World soe sett about with briars and scorpions a man may Escape Sinning? And how purifie himself in a time of Tribulation and Distress as these late yeares have been, when Brothere is sett agaynst brothere, fathere agaynst Fathere and none know where may bee God his Face but goe about Blindlie to seek him as boys in a game at a Schoolyarde?

There were those in the town of Hertford that caused us to bee called *Cooperites*, synce they knew my Master and two otheres of our companie, were of the Cooper's Trade. And those most Knowne to mee were Mr Allan, Mr Bewick and Mr Passmore, which, though they attended the Church of St Michael, by the Square, and suffered in Silence those New Rules of the Archbishop, yet they *walked with Impurity and were not Tainted by it*, and held their Convictions close in their Heartes, speaking what was in Them onlie at our Assemblies which wee held with Doores closed. And neither did wee hold it upon One Holy Day, reckoning, as Mr Passmore said, *there were no set houres for Godlinesse synce wee knowe nott the houre of His coming*. And these Assemblies were given over to the discussion of Scripture but also to Earnest and Sincere consideration of the Affairs of the Nation, so that, when I was twelve, I had as good a Knowledge of the Question of the *French Marriage* or of the exactions of the *Star Chamber* as anie witt at the Court, and, by Mr Passmore was learned in some Manner in the Greek and Latin Authors, which was a grate Pleasure to mee, crying, when hee left mee that *I would have more Cicero* or that *hee was not yet to goe forth without wee read more of Pliny*, for I ever loved his *Naturall Historie*. And it was about this time that this same Charles Stuart made his Attempt to Govern without the due Consent of the People, and then were our Assemblies bitter in their Condemnation of the exactions of the Shipp Monie, or of the tariffs and exactions to which our Trade was made Subject. Whereby I argue, as I have done, that the Kinge's standarde, was *raysed agaynst us*, and the sin of rebellion was nott in us.

It was Mr Passmore who took most Delight in mee, wondering at my Capacity for Instruction and marvelling that *my hande was nott alwaies in my breeches and my mind nott running upon the propagation of my race.* And he marvelled most particularly at my Knowledge and Memorie for the Scriptures and would take Joy in sitting in the Barn, behind my Master's Howse, and question mee as to this Verse or that Chapter, for I knew the Bookes of the Prophets as well as the Bookes of the Apostles. And soe it was I rested among the *Cooperites* and verily they were my Heavenlie Familie and though my Bodie Fathere had been naught but a great Chayne, laid upon my Soule, these Fewe were a *staff and comfort unto mee and my Uncomely Appearance was cast aside, and I grew Tall and Strong in the Lorde, though still I loved not to converse with anie nott known to mee and was in the Town counted a Poor Thing that would start at his owne Shadowe.*

Now all our Propertie was in the hands of my Lord Peters, and it was from such as hee wee laboured to Conceal our Assemblies, synce wee had from him those Exactions that caused us such Tribulations. Synce my Lord was ever one for the Court, which did not prevent him taking his Pleasure at the expense of the Smaller Gentlemen, as that Sir Thomas Lacey who was neare to us and died of his wounds got at *Edge-hill* fight. And my Master's house was gott from him at a *Lease*, which enable his Stewarde, one Thomas Walmer, to come as hee pleased, for this *Walmer* was like unto that Steward that hath doubled his Master's Talents, yet were it better for us, saith Mr Passmore, *if hee had laid my Lord's money in the ground.* And, though the Warres are come and gone, and Oliver who would be King is upon us, as was the King before, yet this same Lord Peters hath still his estate, and soe have wee got naught from our Laboure, but worked to sett up Kings and laboured for Those who are as Fain to Abuse and Persecute those who find Fault with them, as were my Lords Strafford and Laud in the daies of the King Charles Stuart who had as little use for Parliaments as this same Oliver hath now.

Now this Walmer had a verie Madnesse for Knowledge of those Gentlemen who were neare to the Estate of my Lord Peters, holding with his Master, that 'Rebellion is a Disease' and hee and my Lord the doctor to cure it. And when my Lord was in the Countrie, which at that time hee was on occasion, though nott to Labour to Improve his estate, but rather for his Amusement, then was this Walmer, like to haunt the Town, for hee liked to make himselfe a slave and Roast himself for his Master's Wealth, and was, by some accounts, given to Obedience in the Romish practices favoured by my Lord's *pet-priest*. For the Great ever had Privacie in matters of religion, *synce if they were in doubt,* as Mr Passmore said, *they bought the Church.*

It was on a Saturday in June, at some time in my Fifteenth Yeare, that Mr Walmer came to us, as was his Habit, to make his Inspection of the work my Master did, for at that time wee were engaged upon the Coopering of severall Barrelles my Lord required, synce, from his coming into the countrie hee was resolved to Salte his owne Pork, lay up his Ale for Himself and govern his Estates as if hee had no Need of the Town, for *the Mighty know no Law but what is their own, neither are they Governed in the Kingdom, but lay aside Order and Authoritie unto themselves, wherefore it is written I shall cast them down and lay them low yea by their pride they shall suffer yea by their Rebellion agaynst Mee who is their Fathere in Heaven.* And at that time were with mee in the Barn behind my Master's, Mr Passmore and severall Others and wee were at our Pastime, which was Innocent and without Offense to anie save those who think scripture a Matter onlie for the Office of Priest or Bishop, which is to say we read the Bible and talked of it, and, on occasion would this Mr Passmore quiz mee, for my Knowledge of the Scripture amazed him and hee loved to hear me on Chapter and Verse, which caused him to Smile with Delight, for our Assemblies were not held in Mourning and Solemnitie but were Joyous and wee loved to Laugh in the Lord, *for if thou shalt not Smile upon His Face, wherefore art Thou come out of the Land of Whoredoms which is Babylon? And wherefore art Thou afraid to Hide thy Joy for Hee hath said unto Thee to be of good cheer and make Thy countenance to shine for Him and for His Mercies.*

Now they were – when *Walmer* came – quizzing mee concerning the Booke of Ezekiel, which was a common Fancie with them, in oure Barn with the great Doores opened, it being a pleasant Summer's Daie. And though I saw oure *Stewarde of the Talents,* as wee were wont to call him, I saw the others saw him nott, and so kept mine eie upon the Assemblie, & prayed wee might say naught this Walmer would report to my Lord as being *full of Treason and Rebellion*, for in those daies no Man knew his neighbour, for feare, and as wee thought, *Truste was the Nearer Waie to Prison*. 'And of how much,' says Mr Passmore to mee, 'were the foundations of the Side Chamberes of the Temple?' 'A full Reed,' says I, 'of six great Cubitts.' At which they fell to Clapping their Hands and confessed themselves amazed at my Powers of Recollection, which were to mee a Cause for Pride also, though now I see plainlie and know I spake no more than a Tame bird that followes his Master's words with no Idea as to the Sense of them. And hee asked mee some Other Chapter and Verse from that Booke, though now I cannot call to my mind either the Question or my Answere. For my eie was fixed on Master Walmer who stood at the Doore, with his armes crossed and a Smile on his Lips that seemed to say 'Ah ha – now ye're *catched*!' for I knew him to be no Casual Visitor but that hee came on some Errande for my Lord. For hee had his Eare to the Doore, thought it was Open, like anie Spy at Courte. But though wee Continued in oure Talke, hee still leaned agaynste the Doore and smiled and made himself Easy, for, as wee were wont to say, *hee used us as wee might be a Taverne*. And one by one, the *Cooperites* smelt him out there and Turned and he bows a little to them and says – Well, and a fine Boie you have gott yourselves my Masters!' But his voyce saith '*Aye and ye are Like to Lose him!*'

And I durst nott meet the Eie of Master Walmer then, thinking as I did that oure Assemblies were a contravention of some Law or Practice of the Kingdom, which by his Smile and Mannere hee seemed to suggest. But then, as now, Law and Custome were a Matter for Argument and in each parish was a different God served. For where wee found ourselves, were none, as it chanced, of the same Godlie and Learned Presbyters who spake agaynst the Practices of the Court, and though at that Time manie spake openlie of the Rule of *Privy Council*, *Bishops*, and *Statutory Decrees*, yett with us, all the Clergie were for the King and the Bishops, which caused us to seek the Lord after the Mannere I have described. And I count myselfe Blessed in this for None shall seek the Lord on Thy account, be he old Priest or New presbyter and *none shall Poynt out the Waie without*

75

hee Travelles itt. And, as I shall relate there were Those that seemed of the partie of Righteousnesse who were in Erroure, and Right in Justice is hidden from us by the Times.

'Hee is,' saith my Master, 'a stout Boie. And Dutiful and Obedient as hee be Commanded!' At which Master Walmer begins a-smirking, and lays his fingers to his Lips and setts about the duties and Responsibilities of Ownership and the Matter of Oure Tyles (which needed replacement) and of the Long field, the state and Condition of it. All of which is but to remind Us that My Lorde ownes us and is about the Exaction, once agayne, and the curtailment of Leases, the Racking of Rentes and the same cozening his master the King hath practised upon the commonwealth. And hee concludes this Speech with a Hope that such a strong and Lustie boie as I, should nott goe awaste, but might, at certayn Daies and Times be of Use at my Lord's, synce my Lord (as I have sett down) is a Fanatique for Brewing, Salting and Pickling, and othere Matters which may require a *Cooper's* attention, synce hee hath no Love of the Benefit of Commerce and thought to live *out of the waie of Trade.* And yet, as my Master said, What is a Nation without Commerce? And are nott Tradesmen and Mechaniques the blood and Spirit of the commonwealth? And nott those Leeches that sit in *London* the sink of all Iniquitie in the Kingdome?

But Open speech agaynst my Lorde was as Common, with us, as Frost in July, synce my Lorde ownes us as much as the Turk doth his Janissaries or the Archbishop his pet priests, and though, to ourselves, wee may Condemne the Chaynes of Propertie (which the *Cooperites* hold should be held *onlie where it is no cost to Anothere*), yet in the companie of my Lorde's Man, Walmer, can wee nothing say in Truth of what Concernes Us. Wherefore the *Cooperites* teach – *if anie doe Violence unto You guard their Blowes in Thy Heart neither turn Thy Anger agaynst them, for Anger and the Sin of Pride, which is the sin of Rebellion agaynst the Holy Ghost, walk hand in hand and the Lord hath said 'Yea thou shalt suffer. Even when thou art in Babylon thou shalt Suffer and take Thy waie among Stonie Places, and neither shalt thou lift up thy head agaynst thy Tormentors nor take up Armes agaynst Hee who Oppresseth Thee.'*

And, in fine, I am committed, agaynst my Will and better

76

Judgement to goe on the Wednesday next to perform certayn Taskes for which my Trade hath fitted mee, at the House of my Lorde; & with a 'Good Day' and a 'Miracle of Studie' and a 'No such Texte as the Holy Prophet' this Irreligious and Vicious Shoot or Offspring of the noble Lorde goes out into the summer daie thinking hee hath done his Master and himselfe a Service. 'Lo,' saith Nehemiah, when hee was gone, 'Lo wee bring into Bondage oure sons and Daughters to bee Servantes & some of oure sonnes are brought into Bondage already; neither is it in oure powere to Redeem them, for other Men have oure Lands.' Which are the words of the prophet Nehemiah and are the fifth verse of the fifth Chapter. And, though the Prophet spake of *daughters*, yett made I no motion to Correct his Speech, for I saw by this that *Nehemiah* counted mee as his Sonne by which I was much pleased. And was I then in Erroure? To take Him for the Fathere of my Bodie yea even as the Fathere of my Soule? For, as hee spake, it was as hee had had the Engendering of mee and I walked out of the Bondage of hee who *got mee in Darknesse* and thought nott both were separate – as the *Cooperites* teach, holding the Soule and the Bodie to be at perpetuall Warre, but saw them *as things were Asunder yett hath the Lorde joined Them*. Which thing I told nott to the Assemblie, knowing its strangeness to them and knowing, as I now best Comprehend that *Freedom in Worship is a Prison also*.

Then did the other *Cooperites* fall to harsh Wordes on the subject of my Lorde & were much in discussion of the Archbishop of Canterbury, that same William Laud, late of St John's college in Oxford, the Papist and Chaplain to the King who had then, but two yeares the possession of the title, power and was entirely in possession of the Revenue thereof. For hee had then invoked the Name of that Arminius, which was Hateful to Us, and would have his Churches just as hee prescribed for Worshippe, nor would brook Contradiction, synce hee was, as manie said *a Man with no Leisure for Complements and a voyce that would make men believe him Angrie even when hee were no such thing*. And when the *Cooperites* were gone from Us & Nehemiah & myself were alone I said unto him 'Master shall I goe as I am ordered?' To which he gave mee answere 'Behold – wee are servants this day, and for the land that thou gavest unto our fathers to eat the fruit thereof & the good thereby behold – wee are Servantes in it. And it yieldeth much increase unto the Kinges whom thou hast sett over Us, because of oure Sinnes; also they have Dominion over oure Bodies and over oure Cattle at their Pleasure & wee are in Great Distress. And because of all this wee make a *sure Covenante*.' At which wordes hee grasped mee by the Armes and stares into mine eie as hee would see that which was Written in my Hearte. By which I understood I was to goe unto the Great Howse of my Lorde and that such Iniquitous Orderes were a just punishment for my Sinnes but that I was to bee faithfull unto my Familie the *Cooperites*, my Heavenlie Familie even while I was yet in Babylon.

And now it falls to mee to relate the Great Sadnesse of those years between the Coming to Power of the Archbishop and the Time that hee was first imprisoned by the Parliament, which was a Space of some Five Yeares, and was as much the unmaking of mee as of that same Prelate. And though I Turned my face away from Eville yet Eville found mee out. And though I struggled with my Sinne synce it was – as the *Cooperites* teach – through my transgression that I suffered from the Wicked, should I nott then have gone *to wrestle with the eville that was about the City*? May it nott bee Sinne to studie onlie oure selves and oure Transgressions? And should I nott – oh how this Thought torments mee, now at the houre that I must make myselfe quiet and Readie to face Almighty God – should I nott have fought my Fathere that engendered mee, yea, *fought him for the Lordes sake and done battle that he may have had repentance*? Can it be sufficient unto us to *do as wee may be bid and keep oure heartes pure*?

But I went unto my Lorde's Howse & sett up manie a Barrelle for him & was wondrously amazed to see his lawnes and *topiaries* and Tables sett with Gold and Silver and Fine Cloths, though Master Walmer sett mee to work in the Outer Yarde, nor would I have been made welcome to stand at the Doore of the Kitchens there, yea though their Temples are built upon Uncleanlinesse yet are they Sweeter than the Temples wee have built unto the Lorde nd though they bee Corrupted yet hath Hee suffered them to Prosper. And although, on my returning to oure House, I spake plainly and honestly with good Nehemiah of all that I had seen there & I spake openlie of all I encountered, yet was it clear hee feared the Opinions and Influences to which my emploiment made mee Subject, which bred Disquiet between us and made mee exceeding Sorrowfulle. And hee enquired of mee the Practises and Opiniounes to which I had been Subject there, asking mee whether it was with mee as with that *Peter* who denies oure Lorde Thrice. And whether I had spoken to anie of the practises of oure *Holie Familie* (which was forbidden by the *Cooperites*) or carried myself in a Manner shameful to oure People. To which I, trembling, would declare I had heard no Licentious Talk, nor had I suffered anie of them there to come neare to mee while I was at my Worke & neither would I suffer contradiction of anie opposition to that which my Master Nehemiah had commanded synce I was so moved by his Kindnesse to mee. But so it is – a Thought, once Visited upon the Inconstant or Weak Spirit (which I do confess myselfe to bee) may then bee the Fathere to some Action & Weake Soules do enact the Prophet's Vision of them, until they may cry with the Psalmist 'I am wearie of Crying my throat is dried. Mine eies fail while I wait for my God O God thou knowest my Foolishnesse; and my sinnes are nott hid from Thee. I am become as a stranger unto my bretheren and an alien unto my mother's children.'

Thus it was that I looked out from the place where I was sett to Laboure, toward that great Howse that was my Lorde's & fell among the Companie my Master had bid mee to Avoid. Which now I must Report – though the telling Pain mee.

79

9

It was eleven o'clock. The wind had started up again on Putney Hill, breathing a grim life into the skeletons of trees. Somewhere over towards Wimbledon Common, I heard the distant noise of a siren. On the table in front of us, plates strewn with the wreckage of another of Meg's epic meals. Like a field of battle, Rick's plate was littered with potatoes that hadn't quite made it, needlessly spilled gravy, heavily mutilated French beans and savagely stubbed out cigarettes, buckled, like damaged artillery, into the scummy surface of the china. The children were in bed. As the wind battered at the doors of the balcony, Rick talked about witches.

'I didn't realize,' I was saying, 'that there were any witches in Bloomsbury. Apart from Virginia Woolf.'

Meg's eyes flicked between us. 'Actually,' said Rick, 'the title "The Bloomsbury Witchfinder" was stuck on Ezekiel by a nineteenth-century antiquary and it more or less sums up my fascination with him. We're not entirely sure that Oliphant was a witchfinder, and we don't know if he lived in what is now Bloomsbury, although we know he died near there, but in the one footnote I've dug up on him he is referred to, because of that nineteenth-century piece, as The Bloomsbury Witchfinder. But the Oliphant story is a complicated one. In some ways it's a rather nasty, unfinished tale of the kind historians like to puzzle at. But I haven't got time to tell you the whole story.'

The whole story – or at least Rick's idea of what it might be – was, of course, what I had been waiting for. Up to that moment I had been steering the talk away from Ezekiel. Why, I could not have said – it simply did not seem . . . how shall I say . . . *safe*. But now, at this hour, a voice (not Ezekiel's, but a voice like his) whispered 'Ask him. Go on. Ask him about Ezekiel the Witchfinder. But don't tell him what you know. Let him find out.'

Rick had paused, waiting to see how we would take his last remark. Our silence indicated willingness to listen. And so, pulling up his chair to the table and playing with a piece of bread, he began.

'In 1642, the year of the raising of the King's standard, the beginning of the English Civil War, I came across a witch trial in Hertford. It's not part of an outbreak of witch fever, like the holocaust at Chelmsford, where one Matthew Hopkins and his sidekick, a gentleman named Stearne, caused sixty-eight women to be hanged. But Oliphant, like Hopkins or Stearne, is one of those vaguely sinister, tantalizing people who just comes up out of the ground, takes the stage and then vanishes. There's a reference to him much later on as a "finder out of witches", but on this occasion he's just an anonymous deposer of information.'

Meg scooped up a potato from her plate and chewed it morosely. 'So who did he finger as a witch?' she said. Rick seemed almost unwilling to answer.

'Well,' he said, 'I'll come to that. He was involved, as far as I can see, in two witch trials, one in Hertford in 1642, the other in Northampton in 1650. Three if you count his own. But what interested me initially about him was not so much his track record – as far as I can tell he wasn't someone like Hopkins or Stearne who rode into a town and profited from the break up of law and order in the Civil War to make a few bob finding out and then hanging witches.'

'Is that what they did it for?' said Meg. 'Money?'

'Sure,' said Rick, 'they were vigilantes. With the added bonus that they could invent the crime and devise any number of ludicrous ways of "proving" their assertions. But they charged. I don't think Oliphant is quite in that class, the Puritan run to seed. In a way, to me, that makes him more interesting. Just *who* he is and quite how I fill in the gaps in his life I don't know. But what I do know from the available evidence is that he was implicated an unusally high number of witch trials in wildly different places, which is highly unusual. I'm jumping to conclusions, and this speculation isn't supported by evidence as yet, but neither was he someone on the Hopkins and Stearne model who had influence, who wasn't a local gent but who travelled. Because his *own* trial –' He stopped as if he did not wish to go on. Then, with an impatient gesture, he changed tack: 'Actually, the thing that really fascinates me about Oliphant is that I keep coming across him when I'm researching something completely different. He's a man who appears more than he should, if you see what I mean. I happened to be examining the Assize Roll for the county town, Hertford, for 1642 and I came across the trial in which Oliphant appears. What I mean to say is this: he's like those people – maybe you have them in your life, I don't know – who crop up on stations, in busy streets, miles away from anywhere, simply, it appears, because you're fated to meet.'

Rick Mason's Oliphant ought to have born no relation to the creature who was beginning to plague me. My Oliphant, created out of dreams, expectations, received ideas, should have been a quite different creature from the character for whom Rick was reaching. The tools of his trade – court reports, a few stone-faced sentences in Latin – should have given birth to a personage who existed only to clarify our understanding of, say, land tenure in Hertfordshire in the 1640s, or the impact of Puritan ideas on the upwardly mobile provincial gentry (presumably Ezekiel pretended to the title of gentleman). But it did no such thing. It conjured up, for him I felt as well for me, that thin, cruel face, twisting this way and that, the silky beard, the dirty ruff. Above all – it was almost tangible in the room as he spoke – it summoned up that feeling I had had reading the pamphlet. How to describe it? A sudden chill at one's back, as if someone had come into the room very quietly, unannounced, and was standing a few feet away, waiting for something. Someone sick. Someone evil. It would be nice to say that, as a vicar's son, I had a nose for wickedness. But if I am honest, what I really felt as Rick talked was nothing more than fear.

'How like you this Master Matheson? Turn as ye may you shall not escape my Presence and Desires. For that the Wickedenesse and Abomination of This, oure Martyred and Abused Countrie, remains, as ever it was. Seek seek seek and ye shall find, as a Boy that turns over a Stone in playfulnesse, and discovers a Scorpion or a Wife that comes late to bed, hears on the Stair the Noise of some Animal, calls it by name, such as "Jacke my Pet", thinking it to be a Tame Creature of the House, and, at the Turne of the second Stair sees a sleek, fat Rat, that waits for her.'

82

'The trial,' Rick was saying,' was a trial for witchcraft, and there was only one woman involved. She was charged with bewitching Oliphant's horse so that it sickened and died. She was charged with putting a spell on her own children – she had three sons – and she was also charged along with her mother of a pact with the devil. A quite grotesque series of charges, in connection with this. The two women were alleged to have been seen flying around Hertfordshire, skimming the treetops and banking in low cloud. People were prepared to swear that they saw them. It would be comic if you didn't recall that at the end of the trial she (mum was away out of it as far as I can tell) was taken to the local nick and from there, carried out on a cart and hanged.'

There was a silence in the room. Meg was suddenly animated. Hunching her shoulders, sweeping a piece of bread across her plate, she looked at Rick with the malevolence that I knew to be a simple indication of interest. 'Who were these women?'

'Oliphant's wife and her mother. Hahaha. It's a mother-in-law joke. Get rid of the wife and the mother-in-law in one fell swoop. What's really sick about the story is that, from what we know about Oliphant later on, he had something of a reputation as a magician himself. Who knows? Perhaps he wanted her money or her mother's money or perhaps he had abused her so much anyway he was simply carrying out the logical end of such abuse – as the Nazis did to the Jews or the rapist does to his victim.'

'What do we know about Oliphant later on?'

It was I who asked this question and Rick flicked his eyes across at me with what I can only describe as cunning. He must, I had already decided, know about the pamphlet in the Museum. If I had found it on the chance opening of a catalogue, it must have been familiar to Dr Mason. Why hadn't he mentioned it to me yet? And while we were at it, wasn't there something odd about my having happened on precisely that page? What was it Rick had said – 'He's a man who appears more than he should.' Someone whose influence reaches out, long after their death, and, like the stranger we are fated to meet against all the odds, pushes coincidence to the point where we are forced to say 'He's still alive, the evil bastard, *making* all this happen.'

'Er –' He was looking shifty. 'I'd rather not talk about that. The Northampton trial of Anna Stafford was . . .' He stopped.

'Why not?' said Meg. 'Is it too horrible or what?'

'Oh, it's all horrible,' said Rick, 'the whole of the Oliphant saga is horrible. A grotesque and frightening footnote to a disturbed period of our history. But this is . . . I don't know. Look – all I'd say at the moment is, it doesn't add up. I don't want to talk about it really. It's a very odd and spooky story and I don't really want to talk about it.'

'Oh come on,' I said, 'you can't get us all excited and have our tongues hanging out for more and then suddenly tell us "No, this is not for your ears." I suspect you're only trying to whet our appetites.'

Rick looked at me, his head to one side. His voice was quiet and serious as he said 'I don't know about whetting people's appetites, Jamie. I really don't. All this witchcraft business is intimately bound up with that, of course. It has the hypnotic awfulness of pornography. That isn't why I don't want to talk about it any more, honestly. It's simply that I am not sure of my facts. There is something about the story I haven't understood and I don't want to talk about it until I have.'

'Maybe you never will,' I said. 'Not everything has a neat and logical explanation. However much we may wish it to be I don't think there's any evidence that the world is organized along rational lines. It seems to me to be a cruel, arbitrary and crazy place in which things, awful things, happen for no reason at all. You're probably trying to reduce our friend Oliphant to a neat statistic, and he won't go. Why should he?'

I felt that chill at my back again as Meg said, 'What was his wife's name?'

'Why do you ask?'

'I always like to know the wife's name.'

'Funnily enough,' said Rick, 'it was Margaret. Or Meg in fact. Meg is what she is called in the trial.'

Meg laughed. 'I'd have been done as a witch in 1642, wouldn't I? University degree. Supposed to be clever. History of mental disorder. Doesn't make friends easily. Inclined to stare off into the distance in the middle of conversations. Fond of being alone.'

'I wouldn't have let them do you, love,' I said.

She looked at me sharply. 'You, you'd have led the inquiry. You'd have been a witchfinder, you would. You'd have been following this Oliphant round and nodding and winking and leering with him in the pub, about how many witches you caught today. Or else you would have been one of those people who wrote up the sufferings of those poor people afterwards. *Ghastly Affair of the Putney Witches* by Jamie Matheson, printed by Gottlieb & Son.'

I decided to let this pass. 'Did this Oliphant,' I said, 'write anything . . .?'

Rick looked at me oddly. 'Why do you ask?'

'I just thought I had heard the name somewhere,' I said.

Rick shook his head slowly. 'I really oughtn't to talk about it, Jamie,' he said. 'I mean I'm happy to when I know what I'm doing, but at the moment it's not really in shape.' He looked across at Meg, who had lapsed into silence. I looked at her too – the fine features, the afterthought of a chin, the lines of worry around her eyes. Would they have done her as a witch? Was she that much of a victim?

Certainly, as long as I have known her she has never fitted in anywhere. Her father was a naval technician in Portsmouth, a small, meek man, one of those people who go through life without ever revealing their true feelings about anyone or anything. He had died with the minimum of fuss, of a heart attack, when Meg was twenty-four. There were only three people at the funeral – myself and Meg and her mother. I think I suggested we marry a week or so later. His parents were as invisible as he, by all accounts, dying even more silently and tactfully than their son, before Meg had had a chance to meet them. And her mother, too, comes out of nowhere, one of those classless, landless people who found gentility, somehow or other, during the war. Juliet only had a mother and the mother died.

The war in England is such a complicated business. It is no longer a struggle between those who have and those who do not, those who speak for one class and those who champion another; it is, I thought, looking across at Rick's serious face (he comes from six generations of miners), a war between those who retain confidence in some kind of future, even if it's a future controlled and owned by the working class, and those who have begun to suspect that there is nothing round the corner except blankness and silence.

'Actually,' said Rick, 'it isn't quite as simple as that. I think it really is that I don't like talking about him. Do you know what I mean?'

'Yes,' I said.

Then he wanted to know what I was writing and asked me a lot of questions about historical accuracy and the sense of period. Had I read Lukács on the historical novel? How was I going to convey the texture of English social life in pre-industrial Britain?

'Have people say "thee" and "thou" and "forasmuch",' I said. 'I plan on using the word "forasmuch" a great deal.'

'Even when he writes about the present,' said Meg, 'Jamie is short on period detail.'

I waved my arms wildly. 'When I write about the present,' I said, 'I put in the bus queues in Putney High Street, the heavily fortified car parks, the black kid I saw yesterday up in Shepherd's Bush standing over a dustbin, swilling his hand around in the rubbish, and finally bringing out a square, shiny box – at first I thought he knew there was something in it, and then I saw all he wanted was the wrapping. He was happy with that. I put in –'

'You see what I mean?' said Meg, her voice nearly shrill, 'no period detail. Jamie's from another planet. Or if he's from this one he hasn't been using his eyes for the last thirty-nine years.'

'What do I leave out?' I said.

She almost hissed her reply. 'Women,' she said. 'That's one thing you leave out.'

'People who read my work,' I said, 'need to use their imagination.'

'Yes,' said Meg, 'because you're not using yours.'

The tone of this conversation could have been bantering. There were times when we could have talked like this safely. But not now. Once there was always playfulness between Meg and me. Envy, sexual shame, fear – we explored those things almost to amuse ourselves. Nowadays, too often, too quickly, it was for real. Rick was nervous, I could tell. He steered the conversation back to Oxford. At one point I thought he was going to talk about Dewes, then he saw my face and retreated. We talked about dances we had been to long ago, about the dresses Meg used to wear in those days, of how she had taken 'San Francisco' at its word and walked along the High with red and blue flowers in her hair, of how Rick had always loved her and how when I was dead, or famous and married to someone else, she would have him and he would have her. And, by degrees, playfulness returned. Then we saw Rick up to Thomasina's bedroom, where he sat grotesquely adult among the Care Bears and the bright piles of Lego.

Before Meg and I went to bed we went downstairs to clear the dishes. 'How was your day?' she said, 'Really?'

'It was fine,' I said.

It was safest, I had decided, to say as little as possible about what I had been doing. As a result, I felt as if there was a physical gag on my tongue, and, when I looked for some words that might unlock her misery, I could find none.

'Aye,' said Ezekiel, 'on your Tongue now you wear the Steel Trap as we were commonly used to Employ for the Restraint of Shrewes, Scoldes, Hags and Nag Narrows. With my own Wife I employed a Surer Method and one that Provokes the Longest Silence: the rope, Master Matheson, the Rope and the Cart and the Dance over Six Foot of Country Air.'

There was an unaccustomed silence between us as we heaped the dishes into the sink. As the silence – full of unspoken, hateful things – grew and grew, it acquired a life of its own. And Anna was between us. Anna, with her brown eyes and her obedient laugh and the bachelor flat that reminded me of all the places where Meg and I had lived before the children, the big house and all the other encumbrances of age. Was Anna, I wondered, Meg's younger self simply? Were women able to substitute for each other? And when they took tenderness or concern from a man, was there a finite amount of such qualities – were they stealing from each other? Or was love a quality that defied all physical laws – and grew to meet the demand? We like to think of love as like that. Only with love like that can we outface the silence of death. I thought of my father, stretched out on the slab (it was a bed but I think of it as a slab). I thought of his mouth, that had always been laughing or petulant or secretive, and was now as open as a new grave. And, suddenly, I wanted to be able to love Meg.

I watched her at the sink, her thin, dark face anxiously looking out at the night. Perhaps Anna was going to help me help her get through it? I thought, with the crazy logic of the treacherous. Perhaps I was borrowing love from Anna on Meg's account. I went over to her and put my arms around her. 'I love you,' I said. But she didn't respond. She broke away from me, went through to the hall, and flung back the door that leads to where the bicycle is kept. She pointed at it dramatically. 'That,' she said, 'is thy Charger, Matheson – thy Trusty Steed!'

'Aye beldame,' I said, adjusting myself into my Richard Crookback position.

'And it doth belong,' she said, 'in ye Shedde.'

'Right,' I said.

Suddenly vicious she went up to it and kicked it. 'I understand,' she said, 'why that poor bitch put a spell on that horrible man's horse. She probably didn't have a horse to ride off on so she could have it away with some nice man. She was stuck in the house. Like me.'

'They should have had a second horse,' I said.

Meg turned to me. 'You go away on that thing,' she said, kicking it again, 'and I don't know where you go or what you do and I feel I'm losing you and I don't want to. I feel you're slipping away from me.'

I put my arms round her again but she stayed still and quiet and did not lift her eyes to me. After a while she went towards the stairs. I watched her as she trudged up to our bedroom. Does she know? I thought. She can't know. Surely not. And yet, I felt that she did know. Well how though? How does she know if she does know?

I hummed a snatch of a tune by way of answer. One Frank Sinatra used to sing. 'Well . . . it's *witch*craft, wicked witchcraft . . .' Then I went over to the bike. Her kick had been shrewdly aimed. The back mudguard had buckled, and try as I might I could not stop it jamming the free progress of the wheel. Stupid bitch, I thought, angrily. Stupid, neurotic bitch. Just don't you give me a hard time, that's all. Just don't bother me. Or I'll make things awkward for you. I mean that.

10

Next morning, on my way into town, Rick accompanied me. My bicycle had developed a puncture, thanks to Meg's attack and, in the silence that had not really been broken since the previous evening, I walked down the path while she and Dr Mason made their attentive farewells. It was a fine, clear day. The birds in the front gardens, fooled as usual by promises of spring, were rehearsing their jagged arpeggios, their liquid swoops up the scale, and from the huge trees on the corner of the hill, the impatient, businesslike tones of the rookery.

England was one nation, I decided, this morning. On the low wooden platform of the underground station men in bowler hats unfolded their newspapers as children might open presents. A guard smiled amiably round at his constituents. In the trees in the station forecourt more birds sang, and as the silvered carriages rattled into the station the commuters did not jolt grimly forward as usual: they too smiled and stepped aside. Rick did not notice the brightness of the day. He was talking about the seventeenth century, his loud, nasal Yorkshire voice unafraid of eavesdroppers. Indeed, as he talked I felt it necessary to simper round at those nearest to us on the platform, as if to imply that, if they wished to join in the discussion, they were welcome.

'I'm sorry to be so cagey about the Oliphant business,' he said, 'but I won't be so cagey shortly. In fact it's become something of an obsession with me. I have got a lot more on him which as I say isn't entirely clear, but one thing I can talk about is an extraordinary letter I got which I'd like to show you.'

'Please do,' I said.

The doors of the train closed behind us. Rick made for a corner seat and I followed him. 'You see – what interests me particularly about witchcraft, is not its extraordinary closeness to us, its persistence if you like, which makes it not really susceptible to the sort of orthodox historical method in which we were trained. It survives, at some level, even in contemporary urban culture.' I looked nervously round the carriage. There were several elderly women present but they all, at first glance anyway, appeared respectable. 'Open any newspaper, study any popular cultural phenomenon' (this is Rick's customary way of describing what we know as simply 'television programmes') 'and you will find an extraordinary persistence in the kind of habits of thought we are talking about. I was after, you see, tales, popular tales, that dealt with this sort of thing. Oral history.'

'Yes,' I said. Just like ordinary history but even more unreliable. I didn't engage in a debate on the subject though. I wanted, desperately wanted to hear everything Rick was prepared to tell me about Ezekiel Oliphant. In the morning sunlight my interest seemed, once again, a simple, healthy urge towards knowledge.

'After all – the last big witch craze in this country is only three hundred years away. And witchcraft as a felony survives into the eighteenth century. Do you know when the last witch was hanged in England?' He addressed this last remark to a large Jamaican woman, encumbered with shopping bags, who was seated opposite us. For a moment I thought she was going to hazard a guess, but if she had such a thing in mind, she thought better of it.

'Early 1700s,' said Rick triumphantly.

'Good Lord,' I said, without any noticeable feeling of surprise. It wouldn't surprise me, in fact, if they started stringing people up as witches now, this month, this very day. I had a vision of a line of gibbets outside Bow Street Police Station. At the end of sixteen ropes dangled sixteen old women, their necks grotesquely stretched, their faces dead white, their tongues swollen in their mouths. None of the passers by stopped or turned to look. They had wine bars to get to, they had cheques to cash, deals to do . . . So they were hanging witches in Covent Garden. So? So long as they're not hanging me, chum, I don't think I mind too much. This is England. I have a living to make. Leave me out of it. Rick turned to address a plump man in a pork pie hat, deep in a paperback novel. 'This thing is still in the popular mind. It's still alive in that sense and we mustn't think it is something that happened in another country, another time dimension. So I put an advert in several papers, national and local, asking for stories, for lore, if you like about witchcraft, witches and especially about trials for witchcraft. Somewhere, I thought, is an individual or a family with a tale to tell.' As we rattled into Earls Court station the man in the pork pie hat turned solemnly in Rick's direction. He looked as if he were about to burst into a song, a yearning tenor aria perhaps, in which he would tell us he was unhappy, he did not want to travel on the tube train between Putney and Earls Court. He wanted better things. Or was he about to tell Rick to keep his voice down?

'And was there?'

He sounded almost anguished as he replied.

'That's what really puzzles me about this Oliphant business, Jamie. That's what spooks me. He keeps coming into it. At every turn of the road, suddenly, there he is, in a black hat and a black cloak, tugging at his goatee beard and smiling cruelly at me. "There you are, Doctor," he says, "I was there before you."'

And, in spite of the light and the open faces of the commuters round me, I felt a chill. This was how he waited for me (and how he still waits for me, somewhere out there in the rough grass of the field between the hospital and the road, his eyes on the building, watching, waiting his moment). Rick grabbed my arm. 'I got masses of letters and most of them from lunatics, but one of them, the maddest of the lot, was from a Mr Oliphant.'

'Oh come on Rick,' I said, 'the –'

'Ron Oliphant, Flat 33b Hampton Road, Palmers Green. He reckons he is the great great great great great whatever it may be of our friend Ezekiel, the witchfinder. I've got the letter here. It's really crazy stuff. Let me show you.'

From his jacket pocket he pulled out a sheet of lined paper. They always write on lined paper, do the lunatics. Maybe the sight of a blank space confuses them and they feel the urge to start in the top right hand corner and work their way, via the middle, to the sides. This was, quite clearly, a lunatic. He used lunatic biro, lunatic quotation marks round every available proper noun, and a great many very, very mad Capital Letters. All of this made me suspect that he might well be Ezekiel's great

great great great great great grandson. Nowadays Ezekiel would probably be in the National Viewers' and Listeners' Association, writing in to the *Radio Times* with complaints about the level of violence in popular soap operas. The truly remarkable thing about Ezekiel, I thought, is, as Rick says, that so much of him survives.

I looked up and there he was, sitting in the fat man's seat. He didn't speak. All he did was smile and shrug his shoulders, as if to say 'Well, quite. There you are then. Quite.' Sweating slightly, I smoothed out the crumpled sheet of paper Rick had handed me.

Dear Dr Mason,

I read your 'ad' with a great deal of interest, as I come from a family steeped in 'Witches' and 'Witch-Lore' and I am, myself, something of an AMATEUR HISTORIAN. There are truths the 'Bosses' *do not tell us*. The Varsity Men with their long degrees and so on often conceal the real facts from us 'Umble Proles'. England is Rotten, Sir, and in the hands of a few Rich Men who make it a Plaything.

I write to inform you of my most interesting information *for your eyes and ears only* on the subject of my great great great great great great uncle Ezekiel Oliphant, the so-called BLOOMSBURY WITCHFINDER (How did he get that absurd title? Wouldn't you like to know.) It is a strange world and a more frightening and dangerous and evil and complex one than all your 'Oxbridge' rationalization would have us believe. Old Ezekiel is still with us 'in the Spirit' as people say and for those of us who know and have dealings with the Spirit World that is really with us in a real and concrete sense. I was talking with him the other day and he had many interesting things to say about the 'war' in the Falklands and the needless shedding of blood in a cause so that the Iron Lady could satisfy her blood compact with YOU KNOW WHO (or maybe you don't, 'Doctor' Mason). He appears to me quite often, clothed as he was in 'life' and does not think much of the modern way of life, supermarkets and so on, and perverts round every corner abusing little children. I'd kill them I'd string the bastards up who raped that little girl and watch them die with the utmost satisfaction.

You ask, Sir, about Witches and Witch information and I take it this is a Serious Guide not a Which Guide to Which Witch (as you will see though an 'umble soul I can joke a bit) and I must say that witches are not so long dead as many think. The 'struggle' against Dark Forces, lives on even in Palmers Green. If you will come to see me at the above adress I have a most vital piece of information to communicate. ALL IS NOT WHAT IT SEEMS EITHER IN THE PAST OR THE PRESENT OR IN THE FUTURE IF THERE IS ANY FUTURE LEFT IN THIS BLIGHTED BLO-ATED ONCE GREAT NATION NOW OVERRUN WITH IMMIGRANTS AND JEWS. MANY SO-CALLED 'DOCU-MENTS' ARE LIES. HOW CAN WE TRUST THE POLITI-CIANS NOW OR THEN????

> Yours sincerely,
> Ronald Oliphant GCEs in Maths History and Greek etc.
> Age 68 and a half.
> Former Black Belt in Judo and so forth.

I passed the letter back to Rick hastily. 'My Christ,' I said, 'I think that should be sent off to the Director of Public Prosecutions before this old guy goes and turns someone into a frog.'

'Pretty crazy, eh?' said Rick. 'But isn't it extraordinary? And he makes the point here. The same point: "He's still with us." And there are times – I have to say usually late at night or in the dark or alone – when I come to believe him. You know?'

I looked across. Ezekiel had gone. The tube train clattered into a tunnel and the travellers' faces turned sickly yellow in the over-accurate light. 'I know,' I said feelingly. The Jamaican woman rose wearily to her feet. She looked like someone on her way home. A night worker. A night cleaner maybe. There was a fuss once, about the night cleaners – women who worked long hours for no money. Meg had gone to meetings about it. And where were the night cleaners now? Still cleaning. Still trudging back and forth from smooth carpeted offices to homes that were never warm or clean enough. Her shopping bags were crammed with loaves, wrapped in cellophane, and she stood above us, staring at the tunnel as, flat against the window, like something back-projected, a red circle enclosing the name of the station, slid into view – KNIGHTSBRIDGE. Nice part of the world. If you can afford it.

She rolled out on to the platform and the train started again.

'Look,' I said, 'it so happens I have to go up to Palmers Green today.' This was a lie. Why had I said it? Rick was goggling at me. Yet another coincidence seemed to unnerve him. I wondered hectically to myself whether the coincidences the late Arthur Koestler was so fond of describing, were sometimes simply lies. 'I could go and check him out for you if you liked.' Rick looked nervous. 'I don't think that's a very good idea,' he said, 'I really don't. It's just that –'

'I quite understand,' I said smoothly. But I thought –'

He wants to keep Ezekiel to himself. He thinks he's got Ezekiel sewn up. He's frightened someone else will take him over. Well he can't keep it all to himself. And maybe Ezekiel muttered something to me too, about how Rick had always been jealous of me. How Rick would like to be me and not stuck in some dull provincial university. And why shouldn't I do him down? And as Ezekiel talked to me – he was inside me now, buzzing in my head, not crudely manifested as he sometimes chooses – my nice/nasty English face worked furiously. I saw myself briefly in the lighted window opposite. I didn't look quite so nice or quite so nasty; I looked weird, unearthly, possessed by another spirit that was lighting up my eyes and making mouth work this way and that.

I hated Rick, I realized suddenly. This squat little northerner next to me whom I had always called 'friend'. Why had I called him that? Habit simply. I hated his smugness, his slowness, and now his self-important secrecy. Why was I not supposed to know about the Oliphant business? Was I too trivial, of too little consequence to understand such large questions? Rick and people like him have got a theory that describes all behaviour; 'class' and 'morality' are for them primitive taboos rather they categories capable of rational, sceptical examination. For me, now, such words mean nothing.

95

'I'll go up there on my own, Dr Mason,' I thought to myself, 'and I won't tell you and I'll find out why you didn't tell me about the pamphlet and how and why Ezekiel was tried and I'll be there before you chum, long before you, and if I need help there he'll be. I'll go with my new girl who you know nothing about. The red-headed, stubby girl with the small bottom, the tan and the unplaceable accent. She'll be there waiting when I get to the library and we'll go up there together. OK Mr Stuck-Up Mason?' I saw myself once again and this time I did not like what I saw. My face was no longer working or moving. It was as deadly still as my father's had been that day in the hospital. I wanted to shout at it, to bring it back to life, to turn myself back into lovable old Jamie who writes not so good books and will always take the piss out of himself. Jamie, good old Jamie. But I couldn't. It was like looking at my death mask, like seeing myself in wax, a foreign expression stapled to my face.

'You OK, Jamie?'

'I'm fine. Fine.'

As it happened I met Anna going in through the Museum's swing doors. She appeared to have lost weight during the night, and her complexion, which yesterday had promised a certain coarseness beneath the tan, was now of the high definition purity I associate with ski resorts. She was wearing a loose black jersey, a long black scarf, and a pair of jeans that seemed even tighter than yesterday's. They fitted her smoothly, invincibly . . . I realized my tongue was doing rather unpleasant things. I bit it quite hard as I completed the revolving circle and landed next to her looking down at the bright forecourt. Good morning, Troll. Troll, how do you do?

'Where are we going today?' she smiled up at me. I felt that lightness again. Of course. We could go anywhere we wished. There were no restraints on our behaviour. She put her arm through mine as if we had known each other a long time. As if we were always meeting on the steps of the Museum, linking arms and discussing the day's events. If felt as if I had done all this before. 'Palmers Green,' I said, and, wrapping my hand over hers, I steered her down the steps of the Museum. Palmers Green was fine too, her expression seemed to say. If I had said 'Java' or 'the Western Highlands of Scotland', her smile and her glistening eyes would not have lost their nerve.

'I've got a car,' she said. Her car was less of a car than a large, metal handbag. I think it was a Citroën, although it looked as if someone had been trying to turn it into something else, using only a steam hammer. Inside were three or four bags of washing, a pile of books from the London Library, and on the back seat, what looked like a piece of Aztec sculpture. On my seat was a pile of used nappies and a crowbar. 'They're Barbara's,' said Anna mysteriously. I felt fairly stylish, sitting in a strange woman's car at a quarter to ten in the morning. I put the nappies and the crowbar at my feet, and leaned back expansively. She started the engine and, sitting primly upright and well forward in her seat, pulled out into the traffic.

It was only then that the risks involved in what I was doing, occurred to me. What *was* I doing in a strange woman's car at a quarter to ten in the morning? Supposing one of Meg's friends were to be sitting in the car next to us at the next red light? They might well ask such a question. Suppose (this seemed possible, given Anna's style of driving) we were involved in a serious traffic accident?

> Among those travelling in Anna X's car were a pile of nappies, a crowbar, and the well-known screenwriter Jamie Matheson, whose address is 458 Maplake Road, Putney. . .

She was a researcher. That was it. We were doing research. Simple. No problem. I needed some help on the seventeenth century. I began to be quite annoyed with Meg for questioning my integrity. She was a researcher, this girl. That was all. The car stopped at the lights that divide Tottenham Court Road from the Euston Road.

'Kiss me,' she said. I looked furtively round at the pavement. All I could see was an elderly Negro, carrying a large wooden box. He looked at me suspiciously. As I leaned over Anna, out of the corner of my eye I checked the passenger seat of the car parked next to ours. A man in a Homburg hat. Not known to me. He looked on with great interest as my mouth met Anna's. Her lips were dry and soft and opened on contact with mine, as

97

my tongue found hers. It was, I observed on the car clock, 10.03 precisely.

A car horn sounded behind us. 'It's a bit early for this, isn't it?' I said as we started up again. 'It's never too early for this,' said Anna, and, with her right hand, found my knee and squeezed it.

It occurred to me that she might be a Russian agent. It seemed at least a way of explaining her behaviour. Girls simply do not do this to me, I thought, and then 'Hey, maybe they do.' I caught a glimpse of myself in the vanity mirror above the passenger seat. Good-looking Troll. Troll whose hour has finally come. Maybe this girl was the first in a long line of attractive women who would wish to go to bed with me. Maybe I just hit a shoal of them. Like mackerel. Maybe she was the front runner of a gigantic shoal of women down there in the deeps of the city. Maybe I was going to spend the next few years hauling them on board, servicing them brusquely and then turning my attention to the next, floundering wantonly beside me on the deck, gasping for the *coup de grâce*. 'What could I do?' I said to Meg. 'They just threw themselves at me.' 'Oh yeah?' she said. She looked unhappily away from me, and for a moment I felt some of her bleakness and misery. Then I turned myself away from it. I didn't want bleakness and misery. Not even Meg's.

The early sun had faded and the sky was a recessional series of greys and dark blues as we drove up through Hampstead, climbing up through the village to the Heath. We drove along the crest, of the Heath, London over to our right, its apartment blocks as unreal as a planner's model in the growing haze. Through Highgate village, then down towards the Archway Road and Muswell Hill. Out here the streets were striving for respectability, since there was little else to strive for. The endless terraces of grey or yellow bricked houses lacked any style and the parked cars gave no clue as to the social status of their owners. Not quite the town and not quite the suburb. Ideal for Ron. He could be as mad as he liked and no one would report him.

Hampton Road was one of those streets that went on for ever. There was a kebab place at one end, in which a pale, unshaven man was miserably swiping at a huge slice of lamb, turning on a vertical spit. That was the only sign of life in the street. There were net curtains in every house, but none of them twitched. The occupants were away or busy or dead. Should I have telephoned, I wondered, as we parked. But at first sight of the upstairs front window, I knew Ron would not have gone out. Ron was clearly the sort of man for whom a trip to the post box is major struggle. In the window, blocking all light to the room behind, was a sign that read SAY NO TO THE COMMON MARKET. Next to it, in the central panes of the bay, I read NUCLEAR POWER NO THANKS.

'That has to be Ron,' I said, 'no compromise with reality.'

'I wish you'd tell me what it's all about,' said Anna.

'You'll see,' I said.

She pointed to another, smaller piece of paper in the far right hand corner of the glass: ABOLISH MOTORWAYS.

I was looking forward to Ron.

He was in no sense a disappointment. In carpet slippers, baggy trousers, and collarless workman's shirt, he flung back the front door and thrust a sheaf of papers at us. 'No thanks,' he said, 'no thank you very *much* . . . Then he stopped, suddenly curious. 'What are you?' he asked cunningly. 'Carol singers?'

'It's a bit late for that, isn't it?' said Anna.

'It's a bit early,' said Oliphant, 'for Guy Fawkes.' Then he laughed. His laugh was an eery, operatic affair that was in no danger of compromising the stare of his full blue eyes. I saw that, under his shirt, he was wearing a pair of pyjamas. 'I'm Dr Richard Mason,' I said, 'and I've come about Ezekiel Oliphant.'

The man looked out into the street. Once up and once down. He seemed suddenly frightened. 'Is he here?' he said.

'I don't see him,' I said.

He laughed again, a braying, nasal sound. 'Well then,' he said, 'well then . . .' And he flung his arms wide. 'Oh this is a low and carnal misery indeed,' he said, 'for after they are dead they see not what is written in their faces oh when when when will he stop to torment me? When? *This is the filthy dreamer and the cloud without rain! Wait the moment wait the moment Chucky!!*

'Sure,' I said, 'absolutely. But . . . can we . . .' I let this sentence trail away, hoping to suggest that we would be willing to do anything to help the situation to which he was referring

99

(whatever it might be). But he did not like this. He turned on Anna and snarled 'Can what?' I saw that his right arm was thick and his chest well developed. In spite of his age – I would have said he was only fifty or so – he was physically strong.

'Well,' I said, 'work something out . . .'

'About what?' he said.

'Oh . . .'

He shrugged and turned back to the stairs. As he went I said 'Can we come in?'

He turned on me, the blue eyes wide. It was as if he was seeing me for the first time. 'What do you mean "can we"?' he said. 'We all do just as we like, don't we? All the time we do just as we like.' It was only then, in the way in which one sees a parental likeness in a child's face, suddenly, transiently, like picking out a dragon's head in a cloud or some demon shape out of a blot of ink, that I realized he had, to the life, the look of the man I had seen in Anna's flat. I was looking at the ghost of a ghost – the living image of the apparition of Ezekiel, a man who had died three hundred years ago. 'And yet,' I muttered to myself as I climbed the stairs, 'can it be that wee are ever Permanently and Utterly Eradicated? For does not the Spirit live on after us? And, if wee be of the Wickede, live on to Torture and Torment and haunt the scenes of Misery and Pity, where it was pent up in the earthly life?'

For there was there, an idle, oafish fellowe by the Name of Archer, that was a Groome to my Lorde & thought of naught but Vanitie & of his Person for hee was One who affected to know *the style of britches worn in London* (which city hee had heard talk of but never, to my mind, visited) & of *How to Wear a Handkerchief to Advantage* & was wont also to Boast of his Excesses and Improprieties with those hee was wont to style *Oure Burthen and Blessynge* or *The Fairest and Foulest of Us*, which is no more to say than *Women*, for this Archer counted Himself a Great Ravisher and for all I know was hanged for it. At this time I was a stranger to Women, the onlie Shee of whom I had acquaintance being the Mothere of my Bodie, of whom *The Black Beare* was wont to say that shee was scarce Present in a

100

Chambere unlesse it bee as a Miste or Vapoure.

But this same Archer talked of the *Pleasures of Venus* with such Grossnesse and Vile Expression as made mee Faint to hear him and talked of nothing but of *those he had ravished*, saying in my hearing, *if hee were Granted a half-crowne for each Woman hee had ravished, hee would be a wealthy man.* Though I dare sweare now – this *Archer* being a groom – his Intimacies were with Horses withal and the *Hocks* and Forelegs hee loved to speak of were those of my Lord's stable, for no woman of sense could beare, I am assured, his Base and Lewd Mannere of Expression or his visage, which was plump and the colour of Yeaste. And the most of all hee talked of was one *Margaret* that was in my Lord's kitchens, which hee called Meg & by his reckoning was a Willing and Libidinous Wretch. Though I stopped mine eares & let him know his Conversation was not Pleasant to mee, yett still did hee, at the Houres when I was busie with bending and Measuring out the Seasoned Wood, as my Master had taught mee, so hee Poured out Filth from the Pitcher of his Desires and Impurities. I thought him Old in Adulteries & took him to have Committed Whoredoms with her, yea thought him one who goeth in to a woman who playeth the Harlot, even as the Israclites went in to A-hola, and Judged her after the Mannere of Adulteresses to whom it is said 'Thou hast committed Abominations with the Sons of David and Polluted the Ark with the Whoredoms of thy Choosing yea though hast become Unclean in my sight.' But though I thought her then a *woman who had shed blood and upon whose hands was blood* yet I was *Close Mouthed* Oliphant still, for this groom Archer had no reverence for Scripture, and the *Cooperites* say 'Answere not Foulnesse with Foulnesse lest thou become unclean in the Sight of God, but go thy waie as I have Commanded thee.

And yet, so Insidious and without Peere is the Powere of the Evill One, did his Wordes penetrate my Understanding, so that when I went to my bed & my Master kissed mee & held mee in his Armes and spake of the Love hee had for mee, the Picture of the Woman did come into my Minde & took from mee my Strength and the Joy in my glorie. For shee came to mee as an Harlot and a Woman who would Inflame with base Kisses & so *runned up my Soule with Fire* for Pictures and Graven Images can play Tricks with Faith and Righteousness. And was this the beginning of oure Sinne? For though I had no Sinful thought of her, I dare swear this same Archer thought himself to Profit, by the Capture of my Soule for Wickednesse. For Thou has set us about with *Temptation* that wee may Struggle and not be Ashamed & though I thought Myselfe to Laboure for the Lord and step aside from Lewdnesse, yet shee came to mee Unbidden and I was amazed.

It was, I think two or three yeares after the death of the Earl of Portland, the Lord Treasurer, of whom Mr Passmore was wont say that *no man had a greater ambition to make himself thought Great nor stronger desires to leave a great fortune*, and three Yeares before the Archbishop Laud was confined upon Orders of the Parliament, when I was in my seventeenth Yeare, that I first saw this *Margaret* after the Bodie, and untill that daie I had no other Thought of her than that *shee hath wearied herselfe with Lies and Adulteries & her scum shall bee in the Fire; In her first and last is Lewdness.* But the Lord God makes us often to see Bodie and Spirit as two Spheres that shine aboutt each other, as doe the Planettes, so that the Soule may Shine on Us through a Crooked Eie and Lower out from One whose Temple is Adorned and Decked out Gloriously. And how should it bee, O Lorde I saw no Separation in Her that Daie, onlie two Disks of Fire that were One and Shone gloriously, neither could they bee taken one from the Other, as wee may see *the son in the Fathere and the Holy Ghost*?

I was taking out two or three of my Lorde's Barrelles, to stack them in the Yarde, near to the Out house where hee was wont to Kill the Hogges for *salting*, when I saw there at the windowe this Archer, who, with a Winke and a Nod and countless base and Vulgar Expressions gives mee to understand in *Dumb show* that this same Margaret is about to cross my Path. And I would gladlie have turned from her Waie yet was shee upon mee even as I looked and I had no chance to Escape her but turned and looked upon her Face and saw Her.

O Lord how may wee know the Path of Righteousness and Who is it setts Snares about oure Waies, to Deceive Us? And if wee are Deceived and our Reason and Judgement can Avail us Nothing do wee then stumble from Parlour to Church with no Light to guide oure conduct, and no Certayne and Eternall knowledge, that *wee do not Goe about Cozened by that which we take for the Worlde, and all oure Firm and Settled Convictions are but Shadowes*? For in her face I saw no sign of Evill or Disfavour & shee was fair & unto mee as a cluster of camphire in the vine-yardes of En-gedi & O shee was fair to mee & I saith unto myself 'Behold thou art fair my love; behold thou art fair; Thou hast Dove's Eies. Behold Thou art Fair beloved, yea Pleasant.' And my Heart stirred for her & I saw shee was indeed Virtuous and no Harlot yea then God hath shewed mee her verie Soule neither did Hee then Deceive mee, as I thought, for shee betraied no Lewdnesses or Baseness of Expression, but cast down her Eie that shee had come upon mee there & in her Hande shee held a Jug of Water which shee sett down before her, and Turned and went from mee neither did shee Speake but *her Locks were as black as are the Raven's & her cheeks were as a Bedd of Spices*. And I spake nott to Her.

Now this same Margaret, it was reported to mee, was possessed of a Sister, of Tender Yeares (nott above *five summers of age*) & this sister, as I observed in Daies that followed upon my meeting – for my Eie was opened then unto the Companie at my Lorde's house, whereat I sinned in the Eies of the *Cooperites* and yett did I count myselfe Blessed so to Sinne – followed *Margaret* most prettily as shee went about the Gardens neer to the Kitchens & it was through the Offices of Susan, as shee was named, I came once more to Speak with my Margaret. *My Margaret* that I owned after the bodie. Was it in Sinne alone I found her & how may I see her Face without Cries and Lamentations? Wherefore am I Deceived O Lord God & have I gone about too close to seek out Sin? I know nott these things, how they have come to Bee and ask Thy Worde, but Thou hearest not mee & I am alone with my *frost of cares*.

I was, as it chanced Dexterous in fashioning Wood, and had cutt, from the strips cast aside from the Barrelles, a Horse which could be drawn about with Cord & sate at the Doores of the Barn where I was wont to work, fashioning this Creature when this

Susan that was Sister to Margaret comes to mee and asks for whom I fashioned it. 'Why,' says I, 'For Thee little One. For whom Else but Thee?' at which time her sister comes to ask for Her and sees mee. But shee lowered her eie as shee had done Before and by this I knew her to bee virtuous & not as Archer had reported her. 'Come awaie Susan,' says Meg. At which the child Runs to her and begges shee shall have the Horse of mee. At which her Sister scoldes her for Forwardnesse & I was fain to Speak and tell her the Child meant no Harm & 'twas for her I made the Thing, having neither Wife nor Childe of Mine Owne. At which shee blushes most Prettily and I spake no further to her yet was I mightily Disturbed and knew not my Hearte what might bee the Cause of it but that as is the apple tree among the trees of the Wood so was my Beloved among the Women of my Lorde's Howse and in the Daies that followed I kept watch upon her and saw that shee was Good, though still Shee looked nott upon mee.

So it was that I made Enquiry of some that were there in that House and I learned some more of Her. That shee was not, indeed, Bred to Servitude, beinge the Daughter of a Clothier from the Town of Hertford, but that, her Fathere dying of a Fever her and Her sister were like to have been Thrown upon the parish, were it nott that one *Carwardine*, that took Rents for my Lord was Neare to them where they lay and so 'twas fixed that shee and Susan should come in to my Lorde's Service. And neither did shee – it was Reported to mee – have anie Association with anie in that place, synce manie of my Lorde's people were *Catholicus* – and, said hee who told me of these things, *Shee was of good familie and her Fathere was Accounted a Great Puritan by those who were for the King, so that, when the Civill Warres came on he would have been like to have been sett about by the Cavaleers synce Clothiers were alwaies Counted for the Parliament in everie Countie in England.* Although her mother, it was said, was near to being *Catholicus*.

But to mee shee would speak and in her Modestie of Manner and Expression was Pleasing to Mee and I told Her some littel of my Situation and my Place with my Master, at which shee cried to bee awaie from my Lorde's House, *for*, saith shee, *here is*

Naught but Drunkennesse and Folly and none love the Lorde as did my Fathere. So was our Converse Modest and Proper as it should bee between Us synce, because of oure Circumstances wee talked one to the Othere in the Garden as it was before wee were Condemned to eat our bread in the sweat of oure Face, knowing Ourselves Dust and the ground cursed for Oure Sake. And to her I gave a true relation of my Families, both that among which I dwelt with good Nehemiah and also the Family after which I was called in the Flesh, from which I was Fled, from which I had turned awaie my Face. And in our Discourse was much Sweetnesse, yea the sweetnesse that was in Israel that gave Honey where were once no Floweres and Grasses upon the Dry Places of the Deserts. And though I Search myselfe still now to see the Sin in what wee said – each to the Othere – yett can I FIND NO Sinne in Us and all seems as Adam's Kin before the Fall, before was the Flaming Sword and the Cherubim placed Eastward in Eden, when all was Common and Lightsome, yea Lovelie in the sight of the Lord our God.

But in those Daies, often at the Meetings or Assemblies of the *Cooperites* while I did studie or Pray yet my Thoughtes were nott kept upon the Strait Waie of Understanding or upon the City of God or his Temple built among Us as wee prayed togethere, but upon my Soule had fallen the Shadowe of Her Smile and in mine inward Eie was the echo of her Laughter which was sweet to mee & so I was troubled & my Master Nehemiah saw it and was in his Turn Sorrowfull, synce hee saw my Thoughtes strayed. Hee prayed above mee as wee slept and said *Save him O God for the waters are come in unto him & hee is in deep mire where there is no standing.*

Of *Courtship* I have little Understanding, nor thought my Conversation with my Meg was a Wooing, synce wee talked, at oure meetings, as I talked with others at the Assemblies of the Cooperites, and in those yeares between the *Scotch* rising and the summoning once more of the Parliament by the King, wee talked Boldly of the Waies in which Monies should bee raysed and of Mr Pym and Mr Hampden that were resolved to sweep the House of Parliament clean below and pull out all the Cobwebs in the Upper and the Lower Chambers. And about then it was my Lord

Strafford was led to his Execution, and the Archprelate himself imprisoned whereat wee wondered greatlie synce the Power of Presbytery was preached so openlie and none dared to Speak agaynst it, even that *Charles Stuart*, that, so the *Mercuries* reported was run awaie to Scotland for feare of the Parliament.

But yet though wee talked of this, my Mind was not upon these things. I feigned to speak of them with the Concern I affected in her Presence for I thought not hard upon them, or what they might Signify. And in truth when I was with Her I cared nott how it might bee resolved between the King and the Parliament – for I was troubled by a Conflict that sett myself agaynst my chosen Family as was the King sett agaynst Mr Hamden, or the Archbishop agaynst Mr Prynne (for hee who *hath been sett in the stockes now Makes a New Pillorie for the Lord of all the Bishops*). For I knew well my Master would not sanction anie Match between mee and another, synce with the *Cooperites, there was no marriage better than Burning* and they used to say *an Assemblie is the sweeter for the lack of Woman*. And soe I sate in secret with my Meg, apart from my Brethren, at the House of my Lorde and knew both Shame and Sweetnesse in oure Union of Soules. Shame in that I was eaten with Zeal for a House that was ungodly in the sight of my Master Nehemiah and sweetnesse for that to be in Her companie was to taste the sweetnesse of the Swallow's Flight and of the cool Water that was given in the Desert to the Children of Israel. & so was I riven between Sweetnesse and Shame like one who is pulled apart by Horse, as were the *Scythians*. Even as I am Torn now O Lord, between the Sinning and the Sweetnesse and I know nott which waie I may turn. For oure thoughts of each othere were not Carnall, but shee was given to mee in an acceptable Time and was Innocent in the Sight of the Lorde. And in seeking to bee One with Her – surely I sought the Lord God and not the Devil and his Workes? But yet I knowe Sinne to be Sweetnesse, and False Sweetnesse too, so that the Pleasure I took in Her sometimes seemeth *sett about with Snakes and Scorpions* so that oure Blisse was no Blisse & I am deceived in this as in so much else in this my most Unhappy Life. How may I know Her to bee Virtuous synce my Master shee hath Offended? How may I know her to bee of Good Report when so manie hath sworn agaynst her? Send

Thou mee some Certayn Sign or Favoure that it may bee revealed to mee, for I count my owne Death of littel account until this Sorrowe bee taken from mee and until I have the Certayn Knowledge shee be given mee from the Lord God or be at one with Belial and the Demons of Hell and the Sweetness I have tasted bee of fire and brimstone, yea the very stench of hell which is in my Nostrils and Burneth without End. O Lord God grant Thy Servant Knowledge for I am Weak and know nott which waie I may turn in this my Miserie!

I have seldom seen my Master in such a Case as when I told him I would seek to bee married to a woman hee knew nott.

Hee was at the working of a Splay Barrelle, which is to say a Half Barrelle of unseasoned Wood, and when I spoke unto him and in a soft voyce told of my Heart and how I was purposed with my *Margaret* he staied there where hee was over the Wood, & after a while hee strikes his Blade into the Barrelle & still he speaks nott to mee but walked out into the garden that was behind the Barn and stood, his Back turned from mee so that I saw nott his Face, yett was minded how farr Gone hee was now in Yeares and in my Heart was a great Sorrow. 'Thine own Kin shall betray thee and their Backsliding shall reprove Thee; know thou that it is an evill thing and Bitter that Thou has forsaken the Lord Thy God,' says hee. 'Nay,' says I, 'but art Thou then my God that I shall betray Thee when I take a wife in the sight of the Lord who is a godlie and Virtuous Woman as manie will attest? For I have asked Him who is above us all and beseeched him and hee hath made His Face to Shine upon mee, neither is there anie Sinne in the Sweetness of love hath hee not written *that I shall rise and goe to my love and bee clothed in his Affection yea in the Garments hee hath chosen mee in his House neither shall those of mine own Kin have cause for sorrow but goe with mee and see I am well served in Him.'*

'Well then Master,' says hee, 'I see there is Rebellion in Thee. And thou knowest well *Rebellion is as the sin of witchcraft.* As the prophet tells us. So mightily art Thou bewitched and taken from Mee.' & there were teares upon his cheekes but I counted them nott nor thought of anie Pleasure save that which I took in my Margaret, whereat I was much in Erroure. Yea was there

107

Rebellion in my Hearte agaynst Him and all of Oure Assemblies. And was there Rebellion also the length and the breadth of the Kingdome of England in that Yeare and the Yeares that came after. For then was that Great Remonstrance served agaynst the Kinge, was the Rising of the Papists in Ireland agaynst Us and in the summer of the Yeare that followed, being the Summer of sixteen hundred and forty-two, the King hath raysed his Standarde at Nottingham, in rebellion, as I take it, agaynst Us his lawful subjects, and soe was each sett agaynst the other, myself agaynst my Master Nehemiah, Gentleman agaynst Great Lorde, Labourer agaynst Honest Tradesman & in the midst of this discord were myself and my *Margaret* married, nott in a waie of my choosing, but at a church neer to my Lorde's house and soe in oure Beginnings was Dissension and Rebellion & yea it is *as the Sinne of Witchcraft* & before long Witchcraft was of the Business & the Devill hath laid His hande upon Mee. For which I ask the Lorde His Pardon for never was so Peaceable Soule as I born to such Distress and Discorde & never anie such as I *who sought Angells & was Granted Witches, who looked onlie for to see God in the Face and saw onlie the Hideous and Terrible Features of the Prince of Darknesse.*

11

Ron's room, at first glance, confirmed (if confirmation was needed) that he was ripe for restraint under Section 20 of the Mental Health Act. It was piled high with an odd assortment of objects – children's toys, garden implements, second-hand books – which made it look as if he was attempting to form the nucleus of a supermarket. What indicated even more forcibly, however, the precarious nature of the occupant's sanity, were the huge pieces of paper pinned round the walls, offering advice, posing questions, or asserting the transparently false with equal confidence and emphasis.

GET UP EARLY PLEASE RON. And another:

BRITAIN. IS IT A PRISON? HOW LONG HAVE WE GOT? Over the bed was written the largest sign in the room, which said, simply

WITCHES ARE ALIVE NOW AND RUNNING THE ECONOMY. WITCHCRAFT CAUSES HIGH INTEREST RATES.

I nodded towards this sign. 'Does it?' I said.

Ron laced his fingers together. He sounded perfectly sane as he said 'It's just a word, isn't it? It's not a word that's fashionable as an explanation. But it's as good as any other, isn't it?'

He came close to me. His baggy cheeks were sewn with a fine rain of white stubble. His breath smelt strongly of onion. 'Ezekiel,' he said, 'was on to something.'

'I've read *A Cursèd Lie*,' I said. 'I think it's very interesting.' At the receipt of this news, Ron bucked like a centaur on the warpath. His nostrils widened and his eyes rolled. 'You,' he said, 'are the fourth person to read that book in three hundred years.' 'Well,' I said, 'it's not exactly pacily written is it?'

While we were about it – who were the other two? If we counted Ezekiel, although it seemed to me possible that our friend had not bothered to read his own work even at proof stage. How did he know I was the fourth person anyway? The remark gave me an unpleasant feeling – akin to that of an

Egyptologist opening a tomb with a curse on it. I felt that, instead of the observer, I might well be the one being observed. I looked across at Ron. He was rubbing his palms together as if anxious to strike a spark from the joints. Anna sat on the bed and watched him cautiously. I noted again that prim way in which she sat on her bottom – as if it did not belong to her – and experienced another sharp stab of lust. Ron looked between us cunningly. 'And this is your . . .'

'That's right,' I said, 'this is Anna.'

'Yes.'

He leered. 'And she's your . . .'

'That's right,' said Anna brightly, foreclosing any more discussion of her role in the proceedings.

Ron's eyes clouded momentarily as he looked at her, and, for a brief instant a look of real and terrifying hatred invaded his features, as if he were looking not at her but at some nightmare on her shoulder. Then, as quickly, he wiped his hand across his brow and turned to me. 'There are,' he said, 'bad things in the air. There's something foul going on.' 'Absolutely,' I said, thinking we were about to embark on a conversation about the state of the nation. Who or what did he mean? Monetarists? The policy and judgement of Michael Heseltine? The GLC?

Whatever he meant he did not explain it. He bounded across to the far wall, where a large, scrappy piece of paper was sellotaped to the picture rail. It appeared to be a handwritten version of a family tree, but on several of the branches were drawn, quite skilfully, faces, sometimes fully dressed figures. I saw one at the edge of the paper of a man in an eighteenth-century frock coat and a periwig. In his right hand he held a cane which he was using to point to some distant object, and at his feet crouched a thin, ill-clad woman with the face of one of Goya's extras – an onlooker in hell. Next to the man in the frock coat was written *Sam Oliphant, 1756–1805, explains a point of political economy to an Irish peasant.* Some of the other drawings were even stranger. One showed the head of a man about twenty, out of which was sprouting a twisted length of barbed wire. Next to him was written *Paul Oliphant 1896–1916 a jolly good innings considering*.

Ron, without further explanation, pointed to the first name at the head of the paper, which read *Ezekiel Oliphant ? – 1658 (done to death by agents of the protectorate)*. 'Ezekiel,' he said, 'had three Oliphants out of Meg, (here he turned and leered at my companion) 'but of these only Nathaniel and Abiezer survived. Eternal love and one partner for ever has more to do with hygiene and penicillin than anything else. In the seventeenth century you could count on having two partners because one was sure to die. Abiezer, as far as we can tell, was an itinerant preacher belonging to a sect known as John's Day Baptist Men who were a rather extreme form of Muggletonian. But although Abiezer had eight male and three female children out of *Sarah* and Nathaniel had only one male child by his second wife *Ruth* the line goes through this child since all eleven of Abiezer's children died of the smallpox in 1679, serve them right the greedy little bastards.' He grinned fiercely at me, and added 'Don't go looking for immortality in your children, chucky. Because children die. There's no immortality? He did a kind of elfin dance in front of the drawing and went back to his recital. When he was recounting the family history of the Oliphants – in spite of his stern words on the subject of families and immortality – I noticed that his voice acquired a singsong quality, like someone intoning the responses in church.

'Nathaniel's son was christened Reheboam but in 1730, at the age of fifty, he changed his name – as far as we can tell – to George, and seems to have acquired some land in Essex, probably on the profits of Nathaniel's brewery. Did I tell you about the brewery?'

'No,' I said.

'Oliphant's Ale,' he said, 'is still spoken of with respect in parts of north Hertfordshire. More than two pints and you're a bit liable to be sick all over the floor, it has a secret ingredient some people say, which is more than enough likely to be rats or badgers or something. Anyway. From 1730 to 1825, the Oliphants farmed, married and were buried in the parish of Thaxted and would seem to have been respectable Tories, Church of England, supporters of the Game Laws, makes you sick doesn't it?'

'Yes,' I said.

Ronald's finger stabbed at a drawing close to the one I had

noticed earlier, of the man in frock coat and periwig. This was only a head and shoulders, but the massive folds of flesh around the chin, the small piggy eyes and the high brocade collar suggested a Regency buck gone to seed. 'Ernest Oliphant,' said Ron, 'was MP for Otterbury between 1780 and 1815 and he once said that he refused on principle to go closer than fifty yards to the House of Commons. He is most famous for his efforts in obtaining the arrest and then the execution of the Jacobins of New Malden.'

'I didn't know,' I said, 'that there were any Jacobins in New Malden.'

'Of course there fucking weren't,' said Ron, 'but Ernest thought there were. So there were. There weren't any witches in Bloomsbury. *Maybe.*' Here he looked again, rather oddly, at Anna. She shifted uneasily on her chair and pushed back the sleeves from her tanned forearms. Oliphant stared and stared at her arms.

'What's the matter?' she said. He did not answer. Then he moved away from the wall and came close to her. She shifted again nervously.

'What's that?' he said. 'On your arm?'

'What's what on my arm?'

He pointed to a patch of discoloured skin, rather like a strawberry-coloured mole, just below the elbow of her right arm. Anna flushed.

'It's a birthmark,' she said, quietly.

There was silence in the room. Oliphant nodded his head slowly, like a prosecuting counsel waiting for the kill, then retraced his steps to the family tree. He turned and looked back at her shrewdly. He had the expression of a man whose job it is to know when someone is lying. Who knows in the way of, say, a secret policeman, that it doesn't matter whether they're lying or telling the truth since all you want is a result, and given time and the application of pain they will say anything you want. What was unnerving about this man was the way in which he managed to combine the absurd and the threatening. Just as you had decided it was safe to laugh at him, you realized that some of his absurdities were deliberate. That he was allowing you to laugh. That he had you in the palm of his hand, like an actor who knows just when the audience should relax, breathe out and think that all is well. For their calm will be his opportunity, and when they least expect it he will round on them and SHOUT out the word they don't want to hear, the word that gives out the horrors.

'Well,' said Oliphant, 'that's all right. Isn't it?'

He looked back at the family tree, moving his head this way and that as he followed mainstream and tributary Oliphants, down from the Napoleonic Wars, across to overseas Oliphants (there was an extraordinary picture of a man with a bone through his nose which was captioned *Abo Oliphant. Went to seed in the Dead Hill Valley branch of the Australian Resettlement Bureau, 1908 – God knows when*). Eventually, his eyes and his fingers settled again on the line of descent that ran unbroken to the bottom of the page.

Almost at the bottom was one of the best executed drawings on the sheet. It was a carefully shaded, full face of a man who appeared to be in military uniform. Next to his head, however, was drawn a quill pen from which three heavy drops were falling. The last of the drops had been drawn on his face which gave the man the appearance of crying. An odd display for a soldier, I thought. 'Who's that?' I said.

Ron sighed. 'Ah,' he said. 'Roger was a scholar. A scholar and a soldier. He was crossed in his career. There's a book about him I think. The family was smashed badly when corn prices were hit by the French War and young Roger had to go for a soldier.' He beamed at the young man fondly. 'There was a scandal at the University and he had to leave. And he was doing so well. He was a lover of the past, like me. The past has everything to teach us and we do not listen. We pay no heed. I sometimes hear them calling out to us – the war dead and the cholera dead and the witch dead and the voices sound so faint and lost. Oh Ezekiel. . .' The tone of this last remark was so familiar, so close and intimate, that I looked around the room. I saw no one. Ronald returned to his story.

'Anyway. Roger enlisted in the Enniskillen Fusiliers. And from then on the Oliphants were a family of soldiers. Roger's son by Lulu Weiss the actress, Edward, led the disastrous attack on the Bey's Inlet, west of Scutari, in the Crimean War. Four hundred men swam ashore in specially designed garments only to be butchered by a group of Turkish soldiers who had somehow got possession of Old Trouble – the largest field gun belonging to the Fusiliers at that time. Edward survived under a pile of bodies. He was seriously crippled, but wrote an extremely popular music hall song based on hs experiences, *If You Haven't Got a Leg You Can't Shake It*. When he retired from the "boards" he bought a butcher's shop in Enfield which remained in the family until 1940.'

'What happened in 1940?' I said.

The question seemed to upset him. 'War and war and more war and endless devastation, that's what happened you stupid fucking little creep. War and more war and England standing up for the Jews. Why? I don't know. My father fought in that war and he was wounded and he got fuck all and he got fuck all when the shop was hit by a bomb in 1940. Why us? I ask you. Johnson's the baker's didn't get it, did they? And Johnson was fucking the woman on the corner, he was an evil bastard, he was a Nazi, he said we should have carried Ribbentrop in a chaise down Palmers Green High Street, but it wasn't his shop they hit was it.' He came over to me. His head wobbled on his neck like a turkey's. He was simpering. I caught the onion smell again. This time mixed with some odour of material decay – the smell you get off an old house, when its carpet and curtains and linoleum are cleared to face the unwelcome sun. He smelt of ugly secrets, ingrown privacy, a boarding house smell that conjured up a world of empty landings and sour landladies. The new world of landless people.

'The Oliphants,' he said, 'were always tradesmen prophesying doom. And of course our class has been defeated. We went down just as the Cavaliers went down in their day. We are no longer a Manufacturing Nation are we? We're finished chucky. We poisoned the well, long long ago. And you know when we poisoned it? Just when England should have burst into flower. Just when we should have danced our way into our Revolution. Revolution. Revolution. What did your daddy do, chucky?'

'He was a vicar,' I said, 'but he died.'

'What did he preach?' said Ron.

'He preached Christianity,' I said.

'Did he preach the resurrection of the body at the Last Judgement and the eternal life of the soul in Jesus Christ and the condemning of the wicked to eternal separation from God, their casting out into hellfire?'

'He was in the Church of England,' I said by way of reply.

'The Church of England,' said Ron, 'isn't worth the paper it's printed on. The Church of England is a bunch of wankers in my view. People hunger for spiritual certainty and what do you give them? What do you give them eh?'

'Sherry,' I said. He did not laugh. He had gone off into a dream again. His eyes travelled back to the family tree on the wall and he talked, to himself, in the singsong voice. Once again I had the unpleasant sensation of participating against my will in some kind of rite. At first I could not catch what he was saying. I looked across at Anna. She had lost all her earlier pert cool, and was gazing at him in silent horror. Then . . . little by little I made out what it was that he was crooning: Ezekiel. . . Ezekiel. . . still here. . . come here. . . come here. . . my little pet. . . my little animal . . . do Thy work. . . do Thy work. . . Our Father which art in. . . in 1851. . . in 1641. . . I don't know. . .' His voice died away. Somewhere out on the landing I heard a scratching. A small animal trapped in the woodwork. It was deathly quiet in the room. 'It's an amazing research job,' I said, 'how did you do it?'

'You can touch the past in England,' said Ron, 'it's close to you. That's all we've got. Our half-timbered houses. You can reach out and touch your ancestors. They're still here. We build ugly red brick houses over fields but the fields are still there. There are still the old ways in us.'

'Did you go round a lot of record offices?' I said.

Ron grinned. 'I made quite a lot of it up,' he said, and flung himself on to the battered sofa. 'Invented history is quite as good as the real thing. It probably *is* the real thing half the time. People go to war, have children – for dreams or lies. Don't they? They'll go to the wall for an untruth but nobody ever actually suffered for empirical science. Not worth it. Look at Galileo.' He poked his finger at me. 'You have come here for a purpose,' he said, 'you have come here to fulfil your destiny and I will give

115

you the secret. The greatest secret in English history. The most valuable piece of information ever to be revealed even to an humble "amateur".' He grinned. His teeth were large and yellow. 'Then you'll kill the witch,' he said.

I attempted to get some control over the conversation. 'What interested me particularly about *A Cursèd Lie*,' I said, 'is that Ezekiel seemed to have access to material collected by –'

'William Clarke, the Secretary of the Army Council,' said Ron. He seemed pleased about this.' Certainly, Certainly.'

He grinned again. 'If you have read *A Cursèd Lie* you are chosen,' he said.

'Yes?'

'You can read my pamphlet. It's all in there.'

'Thanks,' I said.

'No one has read my pamphlet,' said Ron, 'not even the printer.' I didn't ask how he had managed this. Blindfolded him perhaps. 'But you can read it,' he said. 'You can.'

'Thanks,' I said.

He scurried over to a pile of magazines in the corner of the room and from them took a dusty pile of papers, stapled together crudely. On the front page I read

The Most Important Secret Conspiracy in English
History Revealed and Exposed and the Causes of
Britain's Decline as a World Power revealed

by

Ronald Oliphant

Below this I read

Warning. This book is fully protected by copyright and may not be reproduced in whole or in part except by permission of the author. Any breach of copyright will be prosecuted under the 1948 Berne Convention. Limited edition of twelve signed by the author.

'Good title,' I said.

'I wanted to call it,' said Ron, '*Witches and the Witch Masters.*

But I thought that was a wee bit sensational.'

Anna coughed nervously. 'People love the idea of witches,' she said, 'the idea that it is all women's fault. Irrational ideas are the most evil because –

Ron rounded on her and stopped her with an animal scream. 'SILENCE!!' he yelled.

She froze. Oliphant stooped to the floor, and for a moment I thought he was going to pick up one of the knives on the filthy plates that littered the carpet. I edged forward, slowly, but then he straightened up with a jerk. In his right hand was a shrivelled piece of beef. 'This is the flesh of Christ,' he screamed, 'take and eat. My spirit dwells with the devil and sups and eats with him we are the merriest of devils I cry up the profane as most holy sin is finished, masters, see see where he comes see where he finds me out again because of what has been revealed he co-omes to me . . .' His blue eyes, wide as ever, were full of the terrifying absence I have glimpsed in the eyes of the mentally ill. Meg had had that look once or twice. I knew it. He was staring towards the open door and backing away from it as if something had come into the room. Whatever it was that had come in he did not like it, for, as he backed towards the wall he began to whimper pitifully. He was grinding the dried beef between his two huge hands and it powdered to dust, like dried blood, as whatever it was he could see came closer and closer and closer . . . 'Please . . .' he said, 'please Gip . . . no . . . please my Gip no please . . . I'll give you Jackie Morrow an' you shall ask . . . please . . . no no . . .'

I followed the direction of his eyes. The thing he feared seemed to be moving this way and that across the dirty carpet, until finally, breathing heavily, like an asthmatic in the middle of an attack, he was forced up against the far wall. For some reason I thought of my father; he had developed pneumonia after the stroke, and what killed him – they said – was lack of air. I thought of him gasping in the hospital, with my mother crying above him, and wondered if he had prayed. Or had she prayed? Do any of us – even the priests – believe in the power of prayer? I wanted to believe so much, looking at this sad, tattered wreck of a man. I wanted to be able to spell away whatever it was that was frightening him.

But whatever it was left as suddenly as it had come. We make our own deaths and entrances perhaps. Other people cannot pray for us. Prayer is nothing more than listening to one's voice in an empty room, echoing back in mockery from the walls. Oliphant sank to the floor and then turned to me. His voice was low and urgent. He sounded perfectly sane.

'There are still witches in England,' he said, 'but they are not where you think they are. Study what I have given you. I've been ill in my head and sometimes I get confused. I have some ideas that would get me locked up but I am not all crazy, what I am saying is true, is true. The horrible is sometimes true and perhaps I have said it wrong and been too crude but don't mind that. Get at the truth behind what I am saying to you. There is truth there. When you go up to Worcester College don't look where the fucking librarian tells you the papers aren't there that's all clear in Roger's book the Clarke papers *they* all look at are not the ones. They're in a trunk in the north gallery of the Old Library, marked with the name of James. And it's genuine. Get scholars to check it. It's true.' It's fantastic and stupid and funny almost but the horrible thing is that it is true. No one believed in the camps did they? No one believed they could do those things. In Cambodia they did that too. I saw the pictures of the men before they died. They do. The world is such an evil place Dr Mason and you don't know the half of it there is an evil conspiracy going on. Here. In England. It's as old as old as our history, oh I have proof you see. Proof.'

'We must go,' I said. I didn't want to stay any more in the room with this man. Was there something in the room with us? I don't know. I didn't see anything. Is my father still alive? Sometimes I am here writing and I feel him at my back the way Ezekiel visits me. He wears the big black Homburg and walks me across the Brondesbury Road the way he used to do back in 1956 when I was at Malorees Primary School. He takes my hand and sings 'Hold my hand, I'm a stranger in paradise.' I think he's funny because I'm eight. And then I turn and he isn't funny. He's dead. And it is thirty years later and I am crying because I will never see him any more.

Anna got up and came over to me. I put my arms around her, and, bowing nervously, we retreated through the dirty plates, the opened books, all the grotesque clutter of the lonely or the

118

ill, to the safety of the stairs. *'Look in the Clarke Papers!'* he was screaming, *'It's all in the Clarke Papers they will tell you what to do you have to do it you know . . .'*

As we hurried out to the street I looked back to the door. He came down the stairs and stood looking out at the grey street, his arms raised in imprecation, his white hair wild. For a moment he was a figure of fun again, something risible, like the patient in the asylum in the child's comic. And then he spoke and he wasn't funny. He spoke in a honeying, cloying tone, rather like the one Ezekiel uses when he wants to compel my attention. And I thought 'What have I got to put against the awful, unknowable world and its past but a kind of wounded, petty scepticism, an imagination that is no more than a weak English giggle?'

When we got into the car I kissed her, almost savagely, groping for the button on her jeans, scratching at the line of her thigh, and when she opened and let my hand in, there in the car, in the white street, I felt she was wet and kissed her harder, even more hopelessly, without any thought of who might be watching or what would happened because of all of this. It was only when she pushed me away and straightened herself that I looked up and saw that we had been observed. Oliphant was watching from the doorway, and his eyes, narrow with contempt for what we were doing, could have been those of his ancestor, the long-dead witchfinder, Ezekiel.

12

I couldn't keep my hands off her on the way back. Every time we stopped, and quite often when we didn't, I leaned across the sweet papers, paperbacks and crumpled envelopes that decorated the base of the gear lever, and worked caresses on that straight brown back, up to the neat curve of her shoulders, down to her belly and then –

'Can't you wait, Jamie?'

'No.'

'It's better in bed.'

'Not with Derwent Mate there it's not.'

I sat back in my seat, experiencing none of the glumness I felt when Meg (as so often these days) didn't feel like it, or (worse) approached it with the sort of grim determination she used when hoovering the stairs. I was a sophisticated man of the world. Sometimes women didn't feel like it. That was fine. You were an attractive, sophisticated man of the world. They would get around to feeling like it. Maybe today. Maybe tomorrow. It didn't matter. In the mean time you lounged around in their cars, putting out that lazy, confident charm that made you irresistible.

I caught sight of myself in the mirror again. I looked (I had to admit it) fairly resistible. I seemed to have caught some of Ron's lunatic wildness. My black hair was up in spikes again and my face was flushed. Heated Troll.

None of this was getting me very far with Gottlieb. How did people manage to have mistresses? It seemed, on present evidence, to be extremely time consuming. Perhaps, in the later stages, things would be put on a more formal basis, but for the moment I could not possibly see how I was going to write a major six-part television series, investigate *The Evil Conspiracy at the Heart of England*, have an affair, and maintain reasonable relations with the five dependent women in the large house on Putney Hill. Why was I worrying myself about conjuring up the past, about the times we lived in? (Anna was driving the Citroën down the Archway Road; overflowing dustbins in the doorway and ahead of us, on a crossing, an elderly Greek woman in black, gave the place the air of a run-down Mediterranean country.) Why was I worrying about times past, present or future, when the only real way in which I could experience time, being a practical person, was as a slight ache at the back of the skull? As a voice whispering 'You haven't done this and this and this'? Somebody said that days are what we live in. I live in minutes, seconds even, possessed completely by the sensation of the moment, only to shed it as something new takes over. I was a ripe candidate for possession, I suppose. Hardly there at all really. A series of unfinished sketches, waiting to be given form and density. To be taken over.

Go away, I mouth to myself. Get back, can't you? You're not wanted here.

'I don't want,' said Anna suddenly, 'to have an affair.'

'Me neither,' I said, in the tones of a sophisticated man of the world. My God, did I want another woman losing her head over me? The tears? The phone calls? The suicide bids? The endless bouts of screwing in British Rail hotels?

Not 'arf I did. I'd never had this happen to me before. Was it to be taken away before it had even started? Why didn't she want an affair? I looked sideways at her.

'I don't want an affair either,' I said. 'I just want to go out to lunch with you and go to bed with you and talk to you. But I don't want an affair.'

She laughed. 'That sounds all right,' she said.

I felt sophisticated again.

We were coming down through King's Cross, past the waste of tangled rail and unreachable bridges that lead northwards out of the station. The grey skies had darkened to black. There was rain on the windscreen. I looked out of the window at the gloomy, red brick buildings and thought about what Ron had said. The flashes of reason in his crazy dialogue were, in retrospect, the most alarming thing about him. Method in his madness. Perhaps the way in which the past was tangible was not through a recreation of physical sensation – Ezekiel scratching himself in that chair at Anna's flat, the sour taste of beer

121

unchanging from century to century – but through the mysterious, unknowable things that somehow you felt sure of, in the equally mysterious present. This girl next to me, for example. I could not rid myself of the impression that I already knew her. The way she laughed at things I said. Whole conversational sequences between us had a sort of inevitability about them, a familiarity that usually only comes with long acquaintance. Sometimes I thought she was Meg, Meg as she had been all those years ago in Oxford, in that ragged sealskin coat, smudged eyes and white, nervous face. She felt more like the girl I had crushed to me, dragged fiercely under my wing through the carefully posed squares and gardens of the university, than what that girl had become. I was getting my past back, piece by piece. How could that be?

Perhaps (I didn't like this thought) because the system of my love for Meg had been invaded. Entropy had begun to claim it. It was leaking, holed in the side like a ship in a battle. That particular kiss, that particular morning, were no longer my wife's. Anna was stealing something from Meg, taking away the things that made her what she was. If only people were as closed as machines, never bleeding into each other, never allowing their flesh to be melted or enclosed by another's flesh. Machines are better than people. People go too far.

SCENE THREE.

Int. EZEKIEL's *house.* ANNA *turns from the window her long hair flowing. (Note to self – does Meryl Streep's hair flow?)* EZEKIEL *comes in, his face dark with fury.*

ANNA: What husband – more witches?

EZEKIEL: Aye. More witches. (*He sits on a low stool.*) There are more witches in Bloomsbury than are fleas in a grocer's jerkin. (*Turning on her*) Thee should know well enough. For hast not thou bewitched Mistress Margaret? Confess.

He *crosses to her and pulls at her dress. Beneath her sleeve we see a large red mark, like a birthmark.* ANNA *is terrified but* EZEKIEL *grips her hard on the arm. His face is distorted with rage.*

> All may be well for you my dear. If that indeed is a
> mark of birth only, and in the natural order of things.

I didn't think, so far, that Meryl Streep would fancy it. Whatever
Anna's hair did. Even if it flowed, writhed, coiled, rolled, got
up, sang the Marseillaise and did handstands, I thought
Cavaliers would wing its way back from her agent as fast as Nat
Gottlieb can pick up a phone. And that's fast.

'Jamie. Witchcraft is great. Everyone loves it. I love it. It's
good. People love it. And some vague *plot* – people love that. So
long as it's not too political. But these characters, Jamie – they
don't live – they're wooden.'

'I want them to be wooden,' I said to Gottlieb, 'I feel safer if
they're wooden. You don't seem to undersand, Nat. There's
nothing wooden about Ezekiel, really. I want to make him
wooden in the hope he'll go away. I want to make a joke of him,
you see? I want it to be easy and funny and not too much
trouble. He's at my shoulder, Nat. I–

I didn't go on. There was no point. I knew I wasn't going to
write *Cavaliers* or anything like it ever again. Maybe I wasn't
going to write anything ever again. For once I was at the mercy
of those around me, of unscheduled visits from my past and the
country's past. And I wanted to know, not pronounce. To
understand quite why Dr Mason was being so mysterious, what
was behind these vague threats from Ezekiel and his crazy
ancestor. Most of all I wanted to know what I felt about this girl
next to me. Why did I feel so calm when I was with her? Was I
falling out of love with Meg? Falling away from our safe world,
headlong into a new and terrifying country where there were
conspiracies, ghosts, passions of which you were not in control,
the devil, with his goatee beard and mocking smile, and God the
Father, always merciful but always just out of reach?

We parked in a quiet street near Bedford Square. I took my
new girl in my arms and kissed her on the mouth. I was kissing
her on the mouth, hard, with my hand straying through those
red curls, when out of the corner of my eye I saw Rick Mason.
He came out of a bookshop with a parcel under his arm, hunched against the thin February drizzle. He looked right and left
and right again, like a good northerner, and then he looked

straight at me. He looked for quite a long time, and, because I had the girl's head in front of me, I thought he wouldn't be able to see me. Then, bothered by the image, but still clearly unaware that it was me he was looking at, he started towards us. I broke away from her then and sat, staring, straight ahead of me. When he was about fifty yards away I turned to look at him. Our eyes met, but it was he who faltered, stopped, and looked shamefacedly away as if he was the guilty one. Selfish left-wing fucking northerner. Go and tell her then. Go on. Tell her.

'Are you all right?' said Anna.

'Fine,' I said, 'I've just seen someone I know.'

'Who?' she said.

'Friend of my wife's.'

A pause.

'I knew you were married,' she said.

'I'm going to leave her,' I said. 'I don't love her any more.'

She pulled down the mirror and began to make herself up, calmly, efficiently. Pouting her lips, she drew two scarlet lines across her face. Her reflection seemed to amuse her.

'They all say that,' she said.

'I mean it,' I said.

'They all mean it,' she said.

'But I do,' I said, 'I suddenly saw it just now. I know it's absurd. I've only known you two days. I don't know where you're from or what you think or your history or anything about you. Maybe that's why I think I like you. With you there's only the moment. Never anything either side of it. I've never felt that before. I've always been the calculating little Englishman – "if I do this she'll do this". But I don't feel that way with you. There's just us. Here. In this car. Now.' She had finished decorating her face. Burnished and decked out in a pair of huge gold earrings, she looked like some slave girl, up for auction at an eastern court. She smiled at her face in the mirror and straightened her back. There was that primness about her again. The sudden reserve that made me want to hear her cry the way she had moaned in the flat 'Oh Oh Oh . . .'

'Now,' she said, 'let's go back to my flat and have a really good screw.'

'All right,' I said.

It wasn't as good as either of us thought it was going to be. And when it was over, and I was lying with her under the tangled bedclothes, my arms round her shoulders, her head on my chest, face reddened with the afterglow of lust, her shoulders still damp with sweat, through the door from the hall came Ezekiel. He wasn't wearing his absurd repertory gear, but a dirty white shirt and across his face was a huge scar. His hair was matted and filthy and on his chest was a mass of blue bruises. He sat on the end of the bed, and said in a low voice 'I Beseeche Thee Lorde to pardon this my Wickednesse and for what I did Evil in Thy sight I know is nothing but Just. But I am sinned against in my Time, Lord, even as I sinned against Others, and I Beseech Thee as Thou art a Jealous and Terrible God to punish those who will afterwards be set down as the Great and Pure of Hearte!' He turned his face to mine. 'Nay, Master,' he said, 'for Thee and I are brothers in Sinne and have made oure Compacte on None but our Termes. What is in Thy Heart is in mine and I can reach to the very seat of your Soule.'

Anna was asleep. I wanted to move but could not. He muttered something in Latin that I could not catch. Then he stretched out one claw-like hand, closer, closer, closer . . . I tried to call out. If I call out, I thought, I will know this is a dream. But my lips would not move. I did not want his hand to touch me. It looked so cold, so lacking in life. It was the colour of my father's cheeks that morning when I saw him in the hospital. Don't touch me, I tried to say, please please don't touch me.

But he did touch me. And his hand was like ice on my skin. It grazed my leg, up my thigh, still clammy from sex, and into my groin. The nails were sharp. But, although I was aware of their sharpness, I felt no pain, or rather only the ghost of pain, the idea of it. Neither did I feel at all when his long fingers broke through the skin and reached upwards to the intestine, through the blood and muscle and mess that is at the centre of us (what are we but fragile bags of blood? our substance is our very weakness) until his fingers found my heart. They played with the muscle of my heart as a boy might squeeze a pair of bellows, and then, grown tired of this game, reached up through the spongey thickets of my lungs, and up up up into where my left arm branched out over Anna's nakedness and the rumpled sheets. I looked up and saw he was turning, lightly, but as solid as a hologram. His arm, I saw, that was reaching into me and through me was his left arm, and as it found more and more of my left arm so the rest of his body followed suit. His legs, chest, belly, neck, head and thighs eased themselves into me, pushing in through veins and arteries until they bumped against the skin like a rowing boat against a wooden jetty. One bump, another, and then they had settled, and my arm was not my arm, but his. My legs and chest were not mine but his and I could feel him looking out at the darkened room through my eyes. He inhabited me.

I looked down. My right hand was twisting this way and that but I was not conscious of moving it at all. It stopped, of its own accord. And through my eyes or his I saw a crowd of faces. I was standing above them, looking down. They were shouting something but I could not hear what it might be. I was afraid of something. They were going to hang me. No no no. That wasn't it. It was worse. Something much worse. I was afraid. The roar of the crowd grew louder and, against my will I found my mouth was assuming the proportions of a smile. The lips were being pulled back over the teeth and my breath wasn't my breath: it was his breath, foul-smelling and sour. 'I die,' I said, 'Unregenerate – and What is done Here today is most Infamously and Wickedly Conceived by the Protector – and by all the Devils I once conjured out I swear to be Avenged on this most Perjured and Abominable Countrie.'

Had I said this aloud? Anna stirred but did not wake. What I could not bear was the feeling that my body was not my own. That at any moment he might decide to make me walk off the bed, out into the corridor or that he might turn my hands round on to the girl's face, might make them lace themselves round her neck as she lay there sleeping and squeeze and squeeze until there was no life left in her and her tongue was as swollen as the witch we late hanged at the Cross in Essenden my Lord I did examine her and found the detestable mark of Satan on her body about her privies and after she was put to the torture she did confess and mounted the scaffold and placed her neck in the noose with humble thanks that I, Ezekiel Oliphant, had delivered her immortal soul from the smoke and infernal pain of Hell.

How did he leave me that night? I can't remember. Did he climb out of me, like a stud might leave a one night stand? Was I dull flesh he'd finished with like someone you've fucked and don't want to fuck again? Did I feel used up? Did he turn once at the door as ghosts are supposed to and look back at me and the room and the naked, sleeping girl beside me?

I don't know. All I know is he can do that any time. He can be in my body and make me do things I do not want to do. Things I don't remember. Things I am ashamed of. He can make me hurt people and say cruel things to them and he can make me do what I never did before. Oh I was weak and timorous and facetious but I was never evil the way I can be when it is his arms that fit so snugly into mine, his eyes that look around the unfamiliar world of the present and his thin, whining voice that speaks in my stead. I'm his puppet then, that's all.

And he is out there now, I know he is. I have been writing, now, all day but the sun will go and it will be dark and then he will try and get in here. I have made it worse by writing about him because that summons him up. Of course it does. He is out there. And when the ward is quiet and everyone is asleep and there is only one nurse, at the far end, sitting by her yellow lamp, like the lamp in the museum, he will find a way, at last, in here. He will move softly over the polished floor and stand by my bed. And then he will climb into my body the way he did that day in Anna's flat. But this time he will do it properly. He will make me climb off the bed. He will lead me out past the night nurse because she will be asleep which is why he will come between three and three-thirty (I have been watching her). He will make me dress, although I do not wish to. I will try to say that I want to get well, that I want to stay here, but he will not listen. He will walk me out through the far door that is not locked from the inside because we are not dangerous, and because Ezekiel is clever. He never comes when there are people around, or speaks out of turn. He can make me look reasonable and funny and normal the way I have acted for so much of my life. He can crack jokes about

127

Alfie Barnacle and mothers-in-law and all sorts of things. He knows just how to play me. He plays me to the life.

But he will not be going to London (for that is where we will go) to make jokes or to charm people. He will be going to do something wrong and horrible and ugly, like the things he made me do after Meg left. He wants me to kill someone. I know he does. He wants me to kill them and abuse them and hurt them. And it will be a woman. Of course it will be a woman. Isn't it women who brought us to this? Who lied to us and cheated us and pleasured themselves at our expense? Oh it will be a woman that I will hurt. Sometimes I think I know which woman. And then I think (in Ezekiel's voice) 'What Matters it Which One for All are Equally but Whores and Self-Seekers and All shall be Served the Same way!'

I don't want the night to come. I am afraid.

PART TWO

ORDER OF BATTLE

'Thou art beautiful O my love, as Tirzah, comely as Jerusalem, terrible as an armie with Banneres.' Thus saith the Scripture & even soe is Love that it may perswade a Man who houldes the *Family of the Flesh* as this Mother or that Father, to bee but meer Showe and Emptinesse, to take unto himselfe a Wife yea and to marry her nott among his owne People, but among Those of my Lorde. For after oure Marriage, I returned nott to the howse of my Master but lived with my Meg upon my Lorde's estate, in a cottage granted to her Mother by Master Walmer. And her mother was a Virtuous Woman but wee could not agree as to Religion, for she was of my Lorde's perswasion in this, and was as farr gone in the Old Waies as to long for a Latin Prayere Booke, and other Opiniones and Erroures that would earn her worse than a Whipping in these Daies. But I could nott in that companie advance what I had been taught and held to bee Truth, nor yett her Daughter that was my wife. And soe the three of Us went to Church in Prelaticall style, among those of my Lorde's householde which was such a den of *Robes* and *Candles* as would make the Pope of Rome rejoyce to see it.

But synce the *Cooperites* hold that *Prayere is but a worde to God.* And that wee may pray wheresoever wee may ourselves or at oure laboures or at MEAT or when wee wake from Sleep, so did I offer up to God my prayers for the health of my Master Nehemiah and for my Wife that was then a help and prop in all things to mee. And now I ask agayne how it may bee that love after the bodie should taste so sweet and why Oure Lord granted mee this *Wife of the bodie* that was all to mee yea passing sweet as the laughter of Children, even when I dwelt among Those who walked in Darkness and practised Abominations and went the Waie of the King that was then at his most Bloodie and Unmercifull.

For about that time, nott long ere wee were Married, was

131

published the Ordinance of the Militia, by which the parliament sought the meanes of securing the Kingdome agaynst Popery and in everie parte of the Kingdome were there Rumours and Reports, and even in my Lorde's Householde was the Quarrell in the Kingdome asserted, which came about in this Waie. Certayne of my Lorde's household that were of the *Puritan party* had heard of a Plot to surround and capture the Marquis of Hertford, who staied then at Wells and were desirous of following the Deputy Lieutenant of the Countie that was strong for the cause of the Parliament. And I – being of this companie, made with others, a show and a Parade at Samson's Green which was a Village some four miles from my Lorde's house, & there were manie and Urgente Speeches concerning the Subtil Poysons and Treacheries of the Papisticall partie and of the *need to defend ourselves agaynst those Friends of Spain and France as would have all hanged who were not Catholique.*

And on my return from Samson's Green, Master Walmer met mee on the Road and Scolded mee. & hee bids mee to take my Wages and be Gone, which I was Constrained to do, although my Wife and I had no Place to lay oure Heades synce all oure Dwelling Place was in the Handes of my Lorde & her mother remayned there. O truly is it said *the land yieldeth much Increase unto the Kings whom Thou hast sett over Us because of oure Sinnes, also they have dominion over oure bodies & over oure Cattle at their Pleasure and wee are in Great Distress.*

Thus it was, that, with nothing in my Hands, I sett out for the village of Stavely, and with mee were my wife and oure Childe , for shee was in the fullness of time brought to Bed of Three Sonnes, which though I loved them was a Distress to mee, synce all were sicklie from Birth. And at that time I went nott to mine owne place but came with my wife and childe to the village of Essenden, seeking emploiment, for there were manie at that time that roamed the country *neither Found they the Laboure for their Hande nor did they gain Meat for their littel Ones but went the length of the lanes looking this way and that like Foxes in Winter.* And I rue the daie I came to that place synce there I Gained nothing but Confusion and Tribulation.

Now in the Yeares before the King sett up his Standarde at Nottingham, which as I have written was the time of the Remonstrance from the Parliament and the Quarrell over the Militia (for who shall have the Order of the swords and Musquettes of the Kingdom hee shall also have dominion over the same) & manie spoke of which side they would take if Matters should come to it, but manie who Spoke for One Faction before the event, found they were of the Other when it came to the Conflict. And as to mee I reckoned then that all Formes of Worshippe were as One, and held nott the Meetings of the *Cooperites* to bee the onlie path to God. *For*, said I, *if God is truly in oure Heartes, & if wee may meet him on the Back Stairs or at the Gate of a Taverne or on the Road to Market, how should anie gathering, bee it of COOPERITE or CATHOLICUS or ARMINIAN take it to its owne self, and itself alone, the Conduct of the troubled Soule to the Almighty.* For I saw then there was Godliness in my wife, and shee was of no partie I could see yea shee had worshipped in my Lorde's house in her hearte as I had prayed with Good Nehemiah and verily I said *there is more than One Waie To the Living God*. Which thought I held in my Hearte at that Time as True, though I had Cause to change it Later.

But in that village of *Essenden* were manie Phanatiques who thought themselves the Onlie True Guardians of the Faith & were the verie scourage and Conscience of anie who seemed to Favour the King's Partie or were Backsliders in the Matter of the Presbytery. & it was my misfortune there to find emploiment with one such, for hee was a *Cooper* as was my Master (butt never did two such Different Men followe the Same Trade) & this gentleman's Name was *Smith* & in his Handes I became a Stranger to Myselfe and to my Familie, for hee it was brought Mr *Morris* to mee.

It was with this same *Morris* – as I shall later relate – that I joined when wee went with the companie of Sir Richard Maplake, but long before it came to a Passage of Armes, this *Morris* was loud in his warnings that Charles was aboutt to come agaynst the Defenced cities of the Realm, and that wee had best have a look to anie Traytour in oure midst. And Morris had Intelligence – it seemed – of what was done in the Citie, before anie othere, so that wee said hee *lapped up the Mercuries like a dogge*, for I never saw so much Print as at the Time of the beginning of the Warres, and Opinion was Sharpened long before the Sword. And you could not Question this *Morris* without hee might say to you *Thou lyest like a Traytour* or yett Wordes from the Mouth of a Traytour. And though hee had manie an Oath to sweare on the Question of Monopolies, yet I declare hee had his own Monopolie of Wordes, for none othere, by his thinking, knew the Right Sense of Traytour.

Now this Morris was styled a *Running Lecturer* & was endowed by the Congregation of St Michael and All Angels to preach to us & also by the Tanners, and Weavers of the town. And this same *Smith, the Cooper* that took me in, thought Morris had the Monopolie of Scriptural KNOWLEDGE AND ENLIGHTENMENT & on oure first Sundaie there took my Meg and I to heare him preach upon a text of Isaiah which was *Come ye nations to hear, and hearken ye; let the earth hear and all that is therein*, which hee preached at about six of the evening on a Saturday in August & was a sermon anie who heard it will remember.

Mr Morris was a small and Wizened Man, late of the University of Oxford & tho' hee was nott above twenty and eight Yeares of Age, yett had hee no Haire to speak of & his face was as stamped with Wrinkles as anie Nutt & his Complexion was as brown as a Hazel. Hee was short of stature, with Armes that brushed the Ground so long were they. & as hee Preached hee skipped from side to side as hee were made to Dance upon Hot Coals, & as his Head was sett well downe upon his Shoulderes there were manie who might find him Comicall. But when hee spake his Voyce hath such a Note to it as would drive out anie thought of Laughtere & when hee preached there were Few able to keep their Eies from his, and so were at the Mercie of his Opinions & Rhetorique. For in time of trouble, a Certayn Opinion is a verie Light in the Windowe to a Traveller yea a Pillar of Fire in a Desert Place that draweth on those who Doubt.

Now this Discourse of *Mr Morris* was no *Pulpit Sermon* and indeed hee scorned such Waies but would hop about like a

Sparrow, the Length and Breadth of the Church, a wagging of his Fingers as hee talked of Affaires of State & of TYRANTES and of the RIGHTS AND DUTIES OF FREE PEOPLES & of the Industrie of the Better Sortes of Peoples and the Sloth and IDLENESSE of Great Courtes, by which all well knew what was Signified by his Wordes & by his Leaping and Poynting and Smacking of his Lips. For as hee talked hee made a Great Displaie each time the *Court* was mentioned, & would GRUNT & Scratch at himselfe the while so that hee seemed at time, the verie Modelle of a Dogge with Fleas. Indeed I wondered greatlie also that he Strayed so farr from his Texte but was Assured by *Mr Smith* that on Occasion he would Preach without anie Texte whatsoever.

As I recall myselfe and Meg came, with our Childe, late to the Service, when this *Morris* was at the High Water of his Discourse & as wee came into the nave hee was at the Subjecte of the French Marriage, though hee did not name *Queen Henrietta* yett wee all knew his Subjecte, for hee spake of Shee Majestie and what was Signified by it, saying that Majestie in a Woman was nott to bee judged by Jewelles on Fine Clothes and Finer Wordes but by her Virtue which is above Wealth. & as my Margaret and I come in hee breaks out and rayses two longarmes to the Roof of the Church, crying in a loud Voyce – 'Who can find a virtuous Woman, for her Price is far above Rubies?'

And each Head in the Congregation – for there were manie that Attended there – turns to see where my Margaret stood. For shee was Still and cast Down her Eies and was bedecked with Blushes and they knew her for a Modest and Virtuous Woman. And still this Morris continues to Prance about the Church, from nave to altar and Rounde by the Chancell, but never once Deigning to mount the Pulpit, which hee was wont to terme The Bishop's Privy and by the same Token I have heard him call the Font *a place where you may taste the Clergy's water* and likewise the coloured Glasse of the Chancell was but a Trick to Perswade those who had no hope of God's Mercie that all was well with them. So hee continued and as wee sate, hee seemed to poynte out my Meg as hee spake.

'The heart of her husband doth safely trust in Her, so that

135

hee shall have no Need of Spoyle. Shee will doe him Good and nott Evil all the daies of her Life. She seeketh wool and flax and can work it with her hands. She is like the merchants' ships; she bringeth her goods from afar. Favour is as naught and Beauty is vanitie, but a woman that feareth the Lord shee shall bee PRIZED.' As hee spake the worde – PRIZED – he seemed to Shriek it as if it were Ripped from out of him & after hee spake no further but Gazed upon us as wee sat there. & there was a Silence in the Congregation and none Spake & the Heads of the Congregation were Turned to my Meg, and did not turn unto *Mr Morris* until hee began agayne. But then they turned awaie from us, one, then another, then another, until was but one Face that Looked on us, and that was *Mr Beelse* that was a friend to this same *Smith the cooper* & hee looked long at my wife and I knew nott why but I was mightily Afrayd.

So it was that consequent on his *Lecture, Morris* stood awhile in the Churche Yarde, at which manie came to him and thanked him & then it was *Mr Smith* made us known to him. 'Well,' says hee, *'take Joy in Thy Wife Master Oliphant. Yea shee hath Impressed her Countenance on mee Greatlie so that I know her Virtuous. Nay, Master, shee is a Verie Texte for us where wee may Reade the Virtue wee seek.'* And I made no Answer but inclined my Head to showe how I felt the Honour hee did mee. For I was never one Free with Wordes as some are. But this *Morris* spent Phrases like a woman at a Hosier's who will hold this Stocking then that One up to the Light with 'facks now *this* will do.' And never it does until the whole Shop be Sold her. 'Yea,' says Mr Morris, 'when I preach agaynst the Sloth and Idlenesse of Great Ones I do look for a LIGHT Yea A Candle that will light mee Home and I do Studie Virtue but find it nott. Nay nott in this Countrie that is so Broken on the Rack of the Ambition of Great Ones.' And as hee spake this same LIGHT, so did hee seem to shriek as loud as a Mandrake and looked aboutt him in the churchyarde there, as if he saw a *Troop of Cavaleeres* behind the bush yonder, that would leap Forwarde and take him before my Lords of the Star Chamber to answer for his Wordes.

In conclusion hee asks us to do him the Honour of attending

His lecture on the Thursday nexte at which hee plans to talk of the Free Election of Ministers to which, hee adds, 'And you may hear mee pray for the States of Holland and the King of Sweden, before I pray for CHARLES I.' At which Remark hee seemed to Fright Himselfe, & looked among the Tombstones once agayne as if hee thought *Prince Rupert* and a troop of Horse would come out at him on a sudden with a cry of Death to All Heretiques and Puritans and Here's to the Good Old Cause.

My Margaret made Him no Answere, but remained, with her Eie cast down before her. But I said wee would Hear him Gladlie synce anie that led us to the Lorde was to bee Welcomed. Which was indeed the truth although I told him nott all that was in my Hearte, or how wee had *worshipped in Babylon and found the Waters Pure*. Morris gives mee a Smile as Thin as his Mandrake Screech and adds hee hath Fellowship with One *Beelse* (which was the hee who had stared so long at my Margaret) who hath a TANNERY neer to Mount Yard, & as my Master Mr Smith was sorely pressed for Business – as were wee all in that time and in the times that followed synce *Bellona suffers no Trade but her owne* – I confessed myselfe most Heartily glad of anie Laboure wee could find. Though I may depose that at the Assemblies of the *Cooperites* – which spake as hard as anie agaynst the Idlenesse – none were permitted to talk of anie matter save that which had Bearing on Scripture, for, said my Master *as ye may change your Monie in the Temple so shall ye be served as oure Lorde Jesus served them that hath Polluted it in the Daies of Israel.*

But so it is with Trade, as the *Cooperites* taught mee, that it may bee a Subtil Trap for the Unwary, for it was through my Master's going after Emploiment from this *Beelse*, that I grew in the debt of the two of them. For Mr Smith went from us nott long after the raysing of the Standard, for some Boies that lived hard by him, broke Open his Shop and Laid Waste to all his Goodes, on the Pretense they *thought him too strong for the King* which was never the Case. But in those times manie sought to do Violence as it Pleased them to do and indeed the Time gave them excuse. And I heard Mr Smith went for the Trayne Bands in the Cause of the Parliament, though wee knew littel save that hee were Gone.

I worked at Mr Beelse's Yarde, and my Wife and I dwelt hard by his House, where wee had but one Poore Chambere that was His. I was kept by him nott onlie for my Trade, and for Skill in Carving and Coopering but for anie Task hee needed. And I was glad for the Opportunitie of Laboure and my Laboure proposed and Mr *Beelse* rewarded mee & had it not been for his Sonne that was called Daniel, I would have been well Content there. For Mr Beelse was of a Cold Eie & Phlegmatique Disposition & I think loved no Man well except his Sonne and Mr Morris, that was often in the Yarde with Us. And his Sonne he loved more than was well for him or for the Boie, who was a very Mountaine as to Appearance, & who could scarce draw Breath after three Stairs or a step across to the Taverne to draw Beere for his Fathere, which hee took alwaies in Secret, Mr Beelse not wishing it to bee known hee ever *took a pipe or a glasse*. And this Daniel did nott, as other boies do, play on the Green or Runne to his Fellowes, but sate in the Yarde, chewing on a Rod of Sugar, his Eie so farr into his Cheek it was no easie or light matter to Judge what were his Thoughts – if hee had anie.

And though this boie is nott above ten Yeares Of Age, yett did he call mee as I were a Potboy at a Taverne, saying 'Master Oliphant a word with you . . .' or 'here Sir an you please' as if I had no other business but to serve him as I served his Fathere, which was like to a Yoke upon mee and brought mee no Pleasure but Hardship, for is it not written that *the Children shall hearken unto their Fathers and may nott have the Ordering of those their Fatheres may Command.* For do wee nott all serve Thee O Lord and doth it nott fit us to bee Humble in Thy sight yea Kingdoms that shall nott serve Thee O God shall perish; yea those Nations shall bee utterly Wasted. But in spite of this *unruly boie* I worked as I was bid and wee prospered so that Mr Beelse bought two more Horses besides those that hee used & in a little while I took to *Coopering* a littel on my owne account and bought from this same Beelse the Use of one of his Horses, which Beast wee then owned in Common.

One afternoon Mr Morris is come to oure Poore Chambers to speak of certayn Wakes, Greenes, May Games, Bear Baitings and the like of dove-ales and rush bearings, which Charles had

Blessed and Sanctified in his Booke of Sportes, and some were still desirous of continuing, though they bee on the Sabbath day 'twas no matter. And here was I in accord with Mr Morris, that were hee to have had Beelzebub as his Archbishop, CHARLES could nott have published so Wicked and Profane a Law. And so oure Talk was full of Friendshipp and when I rose to goe to my Worke, I bid him staie a while saying I would be back ere Suppere, and soe I went out and left him with my Margaret thinking it might provide Diversion for her synce I laboured long Houres and *each Farthing was hard wonne*.

And when I returned Home that night, I find Morris gone from the Howse, and my Meg in a silent Humoure. 'Well,' says I, 'and how like you our *Running Lecturer* now?' But shee made no answere to mee onlie sate at the corner of the Table and her Face as White as an Eare of Corn. But what passed betwixt Them that daie shee would never tell mee, save Once shee Confesses that the verie sight of him makes her Afraid, though when I Pressed her as to How this might bee shee would not Answere but turns her Face aside, and grows as Pale as a Flower that closes its Face agaynst the Night. And how it was between the two of them I never Knew but that *Mr Morris* came often times to oure Chamber & sate with her & talked when I was at my Laboures in the Yarde. And though shee never Confided in mee the Matter of their Discourse, yet was shee – as I thought – troubled even by the Sight of Him. And I in my turn was Troubled but said Nothing. Verily the Duties and Obligations wee owe Otheres for oure Livelihoods are Matters as twisted as a Tree that seems wearie with Growing to the Light & turns upon itself like some Aged Creature troubled with the *Gowt* or the *Rheumaticks*. So it was that *the Daies in which wee lived like unnumbered Minutes in a Summer's Garden passed Before Us in a Showe so it Seemed wee were nott Owners of oure Proper Lives but Actors in a Showe that Bowe and Nod and Kiss, nott of themselves, but at the Command of Anothere.*

In the nexte Yeare was more Tumult among the godlie Persons of the Congregation synce then wee had Newes of the great Victorie of Edge Hill Fight, the King's forces being stopped

139

on their Waie to London and Sir Edmund Verney, the standard bearer killed which did cause us to Rejoyce & Master Morris to much Rhetorique and Displaies, although I swear this *Morris* had as great a Horror of Colde Steel as hee did of the Latin Mass. Then was hee at oure Lodging oft times & though I Feared to see him there & what hee said and did when alone with Margaret I knew nott, yet was I Frightened by whatever hee might Purpose & spake nott to anie of what was in my hearte neither to Margaret which was my Wife, and so was I alone with my most Secret Fears and Apprehensions & knew nott who to turn to for I knew myselfe to bee entirely in the Service of Mr BEELSE and Mr MORRIS, & in my wife's face I read the Texte that said *I have sate by the fireside with Oppression and at my Table entertained the Hypocrite and Dissembler.*

Yet did shee not confide to mee the Matter of their Discourse, nor of the Cause of her Distress. And so I came to doubt, nott onlie Him but Her also synce I had feare for her virtue & could nott comfort her in Her Affliction yea though her cheeks were comely and the roof of her mouth like the best Wine for Her beloved and beautiful were her feet with Shoes, I went in and out of the Chambere but I spake nott to her and some Few Weekes after this *Morris* began his Visits and Prayings to Her, shee lay not with mee that was her Husband and though I sought her whom my Soule loved I found her nott. *And I rose and went aboutt the Streetes & in the Broad Waies sought her whom my Soule loved but found her nott. In the Silence of the Morning I sought her and in the same evening did this Silence lie Between us like a Shadowe* and then I knew the Shame of my Desires for I thought of her after the Fleshe onlie, night and morning yea the Joiyntes of her Thighes were like jewelles the work of the hands of a cunning Workman but shee Lay not with Mee and I was Ashamed of her that I loved her with my Bodie.

It was about that Time oure Congregation made an Attaque upon the Coloured Windowes of the Chancelle and upon the person of the Revd *Kimbolton* who was our Priest but durst say nothing, leaving all to Mr Morris whose Wordes Inflamed them Further and Trade was almost ceased. All anie Man would talk of was the Warres and how They went, while I played *Close*

Mouthed Oliphant and hoped for better Times. But still my wife lay nott with mee, and Grew still paler. And still this *Running Lecturer* came – so hee tells me – *to pray with her and doe Battel for Her Soule.* 'For,' says hee, 'thy Virtuous Wife is sick.' And hee looks level at my Eeie as hee spake. And I was Afraid.

Here as I make my Testament I seek nott to Relate the Passage of the Late Warres, for indeed the Newes wee had of them was Scarce and Partiall, synce All Knewe *the Mercuries told a Different Storie.* But in the Yeare that followed Edgehill fight there was a Truce and then noe truce & in the Auguste of that Yeare – with Matters nott mended betwixt myself and Margaret – there came into the Yarde A Beggar Woman that had with Her the Sheet *Mercurius Aulius,* which told the Warre the Cavalier's waie. But as wee had no Othere Newes that Daie wee took it from her, & as I watched – for I was working under the Eies of Mr Morris and of Mr Beelse, these Two fell to and Read of a Great Victorie for the King, at Lansdowne Ridge neare Bristol and Sir William Waller, for the Parliament, compelled to Drawe Back.

Which then I thought to Spell the End of oure cause – synce everie Reverse in a Battel seems to point a Conclusion, though Matters scarce ever conclude as they Suggest – but yet I bring it to Minde for another Reason, for a Man's affairs may take as manie Turns as those of a great Nation, and trulie this was when the Lord made *the hard waie of my life plain to mee and showed mee the Sorrow of my journey.* Which, though it was Harde to bear I took up as did oure Lorde his Crosse, for as the *Cooperites* are wont to say *each Minute is the Lorde's and goe nott about to take it from Him.* For when Mr Beelse had finished reading from this same *Mercury* and wee sate in Distress and in Amazement at the Failure of oure Cause, there comes in from the Howse Young Daniel, the Mountainous Boie who moved slower than a pool of grease on a Summer Daie, and his Face was Pale 'What's afoot?' says his Father. The boie looks at mee then turns his Eie upon his Fathere. 'Oh Father,' says hee, 'tis Star.' Which was the name given the Horse this Beelse and I had then in common. 'What of him?' says his Father. 'Why,' says his Sonne, 'he's sick and like to die.' At which his Father stops and sucks upon his lips and none says a Worde. And the silence grows and I would wish it never Ended, synce no good can come of it. And Daniel looks at mee and his Father also and I play *Close Mouth* Oliphant but did feel myself a stranger to them yea was there a nett to Ensnare mee *neither did I see until then how sett around with Enemies I am for I have given myself into the Hands of those who would Deceive mee neither know I anie waie to find my proper Mind agayne.* And Mr Morris rises up. 'Belike,' says hee, 'wee are Bewitched.'

13

Rose Cottage
Shenstone
Oxfordshire

July

What did I *do* after I got out of the hospital? I just don't know. I know he came in and I know I escaped and got to London but I simply can't recall what I did when I got there. It's a blank.

I'm not going to think about all of that. I won't know how many days have passed since I set out for London. In fact, after I got off the train at Paddington and hailed that cab I have no memory of anything at all. It is all, as so often when Ezekiel takes over, blurred, impossible to place. Sometimes I am being chased across the fields behind the house by mounted soldiers. Sometimes I am walking down an empty London street, on my way to see someone. Sometimes I am with this girl. I have my hands round her neck and I am squeezing, squeezing . . . She's screaming at me to stop but I don't stop. I am going to go on until she has stopped screaming. Until she is quiet and still. Until she is never going to move again. When she is safe, like that, I strip her and look at her body. It's not erotic. I just look at her breasts, her thickening waist, the dark triangle of public hair as if I had never seen a woman before.

But there is nothing to connect these images. I have no precise recollection of what happened in London. All I know is – it was bad. Bad bad bad.

Not only can I not recall the past, I seem to hear the present wrongly too. Sometimes I am in the lane behind the church and I am sure someone is calling my name – 'Jamie – Ja-amie . . .' But there is no one there. And the sounds made by the radio or the television become scrambled. As if my intense attempts to listen to them – to find out if I did do something appalling back there in London – had warped the words out of shape, so that broadcast opinions, the received religion of our

143

society, the sacred words of the news itself, are subject to the same deformations that Oliphant effects on my secret thoughts.

Good Evening. Here is the news at six o'clock. Jamie Matheson, the so-called 'Putney Cobra', has struck again. Since his escape from Lambourne Mental Hospital last week, Matheson has attacked six women in the London Area. The murder of —

Did I? Did I kill her? I don't know what I did. That's the answer.

Sometimes the radio plays old conversations between Meg and me or between Anna and me. 'Do you believe in love?' I am saying to Anna. We are lying in a field of long grass, but the field is one where Meg and I made love, seventeen years ago, behind Magdalen College, the afternoon my brother came to stay.

'I'm surprised you ask that,' says Anna.

'Why?'

'You seem such a bitter person in some ways,' she says.

'I sometimes think I do believe in love,' I say, and she turns her big brown eyes in my direction. She looks hurt now, or rather, as if I am thinking of some way to hurt her.

BEAST OF PUTNEY KILLS EIGHT READ ALL ABOUT IT. READ ALL ABOUT THE PUTNEY BEAST. MONSTER OF MAPLAKE ROAD RAPES TEN WOMEN READ ALL ABOUT IT. WITCHFINDER STALKS LONDON SUBURB
READ ALL ABOUT IT READ ALL ABOUT IT

And sometimes there is silence in the cottage. There is just me and the picture to which I cannot help returning. The image of my father stretched out on the slab. I am staring down into that fleshy cavern and the mouth that will not close. His eyes are as fixed as those on a carcass in a butcher's shop. He will never never never come back to me.

What I am going to try to do now – here in this cottage, where no one will find me, in between meals from tins my father stored here (this was his country retreat), is to write what

144

happened after Ezekiel first took control. To piece together, once more, the person I was then. Try and make myself laugh even. I could do with a laugh. Just as February Jamie looked longingly back at the sixties, at the years in College, the years of no compromise and unadulterated love, so, now, July Jamie looks back at his February self in wonder. Once I was not like this. I was a wry guy. And now, that irony, that very English understatement that I so despised, is what I most crave. I don't want to have to outface life this way. I want to be able to deflect it with a shrug. Perhaps if I summon up my old self – February Jamie – he will climb into my body the way Ezekiel did, start cracking jokes, amusing people, refusing to take himself seriously.

Come on. Come on. Where are you, old Troll? Fit yourself into my legs and chest and arms and head. Look out from my eyes once again and tell me that witches are an optical illusion and the nearest thing England has ever had to a Great Conspiracy is the stock market.

I can't remember how I lost Ezekiel that first afternoon with Anna. I think I may have slept a while. I know that when I woke all was as it should be. It was nearly six o'clock.

'Shall I run you to a station?' said Anna.

'If you don't mind. . .'

She didn't seem to mind. She didn't seem to care what happened in the moments that we did not share. I dressed and followed her out to the car, and when I kissed her goodbye at the station I thought 'We've known each other no time at all. And yet we're always kissing and saying goodbye and – with our eyes at any rate – promising more and more. There's a kind of desperation in it. As if we want more than we'll ever get.'

I got home at about six. I prepared my manner more carefully this time. Adultery doesn't require a high standard of acting, but it enforces a certain willingness to perform. I had decided to be bright and breezy. I was bright and breezy at the traffic lights at the bottom of Putney Hill. I was bright and breezy, as I turned, past the girl's school into Lytton Grove, lined with dark, brooding Victorian villas. They should call it Edward Bulwer Lytton Grove (ha ha ha this is more like it James). I was bright and breezy as I skipped up Juliet's three green steps. I caught a

145

glimpse of her in the basement, wearing her tweed suit and doing what looked like knee bends, but I was still bright and breezy. She would have the World Service on at full blast and one of her gigantic meat stews bubbling away. She would be about to settle down in front of the electric fire with a cigar and a copy of *Woman's Weekly*. 'I'm orff,' I could almost hear her deep bass voice say, 'for a bit of stew.' But I was bright and breezy. Even when she caught sight of me and waved I was bright and breezy. I was bright and breezy right up until the moment when the door opened and I saw Meg, thin and miserable in her white nightdress, and heard behind her the screams of the children. Then my face fell.

'Hullo,' I said.

'Hullo,' she said.

Carefully, like strangers on a railway station, we skirted each other. 'Are you ill?' I said. My voice sounded accusing.

'No,' she said faintly, 'no . . .' There were dark circles round her eyes and her hair hung, lank and unbrushed, against her cheeks. I didn't go up to her or try to put my arms round her. 'How's the English Civil War?' she said.

'A dull little affair really,' I said, 'a series of local incidents that don't add up.' She looked at me listlessly. 'You're cold,' she said, 'aren't you? You're lacking in feeling. You don't find beauty in things. Landscape, faces . . . they're just commodities to you. Things to be pinned down. I think you're more like a scientist than a writer. How do you feel? I don't know. I have no clue. You're a Martian, Jamie.'

I went through to the kitchen. The girls were crowded together in a far corner, whispering over the pastel objects – horses, dolls, bears – designed to train them into motherhood, or romance, or most frequently a queasy combination of the two. They looked up shyly as I entered and watched as Meg followed me. There are always spectators in families. Sometimes the performers modify their act as a result of their attentions. When things are bad, though, the theatre of the row, the tantrum becomes a kind of wilful exercise, a deliberate display. And as Meg and I started again I looked, from time to time, down at those three faces in the corner, raised in a kind of supplication. Well, I thought grimly, this is misery. There's quite a lot of this about. Remember what it's like. Because one day it will happen to you. I make you a present of it.

'Look,' I said, 'see the doctor. Get some pills.'

She was standing in the doorway. 'I don't want pills,' she said. 'I want to be loved.'

I sighed. 'You are loved,' I said. But it didn't sound as if that was what I had said. It sounded as if I had said 'The drains are blocked.' Or 'Suburban trains are unreliable.' It sounded too as if I was criticizing her for something. For what? Not being loved, maybe. Our love was always a question of holding one's nerve. Of making a great show of not trusting the other and then, once the decencies had been observed, allowing in tenderness as if it were a dangerous animal only tamed by our mutual cool. It was an acid business with Meg and I, always, from the beginning, from the day I first met her in somebody's rooms at Oxford. Only now it was all acid.

I couldn't rid myself, also, of the idea that somehow or other she knew about Anna. Perhaps Rick had phoned her? No. That wasn't her style. If she had had confirmation she would be screaming and throwing things by now. Perhaps Rick was planning on a man-to-worm talk with me, soon. I shuddered at the prospect. 'I've always thought that you and Meg were a pretty super couple actually and –'

Meg was talking. 'Why do you look at me as if you hate me?'

'What do you mean?'

'As if you hate me. As if you can't stand the sight of me.'

'Don't be so bloody self-pitying. Please. I have a hard time too you know.'

She looked, briefly, helplessly at me and then at the children. Then she went out into the hall. More out of habit than anything, I followed her. She was climbing the stairs one at a time. For a moment, I thought she was going to do her Cracked Doll impression, and that I would have to respond to that. Then, with a slight sense of shock, I saw that I would not. Our common language was beginning to break down. Her performance merely irritated me. 'I thought you were better,' I said. Her act turned to piteous reality. She stopped and looked down at me. Her face succumbed to the rubbery ugliness of grief and two large tears followed each other, like rain on a window, down her thin cheeks. 'I'm depressed,' she said, 'I'm sad.' I felt curiously glad that her distress could not touch me. Distress is a trap for the unwary. 'What are you depressed *about*?' She couldn't know. There was no way she could know. Surely. Surely. . .

'I don't know,' she said. She sat on the stairs and pulled her nightdress over her knees. 'Maybe because I feel you don't love me any more. That you don't love the children either. I did. I thought you cared for me. Oh you looked cold and peculiar but I thought you really did love me after all. And I liked your coldness and your distance because when I was low or ill I didn't want someone following me down there where I was. I wanted someone on the bank, ready to throw me a line.'

'I'm right there,' I said, 'on the bank. Really.'

'You went ages ago, Jamie,' said Meg, 'you went a long time ago. There's nothing there but habit and silence now. I'm on my own. Oh I don't know why I thought there was any virtue in family or that people really did love each other. All that's whistling in the dark. All you care about is yourself. I'm convenient to you. But if I died you'd just go out and get someone else, wouldn't you? I'm replaceable.'

I thought of Anna's back, of the muscles in her thighs, of her big eyes like a cat's. Perhaps Meg was right. There was no love that could not be replaced by another. There was nothing unique or individual or lasting about love. We shouldn't, really, be using such an imprecise, question-begging word. 'Require' perhaps, was a more accurate term for use in describing sexual relations. 'Need', 'Want', 'Have to have'.

'Daddeee. . .'

It was Thomasina, her elfin face (she has her mother's features) animated by the disapproval she always seems to feel for me. She tugged at my trousers. 'Daddee . . . Gwendoline's got a pencil and she won't let me have it and it's mine it is although she says it isn't. . .'

Meg looked at her daughter bleakly. 'Fuck off,' she said.

I put my hand on Thomasina's head and said, rather stiffly, 'I thought the family was important to you.' I made my voice as sweet as I could as I bent down to Thomasina (what is a family after all but a closed circle of betrayals and adulteries?) and, after I had gone in to the three of them, I heard her heavy tread going up the stairs. Maybe she did know. Maybe someone had told her. I really did not care. I had more important things to think about.

I had been with them for ten or fifteen minutes when Juliet's head appeared at the door. She never announces her arrival, but glides into vision like a mirage – silently, swiftly. . .

'I'm going to change Rabbit,' she said.

What is wrong, I thought, with the definite article? And why are you telling me this? If you want to change the rabbit go and change the fucking rabbit. I managed a smile and offered her, with the smile, a slightly lighter, cheaper version of the approval I offer the children. 'Oh well done Juliet,' I said, 'great.'

'Rabbit needs changing,' she said ominously, 'and *how*. . .'

'It's brightened up,' I countered.

'Has it?' she replied, doubtfully.

She looked at me curiously, as if she was trying to think how I managed to be so hideously, so permanently obsessed with the weather. 'This is not you,' the expression seemed to say; 'you are playing some complicated charade. And yet . . .' Then, as if on castors, she rolled smoothly out of vision, one hand up to her coiffure. She knew when she was beaten. Just to rub the point home I got up and pursued her into the hall. 'It looked as if it might rain,' I said, 'but it didn't.'

'No,' she said, 'it didn't, did it?' And went through the door that leads to her staircase. Once I was absolutely sure she was gone, and not hiding behind one of the coats at the head of the stairs, I closed the door, bolted it, put a chair against it and made the sign of the cross, twice. 'Stay down there I command Thee' I whispered, 'in the name of Beelzebub.'

Just as I said the word 'Beelzebub' the mouse came out from behind Thomasina's duffel coat. It stood looking at me. But did not move.

14

I have nothing against mice as such, and, in the normal run of things, if faced by a mouse, treat it rather like a neighbour with whom I wish to remain on reasonable terms. But this mouse was different. It had a boldness and an insolence about it that, from the first, I did not like. It was not prepared to act the part of a rodent faced by something several thousand times bigger than it, but crouched there, looking up at me malevolently.

It wan't anything to do with the mouse – Dr Masters would say. Ever since I had felt Ezekiel climb into my body back in Anna's flat – he would argue – I had begun dissociating or whatever cant word he uses to try and describe those moments when I am most horribly not myself. It wasn't – and isn't – as I have tried to tell him, like that. When Ezekiel takes me over he does not colour my perceptions gradually, until the line between the real and the imagined is blurred (what are those people saying about me?); he simply takes possession. In the aftermath of these hauntings – as in the weeks since I got out of London – I sometimes do lose focus on things and look out at landscape or faces with eyes that are neither mine nor his, but simply instruments for registering changes of tone, patches of light and shade. It wasn't like that with the mouse. I was fine. It was the mouse that was giving me a hard time. It was a belligerent, self-opinionated, over-confident mouse.

'Psst,' I said to it. 'Psst.' It did a short run into the hall and was stopped dead in its tracks by a pair of Thomasina's roller skates. Its nose twitched. The girls appeared from the kitchen. 'Oh,' said Gwendoline, 'it'th a mouth.' 'Yes,' I said, 'keep away from it. They bite.' 'It'th thweet,' said Gwendoline. Her plate-like face inclined towards the creature. Her blue eyes fluttered concern in its direction. Still the mouse did not move. I advanced upon it.

'Don't hurt it,' said 'Thomasina, 'it's sweet.' The three of them, hands folded across their pinafore dresses, beamed down at the mouse. As far as they were concerned, I thought, the mouse was probably on its way back to a cosy little two-bedroomed flat under the floorboards, with a Daddy Mouse and a Mummy Mouse (rolling out pastry on a board), a daughter mouse and a Little Baby Brother Mouse (on a skateboard). The coal fire would be blazing in the grate and the washing up would be done and a kettle whistling on the stove. It was probably, I reflected, a much more happy and well-adjusted nuclear family than our own. Perhaps we should all get down through the floorboards and ask these mice how the hell they did it.

'They're dirty,' I said, and moved even closer to it. It still did not move.

What was with this mouse? On what inner resources of strength was it drawing? Had it sussed me out as a feeble, irresolute creature? I picked up a copy of the *World Illustrated Atlas* and banged it on the floor 'Shoo,' I said. It did not move. The girls laughed.

'It'th brave,' said Gwendoline.

'It's probably,' I said, 'a witch's familiar.'

'Wot'th a witch'th famlullia?' said Gwendoline, her eyes popping.

I stole closer and closer to the mouse. 'A witch can change herself into a cat, a bat or a mouse, in order to spy on someone or to put a spell on them. For instance – let us assume that granny is a witch.'

They liked this idea.

'Or Mummy.'

This they did not like so much.

'Or both of them are witches. They can turn themselves into a mouse *so that they can keep an eye on me and make sure I fill up the dishwasher*. And wash the kitchen floor. And write a six-part series for someone called Gottlieb who is probably a witch as well. A Jewish witch. They can be terrible.' I thwacked the book hard down on the floorboards next to the mouse. It shot off into the kitchen as if connected to a piece of elastic and Gwendoline wailed, 'Don't hurt it. Pleathe.'

'I'm not hurting it,' I said, I'm trying to persuade it to go back to its Mummy and Daddy and Little Brother Mouse. And its Mother-in-Law Mouse.'

Thomasina giggled. 'Do you think it's a Mummy or a Daddy or a Boy or a Girl Mouse?' she said.

'From its proprietary attitude to territory,' I replied, 'its refusal to scare, its attitude of contempt to me and its ability to get out of range just when I thought I had it in my power, I would say it was a Mother-in-Law Mouse.' Grim faced, I went after it into the kitchen. 'Your Mummy's Mummy, aided and abetted by her daughter, has transformed herself into a mouse in order to make my brutal maleness even more unacceptable than –'

The mouse was by the wooden pew, nibbling a piece of bread. I banged the atlas on the floor, hard. The mouse stopped eating and looked round in a somewhat irritable fashion. I looked round at the kitchen – the piles of unwashed plates on the sideboard, threatening my sense of time. There was breakfast cereal, and next to it a half-eaten joint, and next to last night's baked beans (or was it this morning's? children's tea or breakfast?) were this morning's, or yesterday's, or two-weeks-ago-last-Thursday's papers, smeared with marmalade, curry, tomato, bread crumbs, a whole archaeology of domestic abuse. Why was everything such a damn mess? And why was Meg upstairs? Why was it always *me* who had to deal with things?

I ran at the mouse, slipped on a tea towel, and fell heavily against the wooden pew. The mouse did a spring towards the dishwasher, threw a left just before colliding with it and vanished under the vegetable rack. The girls laughed.

'Come out, you bastard!' I yelled, and fell upon the turnips and the onions and the sprouts, yanking them out of the basket and flinging them on to the floor behind me. To the left of the vegetables was a solid strip of wood (erected by Juliet who attends evening classes in woodwork) and to the right was the dishwasher. The mouse had two chances. He could go through the gap between the dishwasher and the rear wall, which would bring him up against another solid strip of wood, also erected by Juliet, or he could make a break for it. I reasoned that he would probably head for the dishwasher and wait until things quietened down.

But he did not realize quite how seriously I was taking

things. Keeping my eye on the patch of floor behind the vegetables, I began to tug the dishwasher out from the wall. Slowly.
Slo-owly. . .

'If it ith a witch'th famlullia,' said Gwendoline,' it will juth
turn itthelf into thumthing elthe.'

'If it's granny,' said Thomasina, 'it will go back to her flat and
become granny.'

And if it's mummy,' I said sourly, 'maybe it will go upstairs
and get its clothes and make my supper.'

'It's not mummy,' said Thomasina. She sounded nervous.

As she said this, a brown streak of fur shot out from under the
dishwasher and headed for the central area of the sanded floor.
The girls shrieked. I picked up the atlas and headed out after the
mouse.

It knew what it was up against now. There was none of the
let's-stop-and-admire-the-scenery routine. Not a trace of the
it's-my-house-as-well-as-yours attitude. The mouse seemed to
have grasped that it was just a mouse, being pursued by an
irate, thirty-eight-year-old man armed with a heavy book. It ran
up to Juliet's door, only to discover that the door fits flush to the
floor (probably, as Meg once pointed out, to stop her mother
metamorphosing into a cloud of steam and hissing underneath
it, to reassemble herself on the other side). It then retreated to
the cupboard, in which are kept the gas meter, the telephone
directories, and a pair of green wellingtons cunningly wrought
to resemble two frogs.

I ran to the cupboard and yanked open the door. It was
quivering behind the wellingtons, but I was not in the mood for
mercy. 'I want you out,' I said. I had resolved to chase it out of
the front door. I thrust the atlas into the cupboard and brushed
it along the floor, up to the wellingtons. The mouse, now clearly
hysterical, leaped over the telephone directories, and out past
the two doors towards what Meg always calls 'the foyer'. Alone
in an expanse of nothingness, like Cary Grant at the opening of
North by Northwest, the mouse cowered in the middle of the
expanse of dull red tiles, as I carefully closed the double doors
behind me. From a safe distance Thomasina called 'Please don't
hurt her.'

'It's a she-mouse, is it?' I said.

'Please, Daddy.'

I had no intention of hurting it: I just wanted the damn thing to go away. I moved slowly towards the front door, the atlas in my right hand. My plan was to swing back the door with my left hand and at the same moment unleash a series of sharp blows on the tile floor, with the atlas. The mouse seemed to have reverted to its earlier wait-and-see policy. Now I was close to it I saw that, like many undomesticated animals, it had a mangy, sordid aspect. Its fur was grubby, its little yellow eyes empty. It brought home to one the many negative features of being a mouse – the long afternoons in search of food, the risky, pointless journeys through the shadier fringes of human habitation. This mouse looked as if it had seen better days. Perhaps its public advertisement for itself was a cry for help rather than a piece of bravado. Perhaps it wanted to be found and caught and given the Gavin Maxwell treatment.

'Look,' I said, 'go back to wherever you came from and leave me in peace.' I began to bring the atlas hard down on to the floor and lunged for the Banham lock. But the mouse, instead of breaking away from the noise, headed straight for me as I shouted *'Get out get out get out.'* There was something that surprised me about the way I said this – as if I was struggling against some private fear or an external enemy that posed a real threat. *'Get out get out get out!!'* But by some trick of chance the mouse, that was heading in, not out, put its back between my second fierce stroke down of the atlas spine and the hard wooden tiles. There was a crack, a splitting mass of fur, and a brief, ugly spillage of blood across the floor.

But it wasn't dead.

'What's happened?' yelled Thomasina.

'Nothing,' I called back. It was still moving. Broken-backed, bloody, the ball of living tissue was crawling towards me, pulling in all directions. Put it out of its misery. Oh Christ. With what though? I looked wildly about me. I did not want the children to see what had happened. Shoe. Use your shoe. But take it off first. Feels less like murder. Oh Christ. I fought with my laces and pulled off one heavy grey boot. What was left of the mouse was still seething piteously across the tiles. From the hall I could hear the girls' voices. Get it over with. Get it over with. 'Sorry about this old son,' I said, and brought the heel of my boot hard down on the struggling mass of flesh. To make sure, I ground it in to the surface of the floor. There was a crunchy, smeared sound, and when I lifted the boot the flattened mass of fur had no life to it. I bent down to the creature and tentatively turned it over. Its paws were flattened into its body and its teeth, grotesquely isolated from the jaws, were broken pearls sewn into the skin. I looked down at my finger. The tip was stained with blood. And, behind me, I felt that chill, as if someone had opened a door, as if someone or something were standing quietly behind me, watching. I wanted to turn but could not. It's the girls. One of the girls has opened the door. But it wasn't the girls. Whatever it was, or wasn't, stayed at my back. Get the blood off your hands. Wash the blood off. But then there was a rush of air, as if the temperature of the room had changed suddenly, and the mouse, to my horror, twitched once, twice more and only then was finally stilled.

As I stood there, looking with dismay at my finger and at the underside of my heel, daubed with blood and fur, from upstairs came a long, ghastly shriek, the sound of someone in agony. There were no distinct words, no tone even, just a prolonged, desperate, animal wail, of the kind dumb creatures might make if they could find expression for the lack of heart in what we are pleased to call humanity. It sounded, I thought, like someone dying. I didn't recognize the voice. It seemed to have been changed out of anything in the human register. And then I remembered that first attack in the house at Lewes. It had scared me then – for some reason I found it more frightening now. Or was that simply because of the earlier coldness at my back, the sensation that, this time, something or someone was doing it to her? It was Meg's voice, without question.

I slipped my other boot off, turned, and ran for the stairs.

15

She was lying half out of bed, half in it, and the first thing I saw was blood on her nightdress. For a moment I thought she might have tried to cut herself and then I saw that her nose was bleeding – there were great swathes of crimson across her cheeks and upper lip. She was still screaming and her hand, like an automaton's, went up to the blood, then down to the white material of her nightdress. She rubbed the blood in to the linen then went back for more. And all the time kept on screaming. Not like a child, or at least, if it was like child it had gone beyond the attention-seeking stage. This was a private act, horridly mechanical – again and again and again.

When she gets really bad she can't breathe and there's nothing you can do except hold on to her until it's all over. One doctor said it was to do with her mother, another said it was due to me, and yet another (clinical) made her sound crazier than she actually is, by defining her state with words longer and more disturbing than, say, anger or possession. When she was clear of it that first time, before things went bad between us again, she said – 'I just feel I've had enough, had enough of all of it, and I scream and shout and don't stop. It's like having a devil in you.'

I grabbed her by the shoulders and held her down on the bed. Outside I heard the girls' footsteps. 'Go down,' I shouted 'and stay in the kitchen.' 'Just go *and don't go in the hall!*'

She was making recognizable noises now. Swearing, softly, blindly . . . 'Fucking stupid fucking cunting stupid bloody go on you stupid little fucking cunt stupid little stop it stop it stop it . . .'

'Please, Meg. Please.'

She's very strong when she's like that. One hand came up and scratched at my cheek. I grabbed her wrist and forced it back on to the duvet, its white lace spattered with blood. I was kneeling on top of her now, astride her exposed thighs, which thrashed this way and that in fury. Suddenly she snaked her chin out and bit my hand hard. Instinctively, I raised the other hand and hit her across the face. She lay still for a moment. Then, in an obscene, parodic gesture, she began to move her hips up and down, jerkily. She stared up at me, cunningly. 'Go on then,' she said, 'fuck me fuck me fuck me fuck me go on poke it into me poke it into me *get it out go on*. . .' She started to laugh. One hand grabbed for my prick.

'Meg –'

'Meg Meg Meg who's Meg? Who's she? Never heard of her you just want something to stick it in don't you? Go on get it out get it out get it out stick it in isn't that what you want to do that's all I am just a lump of meat aren't I?'

She let her hand fall back. Breathing heavily she watched me for a while with what I took to be real dislike. There was sweat across her forehead and the blood now smeared across her temples made her look like a Red Indian. Her blood was on me too, mingled with that of the dead creature downstairs. She's crazy, I thought, dully, she's actually gone.

'Are you doing it with someone else?'

'No,' I said, after a pause that lasted too long, 'honestly.' I sounded gentle, sincere and effective. I didn't want, at that moment, for it to be true. And my conviction seemed to shame her. She curled up into a ball and turned away from me on the bed. Her thumb went into her mouth. 'I'm ill,' she said, 'I'm mad and I'm ill. I'm crazy.' I didn't reply at first. Then 'What started it?'

'I went to sleep,' said Meg, 'and I had an awful dream.'

'What about?'

She rolled back towards me. She looked scared. 'I keep having it,' she said, 'over and over again.'

'What?'

'There are these people in . . . historical dress . . .' A pause. Her voice became pleading. 'I mean that isn't surprising, is it? You're writing about the seventeenth, the seventeenth . . ., you know . . . they're all wearing those clothes, those clothes. . .'

I tried to joke her out of it. 'Look,' I said, 'I'd be very offended if you didn't dream about the seventeenth century. It would show you hadn't been listening to me. You should be dreaming about 1650 and Puritanism and Witchfinders and –'

Here she grabbed my arm. 'Why am I dreaming that?' she said, 'I dreamed it before you said it, didn't I? I can't remember. When did we start to talk about witches? We weren't at first and I was dreaming I don't know which came first you see, I don't know. Why are they hanging these witches? Why are they taking them out on rough wooden carts and putting them up ladders and kicking them out into space. Why?'

'Meg,' I said, 'why do people do awful, cruel stupid things? I don't know. Nobody knows. They just do.'

She pulled hard at my sleeve. 'They're putting something round my neck,' she said, 'they're going to strangle me, I can feel the rope round my neck.' Her thumb crept back into her mouth. 'I don't think you should write about Ezekiel Oliphant. I don't think you should even think about him. When you write about evil things – they happen. . .'

'Sometimes they do,' I said with a confidence I did not feel. 'It is called coincidence. History is full of ugly things. They happen. His wife . . . .' She was nodding furiously. 'Yes,' she said, 'his wife.'

'Meg –'

'Things happen,' she said, 'again and again and again. Don't they? Isn't that all the lesson we learn from history? People make *exactly* the same mistake again and again and again. They don't even have the imagination to escape the awful, dreary inevitability of it. War, adultery, I don't know . . . how can people be so stupid? How can there be progress when people are so stupid?'

'Some people,' I said, 'can try not to be. Some things change. There are good acts among the mess and the filth. . .'

She looked at me oddly. 'Not enough, and since we've stopped believing in good and evil there will be less and less. We'll be swamped by the past, by the darkness, don't you think? And you see – the things you're playing with, talking about to amuse yourself, you won't be able to control them.'

What she's saying, I thought, is irrational. Why then does her voice sound suddenly so clear and sane? And isn't this what I think, privately, about Oliphant? I don't dare say it out loud. But it is what I think.

'You've got your story, Jamie. But you mustn't write it. It will come true if you write. All your stories come true you see. And this is such an evil horrible frightening story. I liked your soap opera story it was comforting but there's no comfort in this story. Please don't think about it Jamie.'

'What do you mean – my stories always come true?'

'You said you loved me once and that was a story and it came true because you said it and I believed it. And you said all sorts of other things and they all came true of course they did. Didn't they?' Her hands gripped my wrist. I looked down at her knuckles. She has housewife's hands, I thought, worn and bulged from washing and cooking and caring for my children. Hard working hands like in the country song. I thought of Anna's hands, small and tanned and helpless.

'You do still love me don't you? Don't you? Say you still love me. There isn't anything if you don't love me. I'll die if you don't love me. Please love me. Please. . .'

There was silence. Into the silence, I said 'I love you.' I don't think either of us believed it. To try and make it real I touched her shoulder. But her flesh did not quicken to my fingers. There was none of the instant, physical resurrection of sex. It is, I thought, it is like something died.

'Seek,' said Ezekiel's voice at my ear, 'Seek My Spirit. Seek out the Abominable Shame that found me out. Watch. For in Some was made Incarnate the Hellish Principles of Satan and in others the Light of Our Lorde God that will alone be There to Save Us. Choose Master. Which is the Good Woman? Which is Shee who Hath her Compacte made with the Evil One?' And then a chuckle. 'Or is it Thyself, Master, who has his bargain made with Foulnesse and Sinne? Speak. We await your answer . . .' I wanted to speak but could not. I wanted to unwind the years between us. But there were too many years suddenly. You can't make love happen, I thought. It's there or it isn't. And something is killing it in me, piece by piece.

The doorbell rang.

'That'll be Rick,' she said.

'Oh.'

I felt alarm, then anger. 'What's he doing here?'

'He forgot some papers or something. He rang.'

'Oh.' It looked as though I was going to have the man-to-worm talk earlier than anticipated. Or perhaps he was going to tell her. I heard Thomasina go out into the hall, and ran out after her. 'Don't go in there . . . But I was too late.

'Oh Daddy you hurt it.'

'Hurt what?' Meg appeared behind me on the landing.

'Nothing.'

The doorbell rang again.

'What did you hurt?'

'I didn't hurt anything.'

'Oh Daddy –'

'Let him in.'

I ran down the stairs and saw Rick standing over the bloodied corpse of the mouse. The children were looking at it with the chastened curiosity that death seems to provoke in the very young. 'It'th thquashed,' said Gwendoline.

'Yes,' I said.

'You thquashed it,' she continued remorselessly.

'I'm afraid I did,' I said.

Rick looked up at me. I could not credit, from his expression, that he had seen me earlier in the day. He didn't smile, but then Rick doesn't smile much. If he does it's usually a shared secret between him and his jersey. He was wearing a long black overcoat and carrying a briefcase. He looked more like a city gent than an academic. Behind him was the cold, black evening street, and one determined commuter, collar up against the wind, on her determined, formal path home.

'Ith it dead?' said Gwendoline.

'I think it is,' I said.

Rick shut the door and came into the hall. He put the briefcase down and rubbed his hands. The coat made him look even smaller than usual. 'What the hell were you playing at today?' he said.

I started to make puzzled sounds.

'Oliphant phoned my office, What the hell were you playing at?'

I gulped nervously. 'I thought –'

'Is Meg upstairs?'

'She's asleep,' I said. She had gone from the landing. Perhaps she was asleep. 'Get your papers and go,' I said.

'Why did you go there?'

'No business of yours.'

'The Oliphant business,' he said, 'is a very peculiar –' Whatever he was about to say, he decided against it. . .

'Tell me,' I said, 'the Clarke Papers. . .'

He didn't want to tell me but his urge to justify his scholarly record was too strong. 'Were bequeathed to Worcester College by his son. They're still there for anyone to see. Why are you interested in the Clarke Papers?

'No reason,' I said.

'Listen,' he said, 'don't mess around with things you do not understand. This is my affair. OK? Keep your horrible, grubby little hands out of it.'

'Did you get any good stuff on Ezekiel today?' I said. Anything to keep him away from those stairs. I must get him out of the house as soon as possible. He paused, with one foot on the stairs. 'Ezekiel Oliphant,' he said, 'was probably the kind of evil bastard who preys on women. Who desires them, feels guilty, then blames them for his guilt. Bit like you really.'

I simpered.

'But there's a lot more to the story than that. And you wouldn't understand it so keep away from it. I don't want your big feet treading all over it. It's mine you hear – mine. Mine.' It was curious. There was something of Ezekiel in his tone. A whining, unpleasant, possessive quality. It didn't sound like Rick talking at all. For a moment his eyes were bright with something that looked like greed or lust. Then the gleam faded and he was good old Rick Mason once more. 'I always liked you Jamie,' he said, 'I thought you were quite decent. Wet but decent. But I think you've gone corrupt and rotten. You don't believe in anything any more. About society. About personal relationships. Everything about you has gone soft and . . . bad. You've gone rotten. I was going to tell Meg about what I saw today but I can't face her. You'd better tell her though.' I listened for sounds from the upper landing. Could Meg hear this? He came closer to me. Over by the door the children stared at the mouse.

'I love Meg,' he said, 'I've always loved her. I think she's

161

brave and clever and beautiful and decent and if you do anything, *anything* to hurt her, I'll come over here and so help me I'll kill you.'

'You and who else?' I said.

He went over to the corner by the kitchen door and picked a pile of papers off the floor. Then he turned to go. 'You were a bastard to old Dewes,' he said, 'and I should have known then. You know who you remind me of? Ezekiel bloody Oliphant, that's who.'

'Have a Care then Master Mason . . .' I said, and as I spoke I felt the hairs on the back of my neck prick up. I felt a power come into my voice and my fingers as I stabbed them at his chest in the kind of gesture a prosecuting counsel might make. '. . . lest I Saddle up my Horse and Betake myselfe to the University of Lancaster and Declare your membership of the Detestable Communistical Crewe and of your Utter and Complete Lack of the Virtues Necessary for Those set in Authority of the Youth of this Kingdome, Disturbed as it is by Riots, Civil Strife and Insolence before appointed Officers!'

I was laughing as I said this. He wasn't. I don't think he was worried about anyone knowing he was a member of the Communist Party (does anyone care about that any more?), I think it was my voice and my angry, relentless fingers that silenced him. Maybe it was that he saw that I had made a choice and that my politics were no longer his politics. That, if it came to it, I would pursue him with the fury and hatred I once reserved for policemen, magistrates and teachers who thought they knew something I didn't. A few minutes after he had gone, Meg came out. 'Did he go?' she said.

'Yes,' I said coldly.

She started to cry.

The odious Sinne of Witchcraft may cunninglie ensnare those who Struggle to Followe the Path of Righteousnesse, and anie may bee cozened into Witchcraft, as was our Mother Eve. And though the *Cooperites* teach us that *wee must take the Neare Waie agaynst Sinne* which means that each must Examine his owne Hearte and Conscience before hee seek to cast out the Sinnes of

162

another, for *let him who is without Sinne cast the first stone,* Yet there is a Godlinesse resides in oure conception of ourselves, what wee may bee. And certayntie in Matters touching Faith is the onlie *sure light,* for without we bee certayn of oure God and how wee be sett round with the Devil's snares, how may wee Fare from one Citie to the Nexte? Or ply oure Trade? Or Teach those that come after Is the Waie to Godly Manners?

For I had Doubted Margaret and soe it is the Evill One does his work and *comes in by anothere doore while we are sleeping.* Think nott hee will nott come for you or the Nexte one, for hee does his Worke while men SLEEP and if the Soule sleeps, why the Devill comes in to Pollute the Temple which should bee the Lorde's. But how O Lord may wee Know if a Woman be tainted with the abominable Sinne of Witchcraft? And how, if shee bee so Cozened by the Devill and his Workes, may shee know the wicked work shee does, until shee Repent and come to Heaven and His holy GRACE. For there are those, as I have heard, that will die, and boast of their Master Satan, who can still work his work and make anie Suffer that Turn agaynst them. And in that same Yeare At Newbury, was credibly related by gentlemen, commanders and captains of the Earl of Essex his armie, some of the Soldiers being Scattered by the reason of their loitering by the waie of gathering Nuts, Apples, Plums, Blackberries and the like espied on the Rivere being there adjacent a Tall, Lean and Slender Woman *treading on the Water with her Feet with as much Ease and Firmnesse as One should Walke or Trample on the earthe, where, having taken aim, Give Fire and shott at her shee caught their Bullets in her handes and chewed them, which was a Stronger Testimony than the water.*

But what I could nott credit was that Satan should so Artfully work upon my Meg, which I said, when they Accused her, which they did the Night Mr Beelse's sonne told us of the Sickness of the Horse, which died that Evening, though none could Discover how this thing should bee. 'Well then,' says Mr Morris,' goe to Her and Examine Her. For wee would have an Answere.' 'I will not credit,' says I, 'that shee bee a Witch.' 'Indeed,' says Morris, 'but this must be put to the Test.' And in my Heart was Doubt and Uncertaintie which I doubt nott showed in my Face. For the Holy Scripture attesteth to it and to the *cunning waie the Devill may put oure feet aboutt the Net and Snare us.* And why, I knew nott, but yett my Margaret had become as a Stranger to mee, which first I put to Mr Morris and yet, if shee had Feares of Him shee told mee nott of them. And who shall 'scape Sinning if the Devill counsell Sweet enough? Am I to say 'Nott I Lorde. Nay neither my Wife or Shee who dwells in my House, for *I am stronger than anie Temptation Ye may send agaynst Mee.'* Is nott such talke most Blasphemous and Irreligious and denieth the verie Texte of the Bible as one who would say 'Why Masters there are no Witches wee may Fear.' And does awaie nexte with all Other Matter of the Scripture and leaves us meer Lumps of Clay that *take a fewe Steppes and then are Gone.* And as I went into Her that night I thought of the Wife of Essenden when I was a boie that was taken for a witch and swimmed in the water there and swore shee was no witch. And yet I stood behind the Cart the Daie shee was cast off from the ladder and Hanged and heard her cry upon the Devil to come and aid her. And it was said the Devil sucked her *fundament* and there were marks upon her, which when my Brother and I heard did provoke us and compound oure Night Fancies. All these things were in my Heart when I went to her and told her of what was said of her, and Prayed shee Confide in mee and if shee bee guilty of the Sinne, confesse it Freely. 'For,' says I, 'I have a care for Thy Soule as I love thee. And care for nothing but my Clear and Honest Favour in the sight of God. Wherefore answer mee these charges if they bee True or nott, for they are sure you have Bewitched the Horse and I am troubled by your Silence and that you will not Lay with Mee.'

But shee answered nott, and sate upon her Handes by the Hearth. And though shee looked upon mee piteouslie she made no Sound, though I heard her breaths come quicklie. 'Come,' says I, 'if this bee nott True it may bee proved. For the *Lord's Waies are just – neither hath hee led his servants into the Wildernesse and Given them nott Food and Drink but Hee hath sett their feet upon the Strait Waie and made them to Marvel at His Love.'* But shee gave me no answere to this, and sate and would nott Speak though shee breathed still as One who is hard pressed. Whereat I went out to Mr Morris and Mr Beelse, whose Sonne was there beside him and Told them shee would not answere. At which Mr

Morris saith 'Well then shee must. And shee must bee Examined. And taken to the Justices.' Which sate then at Hertford, though none knew rightly when synce the Warres had all but *chased out the Assize*, 'And,' says this *Morris*, 'before wee take her thither some fewe of us must examine her. And watch by the Howse withal, that shee may nott suffer her Imps to come and goe as they please.' At which I was very much frightened, but kept my owne Counselle, there being severall otheres with him there, that were his Followers. And as I turned from them and went to goe back into my Lodging, Young Daniel comes forwarde and, with his Eie upon mee, says, 'I have seen a thing like a cat leave her Chambere and seen it come agayne. But it had nott the shape I knewe nor would it come when I called but was like a spirit that knew onlie its owne Mistress.' At which his father sighs and Young Daniel, keeping his Eie upon mee all the while, says 'It is true that I have seen it.' 'Well,' says Mr Morris, 'We will watch and she shall be examined ere wee take her to the Justices.' Which then, at Hertford was Sir Richard Maplake.

That there bee those Falsely Accused of the abominable Sinne of witchcraft I do nott doubt, neither than that some bee called Witches and are None, but I was much afraid synce, when I went in to Meg agayne and spoke gently to her withal, shee seemed nott to know mee & stared past mee at the Wall, whiles I spake to Her. 'Why Meg,' says I, 'there are those here as would examine You which must bee done.' At which shee starts a-shaking as of a Fever and I counselled her to say a Prayer. 'I cannot,' says shee. 'Why Margaret –' says I, 'it will goe hard for you if you bee nott able to say a Prayer.' 'A woman was in oure village,' says shee, 'that gave suck to the Devill, and shee could not pray, for Mr Clarke, that was the Priest there, examined her. I cannot pray. I know nott why but I cannot.' And shee turns Her face awaie from mee and shee spake nott agayne. Neither when they came in to her did shee seem to know them. 'And soe,' says Mr Morris, 'you may leave us.' And when I was gone they searched Her and on her Bodie was found the Devil's brand, which Innocent women doe nott have.

That night, and the night that followed, I slept at Mr Beelse's

Lodging, for I was afraid. And Mr Morris and four other persons watched over agaynst oure Chambere, which they did on three Nights and Deposed, before the Justice, when wee went there, that shee had called up half a dozen Angels, in the shape of kitling, polecat, spaniel, toad, and one said hee saw a Child without a Head. It was, I think, the Fifth daie wee took her to the Assize and I Went in to her and asked her if shee knew what was said Concerning Her by Honest and Godlie persons. For though in my Hearte I Had Questioned Mr Morris's opinion concerning Her, there were now so manie testified as to the Truth of his Report as made mee Ashamed. And I asked God's mercie of my Disbelief and of my Doubts concerning Him. At which I went to Mr Morris, declaring to Him my confusion at which hee says – 'there bee those that love nott the Lorde and will nott Discover Him, but ye are nott one such. *For though thou hast doubted yett is the Waie made Plaine for unless ye trust in the Lord will ye be Cast out, for there is no waie except through Him.*' Before shee was taken from mee I went in agayne to her and begged her, on my life if these things reported of her bee True, that shee might Confess, because, of the Love I had for her I would pardon anie Sinne synce how are wee to be spared unless by the Action of His Mercie. At which shee fell to crying, saying that shee was no Virtuous Woman and noe Crown unto her husband; but was One that maketh ashamed & as rottenness in my Bones. Before wee took her to the Assize, Mr Morris counselled mee, saying that shee may yet cry her Innocence and put herself upon the countie. 'For,' says hee, 'the Devil may soe work on one who is a Witch and Unless shee confess and Repent she hath no waie to Salvation. Wherefore I counsell that you bee the one to bring the Charge agaynst Her synce it bee agaynst your Breast shee has worked her charms.' And hee questioned mee further concerning Her familie at which I told him of the Latin Prayeres her mother favoured and hee says, 'Consider, how such things may nott bee Charmes, or how shee hath acquired the Knowledge and Instinctual Understanding that led her to these Waies.' And hee counselled mee to work upon her and to obtain the full particulars of her Imps.

When shee heard it was at my charge – as also of the other

166

gentlemen – shee was brought to the Justices, shee wept agayn and made Confession to Mr Morris, that was there & did freely confess that shee had three black Imps named Wrynose, Jesu and Panu, which sucked on the lower parts of her body. Shee had sent also to our Sonne an imp in the likeness of a grey kitten to suck on Him. And having Confessed all shee wept and implored forgiveness of Us at which wee Rejoyced.

But even as I had Doubted when first shee was Accused, because of the Love I had for Her, so now, when it came to the case that shee bee taken to the Assize and the depositions agaynst her heard, I was fain nott to goe and to doubt the Truth of what was Asserted agaynst her. For I knew shee must bee hanged. But this same *Morris* sate with mee and prayed and made the Waie plain to mee, that though I may doubt and Lament, I must goe with them *for I must Show my Good Intent to them*. And hee looks mee in the eie straight as hee spake. And I was Afraid.

Soe it was I went to Hertford Assize to speak agaynst her. And in the Court shee confessed that shee had cursed a Colt that was a gentleman's nearby to us and had suffered the Devill come to her in the Howse when I was awaie and hee was dressed in black cloak with silk points and had given Imps to her with which shee was wont to do much Mischief. And shee called on the Lord for mercie when Sir Richard given her to be hanged. I would have gone from there but Mr Morris would nott Suffer mee to go, synce wee must have a care *for her Sincere Repentence*. In which Cause hee did enforce mee to stand with Otheres that were there that prayed for her Soule when shee was taken from the gaol to the Gallowes on the North Side of the town and there cast off the Cart and Hanged. Which I could not suffer to see but turned my face from it, though shee called upon the Lord for his Mercie, for there was doubt in my Hearte still and Waywardness and Rebellion and still I could not Trust in the Lord or in the Righteousnesse of his Waies. But I was afraid to let them that were with mee see my Unbelief, and I was ashamed that I could nott Loathe her Sinne as shee Confessed it, for shee owned herself *to rejoyce that her Abominable Compact was discovered*. But I went from there and kept my owne counselle, saying 'I cannot find one wise man amongst you. My daies are past, my purposes are broken off; even the Thoughts of my Hearte. They change the Night into Daie; the light is short because of Darkesse. If I wait, the grave is mine howse. I have made my bed in the Darknesse. I have said to Corruption, Thou art my Father; to the worm, Thou art my mother and my sister. And where is now my Hope? As for my Hope who shall see it? They shall goe down to the bars of the pit, when oure Rest togethere is in the Dust.'

16

I think back, now, here in the cottage that belonged to my
father, as the hot July day begins to fade, and try and decide
whether Meg did know. Impossible to decide. Certainly she
knew in the way in which we know the most important things
– by how I looked at her, how I touched her or didn't touch
her. Perhaps, for people like me, who never say quite what
they feel until the feeling is safely past them, such sign language is the only truth.

The silence between us – in the days that followed – became
more subtle and more loaded with guilt and misery. From an
angry silence it graduated to a polite silence, and from a polite
silence to a grim exchange of necessary information. 'Where
are you off to today?' 'I'll be a little late . . .' The only thing that
can break such a silence is the truth – shouted or cried or
whispered, it doesn't matter. At least after the truth, whatever
is left, there won't be the silence. But I could not find a way of
telling her. I was already too frightened of her misery to have
the courage to add to it. And so I hugged Anna's image to
myself, allowed it to nourish me, while she grew paler and
quieter and more stooped and, suddenly, old. *Affliction stamps
the soul to its very depths with the scorn, the disgust and even the self
hatred and sense of guilt that crime should logically produce but
actually does not.* Well – and what if I was the criminal? Someone's got to be the criminal, haven't they? And she was sure as
hell determined to suffer.

I started to phone Anna, early in the mornings, after Meg
had taken the children to school. They weren't long conversations. She'd ask me what I had been doing. I'd tell her about
Gottlieb or some little thing I knew would make her laugh.
And her voice was very quiet and small and nothing commit-
ting was said by either of us, but with each call, and each
lied-about drink after the library closed, the calls and the
drinks and the kisses (there were only kisses now, nothing

else) seemed sweeter and more necessary. That's how it goes always, I suppose. Nothing new in it. Why should it feel so unique and sweet? I don't know.

I can't remember when we went to Oxford, or indeed quite when I determined to go there, but I do know we talked a lot about the Oliphant business. I had consulted several books on witches and witchcraft but could find no mention of Ezekiel. There was plenty of horrifying stuff, but no reference at all to Oliphant or to Essenden. Not that I searched very hard. I had put Ezekiel to one side. If I was honest I would have said that he had begun to frighten me a little.

And then, one night, I picked up Ron's pamphlet. Meg was asleep. I was alone downstairs, drinking. And its weird blend of the comical and the grotesque caught me, until I found I was reading as I had first read *A Cursèd Lie*. I was caught, magicked, spellbound – all those words a rational age uses to describe the uncomfortable power of narrative.

'. . . throughout History men have attempted to find the key to the way in which the society in which they live is constructed. In the nineteenth century, for example, writers like *Macaulay* (though what does he know?) believed that the history of society was a long, slow climb towards justice and humanity, and that all the liberal ideals to which people feel able to subscribe in between bombing and starving and shooting each other actually mean something. In the twentieth century the 'Marxists' – as Marx said 'I am not a Marxist' and if he isn't a Marxist that is good enough for me – attempted to describe a situation in which something called the PROLETARIAT – or working class – struggled against the BOURGEOISIE and eventually overcame them. But, if Dresden and Hiroshima make Macaulay's liberalism look pretty bloody stupid HOW MUCH MORE DOES THE PRESENT APATHY OF THE WORKING CLASS GIVE THE LIE TO EASY MARXIST ANALYSIS OF WHAT IS WRONG WITH BRITAIN AND SO ON WHO ARE WE TRYING TO FOOL PLEASE MESSIEURS OF THE TROTSKYISTS AND COMMUNISTS NOT FOR ME A START I AM VERY MUCH AFRAID.

The fact of the matter is this. In the West, Marx's beloved proletariat are a cowed bunch of bozos only interested in 'bingo' and the everlasting telly set. In America the heartland of capitalism they supported the Vietnam War and they voted for Ronald Reagan and generally behaved like a bunch of Turkeys enthusiastically advocating the continuation of Thanksgiving Day by all the means at their disposal. *Stupidity does not create justice my friends.* Let us pass on to consider other 'theories of history' which have been adumbrated and it may be worth our while to consider them before disposing of them. For I too have a theory. And it is not a theory but a truth. A true story that none of you will have heard. That none of you will believe. That none of you will want to believe, but it is nevertheless the truth and I will make you listen to it and remember it and when you have heard me through you will see that – odd and terrifying as what I have to say may seem – it is none the less the whole and certain and unvarnished truth about the island in which we have the misfortune to live.

Take Spengler. I have not read Spengler but as far as I CAN SEE HE MAINTAINS THAT THE WEST IS IN DECLINE. Surprise surprise. All 'theories of society' from Calvin to Hitler preach that there are forces that shape us over which we have no control. This is their very charm, of course. Nothing is to be done or thought. All one has to do is to line up behind the theory – or more usually the jackbooted advocates of it – and wait for the millenium to come around. Best of all one does not have to think – a process which humans have always found tiring.

The imperfections of English society are not, I fear, to be explained away by our failure to live up to the ideals of Tom Paine or the woolly pragmatist Burke. We are not poor, isolated, greedy, and lacking in moral fibre because we did not read the ideas of Benjamin Disraeli correctly. Oh History has a lesson to teach us and we are indeed bound by 'forces' out of our control but those 'forces' are not so cheap and easy to describe as so-called 'thinkers' have assumed.

Upstairs I could hear Meg cough. I put down the manuscript. If only he wouldn't write so persuasively. The central heating was off now and I felt a little chilled. I didn't want to read on. But I did.

. . . I am afraid, gentle reader, that I am going to bring out a conspiracy theory and I expect you will not find it to your taste. You are too clever for such things. You are well read and you have two children and a nice clean English house and you don't want to hear about conspiracy theories especially from someone who you suspect of being a little bit less than normal. I am as normal as you are chucky and what I have to say is in deadly earnest. It's not 'The Jews Done It' or 'The Blacks Done It' I am afraid, touching though those theories are in their incompleteness. Why, I ask you, my reader, my *frère semblable*, my white middle class English person, or working or upper – I don't really care – why are we living in a country that forty years ago had a seat at a table at the Conference that decided the fate of the world, and now we are despised even by the Pakis and the Niggers who come over here from colonies we created and administered only to howl 'racist' every time we open our mouths? Why, I am sorry but I have to ask these questions, should the country of Shakespeare and Elizabeth and – yes yes yes – Oliver Cromwell have fallen into such an appalling mess? Why is it that the telephone boxes don't work, that the traffic all goes one way, slowly, that the television programmes are getting worse and the youth of the country look forward to a decade in which none of them will ever work again? I'm sorry to ask these questions but I must. You probably don't like to think about the mess you are in. Oh yes there is someone to blame I am relieved to be able to tell you – but I must also say that blaming him will not solve our problem since the very thing that made *him* the architect of our present miseries is still alive and well and making trouble and our refusal to recognize it, to face up to it and to speak out against it is the principal reason why we are the banana republic of Europe, the fag end of nothing, the laughing

172

stock of East and West. I think we should face that challenge and, unlike some others in this country I think that Englishmen and Englishwomen have a great deal to give and that they must be simply taught to be proud of what they are. I'm so sorry I'm not a Muslim. Sorry sorry sorry I don't do Reggae round my front room. I say what I have to say because it is the truth.

There is, and has been, an unbroken line of individuals, traceable back to the seventeenth century and beyond who have combined, for private greed and profit, often for motives of sexual gratification, to extort money, to betray and corrupt what we like to think of as the English way of life. Although external evidence as to the activities of this chain of groups is hard to come by and the key document belongs to the period of the English Civil War, there is no doubt in my mind whatsoever that these people were active in their work of corruption and evildoing well before that date. From my researches I have been able to discover little of their 'infrastructure' (it is and remains a well-guarded secret) but I have a good idea as to who the principals involved are. Before I name them let me prepare the ground.

Belief in the supernatural is unfashionable, largely because of the difficulty of examining 'supernatural' phenomena, and largely because the burden of proof is too heavy for those concerned to prosecute it. It is very difficult, for example, for an author to 'prove' such and such a critic ruined his career purely for personal reasons. His perception that such is the case is based on his view of the critic in question and his own estimation of the work criticized. 'Oh no', says the critic, 'it is pure coincidence that I slept, or failed to sleep with Mr X's wife. My view of his work is my view of his work.' Historians often speak, blithely, of the 'causes' of historical phenomena. Who 'caused' the First World War? Who precisely is responsible for the Holocaust? It is my contention that such talk is of no more significance than the declaration in 1642 by Elizabeth Hardacre of Essenden, that Meg Oliphant had bewitched her two daughters to death. Modern medicine 'blames' the virus or the microbe, and lately, I observe, even such humble servants of man as butter or meat, for the cruel ways which, even in the civilized West, we are deprived of life.

Yes, gentle reader, it is my contention that since the fourteenth century an influential group of witches and witch masters have been deliberately undermining English society. And you laugh. My 'witches' are not even the crones of popular imagination, although the witch movement did indeed include such poor deluded women, who confessed excess after excess, often unaware that the very people to whom they were confessing were themselves the true witches and witch masters. The so called 'witch craze' can only be understood, in my view *as a terrified response from the witch establishment that the game was up.* For when the witch craze ran out of control, as in the English Civil War, it did so for the very good reason that some of those involved, realized that they were on to something. The establishment cover up was swift, ruthless and brutal. It is quite as ruthless today, except that now it uses the liberal false-speak, the jargons of feminism and sociology to conceal what it wishes to conceal. The deaths of Hopkins and Stearne are one thing. The strange case of Ezekiel Oliphant quite another. Oliphant was killed because he was closer than anyone else to the heart of the story, to the central, critical power point in the history of English witchcraft, the man who pulled the switches, the High Witch of this country. I refer, of course to

I turned the page and read, in capitals on the next sheet, the words

OLIVER CROMWELL.

Brilliant. I like it. Oliver Cromwell. Go it, Ron. Ollie on his broomstick. Ron – you are nothing if not original. I had my laugh. Don't tell me, Ron – Ireton was a warlock. The Long Parliament was a coven in drag.

Then I stopped. Of course, I thought, our contemporary

vision of witches – black hat, broomstick – is a cartoon designed to provide reassurance. What people like Oliphant meant by the word *witch* was far more insidious. A witch was someone evil who had somehow managed to get control of you. An assembly of witches wasn't a chorus line of female pensioners – it was an image designed to evoke all that is most unwelcome and uncontrollable in society.

And are you saying, Jamie, I asked myself, that a nation's life is simply a chapter of accidents? Surely you allow the Masons, the Communists, the neo-Nazis, a degree of influence. Under the surface all countries are veined and marbled by a map of alliances and conspiracies – England more than most. It is a very old country. I looked down at the pamphlet once again and read

... Cromwell, as Clarendon described him, was a man who had 'all the wickedness against which damnation is denounced, and for which hell fire is prepared, so also he had some virtues which have caused the memory of some men in all ages to be celebrated.' Yes indeed. If it were not for a close and detailed reading of a paper written by an ancestor of mine, I expect I would never have discovered the appalling truth about Cromwell or his agents.

In his *A Cursèd Lie Put About by the Government and a Shorthand Taker Thoroughly Rebutted* by ancestor Ezekiel Oliphant makes very guarded reference to the conspiracy. It is not surprising that Ezekiel was careful, for the target of his abuse, William Clarke, the Secretary of the Army Council was, my argument will show, a high witch master, and implicated as deeply as anyone in the history of the English witch movement. English witchcraft is a movement closer to, say, Masonry than to some underground, outlawed conspiracy, but that does not, in my view, make it any the less sinister, and, indeed, when you read of the doings of the High Witches of the Brotherhood – an unbroken line that stretches from Cromwell, through Charles II, Newton, William Hobbit of Lewisham, William Blake the poet, Lord Castlereagh and the Duke of Wellington, Harry MacTaggart of Ealing, Disraeli, Edward VII, Jack the Ripper, George Citrine, Winston Churchill, and of

175

course the 'Continental' Witch, Jean-Paul Sartre.

Sexual perversion is, of course, a traditional ingredient of Satanism and the repression of the Puritan's sense of sexuality must have had something to do with Cromwell's recruitment to witch activities. There is little doubt that the ingredients of seventeenth-century Satanism are much as they are for the frustrated housewives of Essex, who today, strip off in front rooms for the benefit of *News of the World* journalists. What is certain is that the sense of evil that they generate is far far more real. For these witches – as do all the witches of England – mean business. They will kill and torture and lie and betray in order to hide their hideous conspiracy – the pleasure that lies for them in consummation of their passion for Satan and all the children of the Evil One. There may be a witch next to you my friend but do not imagine that you will recognize him or her by a mark on the body or the howl of a familiar. The witch is a man or woman like you. The difference is that he or she is wholly dedicated to evil. Perhaps you believe that evil does not exist. Is not a useful word. Perhaps you explain the screams of the children Myra Hindley and Ian Brady tortured as a symptom of something or other. If so you are probably of the party that would recommend the release of these good and harmless folk. Perhaps you believe that our friend Mr Nielsen, with the bodies of his homosexual pick-ups in the garden, or Peter Sutcliffe, hearing the voices on the gravestone and going out into the dark streets of Chapeltown to seize women and stab them through the stomach again and again – these are 'ill', these are 'unfortunates'. If you believe that in your soul, if you feel no chill of terror when thinking of the screams of the dying in this or that war, then by all means turn the page and 'have no more of me'. But if you want to explain such things. And want to fight them – as well as 'explain' them – then listen to what I have to say.

In 1978 I obtained access to what is known as the 'James Trunk' at Worcester College, Oxford, which is a little known supplement to the papers originally bequeathed by Clarke's son to the College in the eighteenth century. And

176

it was here that I found the document that led me to the weird and horrible manner and circumstances of my ancestor's death, and made me realize to what he was referring in the pamphlet abovementioned. But beware. This is an area in which contamination is rife and I counsel, before you read on, that you examine yourself and ask yourself whether you are indeed fit and able to read what I have to say. For corruption and evil can attack those who study such things and

I looked up. Meg was standing in the doorway.

'What are you reading?'

I started to fold up the pamphlet. 'Nothing.'

'Is it a dirty book or something?'

'No,' I said. I put it in my jacket pocket. 'It's just some piece of nonsense.'

'Oh.'

I was waiting for her to go. She stood there in the doorway for some time, then came over to me. She took my hand but I did not respond. 'I'm sorry,' she said. I did not reply. In the end she went back up to bed. When there was no sound from upstairs, I took out the pamphlet and turned the page. There was no more print. The last two sheets were blank. Scrawled across one, coffee-stained piece of foolscap was the following –

I wish I hadn't started this business. The more I find out about it the worse it gets. He inhabits me. The words run away with me. I'm ill. He's evil. He makes me say these things.

And at the foot of the page he had added

2 and 2 make four. Hold on to that. Do good when you can. Don't let him come again. O Lord which art in . . . of Lord which art . . . into thy hands. . .

17

'I like it.'

'Good isn't it?'

'Cromwell a witch. I like it very much.'

'Who are the current High Witches do you think?'

'Lord Hailsham.'

'Definitely.'

'And Shirley Conran. And the entire staff of *The Times Literary Supplement*.'

'God there's one . . .'

'Where?'

'In that Volvo. You missed him. They often drive Volvos. Safe family car. Lots of room for the, you know, cauldron etcetera . . .'

Anna and I were driving up the M40 towards Oxford. It had turned out she had a contact in Oxford and had herself arranged for me to see the contents of the James Addition to the Clarke Papers. She had done it, she said, to stop me wingeing on about Ezekiel Oliphant (or Elephant as she called him). In her company I laughed myself out of my earlier mood. 'I'll just prove to myself,' I thought, 'that I am chasing something that simply isn't there and then, at last, I can get back to Gottlieb. Tell him the seventeenth century is basically not televisual: 'Now, Nat, the late eighteenth century. . .'

We were driving through a landscape stripped for action – ploughed earth and bare trees – but, instead of the rain of the earlier part of the month, there was now gusty, limitless sunlight. I thought about Juliet, her tweeds, her stew, her thick bass voice. It was very very pleasant to be in this car with Anna. Presumably Anna had a mother somewhere. But it wasn't something we were required to talk about.

As we drove over Magdalen Bridge, a flock of students – gawkily glamorous girls, hunted-looking young men – spilled across the road in front of us, the true owners of the town. One of the girls had on a huge, unseasonal looking straw hat. Anna turned to me and grinned. 'Take you back, does it?'

'Sort of. You were at Sussex, weren't you?'

'Very common.'

'I don't think you're common, Anna.'

'I am. Common as muck.'

'Did you say your dad was a builder?'

'Yeah. And my mother's dead.'

'I'm sorry.'

Her mother was dead. This was very very very good news. Soon perhaps her father would be dead. Perhaps he would fall off some scaffolding. Soon. Then she would be a girl with no family. That was what I wanted. A girl blown into me like paper on the city street, picked up by the February wind.

'What's your wife like?'

'She's nice,' I said, 'you'd like her.'

Anna started to laugh. When she laughed she threw her head back and her red hair shook down her straight back. I wanted to say more things to make her laugh. 'No,' I said, 'seriously. She's had a hard life. She was sent down the pit at twelve. She nearly died in Natural Childbirth Classes.' And she laughed again.

Up past Magdalen to Carfax, where I discovered the traffic system had been altered in such a way as to compel all motorists to go to Abingdon, whether they wanted to or not. Where the cattle market had once been – and workmen's cottages flung close together, to the west of Christ Church – were now only car parks. The shops now looked like shops everywhere. The rundown pub where I had once drunk with Dewes was gone.

We circled back up towards the station, and through a crowd of mid-morning shoppers. It had been near here, in a pub called 'The Welsh Pony', that Rick Mason had told me about Dewes. 'Having if off with some bloke in the Parks, Jamie . . .' And, walking back from the pub towards Merton, he had asked me to go and see him. 'He likes you, Jamie. He really does. God knows why but he does . . .' I hadn't gone. Something else had got in the way, distracted me as it always does. Next morning they found Dewes in his rooms. He had cut his throat at his desk. The blood had congealed all over the manuscript of *The Idea of Liberty in the English Revolution*. He was never going to finish it anyway. He was just another screwed up, hopeless don who wouldn't have lasted two minutes more than fifty yards away from an Oxford common room. It wasn't my fault he was queer. Was it?

'Where now, my dear?' Her hand grabbed my knee. I giggled. 'Left.'

Left past the curious, stunted ecclesiastical folly at the top of Carfax, the cinema (still there), the Italian restaurant where I was sick after finals, and left again past the Playhouse, where the Oxford Experimental Theatre Club were giving us *The Caucasian Chalk Circle*. Does it never end?

None of this, I thought, has anything to do with me. Oxford is just a place I was. It taught me nothing. Its only ideals – in spite of all the big talk about truth and scholarship – are those of survival. 'Listen,' it says to the students, picking their way through the workaday crowds, the tired women in headscarves waiting for buses to Blackbird Leys, 'listen, listen. You don't have to do what they do. You can have it easy.' As we turned right towards Worcester, a young man in a top hat, a full length scholar's gown, and what looked like a long evening dress, cycled past us.

'It'll all be in shorthand presumably,' I said.

'Actually,' she said, 'I have a secret to tell you. My interest in all of this is professional to some extent. I spent a few months working on the Clarke Papers. I know his writing like I know my own. I know about the James stuff too. It's mainly laundry lists as I understand it. But I don't think anyone has ever done a complete job on it.'

'So there could be something there which no one had looked at since 1650.'

'Oh sure. Although I have to say I think it highly unlikely it will reveal that the Commander of the New Model Army was in league with Satan.'

'And what would you think if you saw such a document?'

'I'd assume it was faked.'

'Classic. You're like the man who looks up and sees a witch and assumes he must be drunk. What does it take to settle your rational view of the world?'

'Hard evidence.'

I gestured towards my crotch. She laughed again.

She was still smiling – secretly – as she parked the car, slipped her shoulder bag from under the seat and swung out on to the pavement. 'Now be a good boy . . .' she said. I walked a little behind her as we walked up the flagged path that leads to the Porter's Lodge. The efficient bachelor girl, compact and unafraid. Women without children have some of the neatness of men; they don't trail their lives behind them. After we're finished here, I thought, after we've finally nailed my absurd little obsession, *lunch*. Table for two at 'The Sorbonne', where once Meg got drunk and told me I shouldn't marry her. 'I don't care if you are crazy,' I had said. 'I love you. If you love someone – that's it. Isn't it?' That *was* it. Fifteen years ago.

I followed Anna in through the gate, into a quadrangle, and up a tortured flight of stairs. She seemed to have worked out the geography of the place. Was this how life was going to be from now on? I tried to imagine a similar visitation from, say, Meg, Juliet, Thomasina, Emma and Gwendoline – the sticky, unwelcome caravan of the family, with someone always crying or hungry, going to, or coming from, or failing to make, the lavatory. I was through with that. The sour, dry smell of books caught me as I followed Anna along a catwalk, hugging a wall that was crammed with books from floor to ceiling.

She was talking to a man who looked old enough to have gone to school with Ezekiel Oliphant. The James Trunk, the man was telling Anna, was left by George Clarke to his nephew Herbert Lucy, who had left it to his daughter Anna James. It was of no interest to serious scholars. Laundry lists. Anna nodded and smiled and mentioned the names of several people all unknown to me. The man seemed pleased. Then I heard her ask about Ron Oliphant. Had he been here? The man knew all about Ron. He hadn't been here long, he said, and he had stayed with him while he had looked at the papers. He had got very excited about one item. Here the man placed his index finger to the side of his head.

'Where is he from . . .?' I heard Anna ask. 'Oh,' said the man, 'Dr Oliphant was teaching at Cambridge. Before his illness.' Here, once again, he placed his finger to the side of his head and made screwing motions with it. 'It was ten years ago he came here,' said the man, and laughed eerily. 'I remember them all you see. All. I remember everything that happens here. Everyone that comes through I remember them.'

I walked over to the two of them. 'What did Dr Oliphant

teach?' 'He taught the seventeenth century, sir. He *lived* in the seventeenth century, sir. I think that's what finally got to him. He got some bee in his bonnet about some character – I don't remember. I think he may even have been a distant relative of his. An ancestor.' Close to, I saw the man was even older and stranger than I had at first thought. His skin was stretched over his skull, tight as a drum, and his teeth sat in his shrunken mouth like threatening weapons. No one goes crazy like the learned – and those who aspire to learning . . . think of all those half-mad librarians, guarding all those unread books . . . He turned to Anna. 'Anyway, if you're a friend of Dr Roberts – you're all right. Follow me. Follow me.'

He made a low, sweeping gesture with his right claw, the kind of thing usually done by hunchbacked assistants of Dr Frankenstein when welcoming strangers to the laboratory, and trudged off down another corridor, also lined with leather volumes. They were all bound in the same style, and seemed part of some endless series, though what the series was I could not discover. Some colossal encyclopaedia devoted to things no one but academics could possibly want to know about. *The World Treasury of Useless Information. Roll up roll up: The classification of 40 different kinds of Comedy* by Professors Dull and Boring. *The Idea of Metaphor in the Late Work of Henry James. Form and Meaning in the Poetry of Crabbe. Hearth Tax Between 1856 and 1871.* Can there be anything worse than scholarship without intuition or passion? Than the reduction of the most precious methods of human enquiry to system, unilluminated by feeling? So many books and so little real knowledge in any of them. Real knowledge is something that tells you how to live your life, isn't it? How not to cheat on your wife. How to love and care for your children.

'Careful on the stairs,' said the Quasimodo figure.

Up a circular steel staircase, double back along another corridor, through a heavy pair of double doors, and into what looked rather like a garage. There were several huge tin boxes, what looked like a piece of complicated farm machinery, and in the corner a gigantic wooden thing that looked like a seaman's chest. It was bound with heavy leather straps, and on the side, in gold letters was written

What was not to be done to the trunk was not, unfortunately, legible. Our guide gestured to it. 'All yours,' he said. He turned on his heel and shambled off into the labyrinth of unread volumes.

My first thought was that we had been led into some kind of trap from which we would never escape. My second, that the contents of the trunk must indeed be of little interest or value. And then I decided this was simply another example of our inability to keep up with the past. There is too much of it crowding in on us. My father's papers, I recalled, just after he died, seemed individually precious – each casual bill or formal enquiry to a parishioner worth preserving. And then, later, they were just letters, the way his is just another headstone in a row of them in the suburban cemetery where his ashes lie – if they *are* his, not those of the cremation before or the cremation after.

Anna was head down, arse in the air, burrowing through the box like a dog looking for a bone. 'What's it like?' I said.

'Much as expected,' said Anna, 'dull correspondence about money mainly. None of it in shorthand as far as I can see.'

'It's all a waste of time anyway, isn't it?'

'Why?'

'Even allowing for our friend's capacity for overstatement I just can't *imagine* the document that might give rise to his theory. I can't picture it.'

'The way mediaeval astronomers couldn't picture a helio-centric universe.'

'Our ideas about the past,' I said, 'are not of the same order as theories about the physical world. In spite of Brecht. The past has happened – it's not something to guess about. And I just can't see Oliver Cromwell tied up in Satanism. It just doesn't add up. Isn't this *your* argument, darling?'

She grinned. 'We're obviously beginning to influence each other. But if you found a document that implicated the Protector in Satanism . . . what then . . .'

'My first assumption would be it was a forgery. Like you looking at the witch.'

183

'I'd know if it was a forgery. That's my field.'

'You can't ever be certain . . .'

'Put it like this. I'd know if it was faked within the last hundred years or so. I'd know if our friend Dr Oliphant had done it. And otherwise – who would have a motive? Who would want to prove that Oliver Cromwell was a witch?'

'Hugh Trevor Roper?'

'Don't be facetious, Jamie.' She looked up from the trunk and shook her hair back. Yellowing papers were spread all about her as she knelt, graceful and suddenly shockingly young, among the antique litter.

'It's a question really, of the same order as "Was Adenauer a Nazi?" It only seems unacceptable because, in England history *for English historians*, the truth must never be seen to be sensational. It's like Ulster: continental papers describe it as a civil war – we talk about 'the troubles'. Because troubles pass I suppose. If anything does worry me in your attitude to all this, it's that you don't have a way of making judgements. You want to believe some things passionately – for example you love the idea of a conspiracy *behind* things – but then, at the same moment, you've got this urge to be rational and cool.'

And what's your way of making judgements?'

'I don't worry about such things. I just get on with the job.'

She carried on sorting through the papers.

'How old are you, Anna?'

'What a question! I'm twenty-five.'

Of course. There were fifteen years between us. I suddenly thought of Rick during the miners' strike. No, not *that* miners' strike. The one we like to talk about. The one that brought down Edward Heath. He had arrived on our doorstep with four gigantic men who required rooms for the night. I suppose they were flying pickets. They were big and quiet and confident. Surprisingly gentle. I wondered where they were now. Waiting for another pit to close I supposed. I didn't want to tell Anna about all of that. Perhaps the reason I liked her was that she did not trail any of that mawkish, useless history with her. If we talked politics at all it was the politics of Central America. Global stuff. She was still busy with the papers – the thin light from the one window picking up the lights in her hair, her prim lips closed in concentration. I went to the window and looked down on to a courtyard, closed on all sides. In the middle of the yard below a man in a green apron was carrying a huge pile of old fashioned looking shoes. As I watched, he stopped and sniffed the air. It was, somehow, a feudal scene. Nothing about it suggested the present. I turned back to Anna. She was looking down at a sheaf of papers, mouthing to herself. The papers looked authentically ancient. She ignored me. Suddenly I had had enough of this place, enough of our journey. I did not like Anna's absorption in the papers. I wanted her to look up at me and smile. But she did not.

'Anna –'

She was still mouthing to herself. I leaned over her and looked down at the paper. It was an indecipherable mass of whorls and scribbles and crossings out. 'What is it Anna?' She shook her head at me impatiently and returned to the page. It's exercising an unhealthy control over her, I thought. It's making her eyes bright in the wrong way. What was it Meg had said . . . 'It's a big, horrible, evil story and it will control you.' I remembered Rick's expression in the hall that evening. 'It's my story Jamie and keep your grubby little hands out of it.' And I felt the quiet chill at my back that meant Ezekiel was near. That if I didn't do something, pull this girl up by the hand and run out of this foul-smelling place and into the daylight, he would be with me again and I would be banished from myself, a figure in somebody else's story. I don't want to be in somebody else's story, real or imagined. I don't want to be the object, I want to be the subject please. I don't want to have to think about this. 'Anna, let's go –' I pulled at her sleeve. She turned up to look at me then but at first it was as if she did not see me. When at last she recognized my face it did not interest her. Her attention was compelled by something stronger. She was, as they say, miles away. But that expression's wrong. It was time that separated us, and not just the time between her youth and mine. Not merely a question of decades. But time in the raw – the sort of thing that falls between me and the memory of my father, makes him fainter and fainter with each minute, like a ghost at the approach of morning. 'What are you reading? Can't we go?' She shook her head.

'No,' she said. Then again, 'No.'

'Can you read that?

'Bits of it, it's hard.'

'Is it Clarke's shorthand?'

'It . . . looks like it, but. . .'

'But what?'

She put the papers down and brushed her hands through her hair. The dust rose in a shower about her face – a halo in the light from the window. 'It's . . . someone's playing a joke on us. That's all. A joke.'

'What do you mean?'

'I mean it can't be true.' There was silence in the room.

'Can we go please, Anna?'

'Only,' she said, 'if we take these papers with us.' Her voice was curiously hard as she said this, and her eyes glittered, but not with lust or amusement. I read desire in her expression but it was a desire for something that would not satisfy, that would only create a greater need. And that glitter would narrow to a point until there was nothing left in her eyes but a hard, untouchable light. 'No one'll know,' she said, 'don't look so bloody wet. Come on, Jamie. Come *on*.'

Her voice was shrill with excitment. I asked no more questions but followed her back down the gloomy corridors of the College. Daylight, I thought, will dissolve this feeling. Let us just get out into the day, where reason will rule our judgement. But I knew I reached for this thought too hard, like a man who has lost his way on a mountain and prosecutes his route with a ferocity and singleness of purpose that are, in truth, only a compensation for the fact that he feels as alone and helpless as a child abandoned by its parents in a dark house, inhabited by ghosts, demons and the stuff of bad dreams.

Of how and Why I came to bee of the Companie of the NEW MODELLE, that was raised by the Parliament in the yeare of oure Lorde 1645, it would weary the Reader to relate. For this my Last Deposition before my Execution is intended, nott as a Generalle Historie of the late Warres but a sober and Earnest consideration of things which were of Direct Matter to mee, that therebye I may bee granted the light of his Countenance, synce I am *sorely Confused and sett about & do nott know how I have done the Things which I have done, nor which of them were Righteousness in God's sight nor which loathsome and to bee Abominated.* Otheres may at their leisure Relate the Trialls and Circumstances of oure Age – though I bee sure their Accounts bee Partiall – and it may bee the PROTECTOR will have it soe all ages sound onlie to His Tune and no other Relation may bee Tendered of these Years – but for myselfe I goe aboutt to Question my particular Sinne and the Traps and snares that have *led mee to the dust yea to eat the bread of lamentation and to know myselfe nott.*

Trade was at that Time, when my Margaret was led to her Execution, so Distressed and Confused that there were Few of us in the Village got meat enough. So it was that my eldest son was Taken Sicke *and still the lamentation of the countrie increased and there was no Respite from it.* For the Parliament, as wee heard sent a Delegation to the Kinge at Oxford to seeke a Treatie from Him but he received them most Scornfully & on everie Side wee heard it went nott well for the Parliament and wee were much afrayde the Cavaliers were at hande. Now then, although I prayed much with Mr *Morris* and talked with Him, and hee assures mee my Margaret has made her Peace with Almighty God and that for Her his Mercies shall bee Tendered, still in my Hearte I kept close the Thought to *have a Care of those who would sett up Idols and Worship mere Shadowes of the Living God.* And that the Devill had more Waies to Tempt us than wee could Imagine, nor knew wee Yet how hee went about his Workes but if was for us to spy out the Times, to keep our counselle and *to wait and listen for the Voyce of God* as the *Cooperites* believe. And so was my Fellowship with *Morris no meer Feigning* but the waie I had alwaies followed, which is as was taught mee by my Master and Mr Passmore – to bee Acquainted with Corruption and to know it nott, to Clasp Evill to my Breaste and keep clean Handes withal.

I was joyned with *Morris and some fewe* otheres of the Village, not long after these things had come to pass, and went with them to Sir Richard Maplake's troop that were raysed up, which was at the Time that my Lord Fairfax was entrusted with the commission of a Reformed and Regenerated Armie for the

Parliament. For the troops of my Lord of Essex, it was said were long past anie Stomach for the fight. Although in Truth the matter of oure Joyning was little Debated in the village synce all well saw that *to go Gladlie to the ARMIE was to fight the Lorde's Cause* which when I heard Mr Morris argue it I was much moved. And yet I could not find Fellowship with Him as I perswaded myselfe I must, nor entirely bee at Peace when hee spake, which troubled my Conscience and made mee think of that Rebellion that had led my *Margaret* into the Case in which shee found Herselfe. And my three sonnes I left with the wife of Mr Smith for I could nott care for them & in their features saw onlie my *Margaret*, which was of great Sorrow to mee. But wee went with Sir Richard to St Alban's on Easter Daie, to accompanie his Cavalrie for four of us there, at that Time, were horsed and equipped by Sir Richard, neither did it cause us anie amazement, for there were in this Armie, styled *the New Modelle* – Tanners who yet were Captains of Horse & Major Generalles of humbler stature than those they Commanded. And as wee rode there Sir Richard tells us oure Duties and wee wondered at the Condition of such a Troop, where there was no Insistence on Rank and Condition but an earnest and Honest Address to the Laboures before us. And, though I did not choose it, yet I rode with Mr *Morris*, who was greatly in Sir Richard's Favoure.

Now at that time the partie of the King was in the NORTH-ERN PART OF THE Kingdom, although in the West of the countrie Hee and his Allies had sett up agaynst city after City & it was decided wee should march towards *Taunton* to relieve Colonel Blake, that held that city agaynst the Cavaliers. But as wee commenced our Journey, you would nott have thought that wee had anie purpose but to admire the Spring. For on each tree were white and yellow Blossom so that if one should ask mee now 'You sir, Were you at, as I have heard the siege of *Taunton*?' and pose mee such and such a question as to the mannere of oure taking the town, I should answere him I saw but little of the fight, but have in my Memorie naught but Hawthorn Blossom and the Voyce of this same *Morris* that rode beside mee and never let a ride goe bye without hee talks of *Hell and Damnation* and of how there may be Cavalier upon us at the Nexte Turning. At which I was much Distressed – for then it was I sought to ask myself – though I kept *plain counsell* of it – whether it was that Sinne was a shadowe – as the Cooperites believe – and that *the punishment of Sinne after the Flesh is but of the flesh and but as Sinne itself synce it is in the Thought the Erroure lies and wee are, after the Flesh, as nothing, as Water that One may heare across a Fielde in a Stream or as the late Snowe that melts with the Sun at Easter.* For if I had nott left my Master, and *yoked myselfe – for so the Cooperites term anie marriage – how should my Margaret have been led into Sinne? And as for Her I could nott beare the Thought of it, of what shee had become, both bodie and Soule, synce shee had owned Herselfe the Devill's, but Mr Morris delighted in conversing of the wondrous waies in which Satan had done his work even upon my Virtuous Margaret, for Wickednesse that goeth about in the guise of Vertue was ever one of his themes, whether in or out of Church. As though, each lane was in Mr Morris's Parish and every bird on everie Tree there, but to swell his Congregation.*

Thus it was that I thought mee how if I had done a Wickednesse in lust for her and marrying her after the Flesh and shee had so been led into the Devill's worke – had not this same Morris, in condemning her after the Bodie been most abominably of this world in which wee are but Travellers, nay nott Judges or Governours, for in them is Corruption synce they sett up their Face agaynst the Lord's government? And as I turned these things in my mind and Mr Morris discoursed still I could nott find it in my Hearte to love him even though wee Fought side by side and with each Mile hee swears hee is my *Onlie Brothere in Christ.*

Now at Blandford a part of us are called awaie with my Lord Fairfax to Oxford, and a smaller troop for the Relief of Taunton. And it chanced Sir Richard Maplake would have this Running Lecturer with him to bee of my Lord Fairfax's Partie and I am for Taunton, which pleased mee much as the discouse of this Morris troubled mee and I knew him nott whether hee were Friend or Tormentor, which is all the Vice of the Present Time, synce wee find ourselves in Alliance that are liable to bee broke asunder the daie they Form and Nothing but corruption and the loss of Blisse, bee permanent. And as hee rides awaie with my Lorde, his Nutt Visage turning this waie and that lest *Prince Rupert* leap upon him from the nexte culvert, I shooke my Heade and wondered at the Things were past, missing my Master Nehemiah sorely and saying 'This people draw night unto mee with their mouth & honour mee with their Lips; but their Hearte is far from Mee. But in vain do they worshippe mee, teaching for Doctrines the Commandments of Men.' So was hee gone past the Bende in the Hill & I and my Fellowes were sett on the Road for the relief of Taunton and Sir Robert Blake, who had now unthatched the Howses of the town to feed his Horses, and made Matchlock out of Bedlinen for his Muskets.

And when wee came to Taunton, the smoke of her houses that Burned was seen for miles in the Countrie round. But I saw no sign of anie Battell, synce the Royalists took us for the whole my Lord FAIRFAX's Armie and were gone before wee came there, and made welcome by the governour of that Towne who hath said that *he will eat his Bootes rather than surrender*.

But in two Daies wee turned about and soe began oure Journey agayne, rather as a Sheep that hath fallen awaie and now seeks the Flock agayne wee followed in my Lord Fairfax's footsteps. But as the Scripture has it *how shall ye find agayne the path that ye have forsaken yea I have made the waie plain but ye are in a Strange lande and know it nott*. For when wee came to Oxford hee was gone from there as was hee also from Newport Pagnell and Stonie Stratford so that wee wandered across the Land like Israelites, and were – though I shall nott tell the circumstances here – much troubled with the *Clubmen* that were a group of gentlemen neither for the King nor for the Parliament but for themselves and what they hadd. For so it is that Dissension breeds a Shortage of Pitie for anie person or thing that seems nott to Serve our Pleasure, whereat I rejoyce greatlie I was of a companie that, though it fought its Battles after the flesh yet it fought for God and for God's Victorie and sought onlie His Kingdome on earth. Though I dare say I speak nott of its Commanders of which I shall speak more of *my Lord* will let mee write, synce my eie is tired and my hands weak from where the Officers of the PROTECTOR have bound them.

And indeed, though it may make those that think all Warres and Generalles run as *the greased Wheel of a Carte* to smile and shake their Heads, when wee came upon the Village of Louther, near Daventrie in the early part of the June of that year, wee Rested – *'For,' says Major Loomas*, our Commander, 'I know nott *where my Lord Fairfax may be.'* And so wee staied there as hee gathered Intelligences of the people, and Instructed us to Plunder nott – as did the Welsh at Leicester – nor *ravish* anie women of the Town, as did a Captaine of the King's Armie at Oxford, who was hanged for the offense *for* says hee I come nott to fight for your Cause but for youre halfcrowne and your pretty woman.

Now each evening as wee were Quartered there I walked out on a hill that was nearby from where I could look down into the plain below over and agaynst the escarpment that Rises up above Market Harborough. And there often times in the evening I sate alone and Marvelled at the Courses of my Life and of how it was I was come here, alone & I bethought mee also of the Triall and Deathe of my Wife and how it was shee was ensnared by the Devill and whether it bee Just or Reasonable to *meddle with those things that bee Satan's* or *to take the othere waie from the Man in Black* as the Cooperites counselle. And I asked the Lord in my hearte which was Truth and whether I had taken part with Godlie and Just Persons or *supped with Hypocrites and dissemblers.* But though I asked him the Lorde spake nott to me then. And so I wondered to the edge of that Hill. And saw what first I took to bee a Vision.

For there below mee I saw a Sighte like unto two great Rivers of Silver that flowed towards each other across the Plaine. Yea it was as if all the King's Plate had melted in a Furnace and Broke the Confinements of his Treasure House, or as if some SEA WAVE had coursed past the Land's defences and rode through town and village on the flat lands that Bordered on the Ocean, swallowing all that lay before it. And the last raies of the Sun caught the Silver of the Helmets and the swords there winked and Glinted back to the evening Sky and I saw that these two great Rivers were Rivers of Men, like to a huge Insect that Devoures, that can bee Split or Cutt at and will still Rise agayne and Flow on. And from this Silver Creature – this Great Flow of Light that was like unto a *Volcano* the Mountayne that will belch forth Fire, there came, there, as I listened alone upon that Hill, a great shout like to the noise of an Angel and lifted I up mine eie and I did see an angel above that great Host that was clothed in Pure white Linen & having his breast girded with golden girdle

& hee said in a Loud Voyce *'Fear God and Give Glorie to Him; for the Houre of his judgement is come; and worship thou Him that made Heaven and Earth and the Sea and the Fountains of theaters.'* And as I watched the Angel stretched outt his Hande and from the poyntes of his fingeres there flowed forth Light yea so much light that it was exceedingly sweet and the Brightness of it Dazzled mine Eie and I fell upon my knees and when I looked agayne there were manie about mee that raysed mee up and spake to mee and I saw below that this was indeed no Showe or Vision. For though the Angel was gone from mee yet one that was neer mee, that was from our troop, says 'Yonder below is the Armies of General Cromwell and of Lord Fairfax that meet together on yonder Plaine and I dare sweare there are upwards of 15,000 men that meet together there. And surely when wee meet the Armies of the King wee shall have the Victorie.' At which I fell once more into a Swoon and the Angel spake agayne to mee and I saw His Face in the clouds above us as wee watched though the otheres saw it nott. And from His finger came forth once agayne a beam of light and it travelled across that plaine that was below us on the escarpment where wee lodged and then those that were with mee saw it also and fell to their knees and Praysed God for the Sight of it. And over the land as a mighty column of Light as that Beacon that went Before the Israelites through the Desert, so went the hand of the Angel and the Light that it brought until it came to rest upon the village on the far side of that Plaine and there the Light Staied and I heard a Voyce that said *'Praise Him and Bless His Holy Name and be ye Thankful that the Lord is with Ye and hath taken upon Himself thy Sinnes and made Thine Enemies to bow down before Thee. Holy holy holy is the Lord and Blessed are His People so then Goe Ye Forth and bee nott afraid of thine enemies for soon Ye shall have the Victorie.'*

And I asked one that was neer to mee how was the Village called where the light of the angel's fingere Rested and he saith unto mee – 'NASEBY.'

... confessing this night my most secret thoughts, I do
bethink me of the night, July, last when I first saw the Lord
Protector in the company of the hags who were later taken
at the Assize of Northampton. They were close by to the
river, near to the stairs below the Tower and my Lord
Protector's face was most horribly transformed by the compact he had undertaken with the Infernal Powers, much as
I do recall at our dreadfull Covenante the night of the
King's execution, at which the Imps attendant on Earl
Cromwell, as he was likely to be styled at Our Sabbats –
namely, Pleasantry, Artfull Dealing and the Jackie the
Morrow. 'Stay' I said to him then and hee, seeming not to
hear or see me turned and with a most Aweful Voice tells
me of the Affair at Chelmsford, where many of the Witches
taken were our Creatures and could, were they so minded,
give Names and Times when put to the Torture, as they
will be most certainly, synce Hopkins is of the Business.
Still – truly is it said – the Affairs of a Great and Prosperous
Nation, as Oures, are no matters for Statesmen or Political
Intelligences, but depend on a Higher and more Power-
fulle Influence – if wee are to Deal with a greater Danger
yet than Hopkins – I mean the Witchfinder of Essenden,
styled Oliphant – measures must be taken at Once and the
sternest proceedings against him taken. . .

I don't know whether that was quite how Anna transcribed
those pages we smuggled out of Worcester College that February day. I know, for example, that at first, she took to
improvising seventeenth-century spelling – to amuse herself –
and that when she came to the later stages of the manuscript she
put it into plain English. Neither joke spelling nor standard
English entirely succeeded in neutralizing the atmosphere gen-
erated by the document. It had the unpleasant fascination of the

transcript of some murder trial or the records of the killings of a psychopath. As I heard Anna talk about it or, later, read her transcriptions, I thought of Peter Sutcliffe hearing his voices by the gravestone, or of Nielsen killing those boys in his drab, surburban house. Evil is at once banal, hard to credit, and compelling, simply one more possibility for the only species to mate out of season, or to kill when not in need of food.

I can't remember now quite how the story unfolded, or whether Ezekiel had found some way of letting me know before Anna had even finished with Clarke's manuscript. How we acquire information is often as difficult to assess precisely as how we classify it when we have obtained it. At what stage – I hear you ask – did I 'believe' or 'not believe' what was in the Clarke Papers? I can't tell you. Belief is not such a simple or constant commodity – not for me anyway. Once upon a time I loved Meg, could never imagine loving anyone else or of not loving her. And now? I'm not sure. At nine in the morning I might have the Oliphant business set down for a fraud, a joke, and then later, some image from the papers would return to haunt me. Usually it was the picture of that Stafford woman hanged at Northampton, although sometimes her face would be blended with another picture, that of Margaret, Meg, Oliphant's wife, hanged at Essenden years before. And of course I could not control these pictures, any more than I could control Ezekiel – know quite when I would feel that chill at my back and hear that thin, wheedling voice in my ear.

I suppose I was losing control over everything, the way I felt out on the hills this morning. If I only knew what he wanted, what he was trying to tell me . . .

I get up from the table, cross to the window and look out at the garden and the quiet Oxfordshire landscape beyond. The sky is cerulean blue, there are fields of corn and sloping hills thick with trees. When I put my hand on the window sill the stone feels cold. Hold on to that. Later I will write down what happened on the hill this morning, and try and hold on to *that*.

> . . . I have beside mee the records of the Assize at North-
> ampton at which fifty-three witches were condemned to be
> hanged – one Pleadynge her belly with some success – and

194

read how it was that the first to die there, the woman named Stafford 'howled like a dog' in the court when the sentence was pronounced. Well may the Whore have howled! I have seen her and Three or Four Others in the company of the Protector and the Great Lords of the Army, Naked and displayed openly before the unbridled Lewdnesse of her Masters as they did handle her crying, and touching her most Secret and Privy Parts with 'Where is your God in Heaven? Or in earth, aloft or below or doth he sit in the clouds or where doth he sit with his arse?' And for that the women Stafford was marked as to her body with the very extremity of my Lord Protector's lust, he had ordered her to be so taken up and Sacrificed to those same Devilish Powers whence shee came. O how they screamed in the cart on the way to their Deaths, calling that there was no Love or Justice or Reason in this World, when Great Ones are so Allied to the Principles of Darknesse! And what did their cries seem but the Ravings of Witches who befoul all Noble and Recognized Principles of Authority to support their Own Foulnesse and Shame! But what disturbs mee much is that wee have had to employ Oliphant in this Businesse and that he be now privy to much that is Secret in our Counsels. How to proceed against such a Man? – who seems, in all our estimations to be a most Resourcefull and Cunning Seeker out of the Devil and his Workes, a very Magician himself, who, though hee be laid out and quartered before a Crowde by daylight would yet return at night with this 'What of this Master Clarke?' and his 'Nay but for shame My Lord Protector' and his voice like a wife that hath long lain sourly apart from her husband, curdled in her own misery . . .

It was my Ezekiel they were talking about, although I dared not tell Anna that. And I recognized other things about the Clarke manuscripts – apart from the fact that Anna seemed unable to say how or when they had been faked, if they had been faked, and that they were *quite definitely* at least two hundred years old – and that was the screams of those condemned to die through ignorance, cruelty and the malevolence of those set in authority over us. When I read the detailed description of the Stafford woman's death, I thought of Bukharin brought screaming out of his cellar to be shot, of Röhm shot in bed with his lover one morning, of any man or woman who lived and died by a principle that is, in the light of history, not a principle at all but a trick of the light, a gross error.

And who the hell, as Anna pointed out, would have the skill and time (if it was a forgery it was done by somebody who knew a great deal about the period, and about the Clarke MSS in particular) and the *will* to fabricate such an elaborate hoax? Our friend at the college was no help. As far as he was concerned the James Trunk had been lying there undisturbed, apart from the occasional visit by a bored antiquary, for three hundred years.

'Ron Oliphant didn't have the time to fake this,' said Anna, 'and it is *not* a twentieth-century effort anyway. It was probably reading it that sent him off his trolley.' 'What'll it do to us then?' I said. She grinned at me and cast her eyes down primly. 'Get us hot,' she said, 'Make us Most Full of Luste and Lewdnesse and the Urge to Concupiscence!'

And of course, in spite of those who, like Meg, would like to see lust as a healthy expression of love, there is a close and unpleasant relation between sexual excitement and the torture, cruelty and queasily erotic charade of the witchfinder. Back then, in 1650, the lucky bastards were ignorant of this fact and so could get on with the business of torturing, strangling and prying around the private parts of local women with absolutely no guilt whatsoever. Not so us. Haunted by Freud and his friends, only too dimly aware of the inescapable marriage of pornography and violence, we torture ourselves with images of women in black knickers, swinging from ropes, their faces distorted with what might almost be lust.

. . . under torture, Stafford, it is said by some, revealed to Oliphant what my Lord Protector had done to her and to the Suffolk Witches, Meg Nutting, Martha Houldey and also to the woman hanged at Essenden that was Oliphant's wife, and many of us were in feare that shee shoulde, at the houre of her death make such matters plain but it is clear shee was so weakened by the torture that shee was scarce able to stand or speak in the cart that took her to the gallowes. Except that – as the rope was put around her neck the woman hoist her skirts and, tearing aside her undergarments began to Swear most Abominably saying, as she exposed her belly to the hangman 'There. See where my Lord has marked mee. There. See where he has put His mark' – All the while exposing her privities to those about her, who took her words to mean nothing but that she did Confesse her horrible compact with the Evil One. . .

Sometimes I think that he won't come again. That he has confused me so thoroughly that he will not need to. That he is in me all the time now, that I carry him like a disease, and the healthier and freer I feel the more he is working his way through me, no longer needing the Gothic apparatus of possession to make his claim. If only he had said. If only he had made it clear what he wanted instead of picking me up and using me, making my hands and voice and eyes do things they did not want to do.

Whoever was working me this morning – it wasn't me. That's all. Let me write it down. That was always the method I used. And for years it worked. I was able to spell away my terrors and my longings – and if what I wrote wasn't, for the most part, much more than a compromise, at least it bought me peace of mind. I'll write it down.

I have not been out of the house since I came here. Partly because, if I am the Beast of Putney, they will probably have pictures of me at all the local police stations with HAVE YOU SEEN THIS MAN! underneath them. But this morning I couldn't stay inside any longer. I could feel the heat outside as soon as I threw off the covers. When I went to the window and looked down at the garden. The long grass, the bed of roses by the stone wall, the wooden garden seat with one strut missing, waited in the cool shadows of the morning for the violence of July at noon. Already, on the road beyond the house, the sun was stretching itself like some great, not quite tamed animal.

My father's cottage stands alone on a minor road that leads out of Shierston Village. There is a small front garden and a more elaborate affair at the back. After breakfast (black coffee and an apple) I went out down the front path, and, looking carefully up and down the road, turned up towards the church. There was no one in sight but even so, I scurried up to Hammerson's field, where the footpath begins. I didn't feel entirely safe until I was off the road. 'Hey you – you, sir! Aren't you the Beast of Putney?' 'Who? Me? No no no. I'm *a* beast of Putney, but not the actual Beast, no.'

Beyond the shed in Hammerson's field, where Hammerson keeps a couple of tractors, hay bales, and anything else he can't get into the barn, the path winds back towards the village and then turns sharply up a hill over in the direction of the Stratford Road. As I came down through the meadow grass, bright with poppies, that marks the beginnings of Copper's land the crickets sang mechanically in the growing heat, the river shone over to my left, and suddenly it was as it was when I came here as a child with my father, in the days before guilt and stupidity and carelessness marked my passage towards middle age.

It was the weather that fooled me. Blame it on July. Just as I came into Stoke Bewley, the next village down from us, I turned off the path on to the road. I don't think I believed, at that moment, that I *had* done anything in London. It seemed incompatible with the light and the grass and the cornflower blue of the sky. Ezekiel seemed a long way away. If I was dreaming of anything I was dreaming of my father, walking with him on such a day as this, perhaps up this very stretch of road, his voice deep and droll and resigned. 'This way boy. Don't dawdle boy. This way . . .'

I looked up and saw two men in the uniform of Cromwell's army. They were jogging along easily on two gigantic horses, neither of them talking, in brown jerkins, steel helmets and the yellow sashes of the Parliament. I looked past them to see if Ezekiel was anywhere around (I didn't picture him on a horse – I rather fancied he would be in a cart of some description) but there was no sign of him.

Of course, I thought, he doesn't need to show himself now. He plays tricks with my world as and when he likes. He's not in me. No? I'm in his world. Fine. But if this is the way you wish it, Master Witchfinder, I am cognizant of What hath been done in your Name and Unafraid of Thee or Thy Hellish Practices. And if it comes to a showdown, squire, I can probably make a good living predicting the future. Telling them who is going to win the battle of Naseby. Telling them to get to Marston Moor *and fast*. Mind you – one accurate prediction and I will probably have Ezekiel putting his hand down my trousers and looking for the marks of the devil on my privies.

If it is an hallucination, I thought, I had better outface it. There was no one around but me and these two Parliamentarians. I had better show them that I was not ashamed or afraid of them. I began to walk boldly towards them, deliberately catching the eye of the one nearest to me. He had a fleshy face, a drinker's complexion, and his hands, idling with the reins of his horse, were decorated with three or four large gold rings. If he was surprised to see someone in a pair of white jeans that were not about to become fashionable until over three hundred years later, he showed no sign of it. Nor did he look perturbed by my Fruit of the Loom T-shirt, my plimsolls or my glasses. Perhaps, I thought, he simply cannot see me. I am in his world, but invisible, a ghost, the way Ezekiel is to others when he visits me.

If I was a ghost then it was certainly the case that it was better to see one than to be one. There was none of the chill or the foreboding I felt when Ezekiel visited me. I felt as normal as ever I did in between what the doctor called 'the attacks'. In fact I felt vaguely pleased that at long last I was back there, in the period – I had read so much about. The flowers were the same. The grass was the same grass. Could it be that I was about to be introduced to William Clarke, Secretary of the Army Council (perhaps he was the one on the left), and before being dumped back in 1986, forge an addendum to his minutes of the Army Council at Putney in 1647? In fact, was I in the plot of a Steven Spielberg movie, adapted for British tastes?

As I drew close to them they still did not look down, and, deciding I had better take the initiative, I bowed low and said 'Good morrow Masters. Whither away this fine summer's day? Might I crave your good conduct to Master William Clarke that was of the Army Council that I may impart to him Intelligence above and Beyond his Powers of Discernment? I pray your assistance and do declare myself most heartily of Your Party and of all those that take arms against the Man of Blood, Charles Stuart.'

I thought this was a fairly good effort. They might well, I reckoned, take my outfit for some kind of clown's costume. Or perhaps they would think I was a member of some very, very obscure but ideologically OK Puritan sect: the Grunters perhaps, or the Eighth Day Repentance Specialists. Still neither of them spoke. Then I realized the fat one was leaning down in the saddle, his face distorted with hatred. For a moment I thought he was about to hit me and then his companion leaned across, and with his hand on his arm, said in a clipped, contemptuous tone, 'Let him be.'

I was fairly certain, now, that I was the hallucination and not him. Or if he was a hallucination he wasn't one of mine. Everything about these two men, their hair, their features – one thin, one bloated – everything suggested a quality often found missing in my fictional characters: recognizable humanity. I backed away, slowly. 'This,' I said, 'is some doing of the Witchfinder. He that was late at Essenden and at the Assize of Northampton. I would crave I spake with Master Clarke of him.' The fatter of the men, still looking at me with a kind of weary hatred, leaned down in this saddle and spat on the ground contemptuously. Once again his companion put out his arm. I noticed that the two of them were both wearing swords.

Why hadn't the landscape changed? Surely north Oxfordshire in 1650, if this was 1650, would be unrecognizable? Was this after or before the Enclosure Acts? Shouldn't I be taking Polaroid photographs to show to the Faculty of History at Oxford? Shouldn't I be seeking out a few gentry and asking them whether they were rising or declining? Should I try and find out if Charles were still alive, and if so, what he thought of C. V. Wedgewood's biography of him?

Slowly Jamie. Slowly. This is for real. It's OK. You can't feel him anywhere near, can you? No. He doesn't need to be. But this is easier in a way. He isn't in your head now – he's just showing you things – phantasms, dreams, images. Outface them. That's all you need to do. At least you are in control of yourself. The two riders had sat back in their saddles and were moving off down the road (yes the road was still tarmac but at any minute, I thought crazily, it will shed its skin and, before my eyes, dissolve into a muddy track, the same path that wound this way three hundred and fifty years ago). I shouted after them. 'To what Battle, Masters, may I ask, do you now Betake yourselves? What conflict in the Civil Tumult claims the attention of your sword and Hand?'

They turned back at me, blank now rather than contemptuous. Perhaps I was fading for them, the way Ezekiel did to me. I didn't like the idea of fading, of gutting out, and so I almost shouted, 'Where are the King's forces now disposed?'

The fat man spoke. He had a thick, ugly voice, with something of a west country accent. But there again, it could have been Suffolk. Didn't Cromwell recruit his New Model from the eastern Counties?

'Edge Hill,' he said flatly. They turned from me and were gone.

Of course. We're only a few miles from Edge Hill in the Cottage. I think my father once took me over the site of the battle. From my memory of it, it was a two-all draw. Was there some advice I could give them as to tactics? Perhaps, if I teamed up with a few senior men, I might manage to ingratiate myself with the top brass. Except, of course, that I could remember absolutely fuck all about Edge Hill. All I knew was that the two sides hacked at each other and rode off in different directions. The one time in my life when my knowledge of seventeenth-century history might have been of some conceivable use they have to land me in a battle I know nothing about. Now if this was Waterloo, no problem. 'Napoleon,' I would say, 'the Prussians are coming.' He would thank me for that, afterwards. If this was the invasion of Poland by the Wehrmacht I know just what I'd say: 'Adolf, don't do it. No good will come of it.' But Edge Hill. What about Edge Hill? Who cares about Edge Hill? Who cares about English history, come to that? Or England? The way things are, even if I manage to alter the course of the battle no one will even notice. England is a closed system. Even breaking the time barrier causes little excitement.

It was only when I got to the hill that I realized, however, that if I was not the hallucination (and people seemed, albeit unwillingly, to engage in conversation with me), then was in the grip of a very large-scale affair, as far as hallucinations go. My imagination was not merely working overtime on one half-created character but springing unnanounced, epic events on me – off-the-peg costume dramas, all ready to go. Below me, on the road into the next village, was a troop of twenty or thirty horsemen, and a line of foot soldiers, carrying muskets on their shoulders. At the head of the column was a tall, good-looking young man, bareheaded, holding up a sword that, as I watched, caught the sunlight and winked in silver to the surrounding countryside.

No no no, I thought. This is the sort of thing I never describe. War is not my forte. There must be some mistake. As I thought this, on the skyline behind the line of soldiers I saw a red estate car. Or did I? The soldiers (all in yellow sashes) did not turn and cry 'Behold Masters an engine of strange and wonderful contrivance!' Although for a brief instant the sound of the engine was clearly audible, I did not hear so much as a 'Zounds' from the Cromwellians marching towards me. And then the car – if indeed it was a car, and not some fading image of the modern left on my retina from an earlier world – disappeared from view and did not re-emerge.

I looked at the village on the brow of the next hill. From here, all I could see was the square-towered church and the row of thatched cottages. The square modern houses where the farm workers live are hidden tastefully behind the trees, so as not to offend the susceptibilities of the green-wellingtoned morons who live in the thatched cottages. Much of the landscape round here has little of the twentieth century about it anyway. The car did not reappear. The soldiers kept on coming. This, I thought, is it: like the hero of Ronald Welch's *The Gauntlet*, I have dropped through a hole in time and found myself on the brink of the battle of Edge Hill. And if I know anything about anything, Ezekiel has something to do with this. What if, as well as managing the trick of reappearance in the twentieth century, he decided to restage the events of his life? To use me to disturb the way things happened for him? He might well have been a foot soldier at Edge Hill, might he not?

I looked down the line of soldiers. It didn't take me long to find him. He was at the back of the column. For a moment I did not recognize him without the black coat and doublet and white ruff. He had no beard either. But even in the strange uniform of the Army, at this distance I was sure it was him. He was ten or fifteen yards behind the rest of the soldiers, his musket on his shoulders, and his thin face seemed more innocent, less loaded with guilt. Of course. This was (when was the fucking battle of Edge Hill?) 1643? – 1645? Earlier than the witch business anyway. Or hadn't Rick said that 1643 was the year in which Ezekiel had had his wife topped? Perhaps I was being sent back to 1643 (assuming we were in 1643 – oh what was the fucking date of the battle of Edge Hill?) in order to stop him getting involved in witchcraft and witch finding. Perhaps this young and innocent-looking Ezekiel on the road below me is or was, my tenses are hopelessly confused – about to be redeemed by me and it was for this reason he appeared to me that day in Anna's flat and later on when he really tore at me don't want to think about that that's why of course I must go down there and talk to him and he won't know I'm a visitor from another time because there has to be free will although everything is planned there has to be will so we feel we have control whereas we don't of course we just stagger on blindly till we die knowing fuck all about anything even the date of the fucking battle of Edge Hill.

Get Ezekiel. Get him on his own. Get him away from the others and warn him: 'Have naught to do with Witches Master Oliphant I pray you. I am from another time far in the future and I bring Thee Newes which may change the course of Thy history!' I couldn't see it somehow. Whatever I did with the delivery I was going to sound like the Angel Gabriel in a bad Nativity play.

Get off the road, Matheson. Now.

I ducked down and forced my way through a gap in the its thorns pulling at my T-shirt, scratching my bare arms. I found myself in a corn field, with only the blue sky, and a bird climbing in circles, high above me. I was sweating.

When I was sure I was at a safe distance I crouched down and waited for the line of men to pass. I heard the indistinguishable murmur of voices and the muffled percussion of horses' hooves, and saw the broken flashes of colour. How would I know Ezekiel when he passed? He would be well behind the others. There would be a gap, a few minutes when there would be just me in the corn and the hedge beyond and then a sound of footsteps. One man. Sounding sweeter, more natural than he does when he visits me now. Because he hasn't sinned yet. He hasn't murdered and lied and betrayed his wife to the hangman. There is a time when we know no crime. That was what he was trying to tell me, earlier and later. And that awful time, the horrible thing that happened at Whipps Cross – he wasn't trying to hurt me, he was trying to tell me. I waited. Sure enough, after a few minutes I heard the sound of footsteps. I can predict what will happen sometimes. I write it and it happens. I have that gift.

Ezekiel. Young Ezekiel. On his way.

Of course what had probably happened was this: Ezekiel had been in the Parliamentary Army. Something terrible had happened to him. When he returned to the village he found his wife had betrayed him. He went into the door of their hut or cottage or whatever they lived in and found her with her skirts up to her waist, her white legs clamped round Abel the Miller, pushing her buttocks into him, gasping and squirming and moaning 'Oh yes Abel yes Abel' or 'Oh yea Abel Thou dost love me so well' or maybe just a little gentle moan, like she was thawing – an 'Oh Oh Oh Oh' like the noise Anna made that time in the flat when I kissed her and held her brown body close to me why am I so guilty why do I want to turn back the clock and make it like it never happened why why why do I want to be ten again on this road with my hand in my father's and him saying 'Hold my hand I'm a stranger in paradise' why can't we turn back time why does the fucking clock go forwards, and so slowly?

I was at the hedge. Young Ezekiel was coming into view. He held his musket casually and kept his eyes on the road. I pulled back the hedge and whispered 'Ezekiel, Ezekiel.'

He stopped and looked at me. He didn't, like the other two men, look contemptuous or angry; he looked at me as if he had dreamed me. Perhaps he was dreaming me, I thought. Perhaps this was how all this started. 'Listen,' I said, 'I beseech you.' I had meant to talk to him in the language of the past, or what I thought of as that language, but as I spoke I lost all control of tone and mood, and in due course, of the sense of what I was saying. It made a kind of sense I suppose, but not the sense I wanted it to make. 'Master Oliphant,' I was saying, 'I have the most terrible intelligence to impart – for Time hath no Powere over our Immortall Qualities. Though I am here knowing something of your Past and of your Future, yet I can influence the same onlie as Others about you. *Beware*, Master Oliphant!'

He looked at me, his mouth open, and very slowly started to back away.

Why can't I get my tongue to obey me? What's the matter with you, Jamie? I was half-way through the hedge now. When I spoke again my voice sounded weak and piteous. 'I'm not very well,' I said, 'I'm not well in the head. Can you tell me something? Can you tell me?' He can't have been much more than nineteen. He's just a boy. He's scared. He's scared of the dark and of women. I'll talk to him. I spoke, slowly and clearly, as to a foreigner: 'Where am I? What century am I in? Am I dreaming you? Or are you dreaming me?' He didn't say a word. He turned and ran off down the road towards the rest of the soldiers as fast as he could. I ran after him, shouting. But I don't know what I shouted, or whether it made any kind of sense.

And of the battle that was called Naseby I saw much, for, the same night, Major Loomas calls to us and wee are to make haste to Joyne the forces of my Lord Fairfax and of General Cromwell. Now though I had been horsed when I left for the relief of Taunton, yet now, for a Cause it would weary mee to Relate, neither hath it anie bearing on this my testimonie, which is to concern myself with *how and why I have purposed to seek the Lord both after my Bodie and after my Soule and of whether these two Quests bee seekers after Different Endes and of how the Sinne and Miserie in which I have led myself and those close to mee aftere the Flesh hath anie hope of being Quit or Justified by oure Lorde which is in Heaven*, I had been constrained to joyn myself unto the foot when wee became one agayne with the Main force of oure Armie. And when wee came unto the Forces of the Parliament, I was given a pike and a Musket and pressed in under the service of Mr Skippon that was of the Trayne Bandes in London, and who, though he hath *a lewd manner* yet was a valiant and Christian soldier and calls us *Gentlemen and Fellow Soldiers* which pleased both gentlemen and soldiers.

And oure taske was, as hee informed us, to *seek out the High Ground* which all the Night that followed on that Vision wee did, though I dare swear none knew entirely where wee found ourselves but marched this waie and then that and felt our waie like Moles above Ground, until the sky was grey and then Red and, on a sudden, we Breasted an Incline and came upon the King's forces there before Us. Never have I seen soe manie Coloures – the Taffeta and Damask and Velevet & some amongst us saw their Banneres and Brightnesse and were afrayd for wee were Poor Men and Despised.

Wee drew ourselves up, the Foot in the Centre, & I looked across at their two Extremities – at the Left a Crowde of Fine Horses, that bucked and wheeled as at the Beginning of some Daie of Sportes, whose Banneres, held by the Morning Wind displaied themselves to us in *Norman* array. And one neer to mee says *Prince Rupert* is on their Right Wing, at which I look to my left, but it being then but nine of the morning – oure Scoutes having sighted them a full houre or more before – wee were all still making shift to prepare oureselves. For on oure left side was a thicke Hedge which ran from where GENERALL IRETON had his position across to the line helde by Prince Rupert's cavalrie. This and the winde, which was from the NorthWest and some-what agaynst us, was all that lay in their Favour and Generall Cromwell, as wee disposed ourselves puts Colonel Okey and his dragoons aside the hedge that they may fire into the Prince when hee makes his charge. 'Though,' said some that were neer to mee, that had been at the battle at *Marston*, 'hee will *smoke a pipe or two ere hee come at uss.*' And as wee waited and the worde was given – which on oure part was 'God is oure Strength' wee shook ourselves agaynst the morning for that Countrie is well watered and Marsh and the *ground was less sure than oure Cause.* Wee of the foote were close in the Centre.

And as I looked out at the Lines of the Enemie I saw a Figure some Yardes ahead of mee to my Right Side that Railed upon the Forces opposed agaynst Us, though I saw, as hee spake, his Eie popped as if hee sought some waie to quit his Position, though hee could nott, so closely were the Foot pressed about him. And I saw this was that same *Morris*, for whom the Cavaliers were now *no meer Phantome or Shadowe* but verily before him in the flesh and I bethought mee hee liked it nott. Then came there – it was, I think, at about eleven of the clock – a cry from the King's Forces & from oure left came Rupert's Horse which confounded those who said that hee might stay his Hande. But on hee came, as merrily as to a wedding, and wee were much afrayde at the calls from them which were all of 'Queen Mary' & of the sound of their Horse but stood our Ground prayerfully and called out 'God be with Us'. But still they came.

And then, though the dragoons let fly upon them, Prince Rupert's horse breaks our lines and all to my left is Confusion, for all the Horse is shattered and some fewe of oure Foot break and take themselves awaie from us as they would runne cleare to Northampton. The King's foot came at us across the Ditch that lay between Us and upon our heads brake a wave of Musket shot and a smell I never had caught before, which some that had been a great while in the Armie say is *how ye may know a Battell*. For it is a soure smell, sharp and dry and yet it smells of the Earth too where to it calls the Unlucky. 'They fire . . .' calls one to the side of mee, and up ahead I saw this *Skippon* that was late of the Trayne Bandes, take a ball clear through his armoure. And yett hee did not falter but turns to us and calls above the Noyse that wee are to Presse forwarde neither to bee amazed for God will grant us the Victory.

And though I may have Cause to curse hee who has led mee to the case in which I find myself, yet I owne this Cromwell to bee a brave man, who though hee may be possessed of those qualities the Devill himself hath sought in Man, and though when the Devill had had him in thrall yea hee has worked as Beelzebub and all the Minions of Hell – as I will relate – yet that daie when he led out his Horse agaynst the King's left, where was Sir Marmaduke Langdale, I dare swear wee were fain to cheer at this Adventure. For hee came on steady and sure and like unto the Hammer of God which Stryketh at the Wicked and the King's Horse held themselves but barely, like a lazy Wave that seeks to breakupon the shore but dare nott, since there bee soe manie behind will fall upon it. And wee took Hearte and faltered nott but pressed on as Master Skippon bade us.

Now as wee closed with Them the presse was so thick there

were manie where I found myselfe, that were hard pressed to cutt their way & indeed *wee were more at the mercie of those that advanced than those sett agaynst us.* For wee were borne on and cutt at what was Before us without thought, onlie seeking the light that lies in the othere side of the Line. And soe the two of us – for wee were agaynst the *Welsh* that called in their language to us and stabbed and swore most Frightfuylly, twisted and turned like dancers in the grip of a BEARE soe hard pressed were wee. And as Prince Rupert rides past us down into the Field, to turn agayn, one fellow before mee is Hacked by one Welshman and from his Neck there comes a Gout of Blood, that swells up and out like a Flower that hath one daie to Bloom, and his Fellow calls upon his God to Release him from this his tribulation at which I am come face to face with hee who quit him, a great tall *Welshman, in his hand a long knife.* AT which I thought I was *like to bee his Heifer* untill one behind mee pushes mee on – though I had wished myselfe awaie and I catch this Welshman clean in the stomach and he falls. But I saw him nott where hee lay for I was carried on and sudden the ground ahead of mee is cleare and none there save one of oure Foot soldiers that lies on the Marsh, face up to the sky. Someone hath gone to work on his Face, and nott borne to finish the Worke for his Chinne was all but cutt awaie and though hee made piteouslie to moan no sounds comes from his Lips synce hee was *carved like a joynte* below the lips. And when I looked I saw it was this *Morris.*

Verily is oure Feare of death the thing wee feare and nott the Passing from this World, where there is no Comfort for the Virtuous nor sleep for the wearie not Justice for those who hunger after it. And this *Morris* that feared soe much the enemie, now hee is laid low by them, and his Face cutt awaie most Terribly, can feare no Longer, but, in between cries and whispers for Mercie, slowly comes to Peace, synce what hee feares has come to pass and lo it must bee as God commandes it neither shall ye set yourselves to choose the manner of your Death nor do aught but Yield to the Manner of your going from Hence. As I came up by Him hee breathed no more and knew mee nott and though I had sorrowed much and Questioned much, at his Insistence, and though in Him was the Cause of much sorrowe to mee, both at myself, for what I took to bee my Sinne and at my Margaret who was led astray, yet felt I nothing at his Death. Nay neither *did I rejoyce at the passing of an Enemie nor did I grieve as at the passing of one I had loved and soe was it borne in upon mee that all Concerne of oure Flesh is butt Shadowe and Inconstant Play of Light before Us.* And I raged on up the Field and saw Men come past mee but now they stayed nott, but as wee looked across at oure Right hande sawe Sir Marmaduke Langdale's horse break line and turn and runne for Leicester. And to right and left now whole companies of Welsh gave themselves up to us and cast awaie their Weapons but I ran on up the ridge, for all that was in my Hearte was to clear myself of the Fielde, since the screams and cries of those about mee did much afflict mee and I cutt before mee, not at the Soldiers that faced us but at some picture, as if to hack and cutt soe as to bee quite of those I heard cry behind mee. For I saw manie killed that daie, among them women of the baggage trayne of the King's armie, which oure soldiers said to bee *Irish and of cruell countenance and armed with long knives.* But I took to bee mere camp followers and drudges. And terrible was it to hear them scream for Mercie and to see the blades enter them and the blood Stream forth from their side as they called out in Strange Tongues for Mercie and for Justice. Yet they cried nott upon oure God for hee heard them nott, but let them die where they fell upon the marshy ground.

O pitifull condition of warres. Why should they bee so enacted? And why can None seek to stop the Quarrell that can lead Men to this Pass? What quarrell can it bee that reckons the hacking of a Drab sufficient Argument for its resolution? And how may future Ages fare if they still goe about to seek the Lord's face in the prosecution of Forced Marches, the Gaudy Pomp of a Charge of Cavalrie or the Bloody and Cruell encounter of soldier with Soldier? Yea I mourn even that *Morris* that was the Cause of my tribulation and I mourn all those who fell that daie. What though, on NASEBY field, the King lost all his foot, his guns and Baggage? What though, when the Garrison at Leicester, yielded up to us but three Daies after, the magazine of Armes and five hundred of Horse? What though wee took five thousand Prisoners and the King made haste to Hereford? What of the fact wee took his private Papers so that, as some said *the false mysterie of Monarchie was opened up?* I say if there bee Kinges agayne in England – as well there may – let them have thought onlie for the Safetie and Prosperitie of those they Governe. The daie wee step into the World is Sinning in oure firste Hungeres and after oure Hungeres, come in Angeres, Prides, Conceits, Lustes and all those things that are most shamefully seen in the Prosecution of Warres, to cloak which men give such names as *Valour, Glorie, Great Deeds* and other such stuff as would make anie that saw a battell and the Injustices thereby, ashamed. For warre is no Great Subject as some have thought it, neither is the World so greatlie to bee prized as to bee looked on more than Needful. And as I stood upon that battel yea I THOUGHT MEE OF OURE INNOCENT Assemblies, and of my Master that would nothing of this world save what hee could save of it that might bee of Good Report. Yea *once the smallest fleshlie argument bee sett on foot then is the Cause of Righteousnesse lost and if wee take nott Thy Waies entirely O Lord then are wee among Strangeres and Strangeres unto ourselves also. And are nott Warres and Rebellions and Lustes of the Flesh all of one piece with Witchcraft, that leads us astray from oure Lorde and where hee dwelleth with his Heavenlie Familie.*

Now, though I write as fast as ever I may, yet still tomorrow comes as fast and I may not Stay the light that will break through my Lorde's windowe. And yet I write on, seekng onlie to know the Shadowe and the Substance, how they may bee divided and to chart the Progresse of my Soule, for verily – *in oure flesh is no comfort neither may wee know the Truth of what wee see with mortall Eies.* And yet I pray there will come a time when God will vouchsafe to us the Difference, when wee may see Him plaine.

19

When I reached the brow of the hill from whence I had just come, I found that everyone was running. Not only Young Ezekiel, but all the foot soldiers. The horsemen too were at a gallop, swerving off the main road down into the fields that skirt the hill between ours and the next village. 'Hang on,' I wanted to shout, 'this isn't Edge Hill. You can't have the battle here. You've nearly got it right, but nearly isn't good enough where history is concerned. If Cleopatra's nose had been an inch longer we would have lost the English Civil War. Discuss. *You can't fight the battle of Edge Hill until you get to Edge Hill. Can we have things in their proper order please?'*

But things were not in their proper order. Down the hill towards them was riding a troop of horsemen. They wore cloaks and hats and their hair was long and curled and they looked like the cavaliers in Arthur Mee's *Child's History of England*. Which made me suspect they might actually *be* cavaliers. And they too were determined to fight the battle of Edge Hill in the wrong place. Things were very clearly falling apart. I looked for Ezekiel in the mass of running foot soldiers but did not see him.

There is nothing I can do for him, I thought. It's useless. What will be will be. He will hang his wife and Cromwell will catch him and I will fuck Anna and Meg will not love me any more and my father will die and there is nothing any of us can do about any of it. It's a mess. A hopeless, blind, sodden mess.

The bare-headed man thought it was a mess too. He was shouting at his troops as they rode on towards the enemy, 'For God's sake! Come back here, this isn't Edge Hill, you stupid bastards. What the hell do you think you're playing at? Can we have a little order round here?' He, as Ezekiel sometimes does, had abandoned the attempt to be convincing and seventeenth century, as had many of his comrades, some of whom were yelling back at him 'Fuck off!' or 'Mind yer own business!' One of them nearer to me, a foot soldier who ran after the horses, whirling his musket round his head, was, I could have sworn, shouting 'CHELSEA! CHE-ELSEA!!'

I did not like this at all. To make matters worse, on the road behind me the red estate car had reappeared suggesting that we were once again poised on some razor-thin temporal line between 1650 and 1986. This effect was further confirmed by a fat man who galloped past me on a small and not very efficient looking pony. He was wearing the jerkin, the sash and the helmet, but he had also a pair of horn rimmed glasses and as he passed me he winked coarsely, bouncing up and down in the saddle and said, 'Kills yer bum this does.' Roundheads and Cavaliers were hacking and slashing at each other wildly, although for the most part the conflict seemed shadow play. I could see no sign of blood. The bare headed man, who had a thin, posh voice, was screeching to the scattered figures. 'For God's sake can we have some order! The Royalists are in the wrong place. This is not Edge Hill. We cannot fight the battle of Edge Hill under these circumstances.' Another foot soldier of the Parliamentary forces panted past me. 'You should have seen fucking Naseby,' he said, 'Naseby was a total cock up.'

I had now reached the stage where I did not particularly care which century I was in. All I wanted was to be in one or the other. Perhaps if, like Alice, I shouted at these grotesque apparitions, they would go back into the ground or else start behaving properly – saying 'yea' and 'nay' and caring about Ship Money *or* shouting 'Chelsea' and 'Fuck off' and caring about income tax. Only in the second case, could they please change back into jeans and three-piece suits. 'Stop it, can't you?' I screamed. 'Make up your bloody minds, can't you?' The Parliament men had broken through the Royalist horse and foot and had run on to the end of the field. Clumsily, in no particular order, they wheeled round and prepared to round on the Royalists. But the Royalists, whether in response to one of their own leaders, who was also yelling at them to desist – except I don't think he used the word 'desist'. Or maybe he did. I don't know.

The Royalists did not face out this new charge. They wheeled their horses round, as did the foot soldiers, and headed back up the hill. I was some sixty yards away from them, and it was only now I saw the youth I thought of as young Ezekiel. Quite clearly young Ezekiel had got out of soldiering and into witch finding for very practical reasons. He was standing open mouthed at the spectacle before him, showing every sign of what a few hundred years later would have been called funk. 'Ezekiel – ' I said, but before I had time to continue he gave a low whinny of terror and stumbled off up the field. I could not tell whether his terror was caused by me or the advancing group of attacking Parliamentarians and retreating Royalists. I turned and ran after him, the horses thundering up the hill after me.

I decided to resort to seventeenth-century speak. 'Master Oliphant,' I called after him, 'I have matters of grave import to discuss with Thee, which pertain to the Doings of – '

'Shut up,' he cried at me reedily, 'shut up and go away. Please.' I ran on after him, marvelling at the pleasures of being a phantom. It's so much more fun disturbing people than being disturbed. He was a fast runner, was young Ezekiel.

The horses of the Royalists were now passing on either side of me, their riders screaming back over their shoulders. One horseman had lost all control of his mount and was slumped low in the saddle as he passed me. The few of the Parliament's men who had caught up with the King's soldiers were not thwacking them with their swords or stabbing them in the back but yelling at them to turn round. Why were they doing this? Ezekiel and I ran on through the long grass of the field. We both seemed to be about as unfit as each other, and after a while the horses were replaced by infantry, first of the Cavaliers, who staggered along ineptly, clutching at their cloaks like ladies at a summer ball, and then by a wheezing, guffawing bunch of Puritans.

I caught snatches of dialogue that only served to underline my confusion:

'It *is* a cock up.'

'It's all Charles's fault.'

'We said the third hill to the right, didn't we?'

'I'm *furious*.'

This last from a rather camp, bald man who was flourishing a drawn sword in front of him as he ran. As the figures ahead of us crossed back up to the road and over to the fields that lead down to the river, Ezekiel, after a nervous glance back at me, swerved off to the right. I followed him. The two of us had settled to a slow jog now, with him about ten yards in front of me. I felt suddenly pleased to be attacking him for once, to be in command of myself, pacing it out across the grass. 'How does this feel?' I said. 'Makes a change does it? Boot's on the other foot?'

He didn't answer. I heard him breathe harshly as we ran on. The soldiers over to our left were careering down towards the river. 'You climb into me,' I said to him, 'you get into my head. Don't you? How's this feel when I get into your world? How's it feel?'

He stopped. Away over to our left I saw the troop of horsemen reach the river. They didn't stop, most of them. Perhaps they didn't know how. The horses reared up as they entered the stream and their riders beat out furrows on the smooth surface of the river. There was no distinction now between Roundhead and Cavalier. I saw swords raised, heard shouts. One man leaped at another and the two of them toppled into the stream while all around them the horses bucked and reared. Beyond, on the other side of the river, the calm, under-stated English countryside stretched on towards Stratford, the neat fields and neater hedges preserving their calm in the presence of armed conflict, like a gentleman who observes an unpleasant scene in his club and passes, without seeming to see it, for the sake of decorum. Ezekiel was slowing to a halt. I stopped too.

'Who are you?' he said.

'You know,' I said, 'you know all about me. You wait for me and fuck me up and make me do bad things. I know all your story. I know all about you, Ezekiel.'

He turned towards me. He looked younger than nineteen. 'Why do you keep calling me that?'

Maybe we do dream each other. Maybe the real flesh we think we touch is only a dream and in the dream it's solid. And maybe we see each other in dreams long before the dreams we call 'now' or 'reality' or whatever fancy name we care to use. Why, otherwise, should lovers talk of 'having known each other before'? Certainly with Anna I felt the presence of shadows I could not explain, and imaginary family relations rose between us as we kissed or talked so that sometimes I was her father, sometimes her brother, and then of course, the lover, but not just *a* lover, the lover she had waited for, known, dreamed, long before this most delicious part of the reverie, the one that whispers 'here and now' at you, and whispers it so sweetly and seductively you take it for the truth, until your inevitable and bitter awakening.

'Who are *you*?' I said.

And this young man too knew me, or thought he knew me, or was held by something in my voice and manner that he couldn't be said exactly to recognize, rather to remember, and all our attitudes to each other seemed suddenly, terribly familiar, so that I knew exactly what he would say next and how he would say it and was not surprised when he said it.

'We,' he said, 'are the Society of the Sealed Knot.'

I thought this was a delightful idea. 'And what do you do?'

His voice was now sounding like a gramophone that had run out of power and was slowing down. 'We dress up,' he said, 'in the costumes of the English Civil War and we fight their battles again. We fight Naseby and Marston Moor and today we're fighting Edge Hill except it's gone wrong.'

I laughed with pleasure at the idea that a battle could 'go wrong'. That it had a second life, in which the deaths were not real deaths but performances, and that it was important to get such performances right. It seemed to me an idea no less charming than enclosing gifts for the gods in the coffin of a loved one. I liked this young man enormously. I wanted to stay and talk to him and I realized that I would have to talk carefully and not allow myself to be tripped up, as I had been on the road. I had said awful things there. Had I said things about Anna and Meg? I mustn't talk about them to anyone. They were my secret. And I mustn't mention Ezekiel. I could see clearly now that this person was not Ezekiel or anything like him and that nothing as ridiculous as my being transported into the seventeenth century had happened. I would be very calm and quiet with him and then go on my way. I smiled warmly. 'Why do you do that?' I said.

'For fun,' he said, 'and it's educational.'

'Yes,' I said.

215

'It's like you're there,' he said, rather dreamily, 'it's like you're back there. Cromwell. Know what I mean?'

'Yes,' I said quietly, 'I do.' He had a pretty, peaky face. I thought I would go over to him and put my arms round him and tell him I was sorry for having frightened him earlier. That I too was interested in the past. I liked his eyes. I thought I would put my arms round him as if he were a child and hold him and make sure he was not frightened any more. As I grew closer to him, though, I saw that his face was stiff with fear. Why was he frightened of me? What had I done wrong? Over by the river the ridiculous bank clerks, postmen, insurance salesmen and television executives were thrashing round enacting something that never happened.

And then, as I reached out my hand for him I felt that sour breath in my throat, and found that not one, but two hands were reaching for him and they were grasping him by the waist and I wanted to put my hands down between his shirt (his shirt was open) and scratch and pinch at his chest and my hands were not my hands but his hands and I was possessed of a Strength I did not Credit was Justly Mine so that it Seemed as if I was Controuled by Some Demon that would not be cast forth from Mee and I was set to find the Mark which was Upon Him and was – as is always when the Devil will give suck – near to the Privates or Genital Parts For All's One to the Devil and Hee may Suck where he will, kneeling Before Young Men to perform this Office for them and taking their Organs of Generation into his mouth as he kneels with 'I beg you' and 'If it will please you, your Worship' and 'Oh let me suck on this the way a woman will a Bar of Sugar, Master' come on let me please go on stop it what's the matter go on let me please please let me –

'Fucking queer,' the young man was saying.

Why was he saying that? What was the matter with him? I didn't like his face any more. It had gone dark and swollen and it had eyes that were narrow and knowing like Ezekiel's. I didn't like his face and I didn't like him. I thought he was a jerk. People who dress up in historical costume and nancy around the Oxfordshire countryside are jerks and should be fucking stopped by law. Witches? My God witches have nothing on them.

'Get off. Get off. . .'

My hands were on his throat now (had I strangled her? Perhaps I had. Serve the stupid fucking bitch right) and I had forced him to the ground and he was thrashing and kicking and I was squeezing harder and harder and the harder I squeezed the more his stupid face looked like Ezekiel's and the more knowing and wheedling were his eyes and so I thought I'll have to squeeze harder than this. I'll have to squeeze until there's nothing in his face left to bother me. Because at the moment all of it bothers me. The prim mouth and the peaky nose and the fair forelock of hair and the stupid grin and the –

'Hey! Hey you!'

I looked up and saw, about a hundred yards away, a couple of foot soldiers, in Parliamentary uniforms. As I turned they began to run. I looked down and the young man was struggling to his feet and I was running away from him and the three soldiers were coming after me.

I was, then, wearie of the Combatt & sought to returne to Hertfordshire, but knew nott how this might bee Accomplished. For I spake with none of the Soldiers about mee – whence I first got my Name, as Close-mouthed Oliphant.

But at camp that night, after the Field of Naseby, as wee were sate about the Fire, I heard in the Darknesse behind mee, a familiar voice, which shouted Curses agaynst his Captors, and agaynst all the Parliament. Which made mee wonder for the greayter part of oure prisoners were Welsh but this was no Welshman and I seemed to know his voyce. So I went up from my Place and went out into the Shadowes beyond the fire, where were some twenty or thirty prisoners bundled together with Cords. And at once as I saw Hee who gave the Shout, that this was that same Beare whose Hande I bit full *fifteen yeares* past at the village of Stavely, for this was my Cold PRINTER Father, who seemed nott a Daie older and Twice as Quarrelsome.

But what astonished mee the most was that this same Black Beare, this *Thomas Oliphant* – who to mee was nowmore than a footstool, a knife or anie instrument to hand synce hee has had onlie the Engendering of mee (for as the *Cooperites* teach

'Paternitie is in a single embrace & Motherhood is in the first embrace with a Stranger). Yet though I had held it as a *true teaching* yet now I had the Proof of it for I looked upon him as if hee had been anie John or Andrew met by the Wayside. Hee was far gone in Drunkenness – as were manie of the Welshmen wee took that daie – & much as hee Abused the Officers that sate by Him nor paid anie Mind to his Discourse, which ran, now on the Capital Necessity for the King's PEACE, now on the near Approach of the Wickednesse of Universall Presbytery, now on the Sinne of 'plain silly fellowes' such as wee who would claim to Read and Interpret the Bible. These are the same,' says hee, 'that would mistake bookes of Magick for Conjuror's Book & seek to Confound the Learned and Schooled.'

But at his Wordes I bethought mee of that *Morris that* lay on NASEBY field withal, & of how Jealously hee guarded the Textes and Sayings of the Prophets, saying *that hee that wandereth out of the Waie of understanding, shall remayne in the congregation of the dead* & reflected that Learning may bee a Perverse and Malicious Wounding of the Spirit or a Tedious and Dusty enslavement to Example. Hath St John, whom Jesus loved, said *And now little children abide in him; that when hee shall appear we may have communion and nott bee ashamed before him at his coming.* And such Learning may bee but a *by-waie to hell* synce at His coming wee shall surely speak as the Apostles spoke when the Daie of Pentecost was come & there came a sound from Heaven as of a rushing mighty wind & it filled all the howse where they were sitting & there appeared unto them cloven tongues as of Fire and it sate upon each of them.

'Hold –' says the Officer who had guard of Him, *'enough.'*

At which I stepped somewhat closer & begged him let mee have a worde of this Man. 'For,' says I, 'inasmuch as wee are God's Armie – so may wee Endeavour to *convert the Heretique* & use Reason and Argument to plead oure Cause which is that each may find his owne waie to God & nott goe about under Instruction at each turn of the Road that leads us out of this worlde to where Our Father & his Holy Son which are the spirit of Love & Comelinesse. 'You may talk all you will,' says the Black Beare, 'but by my *arse* you will nott finde I argue anie

Cause butt the King's. And you shall finde ere long the Parliament will Argue it my waie. For if such fellowes as you are presume to Study & Understande the Word of God, then what Authorities may hold you in Worldlie Business? Or do ye nexte seek to have the Ownership and Controule of all Estates? The Sharing of all in the Kingdom and the Abandonment of Oaths of Loyalty to the established orders of Religion and Land.' And I made myselfe nott knowne to him but went & argued the Matter, marvelling at how a Warre may change a Man's opinions.

I learned from him my Mother was long synce Dead, and that hee had journeyed from oure Village, which was Stavely, to Oxford, with one *Hargill* who had sworn there was Emploiment there. But on their coming neer that Citie they had been stopped by a group of Cavalier gentlemen – and in fine, on promise of shoes and *fourpence* had joyned the King. By which I saw his Argument was founded, nott upon Reason or the love of Justice, butt upon a desire to feed at anie man's table who would take him in, of which I attempted to perswade him, for I had some care for his Immortall Soule, though in truth I cared nott still to reveal myselfe to Him. But hard as I might argue the Case, hee proved as Stubborn now hee were Bound and at my Mercie as ever hee had when I was scarce up to his Chaire. O verily this poyson of oure Flesh lays upon us like a cloud of Ignorance and Folly and our Familie after the Bodie is but cheap and worthless Raiment, such as was *shared among thieves and left after the spoyle were Divided.* And how may one night's thoughtless and Improvident Lust – or ten or twenty, nay or a lifetime's? – worke anie magick on our Flesh – to transpose it into something fit in the Sight of God? Nay – kinship in oure Soules is all wee may hope to seek with Profit and Advantage. How then, if I had fallen upon his neck and called him 'Father' and hee mee 'Sonne'? What thought would hee have had except hee might scape a whipping and gain some Advantage by oure Discourse? And what was in my Hearte towardes him? Then as ever – nothing save the Deesire to save and sanctify his Soule synce hee was so deep in sinne for in his Mind was naught but Vanities, jugglings, cheats, games, plays, fools, apes, knaves, rogues, thefts, murders, false swearings, adulteries and that of a blood red colour. For hee boasted of how Cheap hee had bought this or that Woman synce the Warres began, and of who hee had *ravished* and of how much Plate hee had taken from this or that City so that, though I besought him to Return to the Waie of truth synce *the bodie without the soule is a dead carcass nay if it bee alone is but a dead carcass also for what is oure bodie but a most pitifull and impernanent house for Appetite and Lust*, hee answered mee with Laughter. And I grieved to hear him still so deep in Sinne but knew nott how I might Proceed. At which I heard a Voyce behind mee that saith – 'Leave him for hee feedeth on others, a deceived heart hath turned him aside.' And I knew the voyce that spake unto mee and turned aside from the Father of my Bodie and saith 'Remember O Jacob and Israel – for I am Thy Servant; thou hast formed mee. Thou has blotted out as a thick cloud my Transgression.' Which are the wordes of the prophet Isaiah and known to mee for there in the light of the fire his armes outstretched to mee, his old nose as sharp as ever and teares upon his Eies, was hee who took *me in when I was a hungry and cold* yea my Master Nehemiah which was and is, the Father of my Spirit. And I never looked agayne upon the face of hee that used mee so Ill when I was a boie and know nott what became of him, though all oure prisoners were taken in Good Order to London and were shown the People & manie of the Welsh found themselves amazed that they were Spared so eas-ilie. Or hee lives in some Taverne or Alehouse or whores his waie through the Weeke. Or hee laboures in the Protector's service I know nott neither care I. For I see clearly now that my first sinne, which led mee to so low a Case was to go agaynst the principles of the *Cooperites* that had taken mee as one of Them whereat my Meg was led to sinne & if I had not so polluted up my spirit perhaps shee would have lived yet.

O ye that will come after us hearken to the voyce of one who would live in the Spirit – whose wordes would seek to echo down the YEARES and warn of how it may bee when wee are fallen awaie from Righteousnesse and have weighted oure Soules so they bee Havie, Impure and things of Clay. For I would have it alwaies so – that Men should seek His Light and His Truth and soe should walk, nott in contamination of the spirit but in contemplation of His beauties and his Mercies for which I trust this my Testament may outlive my *meer dust* and make my soule to shine brightly as a Pattern for Men. For time, that takes mee in Trust will serve yee the same – neither think ye to escape it or the Steadie Step fo Death. Listen listen listen as I entreat you – those who have ears to hear let them hear or else bee cast out into Darkness. Listen listen listen – unless ye hearken to the voyces of those that went Before ye how may ye come to know the Waie to Righteousness and Truth. O listen listen listen! And as I write I cock mine Ear for an Answere – but hear only Echoes & Silence.

Rick Mason would probably say that we know little of Ezekiel Oliphant, the so-called Bloomsbury Witchfinder. Rick catches glimpses of him prosecuting a trial, prosecuted himself, caught up in another pamphleteer's tale – I know much more about him than that. I know, for instance, that he was an extremely fast runner. That he likes Coca-Cola (after that business at Whipps Cross I drank four bottles straight off, and *I* don't like Coca-Cola). And when he takes me over, sometimes he lets me, Jamie Matheson, go. As I look back over what I have written I can see I haven't described it right. There is a moment when he *is* me – I can't separate myself from him; and sometimes, as in that business in London after I escaped from the hospital, I black out and for a day, or two days, remember nothing of what happened after he came.

But sometimes, as in this instance, after the unsavoury discovery that Ezekiel was not only a witchfinder, a coward and a psychopath but a bit of a nancy boy on the quiet as well – once I was away from the youth and the two men who joined him in the chase, I can leave him in my body and watch him as he talks or drinks or has a pee, or as in this instance, runs like blazes, and when this happens I *know* facts about his life, in the way in which one knows someone is an enemy or a friend. I couldn't tell these things to the likes of Rick Mason. He'd ask for evidence. But that doesn't stop me knowing that they are true.

Ezekiel joined the Parliamentary forces just before Edge Hill. His wife was against it. 'Ezekiel,' she said, 'who needs it? Maybe the King will win. Maybe not. Maybe the Parliament will win.

Let's wait and see, shall we?' They argued a lot about politics. Ezekiel wouldn't have it. 'A man's gotta do what a man's gotta do,' he said. He felt, poor mutt, that he was taking some world-historical decision, the way all young men do when they espouse a cause, be it ship money, democratic centralism, or immediate revolution by absolutely everyone. He went to the battle (they were gaining on me) and unfortunately, the night before, he quarrelled with his comrades and tried to grope one of them. This did not go down well. No rubbish about gay rights in the 1640s. As a result of which, when the battle was in full swing, a few of them took the opportunity to settle the score with him and, rounding on him, pursued him over the fields with the intention of getting him down on the ground and carving slices off him.

I seemed to have come up against the river again. It makes one last sweep before our village. It blocked my path to the left. I would have to climb the hill up towards Dell's Wood. My pursuers seemed to have slackened their pace. I slowed to a comfortable, jogging stride. Telling myself about Ezekiel was getting me out of it. If you're depressed, Dewes used to say to me, the best cure is to learn something. I started up the hill, dimly aware that behind me, some kind of conference was taking place. Another horseman was coming up from the river to join my tormentors. Pay no attention. Get back to the cottage. Just keep moving.

Ezekiel's friend in the Army was a youth of about nineteen called Install Me with Reverence Arthur. They sat up late in the night by the camp fire chatting about the nature of the Trinity and the urgent need for a war against Spain. They agreed about things. When the war was over, said Arthur, they would open a tavern or start importing linen. Something quiet. It was Arthur who got Ezekiel interested in witchcraft. Arthur was, of course, gay himself but unable to own up to it (it being 1643) and, in late night fireside conversation with Ezekiel, railed against women and specifically against Meg, who was at home with the three little boys, Nehemiah, Saul, and Iscariot (the black sheep of the family).

Gottlieb will like this, I thought. And the thought of Gottlieb was comforting. I'll leave these bastards behind as soon as I get to the wood, and then they can get back to their next assignment – a full scale re-enactment of the Viking invasion of Britain, perhaps. A looting and pillaging weekend in Hastings. Rape £23 extra. In the mean time, Jamie, tell yourself a story. I looked back over my shoulder. The young man was sitting on the grass with his friend. The horseman, in Parliamentary gear, had been joined by a thin, nervous-looking Cavalier smoking a small cigar. As I watched the two of them pulled their horses round and gave chase. The Cavalier was shouting something – 'Hey! Hey you!' I had better ideas for how they might spend their time. How about a two minute Nagasaki special in the Highlands of Scotland – ideal for those with personal and emotional problems they feel are insurmountable. Try our Treblinka Fortnight at a Health Spa in North Wales. Our Dresden night out in Liverpool. Do not miss the Ghengis Khan Under Thirties Weekend on the hard shoulder of the M6 motorway. Understand your past. Learn from the mistakes others have made. It's educational. It's fun.

The horsemen were gaining on me. Out of condition. Too much tinned food. Ahead of me I could see the pines of Dell's Wood. Twenty yards? I'd be safe in the trees. They'd never get the horses in among the trees. Keep going, Jamie. Tell yourself another story. 'What happens next? You want to know what happens next, Nat? Listen. It's amazing. Ezekiel hangs his wife for witchcraft and goes back to the New Model Army to rejoin his friend Arthur, trying to explain that there's nothing funny about him really. But Arthur gets it in the neck from a musket ball at Marston Moor and Ezekiel gets mixed up in the extreme fringes of the army radicals, Everard, Sexby, people like that. Then at the Putney Debates he realizes *there is witchcraft at the very highest level of Government*. It's a red-hot story but what can he do? *Nat, witchcraft is a political issue, Nat, the* –

Twenty yards to the trees. A man is running at six miles an hour on a line AB pursued by two men who are travelling at thirty miles per hour. If the man is running at six miles per hour how long will it take before –

Ten-nine-eight-seven-six-five-four-Oh-h. . . the trees, the trees. I was blundering through the undergrowth. Wading through bracken and thick bushes, as fast and as far as I could go in the sudden cool of the wood. When I heard the explosive breath of the horses out in the lighted field I sank gratefully to the nettled floor and lay as still as I could. I could hear their voices clearly, from this distance. Only one, as far as I could tell, dismounted.

'Who was he?'

'I don't know. Some nutter. He comes out of this bush and starts jabbering. Norm saw him earlier. He thought he was taking the piss.'

'What did he do?'

'Well he come at him. First Arthur thought he was a woolly woofter, but I don't know. Probably some local nutter.'

'Shouldn't we go in after him?'

'Maybe we should tell the Old Bill we've seen him.'

'I think we should get on with the fucking battle frankly. My bum is killing me.' 'Edge Hill is a frost, actually. It never works, Edge Hill.'

'Let's leave him, shall we?'

'Leave him. My *bum*.'

I heard the horses turn and whinny and then they were gone and I was alone among the trees. I dug my nails into the hard soil of the forest floor. I had to get away from here. Soon. There were things I had still to find out. Forget the bloody women for the moment. I had to sit down and think it through calmly. Which information was which? What did I know and what had I guessed? How sick am I? What the hell did I do in London? Was it like what happened just now? Should I go back to the hospital and find out what happened to everyone? Am I the Beast of Putney?

My head my head my head.

I got up and limped off through the wood. The brambles tore at my shoes, ripped into the jeans and T-shirt, but I pushed on aware now of the brilliant July day filtered through the trees ahead of me, but the more I walked, less and less of a white presence beyond the wood, more and more of a real salvation, a brilliant clear open space in which I would not be pursued and confused any more. Give me a clear mind O Lord and let me know what and where I have sinned and how I may make amends into Thy hand I commend my spirit Amen.

I used to make up prayers when my father took the service in the half empty church down the road. And my prayers were always very simple: 'Please can Mum get better', or 'Can I have the plastic lorry from Mac's toyshop.' And as I trudged on, I prayed again, simply for an intermission, for a break from this confusion, this world where nothing is quite what it seems, the past is hopelessly confused with the present, and I do wrong without knowing it. I'm ill, Daddy, I prayed in the end. Please make me better. Make it all clear.

And then it was all clear – as it is when the bastard leaves me alone and goes back to the seventeenth century where he belongs. And I was out of the wood, in the field at the bottom of the cottage garden. No one there. All clear. I limped to the hedge that marks the beginning of our land, up the garden path and in through the heavy wooden gate at the back. I fell on to the sofa in the back kitchen and closed my eyes.

Now. Start again, Matheson. Pick up the story where you left off. What got you to this point? You know what. The fucking Clarke manuscript, that's what. It didn't look like a forgery, did it? Anna said so. And the more you read it, the more she went into it, the more the pieces of the Oliphant story started to fit together, to make a strange, unbelievable, but terrifying shape. Start with you and Anna in Oxford. After you got the manuscript out from the college. Because once you started on the papers, the papers that told you about the conspiracy, it got worse and worse and worse, didn't it? You had no choice. Like a man who opens his eyes one day and sees two of everything, you had been awakened to the unacceptable, the truth no one will believe.

And you were in love, Jamie. That was half the damn trouble. You were falling in love.

20

Anna didn't decipher much of the manuscript that day. She spent most of her time prodding and poking and smelling it. Time honoured methods of dating seventeenth-century manuscripts, I presumed. The prodding and the poking and the smelling only seemed to confuse her more, however. She would hold the pages up to the light, sniff, click, swear and shake her red curls. And when I tried to ask a question she looked at me rather as model boat owners used to respond to eager questions from onlookers, when I was a child at Harpworth Ponds.

I liked her like that. I liked her calmness and her self-absorption. It's funny, writing about her now I feel a sense of calm. We sat on a bench over near Balliol, watcing the morning shoppers pad round their family saloons, and she held the papers close to her, as if frightened her theft might be discovered, squinted at them, but could not, it seemed, much to her annoyance, fault them.

'I'll buy you lunch,' I said.

'Nice,' she said.

I noticed again that faint London tang to her voice. The façade of Balliol caught the morning sun. In the front hallway a group of youths in anoraks stamped their feet and shouted to other, unseen youths further in the quandrangle. All off to the pub. One of them did not shout. Clamped to his head was a Sony Walkman. He strolled out on to the pavement and looked up at the gargoyles. The gargoyles looked down at him – Walkman, CND badge, faded ski jacket. Neither of them seemed impressed by the other. It's lived-in history is Oxford, presenting the visitor not with the frozen images of Cambridge, but blurring the lines between now and then. It's a run-in sort of town. Sitting there with Anna I began to enjoy it – the way I had as a student. I took her arm and slowly we got up and wandered towards Carfax.

'Whatever is in this heap of papers,' I said, 'and I'm not

asking you to tell me – ' Here she gave me that sharp, glittering look I had noticed back in the College. '– there's something about it that worries you. It can't be that the texture and feel of the paper does that. It's easy to fake –'

'What it is,' she said, 'is that if it is a fake, it's an extremely well done fake, and one the forger has not gone to great lengths to advertise. Anyway, if you want to fake something and convince people it's genuine, your first concern would be to make sure the document was one that *could have* existed.'

'Oh I see, so forgery is just as boring as everything else. It has to conform to people's preconceptions. I would have thought that the only charm of forgery is that it gives you the chance to invent completely ludicrous documents conclusively proving Elizabeth the First was a vampire or Cromwell was a Satanist.' I steered across the road and towards an Italian restaurant. I no longer steer Meg across the road, I thought. It's more or less assumed that we look after ourselves when it comes to traffic. Is *that* where we went wrong? I liked the light touch of Anna's elbow as I took her to the left of a double decker. The nearest I get to dancing. . .

'Oh no,' said Anna, 'the one thing that makes me think the document might be genuine is the fact that so far, and I've only read a few phrases, it looks completely improbable. You see the only person with a motive for doing such a thing is our friend Ron Oliphant. And we know from the bloke at the College that he only came there once, ten years ago, and that our friend stood over him because he wasn't entirely sure of him.'

'Yes, but don't tell me Ron wouldn't have found the time to slip in some papers among the rest. Then he goes away and writes his barmy pamphlet justifying his barmy ancestor and waits for someone to take an interest, which in due course we do. He's also got the British Museum pamphlet of Ezekiel's to support his claim. Actually I think Ron probably faked that as well. I'm sure half the things in the British Museum are faked by people anxious to prove some point or other. I'm sure most of English history didn't happen at all.'

I opened the door of the restaurant. She walked in ahead of me. *She likes being taken care of*, I thought. We were shown to a table on a sort of raised marble plinth next to a fountain, and she settled herself, papers at her elbow, with her back to the wall. 'What we need,' she said, 'is some more dope on this character Ezekiel. From what your academic friend said, we know a fair bit about him. We need to know more. And if what we find out in any way corroborates what's in *this*' – she tapped the papers at her elbow – 'whatever precisely is in it, and the *Cursèd Lie* pamphlet, then I think we have a story. Because I have seen the Clarke shorthand originals and I am telling you that if this is a forgery, it's a terrifyingly good one. And if it implicates Oliver Cromwell in Satanism, I for one don't necessarily reject it on those grounds. Cromwell lived in a country that condemned witchcraft as a felony. I should imagine he believed in witches. As did most of the population. As do most of the population now.'

'Where do you stand on witchcraft?'

She grinned. 'Oh, I don't believe in it. I just practise it.'

I was on the edge of telling her about Ezekiel. Then I decided against it. The waiter arrived and clucked round her. She ran a stubby finger down one of the pages. 'We know nothing,' she said, 'about this area. Really. Magic, spirits, whatever you want to call it. We simply don't *know*. How do I know that I know, for example, that I . . . like you. Like you a lot. More than like you. It isn't the way you look, is it?'

I laughed, not entirely confidently. 'I supposed not.'

'There's something . . . something . . . I can't put a name to it. How does my cat know when I'm coming down the stairs – when he's in the kitchen and he can't *see* me at all?'

'You have a cat, do you?'

'A black one, Jamie. And I crouch with him over the rooftops of Bloomsbury every night, waiting for my familiar.'

'We ordered *penne alla Matriciana* and white wine. When the wine came I poured for both of us and said, 'What I really want to know about *that* – indicating the stolen sheets of paper – is whether there are any dirty bits in it.'

She took a deep sip of her wine. My mouth felt dry.

'Cromwell,' she said, 'was a real raver.' 'Yeah?' She cast her eye down the mass of whorls and squiggles: '. . . putting her face first on the floor and renting her petticoats my Lord Ireton entered her from the rear, under the eye of my Lord Protector, who was much excited by her. . .'

'By her what?'

Anna looked up at me. She broke a piece of bread carefully on her plate. The tip of her tongue showed at the edge of her lips. 'By her white arse,' she said, and grinned provocatively.

'You're making that up.'

'I am *not*. Ireton seems to have been a real raver as well,' she went on, 'I mean this is the kind of historical document the world has been waiting for. There's not a lot about Ireton's attitude to property being that of a nineteenth-century Tory, for example, but there's a hell of a lot about his cock . . .' She made a show of passing her eyes across the page, and creased her forehead in a pantomime of scholarly concentration. '. . . purple and distended – about the size of a – Christ I don't believe it. . .'

'What?'

'It's hard to read. I thought at first he was saying it was over a foot long.'

'Ireton's cock a foot long?'

'I don't think it does say that.'

'That would totally revolutionize our attitude to the seventeenth century.'

'Historico-anatomically speaking, yes.'

How long was Cromwell's?'

She made a show of looking further down the page. 'Eighteen inches apparently. This is unbelievable isn't it?'

'Some men do have them that big apparently. There was a bloke in Colorado who had one nearly two foot long. It's true. I met a man in a pub who told me. He'd read it in the *Guinness Book of Records*. So it must be true.' Anna grinned. Our pasta arrived. She wound it round her fork and, jutting her chin forward, opened her mouth. She caught me watching her and grinned again. She had an ability to look as if she was winking without going through the vulgar business of opening and closing one eye. 'There's also,' she said, 'a great deal about Cromwell's hairy arse. And a telling description of him taking off his drawers and buggering, in reverse order, John Lilburne, the Earl of Clarendon, and Thomas Hobbes the philosopher.'

'You are making that up.'

'I am,' she said, 'but how can you tell? How can you tell?' And how, too, can I tell (I thought) that there is something in all of this that cannot he laughed away? Perhaps the very fact that I want to laugh it away tells me.

'I don't want to talk about Cromwell's cock anyway,' she said, 'I want to talk about yours.'

'Why should they have all the fun?'

'Quite.' Raising the napkin to her lips she wiped away a thin trail of reddish brown gravy. She chewed, I noticed, with the same ladylike deliberateness that she employed when driving. Lust, for Anna, was something else over which she liked to feel she had control. Like the notes she used to pass me in the museum, those spiky, neat messages on yellow paper, there was a ladylike precision about her sexual appetite. I felt, as I so often do in the company of women, at her mercy. But I also felt not at all anxious to protect myself. 'We should have our own Sabbat right here,' I said.

'Absolutely. You can scratch me and claw me and shout rude words and tear off my panties.'

'Gee thanks.'

'It's that kind of restaurant. They're *Italians*. They're demonstrative people.'

My cock, although not yet in the Cromwell/Ireton class, did feel ready for a little Sabbat-style airing. I leaned forward in the imitation ironwork chair and crossed my legs firmly. But she was not to be stopped. Pushing the document aside she folded her arms on the table and shook her red curls out at me. 'Where would we have this Sabbat then?'

'Er –'

'Because I am a witch you know. I must be a witch because I steal people's husbands and I'm unprincipled and I once had it off with a man in a lavatory on an InterCity train.'

'Was it nice?'

'Very nice.'

I drank more white wine. 'They have a very nice ladies lavatory here,' I said, 'it's all pink and floral. You could live in it.'

'Does this date from your transvestite phase?'

'I was sick in it once.'

'How super.' Her foot found mine under the table and, at the same moment, I found her hand and clasped it. I was, I realized with some consternation, actually *gazing into her eyes*. I tried, briefly, to look away, but with a shake of her head she seemed to trap my glance once again. . .

'I'm game,' she said.

'Suppose someone. . .'

'Dare you.' Her hand slipped from the tablecloth and groped its way up to my knee. 'My Lord,' she said, 'I have such a veritable and concupiscent need of You between my Thighes as disturbs my most Secret Parts and will not be Denied.'

'Oh Christ,' I said, 'Christ.'

'See you in there,' she said, and with immense decorum she tripped down the marble steps and into the basement. I looked round hurriedly. Not many women in the place. Did they look continent? Answer – not very. Was it an offence to have it off in a public lavatory *with a woman*? Probably. But gross indecency was with men, wasn't it? This felt pretty grossly indecent to me. All the more reason for going ahead with it. I pushed back my chair and, with great casualness, stopping slightly, I made for the marble stairs.

The ladies lavatory had a picture of a woman in a long eighteenth-century-style gown on the door. The door was ajar and I saw Anna through the gap. She was grinning at herself. When she saw me she switched the grin in my direction. I cast a glance over my shoulder. No one. 'Oh my Lord,' she said, pulling down the top of her jeans, 'do Thou Service Mee in great haste for I am –' I slid through the gap and locked the door behind us. I grabbed her shoulders and kissed her hard on the lips. 'I am too,' I said. There was something still, distant and curiously mocking about her, which had the effect of intensifying my lust. I pushed her jeans down to her knees and worked my hands round her buttocks. 'Christ,' I said, rather stagily, 'I want to fuck you.' 'Yes,' she said.

I felt that our lovemaking was in danger of being conducted in a style that owed almost everything to Harold Robbins and almost nothing to us. But having started in this style it was necessary to continue. 'I want to have you from the back,' I said, 'so as I can see your bottom.' She seemed fairly impressed by this manly, forthright request and had the decency not to point out that, given the confined nature of the space, it was the only way in which I was going to be able to have her. She rolled her

231

jeans down past her knees, turned, and, straddling the pink lavatory seat, lifted her bottom up towards me, her two hands grasping the low flush pink cistern.

My cock leaped joyously out of its red Marks and Spencer's underpants. It was the colour of Oliver Cromwell's nose, the consistency of vulcanized rubber, and from the size of the veins, seemed in the middle of a dangerous arthritic seizure.

When I was a child, I used to go to the lavatory with a girl called Ruth Bidamen. I remember that we used to talk quietly and intimately of things that concerned us, while she lowered her blue knickers and, as quietly and subtly as our converse, peed. I don't think I ever did anything apart from lean against the door and chat in a high, squeaky voice. This, I now realized, was what I had wanted to do to her, although it had not been clear to me at the time. I addressed Anna's small, brown bottom with the curious serverity that seemed to have overtaken my performance. I reminded myself of Claudius in some repertory production of *Hamlet*.

'If you are a witch,' I said, 'and you are in league with the Devil then so much the better because that's how I like it and I am going to fuck you. I am really going to fuck you hard.' She did not retort, as she might well have done, 'Well in that case get on with it', or alternatively, match my line with a 'Yea verily thou art the devil and I long for your Satanic Organ up Mee!' She just stood there with her legs apart, straddling the lavatory, waiting. Perhaps, I reflect now, I was rather overdoing it. Perhaps she had got bored. I didn't care. All I knew was that I was about to have it off with a girl in a public lavatory and that, so far anyway, the experience was affording me more pleasure per second than any other activity I could recall.

I was just about to give her a bit of the 'We are both in league with Satan and our orgasms will carry us to the nethermost region of the Pit where we will proceed to have a Whole Load More,' when there came a tap at the door and an elderly female voice said, 'Are you all right in there?'

21

You only had to listen to the voice to know that this woman really was a witch. An elderly, paid up member of a coven. A cat-loving, man-hating daughter of Satan.

'It's OK,' called Anna, peering round at me, 'I won't be a minute.' She seemed to find this amusing. Well, of course, in a sense she had a right to be here, did she not? It was I who was trespassing.

'Have you come?' she whispered to me.

'You what?' said the woman outside. She must have her ear glued to the door. I shook my head. The point of Anna's tongue curled over her lips, and, tensing her shoulders and pulling down her head, she rolled her eyes briefly upwards. 'What larks' her expression seemed to say. I took a more serious view of the situation.

'Do you think,' she went on, 'that you will come?'

'Come where?' said the voice outside the door.

'No,' I said.

There was a long silence from outside. 'Are you all right?' said the voice finally.

I began to pull up my trousers. 'We're just mending the equipment,' I said, 'we won't be a moment.'

'You what?'

Anna too was pulling up her zipper, snapping her jeans round her buttocks, as, outside, the quavering voice started up again. 'Are there workmen in there?'

'That's right,' I said, 'we're mending the cistern.'

'How long will you be?' said the witch-like voice, 'I'm desperate.'

So am I fucking desperate. I wanted to answer. Instead I said 'You could use the men's.' I looked at the two of us in the mirror on the wall – our pink cheeks, our rumpled clothes, our notable lack of overalls. We did not look like workmen.

'Oh I couldn't do that,' said the voice.

'It's quite all right,' I said, 'it's being used as a ladies at the moment.

A doubtful pause. 'Is it?'

'Yes,' I said, 'quite a number of ladies have been using it.' This seemed to reassure her. I was beginning to enjoy my new role of cistern mender. I felt confident about being in the ladies. 'You'll find it preferable to in here,' I went on, 'in here's a terrible mess.'

'What,' said the voice, 'if someone comes?'

'Lock the door firmly against them,' I said.

'It seems,' said the voice, 'unusual.' But I had convinced her. I heard a shuffle, a mutter, and then the closing of the door next to ours. The click of the bolt. I pulled back the door and Anna and I slipped out. There was no one outside. We walked, together, back to our table.

I was beginning to wonder whether someone had put a spell on me. A spell that condemned the victim to perpetual coitus interruptus. We sat down. The waiter approached and I ordered more wine.

'Tell me about your wife,' she said, softly.

'She's a nice person,' I said.

'Yes?'

'Oh yes.'

She played with a piece of bread, watching me. 'Do you love her?'

'I think,' I said slowly, 'I feel sorry for her.'

'That can be the same thing.'

'It can be confused with love,' I said, 'it can *be* love under certain circumstances. But it isn't necessarily the same thing.'

'What does she do?'

'Well once she was a historian. Like you. But now she looks after the children.'

I fell silent.

'What are you thinking about?' said Anna.

'I was thinking about her.'

'And feeling bad?'

'Feeling fairly bad, yes.'

'You don't have to feel bad,' said Anna, 'I'm not her. Your feelings for me aren't anything to do with your feelings for her.'

'No?'

'Of course not. I don't think people should try to own each other anyway. They're not possessions, are they?'

From the stairs emerged the crone who had disturbed us. I watched her hobble back to her corner table with a certain amount of bitterness. Outside the day was darkening and scraps of rain beat against the restaurant's huge plate glass window. 'No,' I said. There was a silence. Then from me: 'But – don't you think – people can *be* possessed. By other people. The other people can . . . take them over almost.'

'I wouldn't want a relationship like that,' she said.

'You might not have any choice in the matter, might you? You might fall in love and then – what could you do?'

'You might be taken over by the spirit of a thirteenth-century monk,' she said, 'but it isn't very likely, is it?'

'So don't you believe in love?'

There was another silence. This time a long, long silence. She looked at the white tablecloth scattered with crumbs and then she raised her brown eyes to mine. They were shining, but not with greed or desire or amusement. With something I couldn't place. 'Oh I believe in love,' she said, 'I'm afraid I do.' The waiter brought us coffee but I did not take my eyes off her face – nor she from mine. The waiter was used to couples like this. He connived, lovingly, at our intimacy, as he poured and retreated.

'This Oliphant character,' I said, 'it sounds stupid. I can't express it. But sometimes . . . I feel as if he were . . . taking me over.'

'You're certainly fairly obsessed with him,' said Anna.

'It's hard to explain,' I said, 'but sometimes it's like . . . it's like he . . . takes me over. . .'

She looked at me shrewdly. 'I don't think you're crackers, Jamie. You're a level-headed sort of person, aren't you. On the cynical side, I'd say. How do you mean anyway, "takes you over"?'

I decided to say no more about Ezekiel. To describe our secret thoughts to another is to betray them. All language is a false translation of thought, even words on the page such as I write here. I look back at my description of what happened this morning, or in her flat, or in the hospital, and am appalled. The resort to fine writing, to attempt to make my meaning clear. And it isn't clear. I haven't anywhere managed to convey what it is like when he invades me. He *doesn't* precisely climb into my body, or take over my tongue; it's much more as if I was doing an impression, adopting a mask, and suddenly found I couldn't get the mask off. If he's a virus, I welcome him in. I encourage him. I start to think *his* way, and start to interpret the signals of the physical world wrongly. But don't we all, all the time interpret the given things around us, not simply according to what they are, but according to some idea of what they should be. And such words as novelists use – 'character', 'personality' – these are merely a desperate attempt to codify what is, in fact, an inchoate lump of stuff common to the planet. All that was happening to Anna and me, that day in Oxford, was that her DNA and my DNA were. . .

Shove it, James. If it's only a question of DNA why do you see her so clearly as you write? Why do you summon up something about her that wasn't to do with fucking or eating or drinking or talking, some indefinable quality that made her precious? That makes her still precious, in spite of what happened afterwards? That makes you want to rush out on to the lawn and knock your head against the wall and say 'Yes yes yes I did. I did love her. Sorry but that is the only way to describe it. And always will love her, however many explanations, all of them coarse or comic, you can devise to account for my behaviour?'

We finished our coffee. I paid and we walked out into the afternoon, our arms round each other. I can't remember which way we turned on the street. I only know we walked a long time among the afternoon shoppers, in the cold rain, and that sometimes we'd stop as if by prearranged signal and without knowing how, our lips would find each others lips and we would kiss there in the street, not for display or security or physical desire, but because it felt as if, by kissing like that, we could make the day go slower, or perhaps stop time altogether, so that we might never have to return to the city where our unshared histories had been made.

It was dark when we drove back down the motorway. We didn't talk much. I held her hand I think, lightly, companiably. And she looked out at the evening and the headlights and the continuing rain. 'Maybe,' she said at one point, 'I do believe in possession. I was brought up a Catholic.'

'Were you?'

'My father was Catholic. I was sent to a Catholic school. I was taught to believe in things far more absurd than possession.'

'Could you really transcribe that stuff for me?'

'Of course I could.'

She looked at me. 'You're not going to tell your wife, are you?'

'I don't think so,' I said.

'Good,' she said, 'I don't want you to. I don't see that this is anything to do with her.'

That is the way I'd like to remember it. Her and me in this car, on our way somewhere, never quite arriving, not bound by any duties or restrictions. I think I told her about Meg and her illness then. About the time she broke down in the High Street because she said someone was following us. About how I loved her and didn't love her. About how she was a truthful person and I wasn't. And Anna didn't have to do anything except make sure those big brown eyes were wide open and the laughs came when I was supposed to be being funny and the concern was present when my mouth turned down and my head lowered and I looked in need in comfort.

Maybe love's a matter of acting, I don't know. But I hold on to that day, transcribe it as carefully as I can and hope this is the image that will remain with me. Hope there will be no more bitterness.

I dropped her at the flat but didn't go in. I drove back, fast, through the empty streets. I wasn't going to tell Meg everything that had happened. But I was determined to talk to her. To talk to her about our marriage – where it had gone wrong and whether there was any hope for it. 'If there isn't any hope,' I said to myself, 'then so be it. If I don't love her I must have the courage to say so and not stay with her from convenience or fear of the unknown. And when we talk I'll know. I'll know whether there is any love left or not.'

For try as wee may, Yet the Lord can Show Us Oure Wayes – and whether they be Comely and Sufficient – and when our Actes here be comely in the Imagination – then also are they Comely in the Sight of God. And of such a Thing is This Love which, though it be of the Fleshly Sort, is yet worthy of the name and of no difference in Kinde or Quality than the love Our Lorde did bear us. For whatsoever is done by Thee in light and love is Light and Lovely so that See what Thou Wilt act what Thou Wilt – all is but One most light and lovely . . . Without action is there no Life and without Life – and is not this New Desire no less a principle than Life itself – there is no Perfection.

I reversed the car into our drive and ran up the steps, preparing the opening lines of my speech. I rang the bell. From deep inside the house a light flicked on and then heavy footsteps made their way to the door. Not Meg's. I felt a sudden prick of nervousness. When the door opened, the first thing I saw was that, in the hall, a glass-fronted picture, a chair and what looked like a pile of crockery had been thrown together. It looked as if a team of burglars had been working for a day to cause as much destruction as they could. The door too, I noticed, was opening in a hideously familiar way. It was sliding backwards slowly, as if by itself. Behind it was Juliet. She was wearing a dressing gown and a turban on her head. She had a mud pack on her face. She looked like a tribeswoman about to undergo a ritual passage to somewhere or other.

I looked beyond her to the debris of the hall. On the lower stairs, I could see the potted geraniums had fallen from the window sills that are set up the stairwell. There was earth and broken petals and smashed pottery. On the wall, just behind Juliet's head, was a huge, scrawled message written in marker pen, just the sort kids use on bus shelters or the ruined walls of inner cities. But the writing was more shapeless than the message familiar to me from buildings or hoardings that have earned the hatred of the displaced young. I could not even read the words. Except – did the end of the message say KILL THEE? You can make words say anything, you can make shapes into any figure you wish, as children do with cloud shapes. It's me, it's not the message, that makes it into the legend

EZEKIEL KILL THEE. KILL THEE. KILL THEE. . .

I looked at Juliet. She was trembling. She said nothing. I

238

waited for her to start to talk, for some familiar, mother-in-law sign that would tell me that what I was looking at was not really there. But she said nothing. I came into the hall and turned back to her. 'Where's Meg?'

She seemed to have been struck dumb. I went over to her and gripped her arm. 'Where is she? What's been happening?' Her mouth fell open. I realized with horror that she had no teeth. Her sunken cheeks gave her the look of an idiot.

'I don't know.'

'What's happened?'

'Oh Jamie,' she said, 'something terrible. Something awful.'

'Where is Meg?'

'She's gone,' said Juliet, 'she's taken the little girls and she's gone out into the night. She's gone out into the world. With nothing.'

If wee may choose One to be the Father of oure bodie – say the Cooperite – then is Death nott certayn, for this Same Father may be hee that had the making of us, stript of the Earthlie Qualities that brought us Lust, Avarice, Envy, Pride and Covetousness & if wee may take agayn a Wife of the Spirit – as some may Take a Wife of the Flesh, then, however cast down in Sinne and Deathe bee shee that was oure handmaiden, so will shee bee raysed and nott dead but live agayn in oure new Elected Sister – as the Cooperites term anie woman with whom they may seek Fellowship. Which shall nott lead them to the Sinnes of the Fleshe but to walk *hand in hand through the Garden which is Blessed as I have seen in thy face beloved in the morning yea when wee took oure Waies together and lay down Each to Each in the quiet places of the Earth.*

And so it was, as I talked with my Master Nehemiah of *Hertford* and of my marriage – the tale of which much affected him – it was as though Time was run back at my Pleasure. For as I told him of what had befallen mee, in everie particular, hee was so Attentive to my Discourse and spake with such Wisdom and Understanding that it was as if hee had travelled that selfsame Road with mee. And, most of all, when I told him of the Businesse at Essenden – which it payned mee much to Relate and of the Cruell and Unusuall work of the Devill upon

239

my Margaret & of my Rebellious Doubts concerning the testimonie of manie of the parish & of the *Running Lecturer* that
play dead on the field behind us, hee spake nott but nodded and
kept plain counsell until I had done when hee says – 'The Devill
may work his Wishes through whomsoever hee may Choose.
Neither is the Sinne of Witchcraft easily or lightly Discovered
and Confirmed. For hee may come to us at NIGHT IN THE
GUISE OF ONE WHO SPEAK Fair Wordes. And hee may work
his Wishes through Kings and Princes and those that sett themselves above us. In truth my son, if I Have Taken Offense at this
that was your sister, synce I have seen you sought her Carnally,
yet if I had met with her and talked with her withal and Gone to
Her in Fellowship, how then should shee and thee have been
cast out from our Assemblie, which grieved mee much and Mr
Passmore that was with us then & was killed by soldiers of the
King these four yeares, which is how I COME TO BE IN *God's
Armie.'* I grieved to hear what he Related concerning Mr Passmore, but wondered more at his Wordes and most especially
when they Concerned the Disguises and Stratagems the Devill
may Assume. For that which wee take to be Godlinesse may bee
none such. As, in the late Warres, manie that seemed for the
Libertie of Religion and Subject are seen to be merely for the
Confirmation of Title and Propertie. By which it is said – *the
Devill may come in the Apparel of a Priest.* And I thought upon Mr
Morris. And I was afrayde.

It was with my Master Nehemiah that I joyned troop that
went with my Lord Fairfax, an honest and gallant gentleman &
with him journeyed to the West Country, where in that year
Prince Rupert yielded up *Bristol* to us & wee prevailed agaynst
the Rebellious Factition of the Clubmen, in that region & everywhere wee had the Victorie. For the King was divided agaynst
himself & surrendered unto the Scotch. To my Amazement my
Master – who practised still the Virtuous and Holy Life of the
Cooperites had no thought that Killing should bee a Murder, or to
Walk with Sinne, and indeed in manie things I found him much
changed, as Warres will alter Opinions. *For*, says hee, *after the
barbarous death of Mr Passmore the Lord came to mee in a dream and
showed me two great figures, one in a black cloak with a Helmet closed*

240

off from the light and the other going Bareheaded as wee were wont to go in oure Assemblie. And as I watched the black cloaked Man smote that hee that went without a Covering and his Face I saw was wondrous Fair yet was there Blood upon it and his cheek was Stained with Blood. And as I watched his Blood fell to the Ground in Particles and Thousandfolds and as Each drop meets the grass there springs up a Souldier and the Souldiers have all a sword and Helmet and a Musket and they march together with a great shout saying BEHOLD WEE SHALL SMITE HIM THAT RAYSETH HIS HANDE AGAYNST US AND WEE ARE COME UNTO OURE KINGDOME FOR WHICH WE MUST NEEDS PUT ASIDE THE USES OF PEACE AND DESTROY THAT WHICH IS RAYSED UP AGAYNST US.

By which Dream hee knew the Cause wee fought were Just and Reasonable. 'For,' says hee to mee, 'how else may wee fight the Devill and Beelzebub unless wee close with him.' At which I would have fain asked him how wee might recognize the Evill One, for I thought then much of my Margaret and *Mr Morris* but I dared nott synce I was much troubled by what had passed. But in truth wee spake so much in those daies, and openlie, between ourselves & between otheres of the Armie & prayed together often in the Manner of our choosing so that our Converse was nott, as it had been with Mr Passmore, *behind closed Doores,* but open and in the Sight of God. Which came to bee the Cause of the Quarrelle between the Armie and the Parliament, for they Feared oure preaching the Word of God as wee chose it & would have had us indoores for feare of the Churchwarden. Thus it was, after the King's surrender to the Scotch, whiles King and Parliament courted each other & the Parliament sought to perswade us all to take oure wages and begone to *Ireland* or *the Americas* wee were Resolute that wee were no meer Mercenarie Armie but free Commoners of England, drawn together and Determined to Continue in oure Concern for the Rights and Liberties of the People. So wee determined at the Heath at Newmarket in the Yeare of our Lord 1647, nor would wee Yield, as may a crowd of Idle Apprentices to the PROMISE OF Sports and Pastimes or of Wages that would tempt us Home. And in all these discussions and Debates was my Master to bee hearde. Very Savage was hee & Satyricall as to the King, who was taken by us from the Scotch at this time & who sate at Hampton Court, wated on by both Armie and Parliament as if it were hee and nott Ourselves, that had had the victorie – 'For,' saith my Master, 'hee hath taken unto himself the Silver and the Gold and the People in the Land of everyone according to his taxation to give it unto Pharaoh.'

Side by side with Him were others that called themselves also *Cooperites*, although, from the Variety and Confusion of their severall creedes, it was hard indeed to Grant them anie Name in Common. For some in oure regiment then, which was *Colonel Thompson's*, said wee should hold all things in common, others said merely that wee should abolish all Controules and Checks to the government of the Kingdome and asked that everie Man might have a Share in electing Officers, while others agayn said wee were but Seekers after Truth whose Businesse was all to ask and nott to Argue oure Thirst Quenched when wee sought so much as never to bee Satisfied. Some called others Levellers, after John Lilburne's Partie and others swore wee had a Need to Elect our Representatives, by which I came to bee an Agitator in the Regiment, of which I must now needs tell the History.

In truth that Armie was more Various and Rich in Opinions than anie after will tell, nor did one Faction end where another began but came together upon Issue as Rivers merge in a plain. And though there were they that called us all LEVELLERS, and some claimed wee were the ANABAPTISTICALL partie, yet,in truth, were I to name each sect or tributary to that Holy River I would outrun the Names of Jehovah and weary myselfe with so Recounting them. For there were there the Cooperites, the Jonson's Men, those that called themselves the *Walking Cooperites* for they prayed as they walked saying *God is motion neither shall ye mock the spheres but take your meat and drink walking and laughing and praysing God*, & there were the Out of COUNTENANCE Men that looked one another nott in the eie, there were True Levellers and False Levellers, those that were all for Honest John and those that said Honest John was a liar, and no good could come of one who called on a Chamber Pot before my Lordes the JUSTICES because, says hee, *I would fain make water.*

O there were some that called themselves Seekers and one who styled himself the Captain of the Rant, there were those who spake of the Parliament of Saints and some few that spoke up, though quietly, for the *good old Presbytery*. Which when I HEARD IT I liked it nott for it called to mind Mr Morris that examined and testified agaynst my Margaret when I was lost and knew nott the Waie. But these names were not Emblems of a particular Partie nor was anie Groupe mindful onlie of itself but Individuals asserted and Pleaded their severall waies to God. It may bee, now, some ten Yeares after, I have mind of what was written after the businesse at Ware & Corkbush Field when the Cause of the Free and Independant Armie went hard and one was shot at the Head of his REGIMENT. Or perhaps I call to mind my time alone in London, after I had come from Northampton. In truth I would remember it as a Time when Men thought they might be Free, where now they see the World through the Barres of a Prison and King Cromwell goes about guarded for Feare of his Subjectes, that they hate and Feare him. And I would remember it as a time when my HEAVENLIE Familie became an Earthlie one also, for wee walked Openlie and told our Truths as wee found them & as wee had once had pleasant Discourse at my Master's, now took it in the OPEN Aire and manie came and listened and debated with Us.

Still was I, even in these Times, where Wordes and Free Confessiouns of the hearte were never more Loved, a Silent and *Close guarded* Man, which perhaps was the Cause of my being elected Agitator, synce one was needed who might Moderate Extreams of Opinioun within the Regiment. And my Master Nehemiah spoke much for mee, saying I was of a Godlie and Virtuous Disposition, neither did I seek to put myselfe forward for *I sought nott the Glorie of Office nor the Apparel of Power but studied to go on my pilgrimage and avoyde those snares of temptation.* It was at this time that wee came upon London and turned out the Presbyters, swords in Hand, for they sought oure Ruine & marched through the Wicked City which caused the Inhabitants to marvel at us greatlie. But wee were not Amazed by their Temples nor by their Palaces and Great

Estates at which they would have men wonder and would nott bee corrupted by that city that Tempted us as a woman should tempt one who is Tired after long Labour, but wee withdrew and camped in the fields by the River below *Putney*, where in the Church that lies hard by the river I attended the Generall Council of the Armie at which Questions of Law and Government were debated between ourselves and oure Captaines.

So do I understand the Truths oure Lorde reveled to Us when he saith that *I came among you and ye knew mee nott*. For now, when I was most like to find this Earth a verie Heaven, & a strong Union between my Brothers of the Earth and those Above, between how the names of things bee called after the flesh here below and how they bee shewn to us by oure Father in Heaven, when all seemed ready to bee Revealed to Us, then was the Vision taken from us. Then was oure faith broken and Betraied. Then indeed was *the body but a carcasse and the Soule buried with it Deep in the Earth*. For wee shall nott see each other's soules except in HEAVEN, where I do hope to meet my Margaret & walk with her in Innocence once agayne.

There were at that Conference at Putney with mee in the Church manie of oure Agitators and nott all known to mee. But before I went into them, my Master saith unto mee, 'Do ye imagine to Fashion out of the Wordes and the Speches of one that is Desperate a Mighty Thing? Yea yea – overrule the fatherless and *dig a pit for your friend*.' By which I knew him to say I should remayne quiet in that Council for feare of certayne Rash and Unquiet Persons, lest I lead us too hastily into a Generall Rebellion, when still wee had the Parliament and the City agaynst Us.

For there were there Masters Rainsborough, Sexby, Everard, Wilton, Aynsworth and others. There was *Clough* the Anabaptist, Thomas Rogers the Seer that sought Jerusalem in the fields by Putney, Master Ellis that I heard took sick and died *when he could no longer wear Green in's cap for Honest John*. And all had, to my mind, more knowledge than I of the Matter of Politics and STRATEGIE. At the High Table of the Council were Cromwell and Ireton and next to them sate Master William Clarke that was a Secretarie and writ much during the proceedings at which I wondered Greatlie. But, as I looked on him, one nexte to me, which was this same Sexby, known to us *Cooperites* as a great and terrible LEVELLER, turns to mee and says, 'Oure Master Secretary is minded to have a full and complete account of what is said here. Have a care lest *Captain Cromwell* do nott use them agaynst us and play us as hee seeks to play the King. Manie who speak here today for the Freedoms and Liberties of England will find their Captaines play them False I will warrant.' For they spake just then of the King and of how wee in the Armie should proceed in the Great and Terrible Enterprise upon which wee are Embarked. And as I noted well his wordes, hee rises – being marked to speak and saith (I do nott recall the full matter of it but this particularly) *'Wee have laboured to please a Kinge and I thinke except wee goe aboutt to cutt oure own throats we shall nott please him; an we have gone to support an house which will prove rotten studdes.'* Which wordes sounded in mine eares and none others in the Assemblie made mee hearken to them & there appeared to mee above the Heads of those that were there an Angel and the Angel spake unto mee saying *Yea is there Witchcraft in the Lande and the Abominable Compact with the powere of Hell is Confirmed and Discovered to bee among us & that same Sinne is Rebellion but nott the Rebellion of a Subject who shall free himself of a Tyrant or of a Father that is ill used by hee who engendered Him which is no Father no I say unto Ye, nott by those who call themselves holy and priests for what is the New Presbytery but the Priest that was and what be hee but a meer Copy and Modelle of such Jesuits and Papisticall Time servers as ever terrified old women at a Country Fair O hear ye hear ye I say unto ye they that USE Witchcraft are the Princes and Great Ones of the Land yea the Priests and the Hypocrites and those that sett thee about with traps for they have polluted shee who is holy and Hanged from the common cart one who would walk in God's Light.*

Upon which above that Angel I saw my Margaret as shee was in Life, her hair down beside her and her eie cast down. And there were two teares upon her cheeks and about her neck was the line of the rope where it had marked her. Which called to mind the Noyse shee made that Daie –though I Turned my eie away from it – and the unconscionable time it took her to make her Peace with God, which manie said was synce shee was Bewitched. From that mark on her Fair Skin came forth blood which flowed upon her raiment & she looked upon mee and I knew Her to bee no Witch. At which I fell in a swoon & knew no more of that Assemblie. Save afterwards I minded what my *True Leveller*, Master Sexby hath said, and was of the Opinion wee fought in some wise agaynst the same enchantments & that it is oure Masters and oure PRIESTS and oure Captains that would lie to us, bewitch and cozen us, and that those that would seek to worship in the Light, gloriously should cast down Priest and Master and Captain and embrace Humility and Innocence. For though Rebellion may yet bee as the Sinne of Witchcraft, yet was this Charles's raysing of his Standarde a Rebellion, was the IMPIOUS Prescription of Formes of Worshippe laid down by such as MORRIS as the Sinne of Witchcraft. & so, as I shall seek to relate, if the night give mee time, was this whole Sweet and Newly Opened KINGDOM of England given over to the devilish and hellish Enchantments of One who Plaied the Witch as no Other – I meane the Lord Protector who would bee King, that same OLIVER CROMWELL by whose strong art I am here confined and must goe to meet my Death when Tomorrow comes, as come, I feare mee, it must.

22

'She's left us,' she went on. 'Left us, left us.'

Us? I wanted to say. Howjamean *us*? Don't you mean *me* or *you*? But you and me, Juliet, will never be *us*. Especially when you haven't even got your fucking teeth in. She groped in the pocket of her dressing gown and fitted the offending implement into her mouth.

'Oh, Jamie,' she said, 'it has been terrifying. Terrifying. Really frightening. Do you believe in the supernatural?' I looked behind me at the street. It was clearly not going to be possible to counter this with a remark about the weather. Although, come to think of it, the weather looked pretty interesting. Ragged clouds across the moon, a gusty wind. . .

'Are you all right, Jamie?'

'Fine. Fine. What is this mess. . .' I went through to the kitchen. Here too, plates had apparently been torn out of cupboards and thrown halfway across the room. The rubbish bin had been emptied over the floor – an obscene mass of potato peelings, stale bread, scraps of meat, and here too, on the far wall, there was the writing. Scrawled capitals bleeding down the white wall. It wasn't the same as the message in the hall. I thought I read the word THOMASINA. And next to it KILL THEE KILL KILL. . .

With her teeth Juliet had recovered some of her customary *élan*. She followed me in.

'What is all this mess?'

'Is all not well in your married life?' she replied.

'Apart from the fact that she's fucked off and torn the house to bits, it's fine.'

'Jamie –' Her left elbow crooked, her right hand flung forward she looked like the contralto in a Gilbert and Sullivan opera about to tell us who was substituted for whom in the cradle. 'Jamie – I saw it with my own eyes. It was terrifying. Terrifying. But I saw it with my own eyes.'

'What did you see?'

She began to tell her story, as only Juliet can. 'I was having my stew with some pimentos, the ones in a tin from Waitrose that are 45p and I heard these crashing sounds.'

This, for Juliet, was almost alarmingly brisk. I was surprised that we hadn't had a long description of the origins of the brand name, together with a disquisiton on the weight, packaging and advertising indulged in by the manufacturers of the items in question.

'I heard these terrible crashing sounds and screamings from the kitchen. I hear every noise from down there you know.' – *And I tape it*, I felt like saying – 'Well I thought at first that something must have fallen over so I turned off the water and the stew or rather I turned it down to a hundred and fifty which is what I normally cook it at and crept up the stairs and stood by the door listening because it was locked because sometimes you do lock it to stop me getting in I know that.' I waited for a lengthy description of the paint used on her side of the connecting door. Or some other key narrative detail, such as the state of her bunions during the crisis. 'All the time you see was this terrible screaming. Terrible screaming as if a troop of devils had got into the house and things were being thrown around and I heard Thomasina give an awful screech a really terrible sound and I realized "Well. Something must be up." '

Brilliant, Juliet. It's nice to have you in the basement. An up-to-the-minute analysis of our relationship any time we need it. And – when danger threatens – there you are, crouching behind your door, plate of red-hot stew at the ready.

'The screaming went on an awful long time. An awful long time. I know because I heard the milkman come the one with the white hair, you know, Mr Klewens, I think he's Polish, he's nice, I heard him come and deliver next door and all the time Thomasina was screaming but it wasn't as if she was screaming it was like someone else was screaming you see. And so I decided to break the door down.' I looked at Juliet's burly shoulders and gigantic rugby player's hands. No problem. Had she lifted it off by the hinges, or just leaned against it casually? 'I went downstairs to my little flat and got a hammer the six-foot one I use for breaking up the paving stones and heavy work like that for instance you remember when I hired a concrete mixer for a day and made a rockery for the little girls even though it subsequently collapsed and I climbed up the stairs and ran at the door that separates my flat from you and hammered at it shouting at the top of my voice *Don't worry darling I'm coming!*'

The perfect image, I thought bleakly, for our marriage. Or for what was left of our marriage.

That shifty, idle, drunken bastard you married is trying to screw you? *Don't worry darling I'm coming and this time I'm bringing a six-foot hammer!*

'Eventually,' she went on, 'I smashed it to little bits, and because I was unable to reach the bolt I shoved one arm through – I have quite long arms as you know' – *like a gorilla's, Juliet* – 'and I still couldn't reach the bolt so I just hammered a four foot hole in the door all the time screaming *Don't worry darling I'm coming* and all the time the screaming and the crashing were going on and eventually, with hammer on my shoulder, ready for absolutely anything a gas explosion possibly of some kind like that one in Tooting I read about or a rapist I am terrified of rapists' – *why Juliet? What chance would a rapist stand against you?* 'And there I was and in front of me next to those wellingtons in the hall she *always* leaves those out I don't know why was a sight I shall never forget there were Meg and the girls only Thomasina was all white and they were looking at this horrid writing on the wall all dripping it was rather like the sort of stuff vandals do it's disgusting isn't it really the whole country has gone mad I think but that wasn't the remarkable thing those flowers you see them those flowers were falling through the air and crashing to the ground and plates actual *plates* were flying through the air of their own accord it was the most terrifying thing I have ever seen and there was this noise in the kitchen and my little girl was screaming *Stop it stop stop it* and then she started saying these awful things Jamie, awful awful' –

'What things?' I had a sudden vision, beyond Juliet's mannerisms, of what had happened. I felt queasy. I didn't want her to tell me. But her voice went on, level, remorseless.

'She was talking about witchcraft Jamie and the devil. I believe in witchcraft of course I think there's much to be said for witchcraft I'm not as agin it as some' – *of course not you are a fucking witch you old bat* – 'but she was going too far. She was saying awful ugly things, some obscenities I have tried to be a good mother and I do not think I have deserved what she said to me ugly foul things she said and all the time these plates and things were flying through the air and it was quite dangerous and Thomasina was sort of choking and her face was all white and she said something about me being a witch and I didn't know whether to laugh or cry actually' – *neither do I Juliet* – 'and eventually I said my darling what have I done what is the matter I do not understand it and at that moment the vase I brought back from Limoges the year daddy died I let you have it I didn't mind actually came whizzing through the air and smashed at my feet in a thousand pieces and I noticed that she had two suitcases with her and she just walked out she walked out by the front door past those tubs I planted last year that never get any sun and she said' – *she said 'I hate you Juliet I hate the way you sit on my life like a great black cloud and talk about how wonderful it was when daddy was alive and how we are so close when we are not if you want to know I think it is you that drove me crazy you and your obscene closeness mothers and daughers are not repeat not repeat not siamese twins why do you keep reminding me of what I owe you can't you give and not expect a return you stupid old ratbag?'* – 'she said "I'm going away from this house. Something evil is happening here. And it's going to get worse. I'm going away and I can't tell you when I'm coming back don't look for me I won't be with any of our friends I'm just going." And then Thomasina her face was all white and sort of twisted looked up at me and said something I didn't understand, a name, it was a funny name only she said it all peculiarly it was horrible.'

'What was the name?'

'Like in the Bible. It was quite clear. Ezekiel, she said. And then she laughed. As if she'd said something clever.'

I went over to the fridge and peered in. She had obviously, taken the contents of the fridge with her as well. At the back was a can of beer and a half-bottle of akvavit. I poured myself a generous measure of each. I looked up to see Juliet eyeing me.

'What's happening, Jamie?'

'Something or nothing, I'm not sure.'

'Are you and Meg –'

'Please,' I said, 'please. Just leave me alone, can't you? Can't you just leave me alone? I have a mother all of my own. OK?' I looked across at her – large black glasses perched at the end of her nose, hands hanging at the sides of her dressing gown, knuckles in the shape of a loose fist. She looked like a boxer at the weigh-in. An old fighter, a little punchy, a little tired. Against my will I felt a pang of sympathy for the old trout. Husband dead, loves daughter to distraction – or thinks she does –and daughter doesn't want the love. There's too much of it. It's grain alcohol on a neat stomach. We're all of us simply trapped by this family business – an infernal circle that is strong enough to make plates fly through the air or obscene slogans appear on walls. Hadn't I read somewhere that the word slogans is derived from the word for spirits? There were enough spirits in this house to set an entire household goods depart-ment dancing through the atmosphere like confetti in a hur-ricane. Enough slogans too come to think of it. *British troops out of Northern Ireland. It's a woman's right to choose. Say No to No Say.* What – when it comes down to it – are these bold words fit for, in their turn, except to frighten old women or make domestic furniture turn somersaults?

'I'm sorry,' she said at last. 'I'm sorry if I've done something wrong. I'm sorry.' She hunched up in the chair. 'Don't be, Juliet,' I said, 'it isn't your fault.' I could have gone to her then to comfort her the way I should have gone, so many times, to Meg, or even to my own father when he was alive. I recall the morning after my wedding when he lay on the sofa of our house squinting at me and, to my surprise, held out his arms to me. But I didn't go to him then, the way I didn't go to Juliet that night. It isn't families. It isn't wives or fathers or mothers or husbands or sons-in-law; it is ourselves that are the bleak thing. Ourselves and the lack of love that is in us.

'I'm not my mother,' Meg had so often said. 'Don't abuse me when you want to abuse her.' Or she might have said 'Love me and love her, can't you? We're one.' But I saw the family like-ness, found it not threatening but human, as the old lady sat there in the wooden rocking chair the poor old bitch made for us out of some kit or other, and still I did not go to her. Maybe that was the moment I lost out to Ezekiel. Maybe that was when the bad side of me started to take over. The worst sin is to glimpse charity in oneself and then shut it down for fear it will swallow you, engulf the hard little thing that we think, oh how mistakenly, makes us what we are.

'I'd better get to bed,' she said eventually.

'OK,' I said, softly. When she had gone I went across to her door, closed it quietly and drew both bolts. There was no point in doing this. There was a jagged hole in the middle through which anyone could walk. But I wasn't going to let the old trout get under my defences.

23

She wasn't at the Tomlinsons. She wasn't at the Carters. She wasn't with Jan the feminist or Susan the schoolteacher or Paula her friend from grammar school days. She wasn't with her brother or the woman next door or the Smiths from Carshalton that we see every year. She wasn't with Rick Mason or Steve Jackson or Dave Prothero or Alan Lewless or the Welch twins or the Muller family from Hounslow. She had vanished. She had disappeared into the tangled city of London, and she had taken the children with her.

At first I was angry, then I was puzzled, and finally relieved. I rang Anna and asked her over. 'How are you getting on with the Clarke paper?' I said. There was a silence at the other end of the phone. 'Well?'

'I'd rather,' she said at last, 'you just read it.'

'OK.'

'Where shall I come?'

'Come here. To my house.'

'Won't your wife –'

'My wife's left me.'

A pause, then a brief, slightly embarrassed laugh. 'Oh. I'm sorry to hear that.'

'Don't be. It wasn't me – it was the poltergeist.'

'You've got a poltergeist?'

'Yes. But I've locked it in the basement.'

She laughed again. This time the laugh was the clear treble. The way I liked it. 'I won't be able to stay the night then.'

'You're frightened of ghosts?'

'Very. Anyway – if you stay all night with me you'll see me change back into a frog.'

'Well I wouldn't want that, would I?'

'See you later.' The phone clicked off. We were strong on banter, Anna and I. I went to the window and looked out into the garden. The sodden trees were empty of leaves. The deserted swing, idle beneath the climbing frame, seemed like a reproach. The only sign of life was Juliet, who was swinging a large axe up and down viciously on a block of wood at the far end of lawn. Perhaps she was imagining it was me. Since Meg's disappearance our conversations had hardly touched on the weather. We discussed, almost without ceasing, Meg's whereabouts. We discussed what the police had said and where to put an advert and who else to ring and I nodded and looked serious, wondering if she suspected that, since her daughter's disappearance, I had done absolutely fuck all to try and find her. Would she have the binoculars out when Anna came round? Entirely probable.

Now that she had made a four-foot hole in the door to the basement, Juliet came and went very much as she pleased. She emerged late at night, carrying armfuls of washing. I would find her on coming out of the lavatory, standing in the hall, looking up at a light bulb. Suppose Anna and I were to . . . and suppose she . . .

I have never seriously thought of killing anyone apart from Juliet (I discount the occasions when Ezekiel, not I, is running things) but in that fortnight after Meg left I quite frequently sat down and calmly and slowly worked on methods of disposing of my mother-in-law. Sometimes I thought I would leap out at her from a cupboard late one night and strangle her. And then I thought of her gigantic physique, her notoriously high reactive speed, and decided that she might well end up strangling me. I considered poisoning her. But how? Never in the entire history of our relationship have I made her so much as a sandwich. I could tip something in her stew. But Juliet's stew would probably neutralize all but the most rare South American poisons. I thought of stabbing, drowning, electrocution, hanging, gassing and burning. And finally walked around the deserted house in a sort of hazy ecstasy, afraid to choose, since the contemplation of all and each of them, of her screaming, choking, frying and spluttering, was so uniquely pleasurable.

I wrote nothing for Gottlieb. He rang once and asked me how it was going. I told him I was very excited. He said he too was very excited. I heard no more from him. I think I was really waiting for Anna's transcription, and found that my immediate surroundings had less and less interest for me. Headlines in the newspaper struck me as merely odd. Someone had blown up a block of flats in Lebanon; women and children had been maimed. I looked at the photographs of the faces of the survivors and noticed the way grief seems to pull the features out of shape, but felt their concerns were nothing to do with me. Once, going to bed, I thought I heard Ezekiel's voice in the darkness, whispering something, but I could not have said what it was he was whispering. I didn't like the idea of his being in the house. I told him to go away, and when he heard my voice he answered: 'Nay, until Ye are Cognizant of the Facts of the Business, I shall be about Ye. For not until ye have a Full Account of what it was that was Done under the Rule of the Unlamented Lord Protector, and How I, too, came to make my miserable End, will there be Chance or Occasion of Restitution.'

'What restitution?' I said. 'What do you want? Tell me what you want. That's all you have to do. What have you done with Meg? And the girls? I miss the girls. What –' But he was gone. I think I heard a laugh in the dark, but I heard no more of him.

How often did I see Anna in those weeks? I can't remember. I know I rang her most days to ask her how she was getting on with the manuscript. I know I went to a film with her once, though I can't remember what film it was. Most of the time I was alone. Not writing, not reading, sitting in my room looking out at Putney Hill, whose trees and houses were as unreal to me as the faces of the bereaved in far off Lebanon. I do know that the afternoon she brought the manuscript round, about three hours before she was due to arrive, Juliet appeared at my door. 'No news of my little girl?'

'I'm afraid not,' I said. I was staring at a blank sheet of paper, my biro next to it at a workmanlike angle. She came further in to the room, anxious to talk. 'Are you all right, Jamie?'

'Why do you ask?'

'I worry about you,' she said. 'You sit up here – thinking.' – I waited for her to go. 'What are you doing?' she said.

'I am Engaged,' I said, 'upon a Most Precarious and Hazardous Task. Which is to Prosecute and Discover Those Who, lately in the Kingdom Have been Discovered to be the Most Notorious and Foul Witches.' She laughed, nervously. 'You are funny, Jamie,' she said.

I turned on her. 'Aye Madam,' I said, 'Thee and Thy Wench are Pleased to be Amused at my Concernes and Mock the Interest which I shew in matters which Touch the very Heart and Substance of these our present Grievances – which are – Want of Employment and Scope of Achievement – a General Lack All and So Must it Be Masters that is abroad. And why not, I ask it of you Madam, should such a Falling Off be not Ascribed to the Ministrations of such Evil Minded Hags?'

'Well,' she said, 'the rain's kept off anyway.'

'About your business, woman, and Hold Yourself in Feare and Readiness for Great and Terrible Events!'

'Are you all right, dear?' she said, backing out on to the landing. I got up and followed her.

'I,' I said – my voice seemed to be getting louder – 'am Sent by Hee who Hath no Peer to Inquire into the Disturbances that have Been Lately Provoked in the Parish of Putney – by which I mean the Most Unnatural Disorder of Nature, and Open Rebellion yea the Transformation of the Very Plates and Decorations of This My Property into Agents of Rebellion, the Unconsidered Flight of my Lawful Wife and the Ceaseless and Illegitimate Intrusion of Thy Most Marked and Perverted Countenance into my Affairs. Get Thee gone woman before I find the marks of Satan about Thy Privities and have Thee put to the torture and from thence to the gallows to Hang before all the Locality!'

She moved off down the stairs. 'There's no need to be offensive,' she said.

But I couldn't stop. I ran down the stairs after her and grabbed her arm. My face was working furiously and my hands were shaking. 'Witch,' I shrieked. 'Damned and Unnatural Witch who Hath by Her Most Evil Practices and Representations made mee a stranger in My House and Home and a Foreigner to These my Children! Degraded and Unprincipled Sorceress I accuse Thee of Sending to mee in the likeness of a Mouse Thy spirit to infect mee with the Principles of the Evil One. Satan himself is about Thy Business, Woman! Begone!'

She broke free of my grasp. 'Jamie,' she said. 'If this is your idea of a joke I am afraid it is not mine. Something very strange is going on in this house and in my opinion you should see someone, a doctor or someone, you have been behaving most oddly –'

I slashed at her with my right hand and she shied back towards her door. 'Aye,' I screeched, 'there's Odd and Odd is there not Beldame? There's the Odd that is the Natural Order of the Created World, and then there's the Odd that is no less than the Malign and Evil Principle which I have discovered here before us. There's the Odd of the Devil and His Works Mistress is there not? And What other Principle is so at Worke on Mee that I am deprived of what is Lawfully Mine!'

She folded her arms at the top of the stairs. 'I always thought that you were quite male chauvinist. But now I know, don't I? And if I were you I should stop talking in that silly way or the wind will change my lad and you won't be able to stop. I shall be looking for somewhere else in the morning. I'm only sorry that Meg – '*Begone witch!*' I howled, '*Begone before I arraign thee and have thee brought to thy Death I command thee Go!*' She opened the ruined door and sniffed ostentatiously. I heard her go down the stairs. When everything was quiet down below I went back to my room to wait for Anna.

She came at about six and I ran down the stairs two at a time to greet her. She was wearing a black polo neck sweater and a denim skirt and her red hair was scraped back from her forehead. She looked like an American college kid with her term paper in her hand. I looked from her to the manuscript, not knowing which I was more pleased to see. Then I pulled her up into my arms and kissed her, there on the steps so the neighbours could get a good long look. 'Are you OK?' she asked eventually. 'You look awful.'

'I have been late at the Examination of a Woman who is Most Surely an Accursed Witch and Whose Obduracy and lack of the Spirit of Repentance Moved mee to Great Wrath.'

'Christ,' said Anna, 'I don't think I can take much more of that sort of thing. I've had our friend Clarke going round in my brain all week. I tell you I'm seeing witches behind every corner.'

'Aye Madam,' I said, 'Now do you Credit that Such Things

can still Affront and Concern Us?' She looked at me oddly. 'Is there a drink in the house?' she said.

The curious thing was – I hadn't wanted to speak in this manner to her. I had started to say something quite different, but found words other than those I had intended coming out of my mouth. This is not a totally novel experience for me. I usually open my mouth and talk without thinking too carefully about what comes out. I'm very aware of the dangers of becoming inhibited. At cocktail parties I can talk for three hours without once allowing my brain to interfere with the free creation of sentences. But this was different. This was closer to feeling that I was on the stage and that suddenly I had forgotten my lines. Into the silence came a voice and it wasn't exactly my voice, but at least it was better than the silence. It was better than the thought that Anna and I had no existence beyond the moment and the moment was about to go. The voice didn't seem to have my timbre, quite. It was rather thinner and more vinegary than mine. There was something old maidish about it.

'I'll leave this thing here,' said Anna, putting the manuscript down with something like impatience. She seemed glad to be rid of it. 'What a lovely house.'

And now there was nothing I could put into the silence. I followed her into the room. Her hips, visible under the denim, ground rhythmically together. I looked down at her legs, followed the curve of her buttocks under the dress, and moistened my lips. 'My God,' she said, 'you look a bit rampant.'

'For Three Hundred Yeares, Madam,' I said, 'I have waited to Feel This Most Sweet and Heated Perception. From Thy Hair to These Two Orbes that burn with such Delicate and Proper Lechery as is Affected by Thee I –'

Her voice rose sharply. 'Stop it Jamie,' she said. Then she grinned. 'I mean you *are* funny but . . . I'm sorry. I just sit there poring over that thing out there and it gets to me, my God you start to think there's something in it after a while. It's all so insidious and plausible. And when you're alone in the flat you look over your shoulder and expect to see bloody Ezekiel Oliphant the Witchfinder walk in at any moment.'

I tried to fight the voice down but it wouldn't stop. 'Madam,' – and now there was a quality in what I said that seemed utterly foreign to me – 'seek no further for Hee who, more than any other, more than Hopkins, more than Master Stearne, more than any Jumped Up Tuesday to All Fools Day Witchfinder is Hee who will at last Purge This Oure Kingdome of Each and Every Hag that Hath Forged the Abominable Compact with Hell.' I bowed low. She backed away towards the window. 'Ezekiel Oliphant the Witchfinder,' I said, 'at Your Service.'

'Jamie, please. Please stop it.'

I laughed. 'What? Afeared of Mee? If there is Nothing you wish to Conceal – what is to fear? All is as it Should be at Daybreak. Cleare and Evident as the Campaigne. But if, Mistress, there is *evil* in you –' 'Stop it,' she said again, 'stop it.'

But I couldn't stop it. I wanted to but I couldn't. It was curious. As I talked I could see her face and it suddenly seemed clearer and more beautiful than I had ever seen it. Like Dante's Beatrice, she seemed above me, capable of helping me and yet – I found myself thinking this consciously – I would not be helped. What was it that soul in hell said to Dante? Carry on with your journey and leave me to get on with my burning. Something like that. I was burning. Something was consuming me. And as it burned me this horrible, thin voice talked on and on and on. 'Let us to My Chambers Mistress and I'll shew Thee a Way to Tickle out the Devil wherever hee may have marked you. Where then, mistress? On Thy Fat rump or about the Thighes? Or . . .'

She backed away into the hall and I followed her still talking. And inside me another voice kept saying 'Look, Anna. Help me will you. I don't want it to be like this. Help me. Please.' But, this wasn't the voice that spoke.

Well – was it me that spoke to her that first day in the Museum? Or me that held her in my arms in Oxford that day and told her I loved her? If it was me, then how can that same person now sit here alone and miss Meg the way I miss my father, as if she was a dead person? Love makes us strangers to ourselves, the prey to any voice that cares to use us. That's a fact.

When she got to the manuscript she reached for it. She was muttering something about doctors (we all reach for the doctor when we are bewitched) but I didn't hear it. I pounced forward

259

and grabbed her arm, pinning it to the chair where she had lain the manuscript. 'Mine,' I hissed, 'mine. Mine. Mine.'

'Jamie –'

'Have a care, Lady,' I said, 'lest You too be taken as was the woman Stafford at the Assize of Northamption, dying Most Unregenerate and Calling all Heaven to Witness that the Witch-finder Oliphant was in League with the Protector and what seemed Most Fair in this our England, was, in Very Truth, Most Foul.'

She went white. She looked suddenly, genuinely terrified, the way you look when you're driving at seventy miles an hour and something pulls out into your path fifty yards ahead of you. There was no colour in her face as she said, 'How can you know about that? You haven't read the paper yet. How do you know about Stafford? How do you know about the Stafford woman? That's the most horrible –'

I grabbed her hand and squeezed it hard. 'Do not Enquire I beseech You,' I whispered, 'too closely into the Workings of the World, lest, what you take to be Meer Shadowes be Proved to bee Themselves the Onlie Thynge of substance. Oh for there are witches – and every sorte of Phantom You May wish – and the Dead may Walk and Controule their Destinies from This, the Dark side of the Grave, where I am so long confined –' My voice took on a pleading note. She shook her hand free and went for the door. The manuscript, I noticed with a pleasure I did not understand, was still safe on the chair. 'I beseech you Fair Lady,' I said, 'I do beseech you humbly. One request. One request I would Beg of You and it Must be You who Grant it –'

'*Get away*!' screamed Anna, '*get away get away get away*!' And, wrenching back the door, she ran into the street. I heard a thump behind me. I turned to see Juliet standing in front of the smashed door. Her arms were folded and her mouth turned down. She looked like a landlady confronting a tenant. 'What are you doing now? You're sick. You're –' I came towards her. I was smiling. With my right hand I made little come-hither gestures. 'Hither, my Pet,' I said sweetly, cloying, 'come hither, my Pet. And what Name do you take for yourselfe Todaye? Art Thou Jackie the Morrow now? Or is it Pleasant Dealing that Wee Have to Outface Here?' When I was close enough to her, I put one hand on her chest and shoved hard. She gave a kind of low grunt and fell backwards into the stairwell. She thwacked and bounced her way down the stairs like a sack of coal going into a full cellar. And when she reached the bottom, she lay still. I watched but she did not move. 'And stay Thou there in Like Manner,' I yelled at her prostrate form, 'until the prince of Evil himself do come to Wake Thee and Make Thy Account to Hee Who Made Thee!'

Then I went back into the hall, picked up the paper Anna had brought and, squatting on the floor, began to read it. She had summarized the contents in a short preface – a typical piece of academic neatness.

SUMMARY

This paper purports to be a confessional diary made by William Clarke, the Secretary of the Army Council, in the winter of 1658. It deals with events some years previously, and touches on the last days of the Protectorate in a way that is at once revealing and unsurprising ('there is an extraordinary series of allegations against the then Master of the Tower, which need not concern us here') but the central section of the manuscript deals with a story, that, if the surface details of the MS were not so immediately plausible, that I would at first wish to describe as some antiquarian joke. If it is such a thing – and I am, I fear, not entirely convinced that it is – who is responsible?

The obvious choice would be Dr Ronald Oliphant, former lecturer in English History at the University of London, who was retired on medical grounds some ten years ago. Oliphant's obsession with his notional ancestor Ezekiel Oliphant (for some reason obscure to me known as 'The Bloomsbury Witchfinder') was in part responsible for his collapse. And it would appear that he is the obvious choice for such a piece of trickery. There is, however, apart from the fact that Worcester College has details of all those to look at the papers over the last ten years, together with an account of the purpose and nature of their visit, an extraordinary fact concerning the physical details of the

MS that I have treated on a separate note at the end. Suffice it to say that this dating procedure suggests, on present evidence, that the MS is *at least* one hundred years old and possibly older.

The gist of Clarke's confession seems to be this. Cromwell, according to his account, had had dealings, as early as the battle of Edge Hill, with a young Parliamentary soldier from the village of Essenden in Hertfordshire, by name Ezekiel Oliphant. Oliphant, from Clarke's account, emerges as a most unpleasant piece of work. He seems to have been a printer by trade and a follower of the Presbyterian faith, but, early in the 1640s he brought a case against his wife, in which she was accused of witchcraft. It was this, says Clarke, that brought him into a very similar position to that of Hopkins and Stearne, the witchfinders.

According to Clarke, Oliphant and Cromwell struck up one of those extraordinarily close emotional bonds that are typical of male relationships inside closed groups, especially closed groups under siege from outside; they ate, spoke and prayed together, very much in the way John Lilburne the Great Leveller grew close to what must be the most enigmatic figure in English history. Such relationships were also, with their stress on 'fellowship', very typical of the emergent Puritan movement, and it was this, it would appear from Clarke's account, that led Oliphant to gain his extraordinary hold over the man who was soon to become the most powerful personage in the land. For Oliphant was by now not simply a self-appointed judge, on the lines of Stearne or Hopkins, but a very sick man indeed, a paranoid schizophrenic who was not only convinced that there were witches under everyone's bed but that he, Oliphant, was on a divine mission to root them out.

It would seem that, very gradually, Cromwell was brought to believe in Oliphant's divine gift of revealing witchcraft. One incident, that dates from around the battle of Edge Hill, concerns a young soldier who was found 'to bee infected with the Foulnesse of Satan' and was more or less killed, on Oliphant's say-so, by his comrades. As far as

I can make out – and the MS is often so obscure as to be hardly comprehensible – Oliphant's obsession with Satanism led him, by a route that would be familiar to all students of the Stalinist purges, to the conclusion that extirpation of the cult of witchcraft would only be possible by using the methods and practices of the cult against itself. Exponents of the War-to-End-War theory, or proponents of the immense value to peace of nuclear weapons, would be interested in and perhaps sympathetic to Oliphant's theory. Like a good practical statesman, Cromwell followed his mentor meekly and became more and more deeply involved in Oliphant's 'sabbats', which would seem to have been a sort of inverted version of the prayer meetings common in the New Model Army. And also – from Clarke's sometimes openly lubricious account – a hell of a lot more fun!

Hopelessly confused, Cromwell was, by this account, terrified to learn of the events in Suffolk in 1645 in which no fewer than sixty-eight women were hanged as witches. Since Oliphant had persuaded him that now he was threatened from two sides – both by the general assembly of witches and by the ignorant mass of the populace who were not aware of the danger from witchcraft and would look askance at the methods used by Oliphant and the rising figure in the Parliamentary cause. Clarke's confession incorporates his notes for each year from 1642 and concludes with a detailed exposition of the plot worked up by Cromwell and those close to him to get rid of this weird and embarrassing figure from his past. Very like that old acquaintance of Hitler's whom he had hunted and killed, years later, Oliphant knew too much about the unsavoury private life of the new ruler of England. According to Clarke, a charge of treason was fabricated against Oliphant and he was hung, drawn and quartered at the public gallows in Whipps Cross, some way north of what we now know as Bloomsbury. If such could be proved to be the case – a matter of checking the Assize Records – the case for the authenticity of the Clarke MS would be strengthened. Clarke is obscure about quite how the charge of treason was brought, although he is categorical that Oliphant was not indicted for witchcraft since the dangers of revealing trade secrets were too great! He also includes a graphic and rather sad account of Oliphant's wife, Margaret and of Anna Stafford, the first woman to die in the Northampton witch scare of 1650, who, according to Clarke, was an associate of Oliphant's. Both women, according to Clarke were 'notorious witches' on whom Oliphant blamed his downfall. Very like the Bolshevik old guard deciding that their summary execution by Stalin was something to do with dialectical materialism, Oliphant could clearly not make the jump into understanding that in Cromwell, he was dealing with a man who was above all a politician. Belief in witchcraft, for the intellectual of the seventeenth century (and most of them *did* believe, or at least refused to commit themselves to scepticism on the matter) was largely a matter of staying well clear of its manifestations – rather like the contemporary creatures who steer clear of politics on the ground that it may incriminate them. All those deep into the witch business – as was Oliphant – who made a practice of belief ran the risk of dying by it, and according to Clarke, this is what happened to Oliphant.

A note about Stafford. The Northampton witch scare of 1650 is well documented; I know of two pamphlets on the subject. What we need to find out is whether Stafford and/or Oliphant figure in the evidence. As to the question of the dating of the MS, I am afraid to say that the paper on which Clarke's notes have been made bears a distinctive watermark – not the one on the original MS of the transcription of the Putney Debates, but none the less a well known figure. It means that the paper was supplied by the old established firm of Josiah Smawlley of London who (here's an example of the continuity of English history) made and supplied paper between 1630 and 1830, when the last of the Smawlleys went bankrupt. So unless Ron Oliphant travelled back in time it looks as though we are dealing with something that is both incredible and impossible to disbelieve. As Einstein said on the subject of quantum theory – God does not play dice with the world. But sometimes I'm afraid he does, Albie. He's been playing dice with it for years *and getting away with it*.

So: let us step off into the void and say we believe the whole farrago. If we do, then you should probably not be reading this MS at all, since it closes with a good old fashioned curse on anyone who reads it. Just so as you know how I felt when I was reading it, Jamie, I'll give the curse first, OK? And if you still feel like disbelieving can I add, for your benefit, that no less a person than William Harvey, the discoverer of the circulation of the blood, made a thorough examination of a witch. Remember too that Dr Johnson refused to believe that the inhabitants of St Kilda caught a cold every time a ship docked there. Maybe there are witches, Jamie – we just haven't developed the technology to sniff them out. Do you like my efficient account of the MS? Aren't I neat little girl? I've done an awful lot of work for you, you selfish bastard, haven't I?

Why? I hear you ask. Well, because I think you're funny and you listen to me and make me feel good when you smile and I feel easy with you and I *think* I'm falling in love with you. Is that all right? Am I allowed to do that? But I never want to own you or tie you down or load you with things you don't want. Otherwise you might have me out on the scaffold and be pulling at my legs, mightn't you?

Turn over for the curse if you dare, Matheson!

I didn't, at first. I went to the fridge, found a piece of salami and tore at it hungrily. Then I went back to the hall. No sound from below. I turned over the paper and read the following:

. . . forasmuch as This is the most Secret and Private Part of myself, I command it bee placed not among the papers that Traffic in Questions of State but among those that Account for Household Matters. For it is a cursed secret and hee who will first Read it is cursed and Hee who reads it after. For did not the Witches Anna Stafford and Meg Oliphant pronounce a curse on the Witchfinder at the houres of Their Cruel Deaths, and Hee himself swear to Return to be

Revenged upon them even as the Hangman reached into His Very Bowelles to draw out his tainted Heart for all to see! And those who have the Temerity to study such Actes as are here described will be *Their* Very Selves compelled to give them Life and Substance once more, so that, a second Time will the Witches be Discovered and Punished and a second Time will Hee who styled himselfe the Witchfinder be Hanged and cut down and Quartered! And so that Ye Shall Knowe I speak, not Idly and in Jest, as some do of such Matters, but in Full earnest and Concerne for my Mortall Soule, Know that my Lord Protector and myself were First Advised of Oliphant's Hellish Compact – made in the name of oure Lorde – when the Devil appeared to us the night we lay at Putney, when wee prepared the Debate with the Elected Officers of the Armie! And know thou the Devil – for hee comes in the guise of a tall black Man and he will offer wine and money for Thy comfort but Accept it not lest Ye be Tainted – as wee have been – with the mark of Satan . . .

It was just as I looked up from that last sentence that I saw the figures. I don't know why I hadn't seen them earlier. They were by the telephone, beneath the notice board. They were of clay, about eight inches high and one of them had a long, pointed nose, a troll's nose you might have said. The other figure was of a woman. Naked. Full breasted. Through the neck of each figure was a needle.

I got up and walked very slowly towards them. They were leaning against each other unnoticed, like drunks at a party. Whoever had made them had sculpted hair, eyes, hands, all perfectly. They lay quite still. I moved closer. I was stretching out my hand to touch one of them – the woman – when the front door bell went. Just once. A short, sharp ring, as if whoever was out there was in a hurry and knew there was someone inside. I did not touch the figure, but peered through the glass at the dark outside. All I could see was a shape. The figure did not ring the bell again.

A tall black man. A tall black man. I stole towards the door. A tall black man. With a speed and force that surprised me I yanked back the door, and there before me, blinking owlishly in the sudden light, wearing the black overcoat that made him look taller than usual, was Rick Mason. He grinned. In his left hand was a bottle of red wine. He grinned again. I saw that in his right was a ten pound note. He pushed the note at me. 'Let's get out and get a take away. I'll pay.'

'Holy Mary Mother of God blessed art Thou among women and blessed is the fruit of thy Womb' – My head started to nod up and down like an old man in the grip of a fit. My voice had that same wheedling quality I had noticed earlier. But try as I might, I could not say the name of Jesus.

24

'Are you OK?' he said. This seemed to be a fairly standard method of approaching me at the moment. I felt rather irritated at the question. Couldn't he see that I was perfectly OK? I was fine. I was bewitched but apart from that I was fine. I had just killed my mother-in-law but apart from that I was fine. I was possessed by the spirit of a seventeenth century witchfinder. Otherwise – no problem. We would have a good laugh about this afterwards. All I needed to do was to get my voice back off the bastard who had hijacked it.

Inside my head I got a good argument going with Ezekiel – telling him to be reasonable, telling him that unless he left me at once and hopped it back to the seventeenth century I would seek professional help. A psychiatrist, a qualified doctor and a priest, not necessarily in that order. If necessary I would use garlic and silver bullets. The trouble was, although I was having a high old time *inside* my head, outside my head I could see that my behaviour might give rise to some concern. You do not expect to be greeted at the door by an old friend saying half a Hail Mary and looking like Vincent Price in a horror movie.

Added to all this, Rick was quite obviously in league with the devil, or was in fact Satan himself. It was very important that I accepted no money from him, and refused all offers of wine. I must make an excuse and find some reason for leaving the house, preferably taking the figures with me. As he stood there, gawping at me, I began to massage my neck, vigorously. It did not, at the moment anyway, seem to hurt. A *tall black man will offer you wine and money*.

'Is your neck OK?' He shut the door behind him.

'I am bewitched Master Mason. Mistress Margaret hath modelled mee in Such Cunning Likenesse I Cannot Think but it will bee More than a Few Houres Space Before I Suffer most Grievously.'

He laughed cheerily. 'Great one,' he said, 'really good. Great one.' I narrowed my eyes and shook my finger at him. 'And Have a Care Master for I Know THEE AND Whom Thou Servest. Think not to entrap mee in the Abominable Conspiracie!'

'I think you're better off in the SDP old son,' he said. 'I came to apologize actually. For being such a prig. I'm still in love with your bloody wife, that's the problem. It's none of my business.' He seemed quite unperturbed by my behaviour. I found myself examining it from his point of view. In a sense – for certain of my friends – this was quite normal behaviour. It might take upwards of half an hour before the joke wore thin. And he was used to my jokes wearing thin. The trouble was, this was not a joke. Not to me anyway. 'And I wanted to talk to you about this Oliphant business.'

Yes, I thought, I wouldn't mind a word on the subject too. Like he's still around, looking for witches and taking over ordinary people's bodies and minds and shouldn't we write to *The Times* about him or something? 'You see,' Rick went on, 'I was being, I don't know, cagey. Keeping it to myself. It's such an extraordinary story. I don't know, I think it sends everyone crazy. Touch of the Tutankhamuns about it. And I thought, well, he's read *A Cursèd Lie* and been intrigued by it. How come bloody Oliphant is quoting William Clarke at us? And I've seen Ron and heard him ramble on and I've even been up to Worcester and found, as you did, there is *nothing* in those additional papers apart from household accounts.'

Sez *you*, Mister Scholar, I thought with secret pride.

'But there is,' he said, 'the manner of Ezekiel's death, which I just can't fathom. And I came across an extraordinary pamphlet I thought you ought to see. We ought to pool our resources, don't you think? And Meg –'

'Where is the Paper?' I said thickly, 'where is the Account of the Crime committed in the Name of Justice and Lawe against One who sought only to Destroy and Defile the Workes of the Evill One?'

He laughed. 'You do that really well. You always were a great mimic. Lack a voice of your own, my boy. Never be a Tolstoy, but a great mimic. It's here O worshipful Master.' He handed me a mimeographed pile of papers. It was headed

A Briefe Description of
the Notorious Life
of the Witchfinder Oliphant, and of
the Horrible and Ignominious Manner of his Execution.
Printed in Amsterdam 1660.

I looked up at Rick. He was smiling inanely, showing a row of broken, yellow teeth. 'Contemporary pamphlet,' he said, 'turned up as a result of my advert. Good stuff. Isn't confirmed by the Assize Roll because there ain't one for the month in question in 1658. But it smells authentic. And it's as kosher as *A Cursèd Lie* as far as I can see. You might get a story out of this and I might get an academic article. So we'd be evens. Where *is* Meg by the way?'

A book? What did he know. A book? My God, I'd be lucky to come out of this alive, never mind write about it. Didn't he know what he was dealing with? Christ, there was something very serious going on here. It was quite clear to me that there was a very large number of witches indeed roaming about the place, many of them in responsible positions. Him for a start, I remembered with a jolt. Lecturer in History at the University of Lancaster. Specializing in Witchcraft. Of course he specializes in witchcraft: *he works full-time for the Devil. An academic job is the perfect cover – all the leisure you want to pry around old books and work out curses. I wonder how long this has been going on. Why did the TLS give you such an unfavourable review for* Say Goodnight to Alfie Barnacle? *Why did the surveyor from the mortgage company dock a thousand quid off the loan for 458 Maplake Road?*

I felt curiously calm about all of this. Now I knew the full extent of what was going on, I simply had to keep calm. There were going to be witches everywhere and I would have to be extremely careful not to let them know I knew what they were up to. To that end I put in a request to Ezekiel to stop using his voice. 'We don't,' I told him, 'want to alarm the Satanists.' And he saw the logic of this immediately because he let me know that it would be quite OK for me to use my own voice and to carry on like good old Jamie until such time as I could get out of the house and begin to deal with the problem. 'Of course,' he said, 'you are aware that it is possible that Anna is a witch.' I told him

I quite understood and if it was necessary to take action against her I would of course do so. I asked him which test he most favoured for the discovery of a witch and he said that on the whole if they floated in water they were probably not kosher. I was wondering, hysterically, where I would find an opportunity of dunking Anna in a pool of water without arousing her suspicions when I heard myself say 'Amazing stuff, Rick. Amazing.' It all seemed familiar. The pamphlet mentioned the affair at Northampton, in which Anna Stafford had been burnt, and suggested Ezekiel had been largely responsible. According to the pamphleteer, Oliphant had later been charged with treason – there was a hair-raising list of charges, all fairly standard political offences, conspiracy, subversion; no mention, from the Crown, of witchcraft. Interest in the case, the pamphleteer told us, centred on the fact that most people were fairly sure Oliphant was a wizard and had only been protected by Those on High for so long because of his magic powers. He had railed against the Protector, said the pamphleteer, although he didn't say precisely what Oliphant had said about him. But at the moment at which he had been cut down, still breathing, and the hangman had cut into his belly and reached up through the entrails for his heart, from the crowd had emerged a large black dog, which had howled without ceasing. This was, the writer concluded, Oliphant's familiar, Gip, and there was a crude picture of the animal on the facing page. 'Fascinating,' I said lightly.

'As far as I can tell,' said Rick, 'the house where he was arrested and held for questioning was very near where the British Museum now is. Hence, I would guess, the tag of Bloomsbury Witchfinder.'

And it also, I said to Ezekiel, explains why it is you are condemned to haunt the place. He said that I had got it in one and I was a very bright boy and would do well and would I please hurry up and give this man the slip because we had urgent work to do. But, I said, isn't he the devil? Oughtn't we to extirpate him while we had the chance? As I asked him this I heard a low moan from downstairs. My mother-in-law was clearly not as easy to write off as I had hoped.

'What he was doing there God only knows. You seem better. I

271

was worried about you when I came in – I got the impression he had finally taken you over.'

I was too busy listening to Ezekiel to answer him. Ezekiel was of the opinion that Rick was not the devil and that Clarke's warning was to be disregarded. He seemed to think Clarke knew nothing about witchcraft. He hadn't got to CSE standard as far as witchcraft was concerned. If you want to know about witchcraft, said Ezekiel, stick with me. You'll be OK. 'What about those figures?' I said to him. 'You must take the figures and make the witch swallow them. Or her familiar.'

Fine, I thought, no problem. Cinch. The question was – who was the witch? 'You know who the witch is,' said his voice, rather weary. 'Don't run away from it. It's obvious. Both of them are witches. Anna and the other one. Either will do. They are both quite obviously witches. I mean – I know a witch when I see one, Jamie.' He also seemed to think it was a bad idea to let Rick see the figures, and with this in mind I took his arm and went through to the kitchen. It was hard making bright intelligent chat about the historical twists and turns of the 1650s while also taking on what Ezekiel had to say. But I managed to get him into a chair, refusing, in spite of Ezekiel's protestations, a glass of wine. 'You can't be too careful,' I said. *'You never know.'* He said that you did know; that was the whole point. Spotting a witch was a question of skill and experience. Outside I heard the rain begin again.

'I've got to nip round and see a neighbour,' I said at last.

'And what do I do with her when I find her?' I said to Ezekiel. 'I'll tell you what to do,' he said. 'Well lay off the seventeenth century stuff,' I said , 'that rattles her.' 'I'm afraid,' he said, 'I am no more in control of this than you are. Just because I've been dead for three hundred years it doesn't mean I know everything. We'll just have to play it as it lays.' I marvelled at Ezekiel's skill in dealing with the modern world as I slipped towards the door.

'You look a bit flushed, Jamie,' said Rick.

'Do I?'

'Are you sure you're OK?'

'I'm fine,' I said, 'won't be a mo.' He smiled again and I went out to the hall. I swept up the figures and ran down the path and into the road. Left or right? Take the car? Could the car be bewitched? Bicycle bewitched. Tubes hopeless. *Due to witchcraft the District line is running eight hours late. We apologize to passengers for the delay and hope they will bear with us until the spells wear off.*

Car. I threw myself at the family saloon – a grey Peugeot. Why hadn't she taken it with her? Turned the engine over once, twice. No deal. Of course not: the 'plugs' needed 'changing'. Or the 'spell' needed 'taking off', as we say. Bus. Bus. Safest on the bus. Can't see witches travelling by bus. Enormously long waits. Witches like to move swiftly, they live in the fast lane do witches. Bus. I clambered out on to the road and headed off towards Lytton Grove.

I forced myself on, past the huge double-fronted houses, each lighted drawing room a beacon of domestic bliss, an advert for the solid and comfortable – *'GET out of the road!'* I swerved to avoid a cyclist as I turned into Lytton Grove. I was about to launch myself out across the road, under the huge, bare lime trees that stand in front of the council flats, when I felt a violent, stabbing pain at the base of my neck, as if someone were pushing a needle from one side to the other, very, very slowly. I stopped and clutched at my throat. The witches were obviously aware that I was on to them and they were determined to stop me. The pain in my neck was intense. 'What now?' I asked Ezekiel. If anyone could get me out of this it would be him. He replied in a tough, urgently pleading voice, 'Don't give up, James, however much it hurts. You can't back down now. You must find both witches, and get a full list of their contacts. They will have *address books full of other witches*. There is *no time to lose.'*

I ran for Putney Hill and the distant roar of traffic.

PART THREE

FALSE AND TRUE TESTIMONY

I lay three Daies sick after the Council at Putney, nor did I speak to anie save Nehemiah. Though from him I later Heard the Council was put under such Delaie by Cromwell, that none of the Businesse there put forward was enacted. Of Masters Sexby and Everard, I heard no more synce my Master declared mee nott fit for Service &, within a month the two of us found oure Discharge. I had purposed to Return to Hertfordshire, but, says Nehemiah, *the struggle there was such and so bitter between mother and son, father and daughter that to return were a penance.* And, indeed, I feared to see agayne the Scenes where Margaret and I had first made oure Acquaintance.

'I have,' says hee, 'a brother near to Northampton where wee may find Rest and Shelter. Hee is, as I, a *Cooper* by Trade & though nott firmly in the Waie of Religion hath a Sound Sense, a loving Family and *is of good Report.*' And so wee journeyed North, passing through *Hatfield* & *Bedford* & clothed as wee were, as for the Armie, were made welcome where wee staied synce manie said *they had nott seen Godlie soldiers till the men of the New Modelle passed through.* And, indeed the talk was much of how oure Generalle had turned out the Parliament, but I had then no Stomach for such Talk but when wee took the Road, alone, the Weather coming on Inclement – for it was November – then did wee look upon the Fields and Hedges & took oure solace from that which is Uncorrupted by Men *and wee lifted up oure eies to the heavens, and looked upon the Earth beneath: for the Heavens vanished awaie like smoke & the Earth waxed Old like a Garment & on it were the New Trees and Floweres & the Turtle was heard in the Land.*

So wee came to a howse on the East side of Northampton, its thatch as ragged as a Beggar's clothes & its windowes soyled & cracked, which was where *Nahum* had his dwelling – for my Master's Father was a Godfearing Man that would have named his children each for a prophet, as Malachi, Micah, Obadiah,

277

Hosea, Isaiah, Malachi, Jonah and I know nott what, save after two boies his wife is delivered of naught but girl children, at which, says hee, *I name them all my Lamentations, for I have runne out of Prophets*. But this Nahum was in no wise the like of my Master, being a chearfull & *wellportered* Man, though Cholerique, who took his glass of an evening. But, though they were at Opposite POLES IN Humour, I never saw two Brothers agree so well as these two, or so much Quiet Joy as in my Master's face when this Nahum comes to the door & seeing him, falls about his Neck with manie Earnest Expressions of Love and Gratitude and bids us both come in and Eat.

Nahum himself had three Sonnes and two Daughteres & though hee worked each daie & was Trusted by the People of the Town wee were in a Hard Case for the Necessities of Life, whiles I was in that House. But never did hee or his wife look sourly on Us, taking instead with Thanks and Kind Wordes oure Labour in his Yarde & indeed when wee had been there under a Yeare he told us *Trade was much Increased at oure Coming, for which hee thanked us*.

Wee had nott been there but above six Months when wee made a Felloweship with Others of that Town that were nearly of oure Perswasion in matters of Religion. & though my Master now scorned our Former Title, saying that a *Cooperite* was one who had as emploiement the Making of Barrelles and no more, there were, in oure Assemblies at Northhampton manie things in common with the Proceedings so dear to mee when my *Mr Passmore had a charge of my education*. There was one *Fitch* a printer that was with us and severall Clothiers of the town and at oure meetings wee both studied Scripture, sang Psalms and prayed to God each in His owne waie & none troubled us. There was talk too of Matters in London & from one that was come from the city I learned of Matters at Corkbushe Field and how one of oure Agitators had been shot at the Head of his Regiment & I was mindful of the words of Master Sexby, whereat I writ my pamphlet *A Cursèd Lie Put About by the Government and a Shorthand Taker Thoroughly Rebutted* which was, in no small part the means of my undoing, and yet I do nott regret it. For manie are now grown so Frightened by the Times they dare nott utter anie Opinion for fear of the *Protector* who as witts may seek to frighten One who dares express the Honest and unfeigned Thoughts of His heart has taken from us all oure Liberties and Handed them agayne as Duties and Prescriptions.

But in truth, when I had finished with that Work I thought no more of Politicks, or of Affairs of state, busying myselfe onlie with my Master Nahum and his Familie and with my Trade and with praysing and worshipping God at our Assemblies. And at night I asked my pardon of my Margaret synce I was now thoroughly perswaded Mr Morris did the Devill's work and by him were shee and I enchanted, but I kept plain counsell of these thoughts & manie there calls mee Grave Ezekiel, which was very TRUTH FOR IN MY Heart was Lamentation and *I prayed the Lord that hee might take awaie from mee the memorie of my abominations & give mee a new spirit within mee; and that he might take the Stonie Heart out of my flesh and give unto mee a Heart of Flesh.*

There was in that Howse – besides the severall Boies that were Nephews to my Master, a girl nott much above fifteen Yeares who was slow in speech and Understanding, but that, notwithstanding, was loved greatlie by all that were there, being Sweet of Disposition and Mild of Temper. She was, indeed, no Naturall child of my Master's brother, but taken up by them, out of Pitie for her condition, which, among the Familie where then shee dwelt, was hard indeed. For they took no account for her Lack of Witt, but used her hard when shee should stumble in some Dutie laid upon her by Her Mistress. Which Duties were, indeed, more Burdensome than anie I yett heard of laid upon Servant by Mistresse. Shee was, I think, of a familie called *Stafford*, that cast her out for her Infirm Sense, having, one said, *the Devill's eie*, synce, when one Orb looked upon the Wall, t'other saw naught but the Windowe. But though shee had nott her Letters shee could *Sing* most prettily.

As I went aboutt my Laboures, in the Yarde, this *Anna* came often and sate beside mee, for shee loved greatlie to watch the woodchips fly as I went to Work, which then was my sole Consolation. 'Close of mouth but Quick of Hand' were their Wordes of mee in that Howse. And sometimes this same *Anna* would come to mee and lay her Hande upon my cheek & look upon mine Eie as if shee would say what lay within her Hearte for which shee could yett find no Word. And then I took her Hande in Mine and spake softlie to her of the Great Love that is the Lord's and prayed shee might have Faith, as our LORD SAITH UNTO THE Leper *Thy Faith shall Make thee Whole*.

When wee were at Meat there also, this Anna sate neer to mee and waited upon mee, bringing both Bread and Water in Due Season, which made my Master's brother marvell as hee took his Portion. Thus wee passed our daies and the Great Lordes of the Armie in London made their Debates & King Charles was led to his execution, which much displeased my Master's brother's wife. But upon this, or on what followed within the Armie or of the Irish Warres I spake nott, saying onlie, if I were asked for my Opinion that my great Desire was to do and to say Nothing.

Why should it bee the Lorde makes some to lack Sense and Understanding? And if wee bee nott in oure Right Minde how can wee Protect ourselves from the Evill & Fatall influences with which wee are Surrounded? How make oure covenante with the Lorde, when wee may know nott ourselves? For even in the Simplicity of Children is some Art. For though I saw in *Anna* a Virtuous Simplicity, there were those near to Us, that feared to approach her and threw Stones after her, each time shee strayed from the howse of my Master's Brother. Their names were Lucas & they had a boie of some twelve Yeares that was named Hugh Lucas & also a girl *Jane* of, I think, ten. Once, when Anna had passed them upon the Road I saw Hugh Lucas call out to her & when shee turns to Him he throws a Handful of Pebbles at her Face, at which I ran to him & boxed the boie aboutt the Eares. Later that daie comes his Father to my Master's brother & asks of him where is the *Wild Man* & gives him word hee keeps a Disorderly & Unmannered Guest. At which Nahum calls mee to him & I give to Him a full & Considered Account of what had passed upon the Road. 'You are, as I can Testify a Good and Honest Workman & I will be sworn John Lucas hath no Cause to speak agaynst you. But if you pass him, speak nott to Him – for hee be Quarrelsome & such Fellowes can make Havoc in a House.' And I, for my part, kept our Anna close by mee & used, when I was at my Laboures to Confess to Her things close to my

Hearte that I could nott speak out to Others. & though shee seemed nott to Hear mee yet was her Loving smile answer for mee. Was nott that a Prayer wee offered then to God, alone in the Yard? For surely Religion must reside, not in the Formes & Manneres of Worshippe, as I once had supposed, but in the Loving Soul. O woe to those false Prophettes that were sent among us, & that taught us Lies and Delusions for the Visions and Deceits of their owne Heartes. They have covered them with Dust saith the Lord and made the Dust to spin in a Great cloud across the Land soe that manie were blinded yea was I also blinded when I saw nott how my Margaret was under the sway of Beelzebub & yet those Devills that were sent to try Her were most readily to Hand. That which torments us is mostly particular. It lies – I mean the Devill – in that Neighbour, in that Offense, in that soft or deceiving Word – yea Hee hath taken the Shape that pleaseth Him, even the Raiments of a Priest or Presbyter. Hee has gone aboutt to deceive us in the holiest part of the Temple & wee must bee Watchful and Vigilant, for as hee hath taken the Formes of oure World & soe transposed them that wee knew them nott – soe have wee fought Sonne agaynst Brother, Man agaynst Wife, Daughtere agaynst Mother yea wee *have taken oure wives for Witches & credited them with the Devill's work & this is all his Strong Enchantment that hee hath laid upon us. O my Margaret I weep that I was mistaken in thy Chastity and Meekness I groan in my affliction, that I was led thus astray & I ask Pardon of Thee. Butt wee are Weak Men & the Light shines nott upon us but is Hidden from oure Senses.*

I think it was nott long after the King was led to his Death – though now my recall of the Great Events that once so much Confused and Perplexed mee – is no more than for the *yeare oure Cow may nott have calved* or *This or That most Notably Inclement Summer* – that I, being at my Laboures in the Yarde one Daie noticed my Anna was gone from mee & soe went forth from that Howse to find Her – synce shee to mee was alwaies most Precious & in Her I had found agayn those children and that Wife that were so sadly taken from mee in the Daies of my Youth. Shee was – I saw – in the Field behind my Master's brother's howse, stooped over some *Grasses* that shee had gathered & neer to Her was the child of this same *Lucas*. And as I went neer to them I heard Him call to Anna, saying 'Go.Go.Go.' And Anna turns to

281

Him with a Quiet and Gentle Face and shee knew nott what was said to Her. But hee agayne shouts after Her, saying 'Go.Go.Go.' and on a sudden Anna calls back to him – though I could nott hear her Wordes synce often when shee spake shee made nott the Soundes of Speech as wee may hear them, for her *false Perception* of Wordes and Sentences made her hard put to Imitate with that Perfection that some consider the Mark of Sense. For though this Anna was not Dumb or Deaf – as manie credited her withal – she had nott a Perfect Understanding of Speech. And consequent upon her Address to Him hee setts up a Keening & his Head falls to one side of his Shoulders like unto a Flower whose time hath come and who must fall awaie outt of the Light & from behind where I was stood I heard one Voyce – which was the Voyce of his sister *Jane Lucas* – which said but one worde at which I was grievouslie afflicted for she said it over and over and would nott Cease from her sounding the Name.

And the worde was witch & Anna turns to Jane Lucas as shee heares it, as a souldier might go to meet his Destinie or anie Man or Woman lift their head synce they felt *now is my Time come upon mee & I must goe to meet my Providence and Justifie myselfe before the Living God that made mee and shall ask mee in the End how I may say I think that I have quitt myself.* And I was afrayd.

25

458 Maplake Road
Putney

October

It is eight in the evening. I am writing this in my study. The door is closed behind me. At my back – a yellow noticeboard, on which is written RING GOTTLIEB THURSDAY. Will I ring him? I don't know. For the moment I am acting the part of the family man once again. I look out into the garden, its apple trees stripped of the last of the late fruit, and marvel at the threatening mildness of October. So much has happened since the summer.

It is Hallowe'en tonight, All Hallows Eve, but there is no such thing as a witch. A witch is just a word. Thousands of innocent women, young and old have been tortured, hanged or burned because of a word. A word somebody found to spell away the terror of the darkness, or the fear that has no name, but is simply *there* even with a newborn child in its mother's arms. Her words, perhaps, turn that fear to love, but somehow the fear survives, and in our memories, those soft words, soft caresses seem like a threat, and we are afraid of our mothers and our wives and our wives' mothers.

I don't want to be afraid of these innocent women. But I am afraid. However well I play the part of a man who has come through, of the good father, the good husband, there is a thin little voice telling me 'No. No. Not really. Won't do.' I sit here and think of the horrors of the last year, and shiver with fright. I think about them as I stare out at the light from Juliet's flat, staining the brown and silver of the neighbour's birch tree, and they are as real, more real to me than any characters I could summon up for Gottlieb.

I'll do something with them. I'm a competent writer. No more than competent.

283

Ext. Day. EZEKIEL's *house.* EZEKIEL *is screaming with pain as the Cromwellian soldiers force him against the wall.*

    EZEKIEL: No no no!

    1ST SOLDIER: Silence fool . . . . . .

I will serve Ezekiel up with a little borrowed social philosophy, make him as safe as one of Rick Mason's statistics. There will be no pain and confusion, none of the unsettling thing – life itself; so I will have spelled away what has happened, smoothed away the grotesqueries and unhappy mixture of comedy and terror that seem to be my life. And people will say 'Good. In *good taste.*' And it will be like it never happened.

In the meantime, unknown to anyone, I set down the chaos of this last year, add to the pile of scrappy papers in my bottom drawer, push the words across the paper without bothing to try and shape them. When I have transcribed the experience, will it teach me anything? Will it teach me to be a good lover, a good father, a good husband, a good Christian the way my father was?

All right. Since Meg says I recognize no other person, am the entire and perfect solipsist, let me try and imagine a reader. Let me conjure up someone to whom I am telling this, the way one might tell a ghost story. And take my preambles – 'This happened', 'This is utterly and completely true' – as mere story-teller's tricks. Imagine I have been here at my desk all the time unravelling the story for you, inventing a mental hospital in the country, a cottage near Edge Hill in the hot summer, all of them simply props to make the narrative more vivid. And think that – as I am being open handed with you – you are about to hear the truth, to get to know the real me. I am with you wherever you read this – with you the way Ezekiel was with me, not exorcised until you close the last page, when both the witchfinder and I will take our leave of you. And perhaps, then, he will take his leave of me.

I am frightened, you see. I am frightened I will never leave this story I am writing. I am frightened in case I am writing the truth, trapped by the present tense of my own story. It seems I do not love my wife in this story. I want to tell myself another tale. Where we love each other the way we did fifteen years ago when I walked along under the Radcliffe Camera in Oxford and crushed her to me and kissed her white, worried face until it wasn't worried any more.

So I go back, as artfully as I can, to re-invent what has happened. And ask you to picture me, in the hot summer, at a table in my father's cottage in Oxfordshire, writing about the winter and the day I ran from this house, a stranger to myself, a stabbing pain in my neck, Juliet lying in the basement and Rick Mason smiling at me with the face of the devil himself. I write that last sentence 'I ran for Putney Hill and the distant roar of traffic' (not a great sentence, but it will have to do) and as I write it, I look up from the page out of the window and see Meg walking towards me across the front lawn. She is wearing a leather jacket and jeans, her hair is cut spikily short and her thin face looks like that of Dickens' crossing sweeper. There are dark circles under her eyes. Everything about her is more jerky, more emphatic than before. There is a black mark on her left cheek and her right hand is heavily stained with nicotine. She has a wild look about her. She is not at all domestic.

Behind her, in the late afternoon sun, come Thomasina, Gwendoline and Emma. They too are ragged and dirty. Thomasina wears a tatty white dress, the other two ragged trousers. They look like tinkers' children. Their names don't fit them any more (if they ever did); they are no longer spoilt little rich kids. They are hard. Hard as wherever it is they have been. Open-mouthed, I put down my pen and look at these four women (I think of them now as women, not as 'my little girls' or 'the girls') – I expect them to see me and wave and smile, but they do not. They come slowly behind their mother – who seems, now, more like their elder sister – in a line. They look as if they are on a mission, but whether of vengeance or mercy it is impossible to say.

Do you think I treated her badly? Is that what you think? Where do you think she went after she left me? Do you find me spiteful, irritating? Perhaps you think she went with another man? Maybe she did. *I* don't know. She's downstairs now, as I write, with the children, but I still don't know quite where she went in those missing months between February and July. She's never told me. Even now, when I face her across a room, I don't know what she's thinking or how she feels. She has become a mystery to me.

I opened the door of the cottage and watched them come up the path. They filed in past me, blank-faced. 'What kept you?' I said. None of them answered. Meg sat on the sofa, reached into her pocket and took out a tobacco tin. Fairly expertly, she began to roll herself a cigarette. I closed the door, shutting out the sweetness of the afternoon and came back into the room. 'Where have you *been*?' I said.

Meg looked at me. Her chin was set, hard. *She dislikes me*, I thought.

'How sick are you?' she said at last. 'I rang Rick Mason. How sick are you?' I didn't answer this question. 'I can never tell,' she went on, 'with you – whether you're acting or whether you mean it, or what. I don't where I am with you. Are you ill?

I bit my finger. Over in the far corner Gwendoline and Emma had opened the fridge and were going through its contents, expertly. Thomasina sat on the sofa, yawned elaborately and affected to take no notice of what was going on.

'Ezekiel . . .' I began, slowly, in a thick, unnatural voice.

'What about Ezekiel?'

She lit her cigarette, drew on it deeply and watched me. She had lost weight. She lay back on the sofa and spread her legs wide. She was wearing long leather boots. 'I know all about Ezekiel,' she said finally. 'All about him.' Then she smiled. I didn't like the smile. Her lips came well back from her teeth but the eyes didn't change at all. The smile was followed by another deep inhalation of cigarette smoke.

'This witch has got A levels in Ezekiel,' she said, 'this witch is one ba-ad witch. Bad bad witch.'

'Nast-ee . . .' said Thomasina and giggled.

'Stop it,' I said.

'Stop what?'

'Stop what you're doing.'

Now, you see, now I adopt the pose of the conscientious

narrator, the one who wants, however difficult it may prove, to tell you exactly how it was, who has a contempt for the cheaper tricks of narrative. I am forced to look back and ask quite what I thought and, perhaps more importantly, how I thought it. But as I look for the consciousness that boils and simmers into speech or the articulated thought that is supposed to precede speech, I cannot find it. All I can say is this – she threatened me that afternoon. She looked like one of the Furies and her daughters did not seem my daughters at all. If I wanted anything, I wanted for them not to have happened. But I knew, from the leisured way Meg drew on her cigarette or the way Gwendoline and Emma began, methodically, to spread cream cheese on to a piece of dry bread, that I was going to have to face this out.

'Have a care,' said Ezekiel, 'For this is a Cunning Witch.'

'He's talking to you now, isn't he?' said Meg. 'Yeah?'

There was a long silence. On the road outside, two or three of the local youth passed by. One of them had made a brave bid to belong to the 1980s by dyeing his hair green, but it was clear his heart wasn't in it. The only course of action for young yokels is to get on and become old yokels as soon as decently possible. The sad attempt at fashion was shamed by the perfect green curve of the field behind them, the long declining light of the afternoon.

'Gently,' said Ezekiel, 'go Gently with Her.'

'I got that,' she said, 'voices in my head.' Then she got up and crossed over to me. She reached out two scrawny arms and pushed her palms towards my face.

'What's up?' I said.

Her voice sounded low and canny. 'There's something,' she said, 'in there.' Her fingers touched my forehead. 'How's that?'

'It's OK,' I said cautiously.

'How nice to be you,' she said, 'how nice to be the centre of the fucking universe. I bet your voices tell you what a great cheese you are. A real little Joan of Arc. My voices always told me how wrong I was getting it.'

'Maybe they weren't your voices,' I said, 'maybe your lines got crossed.' How did she know when he was talking to me?

Did my mouth move or what? If he did his materialization stunt, walked into the room now and put his buckle shoes on the table, would she see him too? Would she round on him and tell him where he was getting it wrong?

'There was a man,' said Thomasina, 'on a road outside this town and when he saw us he came for us, just ran after us like that we were staying with Mary then in the north somewhere –'

'Shut up, Thomasina,' said Meg.

'Where have you been?' I asked her.

'All over, we've been all over.'

I had a vision of her and her daughters sleeping in ditches, under the stars. Of linking hands by some stone circle in the middle of nowhere. Of being outside the wire at Greenham Common in one of those polythene draped lean-tos, while the rain came down and plump local constables patrolled the perimeters of their camp. Goddamn witches. Goddamn motherfucking witches come up here and dance round our goddamn missiles and jump up and down on our silos.

'By the side of the M6 motorway,' said Meg, 'I sat down and wept. In the shopping centre in the middle of Birmingham I sobbed my heart out. In a McDonalds in the Old Kent Road I wailed and screamed and did my pieces. Outside the employment exchange in Newcastle upon Tyne, on a cold day in late March, I *really* got cross.'

'Look –'

'What about those voices in your head? Maybe you should just listen to them. Maybe you should do what they say. I don't know about those voices. Maybe they're telling the truth. *There* – there he is again. I saw him.'

Ezekiel's voice buzzed in my hear. 'A most Consummate and evil Witch,' he said. 'Before shee may infect Thee with any more of her Chimney Corner Fancies and Hobgoblin Tales, Take her and Shew Her thy Door. OR –' here his voice dropped confidentially – 'take her by the Neck and –

'What's his advice?' asked Meg. 'Strangle the bitch? Or Ye Bitche?'

There is no more awkward knowledge than that given to one's sexual partner. When you have been living with the same woman for nearly twenty years, that knowledge can outbluff almost all forms of possession. Ezekiel sounded rather peevish. And not at all seventeenth century. He sounded like a boy called Royston Haliday, with whom I was at primary school. 'She's being really unfair,' he said, 'she really is being unfair.'

'Ah,' said Meg, mock motherly, 'have we had a hard time? Have we been a bit fruitcake?'

'I've been in a fucking mental hospital,' I said. 'I've had a rather serious mental breakdown and I've stumbled on something that is extremely sinister and threatening actually.'

Ezekiel pitched in in my defence. 'He has actually,' he said hotly, 'and also in fact he has been in the grip of satanic possession by an undead monster of evil from the middle of the English Civil War.'

She seemed to have the knack of getting under Ezekiel's defences. A lot of his old *élan* was not there, I felt. He had a distinctly moth-eaten quality to him. He reminded me, as she spoke, more and more of a fictional character, and, in particular, one of mine. I was rather hoping he would do a number on her – one of his finger-wagging, eye-rolling jobs – but so far, no deal. It is a terrible thing to fall into the hands of the living God but it is pretty fucking terrible to be married to an intelligent woman who does not take you seriously. Even if you turn round to her and tell her you do not love her she just laughs. She knows you do not love her. She knows you have about as much capacity for love as the North American tree rat. She stays with you for entirely different reasons. She likes tree rats maybe.

She was looking good, I thought, very good. And then *how much does she know?*

'What have you been doing?' I asked.

'Studying witchcraft,' said Meg. 'I started just before I left. I read a great deal about witchcraft before I left. I read Halbertstein on *The Impact of the Witch Craze on North Shields 1564–1688*, I read C. H. L'Estrange Ewen, *Witch Hunting and Witch Trials*, *Witchcraft and Demonianism*, Wallace Notestein, *A History of Witchcraft in England from 1588 to 1718* –' A voice occurred in the room. It hovered, uneasily, somewhere over my left shoulder. It wasn't the Ezekiel voice I recognized, but it could have been him. It sounded lighter, younger. 'A most Contemptible Volume,' said the voice, 'and One which contains Erroures and False Opinions, likely in the work of One from the Far off Americas!'

Meg grinned at where the voice was coming from. She obviously felt she had Ezekiel where she wished him to be. She looked like Martina Navratilova tempting a young and inexperienced player out from the base line. The girls, too, were following the direction of her gaze. I looked behind me, and, like a photographic print going through the bath, saw the shadowy outlines of a figure. But not the familiar character in black hose and doublet. No beard. A much younger man. In his twenties. He was wearing a loose white shirt and a pair of what looked like rather grubby riding britches. His hands were covered with clayey soil. He didn't look like the young man I had seen that morning on the hill, but I knew at once, without having to ask, that this was Young Ezekiel. He would have stood a good chance in any screen test for the part. He was square-jawed and blue-eyed. He was blonde of hair and regular of nose. He had unobtrusive ears. My God, I thought, I should be so lucky to have such an alter ego!

I liked him. He seemed open and friendly and decent. He looked like the sort of man who would go in to bat on behalf of your average witch. A reliable, frank, lovable cove. But of course he was only twenty or so. He probably hadn't met Meg, or Anna, or any of the other harridans who ruined his life. He was probably down at the tavern for a glass of sack and back to his mum for clean shirts. Life hadn't got to him yet. Typical of a woman to summon up a younger man, I thought, and then noticed that Meg was not looking at him in a welcoming manner.

'Look mummy,' said Emma, 'there's a man appeared in funny trousers.'

'Don't,' said Gwendoline, 'be tho thtupid.'

Ezekiel paid no attention to any of this. He stood just behind me, looking rather sulkily at Meg.

'If,' went on Gwendoline with seven-year-old scorn, 'if there'th a man in funny twoutherth *how* did he get in pleathe? Or ith he a *ghotht or thumthing I wonder.*'

Emma was not dented by the overweight irony of this last remark. 'Yes,' she said.

Gwendoline looked across the room at Ezekiel, screwing up her eyes as she did so. A cunning look came into her eyes. 'I thee him,' she said, 'he'th got a huge white head and hornth and a tail.'

'No he hasn't,' said Emma implacably, 'he's got funny trousers.'

'*All right*,' said Gwendoline, looking across at me and raising her eyebrows in elaborate pantomime, '*all right. He'th got funny twoutherth. Huh. Let'th jump at him.*'

Emma liked this idea and the two of them ran across the room at Ezekiel. They jumped in the air and snapped their fingers in his face. They gibbered and shouted at him. They made Ghostbuster noises in his ears. They tweaked his britches and stuck their fingers up his impalpable nose. They joined hands and danced round him in a ring, shrieking and laughing and whistling. But Ezekiel paid no attention. He sat between Meg and me, real with the load of adult misery and adult knowledge. From time to time Thomasina looked over at her sisters, but mostly she kept her eyes on the ground, encased in the sad privacy of ten years old.

'What's always fascinated me about exorcism,' said Meg, 'is that it uses the very instruments most precious to what it professes to hate. Cast out ignorance with ignorance. If I was exorcizing a spirit I wouldn't read it the Bible. I'd read it a book on mathematics or philosophy or an honest attempt at history.'

'You'd bore it out of the afflicted one's body would you?' I said.

Meg yawned and ignored me. When she spoke again it wasn't to me but as if to the young man sitting between us, winding his fingers into each other, chewing his lip. There was clay, too, on his boots, I noticed.

'He twisted your head,' she said to him, 'and there are always people like him around, aren't there? Gibbering on the edges of the sex war. What is it you and he hate so about women? Why can't you bear the life that is in women? Why does it have to conform to your idea of what life is? All through history people like you beat and tortured and raped and tried to destroy women. Why? What did we do that was so wrong?'

It wasn't Ezekiel who answered, but me. 'You were there,' I said.

'Woman,' said Ezekiel in a high clear voice, 'synce my Arrivalle in This Temple of the Unclean, this Soiled and Fretfull Assortment of Warring Factions, this Oure Beloved Englande, now at the Mercie of Turke, of Blackamoor and Jewe, a lande where God hath turned away His Blessed Face and gone a-weeping into the Wildernesse. And for why? For that the Principalle and Chiefe State of Ordered Governmente, which is to say the Law as established and Described in Home and Place of Public Assembly by Man, who is, and always shall be Defender, Counsellor, and, where it be Necessarie, Scourge to the Infirm and Feebler Sex!'

I wondered where Ezekiel had been in 1986. Not that it mattered. Set him down anywhere, what would be the difference? Meg leaned forward in her chair and raised one thin finger at me. I looked away from her pettishly but she found my eyes again. 'I want him out,' she said, 'you hear me? Out out out.'

But Ezekiel sat there, refusing to scare. And as I watched him, his young, fresh face began to blister and pimple like an oil painting subjected to heat. His skin leaked corruption, prickled, as with the marks of some disease, boiled up and cratered down, then slowly dissolved into a mass of fixed wrinkles, puckered and set to the consistency of old age. But old age, it seemed, was only another possibility, for as soon as he had acquired that mask, it began to fade and he was becoming youthful again. You could count the years as he sloughed them off. Here comes the War with the Dutch. Look out for the Instrument of Government. Steady, steady, steady – it's the end of the Rump Parliament. And here (the rate of change was slowing now, and out of the shifting patches of his face was emerging the man I recognized from Anna's flat: beard, long hair, and narrowly focused eyes) here at last is your friend Ezekiel as he might wish to be remembered, as perfumed and stylish as ever. The Witchfinder of Essenden. At your service.

They're going to fight for my soul, I thought. Then, *I do not believe in the existence of the soul*. But how often do we fight for things in which we cannot quite believe? Over and over again. And perhaps 'belief' is too simple an idea. Perhaps there is only the struggle, with ourselves or with others. The crawling towards the light and never reaching it. The hopeless journey in the direction of hope.

26

For a moment I thought they were going to play cards for me. They had the look of gamblers squaring up to each other. Then it occurred to me that Meg would get physical with him. But there was little point in that. How can you get physical with a ghost? We all want to dig up Hitler and throw stones at him (I am told his wax image at Madame Tussauds has had to be placed behind a glass screen to save it from damage) but it's too late. The crimes of Ezekiel Oliphant have happened. They have in a word, *worked*; they're safely into the bloodstream of history, poisoning men's view of women, women's view of men, souring the mind of one unimportant little screenwriter called Jamie Matheson.

And yet . . . and yet . . . Meg had a dangerous look about her. Was she going to read him a lecture on the subjugation of women? Was he going to be made to vanish by dint of a lengthy quotation from the works of Adrienne Rich? I, I reflected, might well decide to vanish, should Meg choose such a drastic course of action. But, for the moment anyway, she seemed content to meet his gaze, unafraid.

It was some time before I started to talk. And when that began, I knew that something was being exorcized. My voice had the booming, self-important intimacy of someone talking to a shrink. And Meg's silence wasn't natural. It was a patient, let's-help-you-dig-your-own-grave silence that I recognized from my long and pointless seessions with Dr Baumgarten, Gottlieb's analyst. 'Why do you say that?' I expected her to say at any moment. Although she did not. She was also cheaper than Dr Baumgarten.

'After you left,' I said slowly. 'I went through hell. It felt like I was in hell.' Ezekiel nodded self-importantly at this remark. *Nach*, his exression seemed to say, *your wife leaves you, you go through hell. This is something of which witchfinders are well aware.*

I'm not entirely sure, actually, that I used those words. In telling a story to a page, even as hurriedly as I am doing (the truth is no respecter of style) there is one approach to pace, to the climaxes and main points of the story. To tell a story with the voice, as I did on that afternoon with Meg, is a different matter. There is no time for an attempt at Jamesian complexities of psychology (not, you will have noticed, that I go in for that much). The storyteller, like the analytic patient, reaches for an effect, hears silence, redoubles his efforts, and then, blind to indifference, consciously loses himself in the tale, only to surface at the end, aware of being overheard, gladdened by the thought that he has shared his very self with another.

'I found those dolls you'd made by the phone. I got these violent pains in the neck.'

Of course, Ezekiel's face seemed to say. *What do you want? Someone makes a doll of you and puts a needle through the neck, you get pains in the neck, don't you? Now if you got pains in the chest that would be worrying.*

'I just don't know, you see. I don't know what I believe and what is and what isn't. I'll start from the beginning. After you left. Why did you make those figures? Was it a joke of some kind? What were you trying to do?'

Look I gave her a version of those events, that's all. I lied, the way I had lied about Anna. I didn't mention Anna. I thought that maybe I could get her back and not mention Anna. I thought Anna didn't mean anything to her. And so, I suppose, not much was exorcized that afternoon. Even much later when I told her, I didn't tell her everything. She wanted to know of course. Every single fucking detail. She wanted to know when and how and why and what it was like. She wanted me to betray Anna to her the way I had betrayed her to Anna. And I couldn't bear to hurt her – still can't – so I lied and lied and never said quite what I felt. Never used the word 'love' – dangerous word. She couldn't let herself think I had loved the woman, could she? So I told her what she wanted to hear. And still the ghost would not go away.

It is only to you, gentle reader, I tell these secrets. You're the only one who knows. I'm whispering the truth to you, nothing but the truth. These other people, Meg, Anna, Juliet, Ezekiel – they are all shadows. They don't count. And when I have finished, then Ezekiel will take his leave. Oh, sometimes I might misremember a line, improve on it a little. I want to make you laugh, you see. And I want to frighten you too, from time to time. I want to do both. I want you to share that February evening with me, when I ran out into Lytton Grove and the throbbing at the base of my neck began, and Ezekiel was no mere prop but a living being, as real as the day he denounced his wife, or was himself denounced.

I ran up Lytton Grove towards the phone box, outside our local grocer (*Raj Kumar OPEN LATE*). The phone I had used to call Anna, sometimes, in the evenings, at the beginning of the affair. I knew that I could not afford to scare her. I knew that I had to sound calm. Looking back at what I wrote in the summer, I see I describe myself as 'talking to' Ezekiel, but that's a crude way of describing it. I find it impossible to portray adequately my state of mind, since the moments when I have been able to write about this, have been precisely those moments when I have not been possessed. In fact when Ezekiel has taken control, he blocks out all other signals. There's no voice but his. It takes different shapes. It adopts a contemporary tone, a pastiche 1650s tone, a camp tone sometimes – it is a protean voice, one that can fool me into thinking it is my own. But what it says is the most impossible thing to describe. What it says is: 'That woman you slept with. That woman in whom you confided. She is a witch. She is trying to kill you. You have to kill her. And quickly.'

'Hi, Anna – look, I'm sorry . . .'

A silence at the end of the phone.

'A joke that got out of hand. Sorry.'

More silence.

'How did you know about the Stafford woman, Jamie? How did you know they hanged the Stafford woman?'

'Because, my love, you told me.'

'I didn't.'

'Darling, you did. You *did*. That's how we receive information. Sleight of hand. How do you think conjurors work? This whole witchcraft business is about the misinterpretation of signals. You told me, I stored the information, and then surprised you with it. A simple writer's trick.'

'I didn't tell you.'

'Darling – do you remember everything you've said? Don't you ever misremember things? Admit you do. You've been working hard.'

'Jamie – *I swear I didn't tell you.*'

Very obstinate, witches. They get an idea in their head and it's impossible to shift. It's a shame that we are no longer able to use the strappado, the garrotte, the immersion test or the Merry Table of Ezekiel Oliphant, in which the witch is impaled on a flat board studded with spikes. It really gets good results, that does. If the Metropolitan Police didn't have their hands tied by a load of wet liberals they might get some convictions at last. Since the abolition of the witchcraft laws in 1726 *I have conclusive proof that witchcraft has reached epidemic proportions in this country. And what is done, I ask, about this menace? Nothing. We have to go cap in hand to these unscrupulous women.*

'Darling, you did –'

I heard doubt in her voice at last. Assert anything for long enough and people will believe it. Cigarettes are good for you and make you popular. Beer makes you strong.

'You did, my love, you told me.'

'Did I?'

President Reagan cares. Nuclear power is not dangerous. *Say Good Night to Alfie Barnacle* is a good novel. I can't fail if I go on like this, I thought. Perhaps she did at that. Perhaps this whole affair is nothing more than misrepresentation. Perhaps, dear reader, you doubt me enough to suppose that, here and there, I have been wilful in misrepresenting certain things. Perhaps you think I'm trying to make myself look good. But I tell you that there are things I remember just as I have described. And they will not go away.

'Oh maybe I did. Jamie, I'm so bloody –'

'Can I come round?'

'Could you leave it a couple of hours? I have some work I must –'

'I must see you.' Was this it? Was it that after Meg left I started to lean on her, want more from her than she wanted to give? She always held something back from me, that's true. She could see that when I start on a person I want all of them. I want more and more and more. And when I've got it all, when there's nothing left, as with Meg, I walk away. *Done that, bought the T-shirt. Now what?*

Perhaps she had been cold with me at a previous meeting. I don't remember. What I remember is the vivid pain in my neck and the voice telling me to be gentle and nice with her, to get over to her flat and then hurt her, tell her she's ugly, unnecessary to me. Or was all of that later? The trouble is each moment that I describe is infected with the present. I conjure up myself then but I am no longer reachable. And by the same token in each living moment, we feel we know our futures and act on their knowledge. No such thing as history. Now I had persuaded her, Anna's image broke free of Meg's. She was once more the agent of my salvation. I would tell her everything. She would get rid of Ezekiel. Set a witch to find a witchfinder. Find 'er first. Find her. 'Anna, I do love you.'

A nervous giggle. 'You're not so bad yourself.'

'I must come round, love. Does your neck hurt?'

'Does my *what*?'

'Your neck hurt. A sort of pain at the base of the neck?'

'What are you talking about?'

'It's this bloody Ezekiel character, my love. He's rather taken me over.'

'I noticed.'

'When I'm out of it I can see quite clearly. It's you I want. You're like an angel, you just get me out of it. I concentrate on your face and I'm OK. But he gets in the way and makes me doubt you and then everything goes – sorry, you'll think I'm barmy.'

'You sound –'

'Are you sure your neck's all right?'

'My neck's fine. Look, Jamie, I have some work to do, I –'

'Don't worry, darling, I'm coming over. Just hold on.'

'Jamie –'

I slammed the phone back on to its cradle. Some enterprising Putney youth had taken a hammer and smashed out the window pane to my left. He had done a craftsmanlike job – vandalism is one of the few things left that British youth does with real love and care – and there were no stray fragments of glass

298

adhering to the side of the frame. It was hard to tell, looking at it, which were the frames with glass and which was the fraudulent square. I found myself looking at the window, thinking 'The best glass is the glass that isn't there, or looks invisible. Vandals have got *really* good taste.'

I looked through the empty square in the telephone box. No sign of Rick. Would he follow me? I had a sudden, horrible vision of running up from the tube, from the wicked neon of Tottenham Court Road (say) or somewhere out there in the spoilt yet rational city, to meet Rick Mason, grinning at me, holding out a bottle of wine and a ten pound note. I ran for Putney Hill.

When I reached the main road I looked up towards Wimbledon but saw no buses, no taxis. One old man on a bicycle. That was all. I ran across the road, and, twitching glances behind me as I ran, staggered crazily past the Polytechnic, towards the lights of Putney High Street. Running seemed to make the pain easier. Was the model only effective when a certain distance from base? Like a shortwave radio. Should I have left it all at home? No. This figure I kept in my pocket *was* me, wasn't it? Meg had thought of it as me. The other figure was Anna's. I had to get to her. She would save me. *If this is anyone's fault it's the witchfinder's.* At least I knew which side I was on. I reached the Hill and glared up south, towards Tibbett's Corner.

A roar behind me. Damn. A bus. Fifty yards to the bus stop. No one waiting there. Oh stop you bastard can't you? Stop! I could hear the driver gunning his engines. Nothing they like more than drawing away, just as another would-be passenger tries to fight his way on board. Stop you bastard. It was stopping. And an elderly lady was winching her leg on to the platform. The conductor had her left arm and was bending his body in sympathy with hers. A courtly, old fashioned scene. Stop you bastards. Stop.

She was on the bus. Very, very slowly the conductor turned up towards his bell. Had he seen me? Fifteen yards. His hand was on its way, travelling in a slow arc, like a lazy swimmer's arm, towards its target. Ten yards.

'PLEASE!'

He turned round and saw me. He put his hands on his hips

and grinned. He wasn't a contemporary bus conductor. He was straight out of the fifties. Out of a black and white (he was white) British film: a comic, lovable, durable, British cockney. I could imagine him about to say 'Lawks' or 'Bless me soul' or 'Gawd bless yer Guv'ner.' I stopped and we looked at each other. The pain in my neck had disappeared. 'Easy,' he said, 'you look as if all the devils in 'ell were after you.'

I panted and snarled at him for a bit. Then I said, 'Why do you say that?'

He grinned. 'It's only words. It's just an expression – don't mean anything.'

If I bee sett to call this one Traytour or that one Jesuitte, though the One may bee as Faithfull as anie to the Nation & the other bee as True a Protestant as ever Lived, there will nott bee much Space between the Accusation and the Proof of it. Was it nott ever thus? And how else shall Lawyers & Judged find emploiement except by shaping the World to the Needs exacted upon it by the Intemperate Fancies of the Vulgar?

Indeed it was nott long before I heard that Charge agaynst my Anna, from otheres in that Town of *Northampton*. And though, at first they whispered it behind their Handes, fearing to make a Deposition before the Justice, yett, as the daies passed, some said it openlie as shee did pass them – if shee went forth at all, which was nott often – & soe my Master's brother comes to hear of it & sends for mee & asks mee of the girl, how I may report of her. 'Shee is,' says I, 'as Virtuous and Honest a Gentlewoman as anie I have yet encountered.' And Nahum nods slowly and says nothing but that *John Lucas* is nott an honest Man and yet hath Befriended manie in the Town.

I have no Knowledge as to how the Matter came to the Eares of Master *Wavell*, that was oure Pet Priest there – and, to my mind, a Common and Ignorant Fellow – but on a Daie hee comes to the Howse & asks mee if I may lead him then to Anna. 'For,' says hee, 'I must Hear her say her *Catechism*.' 'How can that bee,' says I, 'when the wench speaks nott to anie?' 'Nay Master Oliphant,' says hee, his eie seeking Mine, 'must wee nott all say the Lord commands us, and repeat His Scriptures as

300

wee may bee taught?' And hee lookes narrowly upon mee for hee loved nott the Waie my Master and I took to the Lord God but thought himself the onlie True Authoritie for the blessed wordes of the PROPHETS and the True and Holy testament and parables of oure Lorde Jesus Christ. Much as oure present Generalle would have alone unto Himself the Ordering of the Lives of his Subjects. 'Well then,' says I, 'you must come another daie for shee bee nott well.' Synce I knew well it would go agaynst her if shee knew nott her Catechism. 'Indeed,' says Master Wavell, 'I think you would nott Quarrelle with One who asked a Virtuous Woman to say her *Lorde's Prayer*.' 'Why,' says I, 'are there some hereabout who say my *Margaret* is nott Virtuous?' For verily I had thought wee were aboutt another Case. And I collect myself & say unto Him, 'I'll swear oure *Anna* is no Witch as some have Testified.' 'No?' says Master Wavell, 'and mayhap this *Margaret* neither.' 'And with a smile as thin as Milk and Water hee went from mee.

I have spoken with those that say the Pattern and Image of oure Lives is no Fixed and Settled Thing, but as much at the Mercie of Argument as the nexte Wave in from the Sea may bee affected by the Wind or Tides. And these would say that *Ptolemy* or *Plato* may have as much to do with the formation of oure Manners and Opinions as is our Commerce with those that Serve, Command or Recommend themselves to us. Which, if it bee taken with the Arguments of the *Pythagoreans* – as Mr Passmore described them to mee – that the *soul* itself may Migrate after Death & find itself in the Bodie of Another – wee may Argue that it was, verily, my Margaret I looked upon when I held this same *Anna Stafford*'s hand up to my Cheek. But for my Part, I hold the soule of Man to bee a fixed and certayn thing, a verie *North Star for Sailors* & that each must guard his & Cherish it & Keep it. So it bee that what I write now here may this Night bee burned by the Officers or that the Truth of it bee taken up & twisted out of Shape by all the Ages that are yett to Come. For wee know well that Reputation, Great Office, Cunning Art, Power & Authority of the *Generall*'s art, all are laid waste by Time, which takes oure poor Prides and Conceits & shews them back to Us as Grains of Sand that lie upon some Beach and are Trampled low between the Sea and the Land. But love, as I do think, may yett Survive as an Example yea though the Devill goe aboutt to Snare us & give us False Prophecie so that wee know nott what may bee Love & what Conceit & Erroure of the Fleshe. And here it is of *Love* I wish to write for sure in all my Wretched & most Miserable Life I think I never acted it but the Once. For a Man may *think* or *dream* or *picture Love* but unless hee Act & by His Workes demonstrate God's Holy Love for Man then is hee but an Emptie Thing.

O send Thou mee the Fortitude to tell it Plain & make this Love of Mine most Fast & Secure, so, yet there bee neither mee nor Pen & Ink nor Fields beyond this Howse nor England neither – say the World bee all as Barren as some Rock upon the farre Bermudas, yet let this Love last & shew itself a Beacon to some Weary TRAVELLER who trusts nott the Lord & hath, as anie who hath his feet upon the Pit may Testifie, no Secure and Lasting Belief in the Lorde, nor, by this Token, in the Things that Nourish & Bless us – as the State of Matrimonie, the Wise and Prudent Management of Friends and Family, Thrift, Diligence, Honesty & those severall Virtues that may teach those who will come after us to say 'Here was it *well done*.'

That same Night after Master Wavell visited us I went to Anna & asked of her if shee could say her Lorde's Prayer. For, though shee spake few Wordes after her own Endeavour, yet had shee some ballads or Pretty Rhymes I had heard her sing. I took her some waie from the Doores of the Howse, by a Field that was there, turned her to Face mee, & with my Armes upon her Shoulders thus, began: 'Anna, do you Knowe Youre Lorde's Prayer?' And shee, after much hesitation: 'I think so Sir.' – 'Well then . . .' Her mouth, though her Eie showed Want of Sense, was Shaped to saying the Sweetest & most Reasoned Sentences. Yet, as I studied Her & saw shee fought to Utter oure Lorde's name shee could nott doe so, at which I was much Disturbed. 'Why Anna,' says I, 'what's amiss?' But though shee struggled agayn still the Wordes rose nott to her Lips. But I was nott Dismaied, taking her Arm & urging her in a quiet Voyce, first that shee should sing mee some Ballad shee was used to, then Reminding her, with Gentlenesse of the Blessed Wordes, which, at length, she begins to say with mee & ends by Repeating the Oure Father in a low & clear Voyce at which I was much Affected. 'There Anna,' says I, 'if yon *Wavell* asks you to Repeat the Wordes you are Assured of Good Success in the Exercise.' But shee looks back at mee & shakes her Head, slow-lie, as solemn as a Church Bell. 'I cannot,' says shee, 'for I am afeared of them.'

I took her Arm agayn and walked with her toward my MASTER'S BROTHER's Howse, turning these things over in my Mind, how manie may bee accused of False Testimonie & how the Practice of Witchcraft may bee Hidden from those who walk nott in God's good Grace & I called upon the Lord for Advice & comfort, saying unto him *Hear thou my Plea Lord for I have stood upon ground and thought myself in a sound Place and I was lost & I have walked in a Great Light that yet Hid Light from mee & how may I know Thy Truth and Thy Light from what is the enemie's & how may others bee led to it*. For I knew Anna was no Witch. And yet still I was Afrayd.

27

It's just an expression – it doesn't mean anything.

I am bewitched. I feel I am in hell. Fire and brimstone. Just expressions. As I looked out at the London night – the Thames at Putney, in a huge black curve from Hammersmith to Wandsworth; the Fulham Road, crowded with the leisure-seeking young – London seemed an evil place, ripe for destruction. *Wee are condemned. When all the profit and Residue of the late discovered Oyle in the Northern Oceans be spent – then what of us the Late Lamented English? For are wee now any more than a Chequers Piece to the Aged Captain of the Americas? A hand stool for the Arse of His Generalles? See how the Young and Olde parade through the Markets, naught in their head but the 'Let's Buy my Masters! While wee are above Grounde shall Wee Use up the Last Drop of Currencie! Here's to the Nation of Wine Barres and Fast Food Restaurants! A Health to Stereo Headphones, McDonalds Hamburgers, Pulloveres in the French Manner! And a murrain on all formes of worshippe and Decencie!'*

Opposite me, a woman of about sixty was sorting through a collection of brown paper bags. From one of them she took a sandwich and as we lurched into Kensington, she munched on it. Her eyes did not register those around her. She was a solitary. She could die tonight and no one would notice.

I felt in my pocket for the two figurines. The needle of one pricked my figure, and, cursing, I pulled my hand away. When I looked down I saw I was holding the doll that looked like me. A red bead of blood had fallen across its chest. I hadn't wanted to bring it out. I gazed at it stupidly.

'Wochoo got there?' The crone opposite, her mouth full of sandwich, was leaning towards me.

'Nothing.'

Harrods was behind us. Like a floating city, strung with lights. The old woman came closer. Her clothes, I noticed, were thick with dirt and her wrinkled fingers would not straighten.

As she reached for the doll I saw not a hand, but the claw of an animal. I pulled the figure away from her.

'Doesn't look like nothing to me, dear.'

'It's nothing.'

There was no one else seated near us. The conductor was sitting in one of the seats to my left, head back, eyes closed. He seemed to have finished conducting for the night. And the bus too was breaking rules. Its huge engines were being indulged, roaring with pleasure, as it carried us on through the black February night – Hyde Park, Victoria – the infernal omnibus, I thought, as I looked at the old woman's face in the sick light.

'It's a charm,' she said. 'It's unlucky.'

'Yes,' I said. The pain in my neck had come back. It was throbbing like a tightly bound wound.

'If you don't find the person who made it,' she went on, 'you might die.' She cackled, as the bus, like an unladen boat in heavy seas, swerved into another corner. 'My mother was a witch,' she went on. 'If she looked at a person the wrong way, that person might die I tell you.'

'Yes?' I put the figure back into my pocket.

'Find the person who made it,' she croaked, 'find them and hold them down and do them some fucking damage.'

I got up and rang the bell. 'Sure,' I said.

She wiped crumbs from her mouth and sat back in her seat. 'You look white, you look white and ill.'

'I'm fine,' I said, 'I'm fine.' But as I stepped off the bus I put my hand once more up to my neck. I glanced back at the old woman and she was nodding at me like a mechanical toy. 'I told you so,' her gummy eyes seemed to say, 'I told you so.'

It was all very well telling me to find Meg. Meg was gone. The trouble was, in this state I couldn't think straight. How could I have doubted Anna? That bastard Ezekiel confusing me. Anna was at risk, wasn't she? The pains in her neck were probably starting up right now. Anna would help me; Anna with her red curls, slim hips and bright brown eyes.

It wasn't surprising that Ezekiel was trying to stir things up between Anna and me. He had, quite clearly, gone well over the top as a witchfinder. I mean there are witches, but not absolutely everyone you meet is a witch. How can you begin to function that way? Unless, of course, the figurine of Anna was a kind of double bluff, to allay suspicion. No no no. That way madness lies. Anna will help me. I ran up Whitehall – ghostly, formal street. From here the man of blood stepped out one cold January morning on to the scaffold. Hasn't changed. The same elaborate dignity of the buildings, a cloak for all the complicity and intrigue of government. Witches in government, of course. Since Cromwell's day. Witches in three-piece suits smiling and nodding and talking about the EEC and all the time in league with the infernal imps, witches and monsters that lie out there in the dark waiting for us. Got to get to Anna. Put my arms around her. Tell her what Meg is trying to do.

I picked up a taxi on the corner of Trafalgar Square. Bloomsbury please. I would see Anna and it would be all right. I would go into her bachelor flat, which was like the first flat Meg and I had lived in, in Notting Hill Gate fifteen years ago, and time would slip backwards. There would be no children, no mansion in Putney, no mother-in-law in the basement. We would be young again, and my father would be alive. Of course. He'd be alive. He'd come in to Anna's flat, and sit on a stool by the window, and say, 'Well, boy. Call this living?' And when he left, his weight would have drilled four neat holes in Anna's brown carpet. Those holes would be all that was left of him.

'Five quid, guv.'

To my right were the black railings above Anna's basement. I reached for the dolls in my pocket. Once again the needle caught my stumbling fingers and I felt the point sting me. I paid the driver and walked to the edge of the railings. There was a lamp burning in the far recesses of the room, but, although she had not drawn the curtains, I could see only the vague shapes of furniture. Had she gone out? I hurried down the stairs and rang the bell. After a minute or so I heard her voice.

'Who is it?'

'It's me. Jamie.'

'Jamie –'

'You've got to see me, Anna. What's the matter?' As I said this the door jerked back and she stood before me. She didn't look like the girl I knew. Her hair was neatly tied in a bun. She was wearing dark overalls, spattered with paint, and although her sleeves were rolled up beyond the elbows, I did not notice her forearms. I saw that reddened mark on her arm, perhaps because she was picking at it nervously; it was raised, angrily, I noticed, like a blister.

'You look terrible, Jamie –'

'I am terrible.'

She made no motion to move or to let me past.

'Is your neck all right, Anna?'

'My neck's fine. Jamie –'

'Please let me in, darling, please. Something's happened.' I pushed past her into the sitting room. It smelt of stale cigarette smoke. I turned and produced the two dolls, thrusting them at her. 'I found them in the house and something is going *on*, Anna, I can't move my neck hardly, why are you rotating your neck like that, it's hurting isn't it?'

'Jamie, it's just you going on about it making me self-conscious. I don't know, I just can't cope with it if you want to know, I have had witchcraft up to here, I don't want to think or speak about it actually.'

'Well I'm not *mad* about it am I? Since it's being used against me by my fucking wife I tell you there is something going on. I so wanted to see you.'

'Well I wanted to see you, Jamie, but I don't want to talk about witches or anything like that or –'

'There's a funny atmosphere in here, Anna – what's up? You look so tense, what's the matter, is she getting to you? Is it getting to you?'

'It's not getting to me, I –'

'What's wrong, Anna? What's wrong?'

She stopped moving her neck and came towards me. Her voice had a slightly hysterical edge to it. 'He lived here, Jamie. He was here – in a site on this house. He's still bloody here I think sometimes. You try to get rid of the past but it traps you, doesn't it? I mean your wife is *there*, isn't she? I don't know, you pick me up and put me down and –'

'What is the matter, Anna?'

'This,' she said, and almost running to one of her low book-shelves, yanked out a pamphlet which she tossed to me.

307

'What's this?'

'Page ten,' she said sharply, and went out to the kitchen.

I sat on the floor and turned the pages. Not a lot seemed to have happened in Bloomsbury. Roman Bloomsbury amounted to a dodgy piece of pottery found on a building site. Medieval Bloomsbury, a series of rather suspect speculations about cart tracks and annual fairs. On page ten I read

> On the site of number ten Cheyne Road, behind the Museum, stood the house of Sir William Devenish. It was here, in 1658, the notorious Witchfinder Oliphant was kept before his trial and execution, according to a letter from 'Antiquary' in *Notes and Queries III* p342. Local legend spoke for years afterwards of the 'hauntings' of Oliphant and one quaint legend speaks of his appearance late one night to a cleaner in the British Museum Reading Room. Dubious as these tales are, we cannot help but reflect on the extraordinary ironies of the Witchfinder's last nights here. Condemned to die a death as cruel as the one he often sought for his victim – small wonder the monstrous Oliphant should be thought to return to roam the scenes of his torment!

I looked up. He was here all right. I could feel him. Stronger than I had ever felt him before. That was what was wrong here. Where are you, Ezekiel? Come on, boy. Where? I got up off the floor, as, from the kitchen, came Anna tugging on a lead. Behind her was a huge, misshapen black dog, and behind the dog came Derwent Mate. The first thing I noticed about him was that he was wearing no socks or shoes and that his face was flushed from some form of exertion. Anna had a closed, determined look on her face as she pulled the dog to heel.

'There's something I ought to tell you, Jamie, 'she said. 'I –' But I didn't wait for her to finish. I was on my feet before the two of them, a great surge of power and anger rising in me. I was walking towards the dog, my arms oustretched, saying in a soft voice, To mee Gip! Come Spirit – Come. And let Us Waste this Abominable Harlot and Her Knavish Companion. Come Gip. Come.' The curious timbre of my voice shocked the two of them into silence. I turned on them and heard myself shriek 'And before this Night is out I will See You before my Master, which is my Real and Living Godde whom I serve and Have always Served, yea though I Talked Freely of God and Saviour Yet it was Satan Himself I served and now Hee calls Thee to Account, and with my Familiar here shall I Cause Thee the Pains and Tormentes you Merit. Away Gip! Away. Away!'

Finally Derwent Mate spoke. His voice had the nervous authority of a primary school teacher suddenly confronted by adolescent vandals. 'Basically mate,' he said, 'cut the funny voices.'

I wasn't there. He was speaking to the monkey, not the organ grinder. I, Ezekiel, drew myself up to full height and pointing that weary, accusatory finger at him, howled out a curse that sent him and the Strumpet back Towards the Filthy room Where they Had consummated their Unclean Desires. 'Have a care Master Derwent,' I yelled, 'for now is my houre. Nowe is it Time for Mee to make Apparent and plaine my Devilish PURPOSES, Which are to awake the forces of Hell and Scourge and Destroy all the Poisonous Hags who have most sorely Mee betrayed and Cuckolded! Now am I Come Again to this Unhappy Kingdome to Claim what the Protector Promised me is Rightfully Mine – and to wound with scorpions They who Have Befouled my Trust! Back Witch Back! Come, my familiar. Come, Gip. Come, Pretty Gip!' With a snarl, the black dog broke his lead and bounded towards me. But he did not, as I thought he would, lay his head in my lap and pant obedience. He jumped for my throat, barking and snarling. I dodged past him and threw myself at Anna.

28

Anna started screaming, and Derwent Mate interposed his body between us. 'Actually, mate,' he began, 'you as far I can see are a married man and I feel –'

'Back you Whoreson Pinchpenny Caller out of Wares and Goods,' I screeched, 'You Vile Peddler of other men's Fancies! Cheapchoice Vaunter with a Dissembling and a Scoundrel Tongue!'

Anna was saying something. Something about how I didn't own her. Nobody owned her. She was a free spirit. If she chose to go to bed with me that was her affair. I had no right to make demands on her. In the last week or so I had been so demanding.

'Demand, woman? What should a Man Demand of a Woman but that Shee be Faithfulle unto Deathe and Tend and Care for Him and Obey Him in the smallest particular of his Commandes! For doth not Hee Owne and Controule her? And is not His Will the guiding and Guardian Spirit of her Poore Woman's Understanding?'

She yelled back at me. 'You don't own me, Jamie. Sometimes I think you're crazy with your constant demands and your looks at me sideways, I tell you –'

'Get out, mate,' said Derwent Mate. 'Just go.'

I grabbed him by the throat and pushed him towards the wall. Anna and the dog made a concerted attack on me. But my hands were on his neck and I did not propose to let go. 'Burn Witch!' I shrieked.' Burn Shee who is too Fainthearted in the Devill and the Powers of Evil. I'll none but the Witches Covenanted to Mee. I'll none of the Essenden Witches, they have no Body to 'em. No, not the Cornish Witches neither, nor the Women that were lately hanged at Northampton Assize. I'll trust None of 'em. Nay not even Shee who Shares my Bed or Claims to bee my lawfull Wife.'

The black dog darted forward as Derwent and I rolled on to

the floor and began to nip at my behind. I was wearing thick cord trousers, but he still managed to make some headway into my left buttock. 'Down, Gip!' I called, 'Away, Boy. Down with Thee Spirit or I'll Tell Thy Master!'

'If you think,' said Derwent Mate, in quite literally strangled tones, 'if you think this sort of thing is funny then let me tell you that I am not amused.' Derwent Mate and I reversed positions, as he got his hands on my forearms and succeeded in breaking my grip. The black dog took a large bite at his behind. He screamed, and Anna in her turn began to scream. I wriggled free of Derwent Mate and staggered to my feet. 'With How Manie Others,' I said, 'hast thou me Betrayed? How many times have You Taken this one's thickeste Fingere, that One's Tickling Rod and pleasured yourself behind my Back? Whore!'

'Fidelity,' said Anna, who was getting into the swing of this quite well, 'is not a subject you can pronounce on, is it?'

'O Distressful Kingdome!' I said, 'when Whores seek to Justify their Licence to God and when Lust is paid out by Lust! O Country Amazed at Itself, at Civil Warre with its own most Cherished and Regarded Principalls!'

'O Fuckynge Scumbagge and Double-Dealynge Hypocritte!' she replied smartly, 'O Male Chauviniste Twerpe!' Then she stopped. I was weaving round the table back towards Derwent Mate. She looked across at me with sudden, almost motherly sympathy. 'Talk to me, Jamie. Make a joke or something love. It's only a cock and a cunt, isn't it? What does it matter?'

To my horror I discovered I was crying. I answered her in my voice. 'Is that all it is?' I said. 'Is it as squalid as that? I loved you, Anna. It isn't just that is it? It's got to be more than that.' Even the dog seemed impressed by my sincerity. I wasn't sure that I was, but I pressed on. 'I know I don't own you, but I thought we . . . I've never felt what I felt for you. Never.'

'It's a casual thing, isn't it?' she asked, but her voice didn't sound so sure, 'we've only known each other a month or so. You frightened me, Jamie, a bit. After we came back from Oxford. It was all a bit fast. You're so sweet and you're funny and I can talk to you not like I talk to Derwent but I was frightened. I didn't want to get hurt. I've been hurt before. I –' But Ezekiel had had enough of this Mills and Boon stuff. He wanted action and plenty of it. He reared up in me, interrupting her speech, with 'I hear Nowadays Naught but this "Cry you Mercy May the good Lord Except *Mee* from the Generalle Charges against Sin and Falsehoode." Alwayes in these Wenches' Pleas you shall hear them Proteste "Ah but 'twas done for Such and Such or This Reason, or That One." And yet what is Their Case but an Argumente in Favour of the Onlie God They Knowe – Themselves! Whore! Malapert Mistress of such Pox Houses, Syphiliticks and –'

But the dog had had enough of this. *I* had had enough of this. The dog bounded over to me and bit me once more in the bum. But his technique of bum biting was clearly improving. He had made a good first attempt at me. With Derwent Mate he had extended his technique, done new, interesting things in the bum biting line, but this was his major work. He had come of age as far as biting the bum was concerned, and he took a clean, mature, savage sweep at my hindquarters. Both I and Ezekiel were impressed. I don't know whether your average seventeenth-century dog bit with as much *élan* as this one. I would guess not. But I and my inhabiting spirit leaped about four feet in the air and, shouting '*FUCKING HELL!*' headed for the door. But the dog, an over-familiar familiar, or at least a familiar unfamiliar with proper familiar behaviour, was not to be stopped. It bounded after me, baying enthusiastically. If it was a reborn sprite, sired from Oliphant's Gip, a lot had happened to it along the way: it had acquired a touch of the Baskervilles, a little bit of Bob Martin's perhaps. And it had, now, a taste for bum. It wanted more bum. It came after me. 'Gip,' I said, 'for that I am Divided from these my Vital Spirits, I beg Thee do Thou my Bidding and answer not the Call of the False Witch who Hath most lewdly and inconsiderately Betrayed Mee! Away Gip! Come away.' It was, now I come to think about it, the worst possible scenario in what you might call the Witch Script: man possessed by Soul of dead witchfinder is pursued, not only by undead soul of witch he has condemned three centuries earlier, but also by *his own fucking familiar*. *Are there no standards left? Is nothing sacred?*

I veered back into the room and yelled at the beast in my own voice, like an Englishman on foreign soil for the first time, who is of the opinion that the natives can be reached by shouting loudly enough in one's own language. *'Get out of here you stupid fucking dog!'* I yelled. *'Go back where you came from and leave me in peace!'*

'Jamie –' Anna was beginning to find this amusing. I was pleased for her that she was able to do so (I tell you now, dear, that I never found it amusing, amused as I was by your capacity for amusement. I don't expect women I fall in love with to behave like giggling morons with no respect for their own bodies, let alone anybody else's, capable of coming up with asinine remarks along the lines of *it's only a cock and a cunt.* It was my cock and your cunt, remember? And then it was his cock and your – oh don't let's even call it a cunt, shall we? Shall we call it the M6 fucking motorway?) but I did not find it at all amusing. I could see that to the detached observer there might be something comic about all of this. I hadn't expected to find her so suddenly, frighteningly detached from all of it. Were you worthy of my love? I don't think so. I don't think you know what to do with love. I think you pick it up with your bright, shiny eyes and play with it and think 'Great. Got some of *that.*' Maybe you even liked me being in love with you. It must have been quite a joke, eh? Only a few weeks and this boy is saying these wild things. He loves me. 'Dear Marge, should I have anything more to do with this man' – oh fuck you and fuck her and fuck all women with their talk of love, or rather with their way of getting *you* to talk about it. I don't want to talk about love with anyone ever again. I know all about that, thanks.

'Jamie –'

'Damnable and execrable Whore! Diseased Child of a world grown Mad for Pleasure! Get thee gone and thy Paramour and this thy Familiar – I'll see thee Hanged before God I swear it!'

The dog and I were now running round the bachelor girl's dining table, like some competitors in a new form of athletic test – the domestic marathon. The dog would leap up from time to time and take another nip at my buttocks. He was gnawing at the corduroy, with each attempt getting more and more of my fleshy rear. I flailed back at him wildly but to no avail. Barking wildly he set two paws on me. I turned back to him and he scrabbled at my chest. I could feel his strong dog's breath on me. I ran for the door.

'Go get him, Gip mate,' shouted Derwent Mate, who had taken advantage of the situation to put on his shoes and socks, 'go get him!'

'Jamie!' Anna was shouting and giggling at the same time.

It's always amusing to betray someone. I betrayed Meg. She betrayed me. Meg betrayed no one. Let's leave the betrayals to the giggling half-wits who can come up with lines like *it's only a cock and a cunt*, shall we? Shall we reserve that for the girls and men who think they're something called 'liberated'? They don't want to own anyone. Not them. Possession is not for them. They were really cool in the womb. When their mothers picked them up and put them to the breast and bottle they thought 'Yeah, but I don't want to be – uh – committed. 'Ezekiel, I sometimes think you were fucking right about this mindless, self-deceiving pile of indulged and indulgent half-wits we call Britain. Ha ha ha betrayal. Big joke. Adultery? It happens every day. Yes, it happens every to morons like you who follow men out of the British Museum and are fucking them about three hours later. Don't expect me to respect you. Don't expect me to say I love you or ever loved you. I take back those things I wrote. I never meant any of them. Bitch. Stupid fucking mindless fucking promiscuous half-witted bitch.

I was running out into the area, pursued by Gip, Anna and Derwent Mate. For a nasty moment I thought Gip was going to catch my ankles, but the fat, black creature was almost as out of condition as I was.

I glanced behind me as I cleared Bedford Square and came up towards the Euston Road. Gip was still out in front. Anna had stopped, and was waving and shouting something. Behind her, Derwent Mate was bent over double. I ran for the lights of Euston Station. But the dog, as befitted an agent of the damned, showed a quite alarming persistence. It was loping along, easily now – about twenty yards behind me, red tongue splayed lasciviously across its open jaws. I was at the traffic lights on Euston Road. Container lorries, broody with cargo, passed with the solemnity of heavy artillery. I thought I would lose the creature in the architecturally-planned no man's land to the

314

south of Euston station, a maze of paths, piazzas, benches facing nothing, and effortfully modernistic sculpture. There were lights there among the trees, but there was the safety of darkness too. Anyway the thing would never get across the road. It was a seventeenth century dog; how could it know about traffic lights and red and green and yellow? How do twentieth-century dogs acquire such knowledge? I might as well have asked, for, when I turned on the other side of the road, I saw it trot neatly across to the middle of the highway, look left, right and left again, and come right on after me, into the gloom of the piazza. It reminded me of some robot, equipped with a heat-seeking device. There was something brisk and formal about it – it could have been one of those commuters who trudge up our road every evening. *Examinate testified that the accused did follow him in the shape of a large black dog and persuaded him to suckle and swear allegiance to the Devil and all his works. He did confess that in the forecourt of EUSTON station he and the dog forged their loathsome Union with the Powers of Darknesse.* It didn't appear to be sniffing the ground or making any attempt to pick up scent. Perhaps it didn't need to try. Perhaps I smelt too strongly of fear to be able to hide.

I decided to go through the station and out through the side entrance to the west. It would never be able to keep track of me – even if it managed to get through the doors. Head down, I ran for the low building at the far end of the forecourt. EUSTON it was labelled, in informal, neutral letraset. Contemporary London can be quite as ghostly as its Gothic or Jacobean equivalents – here, among carefully planted bushes and paved courtyards, I felt myself to be a figure drawn in an architect's landscape, while the lighted box of the station ahead resembled nothing so much as a child's toy. There was a Gothic station here once – huge Doric pillars, mourned by Betjeman. And the station then was raw, acrid with smoke and dust and fog. My father took me through it. Victorian Gothic, don't they call it? Each age parodying its predecessors, until, as now, there are no styles left to parody. The search for a voice is a search for the right thing to mimic. And that, in its turn, is mimicry. So that there are no true voices. Not for me anyway. One minute I am inside my own, underworked fictional world – a place where people *thunk* and *thwack* and *groan* like something from a child's comic; the next I lurch into Hollywood Horror, cheap shocks brave and new, and from there, a short journey brings me to the confessional – easy tears, 'I love you' or 'You betrayed me'; but these confessions too are mere imitations. I don't expect you to believe them. I'm laid out, already, like my father – all you will get of me is all I have of him – the glasses, the cupboard crammed with neatly ironed jackets, the books, the fading memory of a voice that wasn't a voice ever, but a noise like a noise you heard before, a whispering . . .

I was safe. Inside. No smoke, no steam trains. Ahead of me the comforting click of the departures board. Trains were leaving, on time, for Birmingham and Liverpool and Manchester. And on arrival, departure boards (in case you were thinking of coming back) would look just the same and the tobacconists and the snack bars and the car parks and the one-way systems in the town beyond the station would make you feel you were in the town and station you had already left. So there was nothing to worry about. The soft black, studded surface of the floor, the muzak, the passengers who seemed to glide through doors that opened at their approach, the patient, kindergarten tones of the notices, all told you that England was a safe place. Even the anguish of its railway stations is predigested. Listen to our Prime Minister: *It's all right, there's nothing to worry about.*

Actually I find it disturbing that our stations, advertisers, Prime Ministers even, should sound so reassuring. *Why are they trying to reassure us? What is there that's so worrying that they need to sound reassuring?*

Wasn't there another exit? Over to the left? Past platform sixteen? A West Indian guard stood by a pile of luggage, studying a huge watch. A fat woman looked past me into the middle distance. All victims of time, abandoned or tormented by it. I was walking, I found, in a slow, measured way, as if anxious to show the passers that I had no train to meet or catch. I was above all this; I was strictly a tourist on this station.

There was no exit down to the left. I must have been thinking of some other station. Or perhaps the Victorian Gothic Euston ('Come on boy – don't dawdle'). I was in the wrong time, at the

316

wrong address. I turned and ran back towards the line of glass doors. No sign of the dog. I left by the farthest door on the right, and as I came out of the warmth of the concourse into the February night, I saw it. It was waiting in the gloom, still, red tongue and white teeth on display. I ran at it, kicking wildly at its head. 'Beast of the Great Belly,' I shouted, 'Seek another pasture or I will Cut Thee about the Chaps and be Quit of Thee forever. For though I may bee but a Printer, yet is my sword no mere spitfrog and is my Hand no mere Shuttlecock, to pass back Compliments or Curses only.'

"ere . . .' someone was shouting. But they had no need to interfere on the dog's behalf. This dog had no need of the RSPCA. It had no need of friends of any kind. It reared up, snapping at me, as it had done in the flat, and as I threw myself forward into the piazza, caught me on the left heel. I reeled, nearly fell, recovered, and then struck off into the night.

I didn't go back towards the Euston Road. Anna and Derwent were that way. I turned right. North – towards Camden, past a deserted, barricaded parade of shops, and then right again, into one of those sudden, private squares in which London is so rich. Like a quiet reach of water off a busy river, it had a by-passed quality to it. It looked as if the same people had been living there, hanging out washing, calling to each other from windows, marrying and having children for the last three hundred years although the houses could not have been that old. There was a garden – surrounded by railings in the middle of the square, and in the far corner a half-timbered structure on its own, that looked as if it could have doubled as Ezekiel's residence.

Its spell outside the station seemed to have driven the dog crazy. It was rearing up and running at the same time now. Once it fell forward on to my back, and its claws cut through my jersey to my flesh. I put my hand under my shirt and found it had drawn blood. Then, in the pocket of my jacket, I found the doll. I didn't know which one it was but I pulled it out and flung it back towards the creature. The dog stopped. So did I. I saw that it was the figure of me. It lay on the pavement between us. I could see its pointed, troll-like nose, a miniature exclamation mark in the blackness. It did look extraordinarily like me. Meg, of course, would be well aware that, in describing me, one has to go for the nose. In describing her I sometimes go for her lank, black hair, sometimes for her high, nervous laugh, sometimes for that look in her eyes, as of an animal that is being treated kindly but suspects that some form of nightmarish experiment is about to be practised on it. Was her making of the figures a species of revenge for my having used her in fiction so many times, or perhaps – this being her most constant complaint – for having described her so badly? The figurine was me, but it was stone age me. It was the essence of myself.

It was then that I realized: the pain in my neck had stopped. The dog, too, seemed suddenly amiable. It waddled towards the figure. 'Good dog,' I said, 'eat up. Eat up. Nice bone.' I could see the needle, glinting in my neck. *My neck. The neck of the thing she thinks is me. 'Is that what you think of me, Jamie? Do you really think I look like an animal that's about to be experimented on?' We are other people's impressions of us. We are at the mercy of their impressions.*

'Gip Gip Gip,' I cooed, 'eat up. Nice bone.'

The dog peered up at me suspiciously.

'Eat, 'I cajoled, 'eat. Eat. Eat.'

He flicked the model of me up in the air with his nose, with the neat skill of a trained circus animal, and snapped at the doll in the air. He howled in pain as the needle cut into his mouth, widened his jaws, and ran for me. We were at the edge of the railings that marked off the garden in the centre, and, surprised by his weight and the suddenness of the attack, I fell against them and slid down on to the pavement. Crazy with the pain – the needle was lodged in the side of his jaw – the black dog scratched at my chest again and again, as if trying to shake itself free of the needle, and even though I pushed at it with my free hand (the other was trapped as I fell, and caught up against my other pocket, inside which I could feel the sharp point of the needle that penetrated Anna's neck) it clawed its way back up me, towards my face, working up my belly with its nails, scratching aside the fabric until it was digging into naked flesh, and the whole of my stomach and abdomen was running with blood.

'*Damnation to the Authorities!*' I was screaming, '*and to Those Evil ones in Constituted Authority over us! For what is their Powere*

318

but the Verie Hearte of Eville itself and what Their Boasts of Order and Good Government but the bloody mouths of Belial and Beelzebub! Get off me you cunt can't you? Fucking get off me!' But for all my screaming, we seemed fixed in some hideous dance, with me pushing up, only to be forced back as the creature flung itself this way and that, the baked image of myself dangling from its lower jaw.

And then someone was yanking it off me, and two men, one with a walking stick, were beating it back along the pavement. It was I who was howling now, howling like a dog, like a man possessed, howling as Ezekiel must have howled when they cut him open and groped for his entrails inside his butchered, still living body. At the end we all make the same noise, which it pleases us not to call human. 'Where am I?' I muttered. 'What happened?'

'Fucking mad dog got you, mate,' said a voice.

And another added, 'You're in Dayford Square. That's where you are. Whipps Cross they call it. Don't know why. Because Dayford Square is its name.'

I heard from some that were hereabouts that knew my Master Nehemiah when hee was in the town of *Hertford* that there were others hanged as witches after wee were Departed for the Warres & at the Gallowes on the North Side of Northampton were a score of Witches hanged in King James's time. And there were among them some, I doubt nott, who thought themselves as Free of Sinne as I, who tomorrow must die a Traytour's Death, synce I was arraigned, nott for my Knowledge of Master Sindercomb and the others, but that I was said to bee a Sorcerer, as *Dr Lamb* had been. And synce my Black Arts were Judged to bee agaynst the Person and Condition of the government, this most Cruell Death was sought for mee, which I know nott how I shall Beare. As I am sate here at Sir William's house I bethink mee of that same Irish Lord the Lieutenant or his Deputie made to cutt down early & had nott the Hangman slit his Throat he would have felt the Payne of the Hangman's Hands goe searching through his verie Bowelles.

319

I do protest my Innocence of this and all other Charges held agaynst mee – which may bee why they proceed agaynst mee in this Hugger Mugger waie – to kill mee at no Notice at the Common Gallowes hard by here named *Whipps Cross* where few may see the Shame that is done to mee. One told mee in the Tower Master Sexby dyed under the Torture, and *that it were best for mee had I done so.* But I may protest as much as ever I will, yet they will still have Blood. As I consider the Fortunes that have brought mee here, & look back at the Road that was my Lot, I see the Devill's Hand on so manie and so different Proceedings. In the Question of my *Margaret* – whose hand there but Beelzebub's? When Anna Stafford was brought before the Justices – then surely was the Devill's worke wrought. When Guilty Great Ones go Unpunished and Innocent blood is shed by Judges with no thought but to their Future with their Masters in Government – then does the Devill drive the Carriage of State.

Thus am I, no Sorcerer, but brought to a Confession by the Screws and the Rack, taken before the Court & made to Plead the Case of those that are in Authoritie – for I have lately confessed to Crimes I never thought to have existed. Truly Fear is the Devill's weapon & he uses it for his Advantage.

I do recall how Anna Stafford, when shee was examined by that *Wavell*, stammered and stuttered & could nott speak her Piece. Which now I knowe was but the Terrour shee had of the Examiners, as it was, I am assured, in the Case of my owne dear Wife. But none shall know the Bread of Captivity unless they eat of it. And who shall say *I have felt the Poyson of the Serpent that it Stinged mee upon the Ankle unless his Flesh hath felt the Teeth and the Venom thereof yea how shall the Dead speak of their passing to the Living who suffer and Remayne?* Truly, I have heard it said, none knoweth the Road but the Face of the Wheel.

O how Inconstant & Contrary are the Uses of the World! I never thought myself to do God's work as well as when I spake agaynst those that had Deposed agaynst my Anna, having neither Thought nor Care for the Opiniouns or Counsells of my Neighboures. Then was it I stood forth & played no longer *Close Mouth Oliphant*. Then did I testify to the Light of the Lord and to the Devill & his Workes but truly I think some of us see Different

Devills & to find the Lord is to travel a Hard and Narrow Path in which is no Glorie but the Pain as oure Lorde felt in the Garden or at the Place of the Skull which was called GOLGOTHA. For when *I testified righteouslie then did the world turn agaynst mee even as it hath changed oure Youth to Age oure Joies to Cares oure Glories to Dust and our very Loves to Hateful Indifference.* And yet I knew in my Hearte that what I said was Just yea though my brother turned agaynst mee could I nott bee turned aside.

Things fell about thus at the house of my Master's brother. At first my Anna is examined by Master Wavell and John Lucas hath said he saw her *converse with a man in black at the* Crossroads but none others then did testifie agaynst her. And shee was examined in the Lorde's Prayer which shee spake unto them most Clearly. For I had staied with her some three Nightes & made her then my Pupil in the Matter. But there were manie still spake agaynst her in the Parish, which talk I Scorned & walked with her to show I had no Feare of them.

Then – and I could not with anie Truth Compute the Yeare of Time of its occurrence, synce at that Howse I *took no care of Lordes or Generalles or Affaires of State* – was my Master's brother taken Sick of a Fever whereof hee dyed within the Space of a Week. O Righteous art thou O Lord *when I plead with thee: yet let me talk with thee of thy Judgements. Wherefore doth the Waie of the Wicked Prosper? wherefore are all they happy that deal right Treachorouslie?* Why should it bee that Nahum, a Man of Sweeter Temper never found by mee, should bee soe taken? And, consequent upon his Death the talk begin agayn of who it was that could have done this thing – hee being Sound of Health & that within our Howse wee harboured one that was an Undoubted Witch. Sometimes I think these witches bee no more than Motes in the eie of Sinners – a Device sent by the Devill to snare us. Never were there worse weekes than after the Death of my Master's brother – for even his Household after his Death began to speak agaynst her and soe it was shee was brought once more before this *Wavell* that I spoke of & asked nott meerly for her *Lorde's Prayer* but for her *Catechism* & there was talk that if shee had got these off pat then they should swim her for they knew her for a Witch. I onlie spake agaynst the depositions agaynst her which was the Cause of much Distress between myself and Nehemiah & the wife of his brother for her own son was heard to swear hee had seen my *Anna* talk with a mouldwarp on the Heath & seen one boy talk with her & fall into a trance & soe die, which had passed above two Yeares before the present Enquiry. & the more I spake for her the more some said I was of the Businesse.

The daie they took her from the Howse that shee might bee examined I was nott suffered to go with them & indeed it went hard for mee in the Howse then so that it was said by some I could leave at my peace. But my Anna comes to mee and places her Hande upon my Cheek & looks long into my eie & I say 'Well. An you remember what I have taught thee & carry Thyself like a Christian no Harm will come of it.' At which John Lucas, who was there, says 'Nay shee can carry herself like no Christian nor has *yon Close Mouth Oliphant* taught her anie such for hee be as much of the Sorcerie as shee.' And I turned unto him, her hand being still upon mee & said thus 'Truly this is a grief and I must bear it. My tabernacle is all spoiled & all my cords are broken: my children are gone forth of mee & they are nott: there is none to stretch forth my tent anie more & to sett up my curtain for the Pastors are become Brutish & have not sought the Lord therefore they shall nott prosper & all their flocks shall bee scattered. Behold the noyse of the bruit is come & a great commotion out of the North Countrie, to make the cities of Judah desolate & a den of dragons.' And none spake for they saw the Worde was upon mee & still I spake. 'For I am a landless man,' says I, 'and have now no Wife to my Name nor anie Familie save my father in Heaven nor anie Good Opinion or Report save that which ye shall make of mee but *this is a Daughter of the Church that walks nott with bonnets or with Ornaments and is nott ashamed in the sight of the Lord O have a care ye mistake nott Satan and ye bow down before the Devill & his workes yea listen for his Voyce verie Cunningly and answer it nott. This Anna is no Witch.'*

And there, behind them I see oure pet priest who stands in the Shadowe of the Howse and says unto mee: 'Nay Master. But have you now the Knowledge of the Satan makes his Worke? And such Knowledge hidden from Godlie persons of the Parish and from Minister of the church? Belike Master Oliphant you have a knowledge of the Formes and Shapes and Voyces of the Devill? And can you speak to us of the Same? Perhaps, Master Oliphant, you have had Conversation with the dark and Terrible things that wait upon our Sleeping, in the Outer Places where the Soule sleeps and Goodness hides her Face?' And hee smiles agayn once more, like one with Knowledge that may do harm if hee but tell it. And I looked upon the Faces that were round mee, which were some of my Master's brother's familie and those that were with Lucas (for my Master was nott with us then nor took an active part in the business agaynst Anna, keeping *plain counsell* in the Old Waie) and I saw their Faces were nott the Faces of the Righteous. And I saw in their Eie the eies of the Transgressor that winks at Graven Images & in their lips I saw the snare of the wicked and in their carriage I saw nott Grace or Favour but Haughtiness & Conceit & in their Soules I saw the Black Work of Satan and in their Handes I saw the Twisted Uses of Infirmitie & in their Heartes I saw naught but Black, Black as the Pit, Black as the Evill & Sulphurous Places of the Deepest Parts of Hell. And faces that were once Fair turned Crabbed and Old as I looked upon them and Mouths and Teeth Flashed like Lucifer and there was Wantonness there & I saw that they Worshipped the Beast. I saw that they and them that were with them even as had Mr Morris, even as had so manie that were at my Cradle and had acquaintance of mee in Armie or Church, all all all worshipped at the Beast and the Beast spake great things and blasphemies and the Devill was his Servant & the faces of them that were there with mee did Melt and Change before my Eie & a great light came to mee & a voyce came saying; *'Truly the Devill is in Church and Armie and in House and Chimney Corner and in Field and in Farm. Hee doth his work where hee may Find it yea hee may betwitch those that are sent to find out witches and through those that Seem Godlie and Virtuous hee may bee the Instrument of damnation.'* And I looked upon the Faces that were round mee, as they were sett to take Anna to the Justice, but though I struggled to find the Wordes that were within my Hearte I could not speak them aloud. For I was afrayd.

So was my Anna taken and examined & in the Examination confessed shee had bewitched my Master's brother but would not Confess I had aided her in anie wise. And though shee spoke but littel, yet the Rack got words enough from her. And so, my Master's brother being judged her Father as in Law, shee was not hanged but Burned & cried much as the flames were put upon Her. Which I saw nott, for, in sorrow and in Grief I went from thence & even my Master Nehemiah that was good to me, spake nott to mee, for manie said I had Conspired with this Anna agaynst the Peace. And so it was I came at last to London, the Wicked City.

29

I put my hand down to my belly. When I lifted it clear, I could see it was stained with blood. The two men were making half-heartedly aggressive movements in the direction of the dog, which was growling resentfully several yards away. The figur-ine had shaken itself loose. One of the men leaned down and picked it up. It was, I noticed, smeared with blood. The man who had picked it up turned it over in his hands, wonderingly. He had a big square, puzzled face, all knobs and creases. 'What's this then?' he asked.

I pulled myself up by the railings. The pain in my neck had started up again. 'It is,' I said, 'a Figure made after the Likenesse of Mee by the Cozening Witch who styles herself my Wife, and who, Before this Nighte be Done I shall arraign before the Assize to depose that Shee be Guiltie!'

The big-faced man looked puzzled. 'I think we should get you to a hospital.'

'Think you, Master,' I said, 'that any Chirurgeon or Apoth-ecary can Minister to a Mind so Troubled as is mine? Find mee the Woman that was late my Wife and let mee scratch at her and Drawe her Bloode as shee drawes mine!'

His friend turned down his mouth and whispered something. 'Nay but speak your Mind and openly,' I called to him (my voice sounded sneering) 'or are Ye also Bewitched? Is the whole Nation subject to the spells and Nightmare Fancies that are the pleasure of the Lord Protector?'

The dog had progressed from growling to whimpering. The two men were looking at me oddly. And then, from the far side of the square, I heard Anna's voice: Ja-amie – Jamie – where are you . . .?' It sounded very, very far away; it seemed to come from another time. It had the quality of a child in search of a friend in a big house, when the game of hide-and-seek is no longer quite a game. It had a pleading, tentative note, as if to say 'Call it off. Let's stop now. Don't scare me!' Had the two men heard it? I couldn't say. Was it only a voice in my head? *Don't say this dirty tangled city, its taxis, apartment houses, canals, three lane highways, hotel lobbies, markets, tower blocks, are none of them solid. That the concrete and the parks and the queues of traffic are no more than a flicker on the retina. Is she here or not? Just tell me.*

She was there. She was alone, her red hair disordered about her back, her prim chin at a slight angle to the world. She was calling me as if I were a lost dog. And it was the dog, not me that answered her. It reversed its hindquarters into the pavement and, in a series of movements at once jerky and flabby, got itself into the four legs position. It was one of those dogs that clearly suffered from a badly defined body image. It wasn't so much that its neck merged into its forequarters, or its belly seemed like a foreign appendage, propped up on badly jointed legs as if it were some crazy table. It wasn't just an unimpressive dog, a mongrel. It was a mongrel to itself. Looking at it, it was hard to know whether its rear end was about to bark or its jaws to deposit a steaming turd on the pavement before our frightened eyes. It was, in short, a typical, ownerless, twentieth-century London dog. No home to go to, no home to come from. None of the traditional doggy virtues. Only doggy vices. No one to lick, nothing to hunt. Nothing to do with its life but shamble about and shit on the pavement.

It is not Oliphant's dog, I thought, but it might as well be, for no one else will lay claim to it. It's as much his as anyone's. It barked as I thought this, as if agreeing with me, and the two men turned towards where Anna's voice was coming from. It was then that she saw us. The dog barked again, and I followed the direction of their gaze. It was, I discovered, barking at Ezekiel (which made sense) and Ezekiel, who was walking a few yards away from Anna, waved in a cheery fashion at his familiar. The dog barked again. 'Hullo, Ezekiel,' I said.

'Hulloo!' said Ezekiel. He sounded like a bloke I was at Oxford with, called MacTavish. A tall, slightly camp, stooping Scotsman, with a nose like a stork's bill, who was always to be found in our flat, sitting bolt upright among the old baked bean cans, in an impeccable suit, reading new hardbacked fiction at unlikely hours of the day. Anna crossed the road towards us. Her manner was that of a cheery Girl Guide leader, who is determined to make the best of a two week holiday under canvas in hurricane conditions. 'Well . . .' she said, in a barmaid voice.

Ezekiel winked at me and allowed his tongue to drool a little. Then he slid one brown, claw-like hand into her boiler suit. She did not seem aware of this, but continued to look at me with cheery, Girl Guide concern. Ezekiel pushed the fabric of her boiler suit over her shoulders and down to the small of her back. She was wearing a petticoat of grey silk, but, to my surprise neither of the two men, or for that matter, the dog, showed any interest. Even when Ezekiel pulled away the silk of her petticoat and tore at her bra, they went on chatting to her and to each other, and paid no attention at all. I thought at first he was about to fondle her breasts – as I presumed Derwent Mate had done (did he call her breasts 'mate'? Entirely possible) but he wasn't interested in her breasts; he scratched at them but only on his way down to her exposed brown belly. Was he going to flay the skin of her groin? No. He scrabbled at her boiler suit until it fell about her legs in a heap, and then he started to pull, rather testily, at her knickers. He looked at me and winked.

'All I am interested in,' he said in a matey, public bar sort of voice, 'is cunt. Nice juicy cunt. That's all I want. And plenty of it.' He sounded like someone in a beer commercial. I was impressed by his no-nonsense, let's-be-friends approach, which did not seem at all at odds with his gear. He wore, on this occasion, what I thought of as his witchfinding apparel – the full clobber, plus stovepipe hat and curly beard. He was, I felt, a man I could trust. 'I like a bit of cunt myself,' I said, though I could not positively have said that my mouth had moved.

Anna shimmied her buttocks around to allow his fingers into her vagina. She sighed softly as they crawled up into her like some licensed spider, some creature she summoned to please her when there were no men around; on the rare nights when either myself or Derwent Mate or any of the other seven hundred-odd twerps in the British Museum Reading Room were not available to stick their 'cocks' (quote) up her 'cunt' (quote). But it wasn't a loud sigh. It was like the noise she had made in her flat that first time – an 'Oh Oh Oh'. A ladylike sound. Anna doesn't give it away, because she has nothing to give. She goes through the motions of giving again and again and again, and some men are stupid enough to think they're getting something.

Nobody believes in love any more. It's a joke even writing the word down. I feel armed men are going to break into this room and take me away to the *London Review of Books* and shine lights in my eyes and ask me in strong German accents *Vot do you mean by zis, Massezon*? Because it's clearly a ridiculous word nowadays.

'I'm sorry,' she was saying, 'but if I fancy it with Derwent.'

I looked at her. She was bouncing up and down on Ezekiel's fingers, rubbing herself off on him. He grinned at me lubriciously.

'If I fancy it with Derwent,' she said again.

Why did she keep saying this? We all knew what she did if she fancied it with Derwent. She put down her pen and picked up his 'cock' (quote) and shoved it up her 'cunt' (quote) and went 'Oh Oh Oh'. Why did she have to keep telling me this? Or had her brain got stuck on this one sentence, like a fruit machine that can do nothing but PAY OUT PAY OUT PAY OUT. Or (this thought was, for some reason, horrible to me) was it my hearing that was jammed? Was the fault, as they say in telecommunications, at my end? Was there something badly wrong with my end? Was this was this why she had gone for Derwent's end? And what, to coin a phrase, was going to be the end of all this?

'If I fancy it with Derwent,' she was saying.

One of the men had said something about somebody not being well, not being right in the head, and I presumed this was why, after taking a good look at Ezekiel, who was still grinding his spiky fingers into the (presumably) moist cleft below her pubic hair, they had disappeared. They need treatment probably. She didn't want them to go because she said somebody might get violent but they didn't seem interested. People aren't interested nowadays. I saw a man have a heart attack in a bus queue and people just ran for the bus. Well I ran for the bus too. I was late for work. But I did at least worry about it. These days in England people have no feeling for one another. It wasn't like that in 1647. People cared. Yes, occasionally they got it wrong. Occasionally they hanged people until they were nearly dead, then cut them down, pulled out their entrails and groped for their hearts which they then showed to a waiting crowd of citizens. I know all that. But in spite of that, they *cared*. They used words like 'love' and 'forasmuch' and 'whomsoever' and there was not the appalling decline in moral standards I see about me today.

'I don't feel about you,' she was saying, 'what I feel about Derwent.'

I should fucking well hope not, Anna. Derwent is a fully certified jerk and I am a passionate and fascinating character who offered you something more than the word 'mate' every third word.

'But –' she said –

Oh no no no. Don't. Don't say it. She is though. She is going to say. All together now. On the count of three. All together now. I want to hear this one really loud and strong. One to get ready and two get steady and

'If I fancy it with Derwent,' she said.

And why not? If she fancies it with Derwent, why not? There is no such thing as duty and obligation. Why not – if she fancies it with Derwent.

'Has he got?' I asked, 'a bigger cock than mine?' I asked this purely in a spirit of scientific enquiry. I simply wanted to know. While I was at it, I might well have gone on to ask about the relative sizes of cocks in the British Museum. Did people studying, say, Chinese Manuscripts have bigger ones than those engaged in examining Norse Creation Myths? How many whoppers were there in the South Hall? But she looked rather petulant at my having asked this question. She clearly thought it in bad taste. I found this hypocritical. I've cheated on people too, you know, Anna, and I think that only an extremely short sighted person who had no sense of smell and whose fingertips had all been burned off with an oxyacetylene lamp could avoid noticing things like, well, *size*. Because, in case you hadn't noticed, people do not have the same *size* in breasts, hips, bottoms, or even that most familiar commodity (to you) 'cocks' (quote) and 'cunts' (quote). Or do you avert your eyes when Derwent Mate gets out his cock? Has he got one? Were you just trying to impress me?

She was doing something for Ezekiel she never did for me.

329

She was having an orgasm. I thought this was nice for her. The erotic pull of witchfinders must be, of course, considerable. Since so many women are only too willing to be thought of as witches – provided there is no appropriate punishment available – it must be that the witchfinder exerts considerable pulling power. 'I get loads of it, mate,' said Ezekiel, sounding, now, a little like Derwent Mate, whom I now observed on the far side of the square, hanging around like an amateur male prostitute. He didn't seem to mind about Anna and Ezekiel. He could take it in his stride. 'Witches, mate,' I could hear him saying to Oliphant, as they repaired to some neighbouring hostelry, 'are suffering from brand definition problems. We need to give the witch a younger, more professional look . . .'

I didn't like the sound of her orgasm. It wasn't the gentle, mewing abandonment of restraint, the little trembling, wounded gasp with which I am so familiar (I always seem to end up with introverts) – it was a jagged yapping noise, a sound that a machine might make if someone had lobbed a spanner into its engine. It started with her shaking herself backwards and forwards furiously and grew in her throat the way metal fatigue might wear down a strut in an aeroplane so that the crack (his hand had almost disappeared up her) widened and widened until the machine would fly apart, tumbling out well-fed passengers into the freezing sky, two miles up. Well-fed businessmen, starched hostesses spewed out like a garland thrown at some visiting dignitary, the human becoming non-human. And now I saw it in her face. She was no longer hard, metallic, assured. The waves of the orgasm were revealing her to me. Behind her head, like the repeated images in a mirror, appeared Young Anna, Middle-Aged Anna, her Dead Mother (a fat woman in a loose dress who was saying, in a nasal voice *Ye-es dear? Ye-es?*), and beyond her, Anna Writing Her Badly Expressed Secret Thoughts in her PRIVATE Journal, Anna Being Facetious with a College Friend, and beyond that, worst of all, inexpressibly horrible, Anna with Three Screaming Kids *and* her mother (who seemed to have come back to life and acquired a small, foxy-looking man who kept extending his hand to me and saying *Pleased ter meecha Pleased ter meecha*), and beyond *her* was something called the Real Anna. It was hard to

330

see at this distance, since it was the image furthest away from me, but as she started to come, it travelled up the endless line of images, gathering speed, like a cable car out of control. At first no more than a blob, an indistinct mass (at heart we are all formless, shapeless), as it gathered speed it swallowed light from the images that lay between it and me, and as her 'Oh Oh Oh' rose up the scale, whining like a siren until she was barking and screaming, distorted with the pleasure of surrender, and as the 'Oh Oh Oh' became 'Yes Yes Yes' or 'More More More' or 'Go on Go on Go on', I saw that, opposite us, Derwent Mate had joined in the dance and was rocking backwards and forwards against the lamp post, rubbing himself off like a dog, and worst of all, Anna's face was changing and setting. And it was not her face. It was a face I knew but it was not her face. It was my wife's face. She was white and thin and still, and as she watched me, two huge tears, like stones, began the journey down her cheeks. She held out two hands towards me, hands stained with hot water and dirt and time and I thought about the night Thomasina was born and she chanted the same rhyme over and over again and I thought about the night Emma went in for her operation and the two of us paced up and down the corridor ourside the ward, while a Greek vegetable chef stood guard over his child (who was dying) and I wanted to say something, anything, to stop her crying. Something along the lines of 'If I fancy it with Anna'. That seemed to me a calming, sensible thing to say. And, as I thought this, everyone in the square, Ezekiel, Anna, Derwent, myself, and indeed the dog, began capering around repeating the line as if they were the chorus in a Gilbert and Sullivan opera. 'If I fancy it with Anna' I began, and they picked it up: 'If he fancies it with Anna.' Until the whole darkened square was alive with figures, singing and waving and shouting 'If I fancy it with A-nna', 'If she fancies it with Der-went.' And then Anna's scream reached its highest note and Meg's face disappeared and Anna was before me, eyes rolling up into her face, face cherry-red, tongue hanging out, a thin stream of spittle dribbling from her mouth. Ezekiel's hand slid out of her crotch.

It was time to leave.

I stepped forward and took Ezekiel's hand. Ghosts can get

you out of anywhere. And, miraculously, there was none of
Anna's juice on it. It was dry and firm, like my father's hand. It
folded round mine comfortingly, lovingly, and began to lead
me away from the square. As I was walking with a ghost, I had
a ghost's power of leaping, defying gravity, as if I was on the
moon. And Ezekiel started to take great moon-leaps, six to
eight feet in the air, up up up and downward in a curve,
twenty yards further across the square. We cleared the railings
in the middle of the square, landed on the soft grass, and,
when I looked up at him (he had grown huge) I saw that, as
well as having my father's hands, he had his face. He had a
round, red, serious face, horn-rimmed glasses and a wild-
looking tangle of white hair. I remembered how, after he died,
I looked at old men on buses or trains, saw their extraordinary
similarity to him (once I saw an old boy with his glasses, his
hair and his complexion – all he lacked was his expression) and
proceeded, from hatred and jealousy of them (why should they
have life when he had not?) to a kind of love, a mad urge to
rush up and embrace them.

But this was my father as he was in life. He had the same low
serious voice, the same trick of peering over his glasses at you.
He was wearing his black cassock, I saw, which flared up
around him as he rose in the air for another leap, which took the
two of us up up up and on to the roof of one of the neighbouring
houses. From the roof we looked back down at the square,
which was now crowded with people. People I knew, some of
them, and strangers. There was Alan Francis, who went to Chile
in the early seventies and was arrested by Pinochet's police. He
carried a rifle on his shoulders and wore a green combat jacket.
Nat Gottlieb was there, pulling at his hair, and even from this
distance I could hear him mutter 'Frankly . . .' and 'I have to say
that . . .'. There were the Tomlinsons, the Carters, Suzie's dad,
Thomasina's friend from school, Dr Freischutz from the University of Vienna, old Dave Clifford who never married for some
reason and Jools who we never kept up with and the Dawn-
Addamses and the Hitchcocks and the Martins and Anna Beryl
who was Ruby's daughter and all of them were singing, in five
part harmony 'If I fancy it with A-nna!' and 'If she fancies it with
Der-went!'

332

'Pay no attention to them, boy,' said my father, and added with great relish, 'they are a *load of old rope.*'

'*Where to daddy?*' I asked. It was nice calling him daddy. It was the sort of intimate name, I felt, that suited the dead. And he, tolerant old bastard that he was, went along with the game and started to sing the way he used to sing when taking me along that road near the cottage 'Hold my hand, I'm a stranger in paradise.' And I laughed, because I thought he was funny, and he *was* funny let me tell you, and the two of us stepped off into space and flew up above the housetops, hand in hand. 'We'll go,' he said in a throaty voice, 'to Wolverhampton.'

Wolverhampton was where he was born. I wanted to tell him that he wouldn't recognize it, that it was all changed: the grammar school was no longer a grammar school, the town was scarred with one way systems and NCP car parks and McDonalds hamburger stores; that Wolverhampton wasn't Wolverhampton any more, that England wasn't England. But I didn't tell him any of these things. The dead should be treated with great tact. I held tightly as we wheeled above Euston, below us the line of yellow sodium lamps that marked the Euston Road, over to our right the silver and black of the Thames and up to the left, cluster after cluster of dark, compact buildings, Camden Town, Kentish Town, Highgate, Finchley, Barnet, Potters Bar, Willesden, Neasden, Kilburn, Enfield, Tottenham, all glowing dull yellow.

There is no part of England that is dark, I thought as we sailed up higher and, allowing the night wind to catch us, steered south, to follow the line of the Thames. The wind tore at my face. I found that if I thrust out my left leg, and pulled my chest over to the right, I veered to the right, although with almost irritating slowness. It was like trying to control a child's toboggan in thick snow. Air flowed over me and round me like water round a diver, but, paradoxically, I felt heavier, more sluggish. I decided to hold tightly on to my father's hand. He seemed to know what to do. Below us were the lights of the Royal Festival Hall and, to my surprise, he continued to hug the line of the river, moving out west towards Richmond and Putney and Henley and Oxford and – *Dad I don't want to go home yet. I don't want to be nearly forty. I want to go home with you, to your home. Dad I thought you said we were going to Wolverhampton.*

333

'We're not going to Wolverhampton,' he said, 'that was a joke. It wasn't possible for me to go back to Wolverhampton. It was a joke I used to make. I couldn't go back because my parents were dead. And you can't go back to the cottage because I am dead. You must go to your wife and your children. That's what you're on the earth for, boy. To love your wife and children and treat them decently so that when you are dead they will mourn you as you mourn me.'

We were losing height. I didn't want to lose height. I tugged sharply at his hand and pulled us up through the cold, black night. This had the effect of moving us away from the river, and below, only a few hundred feet down, I could see the Wandsworth one-way system, the silver top of a Ford Granada alone in the centre of the four lane highway, ridiculously foreshortened pedestrians, the unkempt roofs of uncared-for Victorian houses at the edge of the main road. Wandsworth. We were too close to home. I didn't want to go home. I wanted to sail on and up through the night, holding my father's hand. I wanted to clear the city and skim over the huge mansions of Virginia Water. I wanted to swoop down on motorways and buzz astonished motorists, then roar off and away. I wanted to loop the loop round railway bridges. I wanted to run somersaults over sleepy market towns and then accelerate off over the dark fields around them. I wanted the two of us to push hard down with our hands and rise to aircraft height, then start our descent, banking over Manchester and gliding down towards the Lake District.

But he was dragging me down. The harder I kicked and pushed down with my hand, the more he, with the grim face I remember, the expression he wore when I tried to break into his desk to get at the unexpurgated copy of *Lady Chatterley's Lover* way back in 1962, bore down on me and forced me back towards Wandsworth, the Putney Bridge Road, then left over the traffic in the High Street and up the Hill, now only twenty yards above the ground.

'I won't, dad,' I said. 'I won't. I'm forty years old. I'll do it my way thanks very much. I'm on my fucking own.' At the sound of the word 'fucking' – a word I often heard him use ('but never in front of your mother, boy') – he started to choke. The dead are never prurient; they want you to use only nice words about

334

them. They want you to bring them flowers and remember their birthdays and pray to them and decorate their graves. They make impossible demands. Demands the living never make. They want you to be romantic with them, too. They pout and simper at you, flirtatiously. They don't want to hear about the time they beat you because you had drawn on your bedroom wall or the time they treated your wife with contempt, or the time they said 'Are you now or have you ever been a member of the Communist Party?' They want it all nice and regular and tasteful.

But I tend his memory not his grave. I tend my picture of him, wild white hair and flushed countenance, and so it is as if he never died but is still with me, even as I write, his deep, quizzical voice extending or withdrawing approval as he thinks fit.

'*Fucking*, dad,' I said, and say now, 'it's just a word. Don't take on. For Christ's sake, dad. You've got to let me be what I want to be.'

But he is falling, falling. Falling and choking the way he choked in the hospital that morning he died. He cannot catch his breath. One hand is held up to me, imploring me to save him, but it is too late. I have kicked strongly up and I am flying high over the river. I look down at him, hear him scream, but do not go to him. I have my own life to lead. He taught me how to fly. *If he didn't want me to fly why did he teach me?* I fly higher and higher and, like Superman, I strike out with my left arm, which takes me back westward and now I see my father hit the deck. He bounces back off the floor with a sick, hideous thud. *Sorry dad. Tough.* And as I rise, full of confidence in myself, I remember, suddenly – there was something I meant to ask him. I couldn't say what it was. It might have been a technical question about flying – what happens in low cloud? How do I land? Will there be any bother from air traffic control at Heathrow? Or it could have been quite a mundane, unimportant point – did you have the car serviced once a month? Or once every three months? Which is the best place to buy shoes in London? Would you advise educating my children at public schools? Is adultery a sin? – I can't remember what it is I wanted to ask him. The fact of the matter is, I didn't get the time to ask, and as a result, I

335

don't know. I don't know what it is, I don't know. All I know is – I don't know it. And this is having a bad effect on my flying. I can't keep a straight course. From out of the darkness a bird comes at me. A big, dark bird. It goes for my face. It should be in its nest, shouldn't it? And what's a bird doing at this height anyway?

But I am losing height. My father cannot tell me how to control it, but I am stalling, losing altitude. The earth is rushing up at me faster and faster and faster, I am going to hit the ground the way he did for Christ's sake not *there*. I can see that I am over my own house. I can see through the roof. I can see Meg and the children at the kitchen table. I can see Juliet in her basement, one leg up on an occasional table, like a country gentleman with the gout. *I don't want to go home.* With a desperate tug I manage to pull both legs out, until they are horizontal, parallel to the ground. For a moment I think I am going to be able to climb again, because the earth is steady now, but as soon as I push off upwards, I curve back towards the earth's surface.

I realize I am headed for a huge sprawl of buildings, like a tennis ball thrown up high by an athlete, at the slow mercy of gravity. I recognize the place. Is it a hotel? A college of some description? Where am I going to land? Somewhere soft please. I hold out my hands in front of me like a diver, and my hands pierce the red tiles of one of the roofs. The building folds over me like putty. For a moment I cannot breathe and than I CAN. It is hot and stuffy and I can hear voices. One of them is Anna's. Another one is Derwent Mate's. What are they doing here? There is a third voice in the room. A stranger. I don't like him. I am being poured into a chair like liquid into a glass and, as my body takes shape around me I see that it is a black plastic utility chair, of the kind you see in hospitals. And the man opposite me, who is a stranger, is not a stranger, but a doctor. A doctor stranger. I have seen, let me tell you, stranger doctors. He smiles at me. I do not smile back. He leans forward across the table and says, quietly, 'Tell me again about this man. What did you call him? Ezekiel? Ezekiel Oliphant? Was that it?' I see Anna and Derwent Mate looking at me. I sit up straight and my eyes glow like a cat's in the dark and I say, 'Master Apothecary. I am most strangely and hideously bewitched by the woman you see before you. Ask me not, either, after Ezekiel, for it is all as one between us now. Seek him and Ye shall find Mee! We are two in One body and Want but my late father to a be a Veritable Trinity.'

I am at peace, at last.

30

'I don't believe a word of it,' said Meg.

We were in the cottage. Outside, the sun had gone behind the hill. A tractor passed us on its way home along the narrow lane.

'For a start,' she said, 'you didn't say anything about that stupid little cow.'

I had not, of course, in my version of events, mentioned Anna. What do you take me for? I think I had probably said things like 'After you left I had a sort of breakdown.' Or perhaps 'I do love you really. I couldn't take you being away from me.' Or even 'After I discovered Oliver Cromwell was a witch, I rather lost perspective on things.' I don't think I said that exactly. Perhaps because Ezekiel was sitting opposite me, and, although my time in the clinic had taught me certain ways of dealing with him, I did not yet feel safe enough to raise the subject of witches in his presence.

I don't think I talked about my relationship with Meg. Not then anyway. The kind of love you feel for someone with whom you have lived, on the whole happily, for nearly twenty years, is not easily or cheaply expressed. It goes beyond flowers and poetry and all the rest of the junk peddled along with that uniquely West European aberration, romantic love. I don't think I could have used the word 'miss' to Meg. When I came in that night, the night the spirits wrecked our house, I didn't 'miss' her. I simply didn't take in her absence.

Ezekiel had rather liked my performance. He winked quite a lot at me, during it. I should have known I was in trouble when Meg turned to him at one point and told him to belt up. Not only that. He *did* belt up. Some witchfinder. He was probably, I thought, a hen-pecked witchfinder. Coming on as a big deal in the local assize, but when he got home putting the kids to bed and moving the broomstick around the floor like he was a fully paid-up member of Men Against Sexism.

I coughed and waited to see how much she knew about Anna.

'Apparently,' she said, 'you went raving bonkers in Dayford Square, up behind Euston there.'

'Did I?' I asked, in a light brittle voice.

'Apparently,' she went on, 'you ran around screaming that Oliver Cromwell was a witch and that you had evidence that many senior members of the Cabinet were, even now, involved in witchcraft.'

'I don't remember that,' I said stiffly. I didn't like the idea that my mental breakdown had a comic aspect. Only other lunatics are comic.

I can remember what I told her. Of course I can. I told her I had gone crazy as a direct result of her leaving me. The shock of seeing the house in disarray, and of losing her, had tipped me over into madness. Quite a credible piece of motivation. If you're dealing with a normal human being. But, as you have probably gathered, normal I am not.

'You took off your clothes,' she said, 'and sang. Apparently. You claimed to be Ezekiel Oliphant the Witchfinder, and you said you had a mission to hunt down all the prostitutes in England. You went on at length about your father. You would think you were the only person in the world whose father died. It's no big deal you know, having a father die.'

'Forasmuch as I, Ezekiel,' said Ezekiel. But that was as far as he got. She rounded on me.

'Just fuck off out of it, can't you?' she said, 'I don't want you round here.'

Ezekiel pouted. 'I don't know how you stand it,' he said, *'and her mother as well!'*

'Quite,' I said.

'You're a saint,' he said, sounding like a TV interviewer. He actually did a quick flick of the head to the left in the manner of such a one, rolled his eyes, and pulled up his knees cosily as if to ask that seemingly impossible thing – a question incapable of producing an interesting answer. Meg turned to me, her face dark with fury. 'Listen,' she said, *'one more word out of you. Just one more word and I will fucking damage you!* You're so *bloody* facetious!'

He nodded a little more but his heart wasn't in it. He stared out of the window, suddenly tired. He looked like a man out of tune with the times. The last witch, his expression seemed to say, was hanged over two hundred years ago. And now look at you all. Feminism. Abortion. Swearing. Repeal of the Married Woman's Property Act. *You should have stuck to your guns. In my day Germaine Greer wouldn't have got as far as her own front door. They have got you on the run, sunshine.*

Meg turned back to me. 'We'll deal with my mother later,' she said.

I didn't like the expression on her face. 'Have you been back to the house?' I asked lightly. Perhaps Juliet was in intensive care. PUTNEY MAN STRANGLES MISTRESS AND ASSAULTS MOTHER-IN-LAW. Not a jury in the land would convict me. Not a male jury anyway.

'You're a bastard,' said Meg, in a tone of voice that suggested that yes, she had been back to the house and that my mother-in-law was still alive, though in some way damaged by my assault on her. How badly damaged? This was the only question. Had someone taken her somewhere else? Or was she still in our basement? Was the only difference now that she was incapable of heavy work? 'You see you say you care about me,' said Meg, 'but I don't believe you. I don't see any evidence of it. You simply say what you think will please the person you are with. Don't you?'

'Why not?' I said. 'It's better than making them miserable, isn't it?'

She drew deeply on her cigarette. I wanted to hear more about what other people thought I had been doing. I was beginning to like this wacky character who took off his clothes and danced about screaming Oliver Cromwell was a witch. I thought he sounded fun. It was a little like hearing about one's exploits when drunk, the appalled fascination as scenes in which you have participated are described to you, and you realize *you have absolutely no recall of them whatsoever*. To be drunk is to live twice, once through yourself and once through other people's account of what you are. The only difficulty being – as I was finding now – how to square the two versions of yourself. This also, as I could gather from Meg's expression, could get to be a problem for one's partner.

340

Was she going to leave me for good? I thought this unlikely. How could she leave a feisty character in his late thirties who ran naked round London squares? This larky and passionate son of a gun? 'Did they take me into hospital that night? After you'd left?'

'Oh no,' said Meg, 'oh no. They took you back to the house, after you'd been to the hospital. You apparently became quite lucid with the doctor. Rick Mason was there.'

'Good old Rick,' I said, 'good old left-wing dependable Rick. The Witchfinder Finder.' Ezekiel joined me in a sneer on this one, but I think it struck both of us as lacking in something. Meg looked across at him briefly and, ducking his head he held up his hands in an appeasing, Gottlieb-like gesture.

'If I had to find a word to describe it all,' said Meg, 'it would be . . . disappointing.'

Ezekiel had lost interest. He stared out at the English countryside with all the passion of a businessman on an InterCity train. The children had gone through from the front room to the ground floor bedroom (my father's room in his last illness) and I looked through to see if they were listening. On the bed, legs crossed, was Thomasina. She looked a weary ten years old, as if in mourning for a love she had not yet encountered. Below her, on the floor, her two younger sisters played complicated games. I thought of closing the door but decided against it. They had had the best seats at most of the scenes from our marriage. They might as well be in on the grand finale. 'I do love you,' I said. Ezekiel looked over at me. He lowered his bottom lip until it hit his chin and raised his shoulders, wearily. He looked decidedly French. I soldiered on. 'What I felt for her never interfered with what I felt for you,' I said. I had the impression that the meeting was going against me. Neither Ezekiel nor Meg were totally convinced by this line. 'I mean,' I said, 'there were times when I doubted it. But now, seeing you now I realize I always did. Love you I mean.'

Ezekiel rolled his eyes. 'Thou hast,' he said, 'fukked up the other one! Hast though not?'

At any moment, I thought, wires will appear out of Ezekiel's ears. *She's making him like this. She's trying to laugh me out of it. She doesn't want me to be significant.* Meg looked at me, her face clenched. Where had she been? What had made this change in her? Everything in her was alive with something. What though? Anger, maybe. 'I don't think,' she said, 'that you have any idea of what love is. Oh once you know, when you sold the pass on what we once believed in – socialism and justice for all the political future of the working class, all of that – I didn't want it to go so easily. But, I thought, I've got *him* and maybe he wants to be an artist. That old thing. To learn to say one true thing. To work and work and work at it until what you write can change the way people think. But that went too, didn't it? You even sold that out for money. Oh you justified it by saying you had to do it for me and the kids and my mother, my God. I never asked you to do that. You did it for yourself. You'd already com-promised the truths you once believed in. That our account of our history matters, say. That the imagination can transform the past and the present into something that can teach and inspire. You'd passed up on all of that. Because there is something soft and rotten in you, something weak. You seek out creeps like Gottlieb and try to please them because you're soft and weak and rotten.'

'You weren't exactly a bundle of laughs,' I said, 'dragging round the house like Lady Macbeth. You only got out of the nightdress when people came for dinner. You looked at me as if someone had covered the surface of the planet in shit and it was my task to shift it for you every day.'

'I was *ill*, Jamie –'

'Well why should I take it from you? Why should I take it and take it and take it. I don't see why I should. You don't need love. You need deficit financing on a large scale. Get someone else to do that for you. Get some big-hearted idiot. Get someone you can puzzle and fool and pull your stunts on. Because you don't fool me *darling*.'

Ezekiel liked this. He folded his arms and nodded his head and looked at her pertly, as if to say 'Follow *that*.' He looked rather like someone at a tennis match, I thought, his eyes now travelling between us: drop shot, volley, half-lob and *oh yes he's done it Jamie Matheson has pulled his talented youngster out from the base line and she really is in trouble now.*

'I knew you had someone else the first time you came back

from the Museum. I knew. I could see it in your face. It's so predictable and drab and disappointing.'

'Is it?' I said. 'Is it wrong to fall in love with someone else? Is that a punishable crime? Is there some by-law that says I can love only you? I haven't heard of it.'

'Love love love,' she said bitterly, 'I keep telling you you have no right to use the word. You think everyone is replaceable. I die, you go out and get a new one. She fucks some other jerk and you run back to me when I show up again. All you need is someone to listen to your fucking awful jokes and your fucking awful stories.'

'How do you know about Derwent? How do you know what happened to me that night? What did happen to me, come to that? Darling –' She shook violently at my use of this word. I glanced across at Ezekiel, who was wincing and shaking his head.

'How dare you talk to me about love,' she said. 'Yes, there's such a thing as love. If it's done beautifully and properly and it is everything, *everything* to the person, then it can be the most important thing. And I loved you like that, Jamie. I did love you. I loved you from the day I saw you drunk on Magdalen Bridge. From the day you put your arms around me in Jake's flat I loved you. But you didn't deserve that kind of love. And it's gone. Gone for ever.'

'How did you find out about Anna? I mean who she is and what she –'

'I told you. When they got you back, Rick Mason was still there in the middle of the cups and the plates and the glasses, and you talked a great deal. You said a lot. You told them all about how Anna was a witch and you were enchanted and how this dog was an agent of Satan and dear old Rick was in league with devil and –'

Things were coming back to me. Rick and I talking in the ruins of our kitchen. Him talking and talking and talking. Rick Mason. Of course. It was Rick who had suggested I needed treatment. Rick who had told Meg. Thanks Rick. There are still people around who think they are right. Even though their method of saving people's soul doesn't necessarily involve burning them alive, they –

'It was,' said Ezekiel, who could see that his boy was on the ropes and needed a little encouragement, 'naught but a Passing Fancie! A between Supper and Bedtime Matter, Mistress. Chide not the Youth for the Natural Heat of His Passions!'

'Casual?' asked Meg, not even deigning to address Ezekiel, 'casual? You are bloody casual, aren't you? With people's feelings you are very casual. Eh? You were obsessed with the bloody woman after a week, were you not? Why? Because you have to make all your emotions dignified and significant and important. You had to justify what was no more than a bunk up. And – wham – you had a passion, while she – poor ignorant confused bitch – had to have a passion as well and now she has failed you in some way, she's denied her passion, and she's a casual thing. Oh Jamie you disgust me. You're so pathetic and predictable and dishonest.'

I decided to talk to Ezekiel. He started to say something helpful to me, along the lines of 'Verily such Women have a Strange Powere over us and Lordshippe is the only Coin in which to Pay Them . . .' but Meg paid him no attention. She went on and on and on, her white, thin face sharp with anger. She told me what a bad person I was, how I had failed her and why she could never respect me and how things had changed, changed utterly. 'This whole business with Oliphant,' she said at one point, 'you have failed to understand. There's a story about Oliphant but it isn't your story. You don't look at *evidence* . . .'

Somewhere in the middle of her monologue (there is nothing more boring than righteous anger, especially when you are the principal cause of it) I broke off and asked Ezekiel to tell me his story. He told me about his father, who had beaten him badly when he was a child, and about his mother, who was a nervous, almost invisible creature, who sounded like my mother. He told me about the Civil War, about Cromwell, about what it was like when they hanged his wife for a witch. He said a great many interesting things, none of which I can remember. Isn't that always the way? You meet people with great secrets or stories to tell, on the days when you're tired or bored or someone else is shouting at you. He was about to tell me something about history, about the secret of history, I remember, but all the time

344

Meg was shouting at me, telling me, now, where she had been since she had left me. She was talking about motorways and late night cafés and tramps and people who had nothing and attacked you and someone called Ella. I didn't understand it. I let all the voices, hers and Ezekiel's and my unsaid answers and defences, wash over me, the way the night air had washed over me the evening we flew over the Thames, and when her voice had dropped to a murmur, and from a murmur to a silence, and she had said something like 'No getting through to *you*' or how sick I was – *'You're still sick. You look sane and you make noises like a human being but you're not really here, are you?'*; then (the silence was, after a while, unbroken) I got up and went through to where the children were.

'Are you and mummy going to separate?' said Thomasina.

'I don't know,' I said.

Emma looked up. 'Is that a real ghost in there?' she asked.

'We can all see it,' I said.

'Do you love mummy?' said Thomasina.

'Love,' I said, 'is like ghosts. Now you see it. Now you don't.'

She looked up at me, miserably. 'Mummy said you didn't love us,' she said, 'just before the poltergeist arrived.'

Gwendoline fixed me with her blue eyes. 'It woth howwid, it threw thingth all wound the houth.'

'If the ghost goes,' said Thomasina, 'will you love mummy again?'

'Maybe,' I said.

She got up and took my hand and the two of us went to the half-open door between us and the front room. Meg had laid her head on her arms on the heavy wooden table. She was sobbing quietly into her leather jacket. Over by the window sat Ezekiel. He looked fat and well-fed and pleased with himself. He looked as if he had just won a good, strong game of tennis.

'Go away,' said Thomasina.

Ezekiel did not answer her. He smiled unpleasantly and looked out at the now shadowy garden. After a while Thomasina let go of my hand and went back to join her sisters. I did not go to Meg.

And then I saw the police car. It drove past the window, stopped a few yards down the lane and reversed back until it was level with our window. The driver looked in at the two of us. At least, if he saw a man in seventeenth-century costume, grinning out at the afternoon, he showed no sign of it. He saw a not very attractive man of nearly forty and a woman bent over a table, crying her heart out. After a pause he got out of the car, and still looking in at the house, folded his arms.

'Meg,' I said, 'I think I may have strangled the stupid bitch.'

31

I did try to strangle Meg once. Not hard. It was a fairly limp effort as far as strangling is concerned. I got my hands round her neck and squeezed a bit, but I lacked the finish of Herbert Lom (I think it was Herbert Lom) in *The Hands of Orlac*, in which he played a concert pianist who had had a hand transplant, the hands, unfortunately, being those of a Monsieur Orlac, a recently-guillotined strangler. As I recall the hands had a habit of wandering off and strangling people while Herbert Lom was trying to get them, without much success, to bash out a piece of Mussorgsky. My hands are the hands of one who hadn't quite the bottle to make a real mental case. They wander off, but can be brought to heel.

And, as I said the words 'I may have strangled the stupid bitch' I knew that I had done no such thing. I might have assaulted her, or hurt her in some way. I might, I had to admit, have done something to warrant the unwelcome attentions of the police. But I hadn't strangled her.

I stayed with the word 'strangle', however. If I couldn't be a writer, or a politician; if I couldn't even be haunted without my wife and children honing in on the ghost and telling him where he had got it wrong; if they were the first in the queue for the possession of the soul of Jamie Matheson – then let them have me. In matters of the heart, first come first served. But I would serve them, not with the Robot Family Man they so clearly wanted, not with daddy or hubby, but with Matheson the Strangler.

'You what?' said Meg.

'I strangled her,' I said, somewhat lamely.

She gave a short, barking laugh. 'Do me a favour,' she said.

Fine. She thought I had no political principles, no talent – she didn't even think I was capable of strangling someone. What the hell was she doing here if that was the case? She could have put all this in a letter, couldn't she? And while we were at it –

suppose she was right? Suppose I did regard women as objects to be used and then discarded? If that were the case – this one was well after time, wasn't she? Was I just hanging around to be insulted?

'Quite,' said Ezekiel.

The policeman was still in the lane. But why – this is the hardest question, this is the million dollar problem – if all this was indeed the case, if I merely used her, needed her simply as a reflection of my male ego, generally treated her as badly as your average witchfinder tended to treat single women of eighty and over, why, when the thought of her leaving me was raised, when a future without her was raised as a serious proposition, did I feel my stomach turn to water? Perhaps she was no longer an individual, but an extension of me (with me, I hasten to add, providing a reciprocal service for her) *I am your wife but think of me as an arm or a leg.*

I am writing this in order to try and answer that question. I still don't know, as I look out at the late October garden, where the fruit trees are hung with paper lanterns and paper cut-outs of ghosts decorate the fence that separates us from the flats between us and the hill, whether I do love her and whether I will stay. Or whether she loves me and she will stay. And in the end, the question is a simple question and requires a simple answer. Yes or No. Live or Die. Stay or Go. It has something to do with the madness of romantic love and something to do with the hard bargains of family life. And yet it isn't as simple as these. Yes or No. Live or Die. Stay or Go. It's to do with the urge towards going and dying and saying no, the urge that takes you away from yessing and living and staying, towards the darkness that's the best thing in the end, the darkness that covers the gardens to the right and the left of us, the darkness that we try, so lamely, to spell away each Hallowe'en.

I'm not against light. I like the sound of newborn babies crying. But imagine the poor bastards who have to live with it all the time. Sometimes I long for the darkness. Sometimes I long for separation and loneliness, the way a soldier might long for peace after a long war. I can't take this struggle with women and children any more. I have a feeling that however creditably I perform, they will win in the end. First into the lifeboats and last into the coffin. Women and children have got it worked out. And worse than that, why should anyone care whether I go or stay, live or die, say yes or say no? It's all one to you, isn't it? People die and get divorced right, left and centre. You can't afford to worry about that. You have the world situation to think about. What's the world situation? I ask. Oh – you say – people dying and getting divorced left, right and centre. People in particular are dull, aren't they? You can always find a reason for disliking them – the way you've found a reason to dislike me. And you do dislike me, don't you? I can sense you do. What do I have to say to make you like me, I wonder?

I could have cast myself as the hero, could I not? I could have been tormented by love, won you over that way. Or I could have seen the funny side, and then you would have seen the funny side too. Jamie Matheson and Friend Share a Joke about Auschwitz. There's a funny side to everything. And a sad side too. And I feel sad tonight, looking out at the garden, remembering how I felt with Meg that afternoon in the cottage, and how it hasn't changed since then. Because this story will end. I will bring it up to date – and what then? It won't be as easy as the old trick: to put myself into the story as lover or poet or decent individual. I won't be able to lie. Because the ending of a story – any story, from the simplest to the most elaborate – is in a simple question, requiring a simple answer. Yes or No. Live or Die. Stay or Go. And the end of a story is its morality and without a moral there is no end to the story.

I made her believe me in the end. Oh I didn't convince her that I had strangled Anna. But I convinced her that I had hurt her in some way, that the policeman standing the summer lane outside, his arms folded, looking in at the house, was after me. I have that gift. I can remember once hiring a car at Liverpool station and convincing myself that it had been built without a reverse gear. I simply could not get the gear lever to any position that would make the car go backwards. And there was no helpful diagram on the knob to help me out of this dilemma. I pulled it and pushed it and waggled it from side to side and finally hailed a passing Liverpudlian. 'This car,' I said, 'has no reverse gear.' He laughed at first. 'Try it,' I said. He discovered that no amount of wrestling or pulling or pushing could make the gear lever make the car go backwards. We were, so to speak, away. After that there was a queue of people who were all unable to make the gear lever what it was supposed to do. Each new Liverpudlian was subjected to the combined wills of about twenty people, for all of whom it was an article of faith that the car was not equipped with a reverse gear. I felt like the founder of a new church. And when, much later, when everyone had gone home, and I shyly gave the lever a twist and a wriggle and it went, without complaint into reverse gear (my God this is the twentieth century – they just don't make cars without reverse gears) I felt, just a little, disappointed.

'What did you do to her?'

'I attacked her,' I said, 'I'm sure that policeman is watching the house.'

She wiped her eyes. 'Don't be ridiculous,' she said, and looked across at him. He looked back.

If you want a criminal you need a policeman. If you want a witch you need a witchfinder. He had that mean and evil look policemen get when they have nothing much to do. He did not look like a man who was enjoying the afternoon. If he was just 'enjoying the afternoon' for God's sake, why was he enjoying it outside our cottage?

'Did you really?'

I could see the scene as I described it. 'I got out of the hospital and took a train to London and went to her flat. She was in, but I checked through the window Derwent Mate was mating around. I waited opposite for about an hour. Sometimes I'd cross the road and look down. I wanted to see if they were fucking. I actually wanted to see what it looked like. They weren't. They were talking.'

The policeman over the road took off his hat and strolled out of vision. A decoy. Clever. I like it.

'Anyway, after about another quarter of an hour, Derwent Mate plodded up the steps and two of them kissed goodbye. It was funny – she kissed him just the way she kissed me – intimate and public at the same time. Well. When she had gone back inside I went down the stairs and knocked at the door. As soon as she answered I grabbed her. I pushed her into the hall and started to hit her. She shouted but there was no danger of anyone hearing. The flat above is empty. There's no one on the street at that time of night. It was about nine I think. She fell to the floor and I just kept on shouting and hitting her and telling her she was a cow and a whore. I don't remember. I was mad, you see, mad. Then – I don't know – she went all soft, sort of gave up. She was breathing OK. She just went horribly quiet. And I remember thinking "Oh my God. I've hurt her. I've hurt her really badly." Then I ran. I ran to the station, and I came here. I don't know how long I've been here. I just wanted somewhere to hide you see.'

Outside the policeman came back into vision. He opened the door of the car and said something to his mate. They would have checked with my home. What would Juliet have told them? Was Juliet capable of speech? Meg was looking at me narrowly.

'You've done something,' she said at last, '*something* stupid.'

The policeman yawned. I was getting more desperate by the minute. 'Can you just take me away from here?'

There was a silence. Outside the policeman scratched his cheek. She got to her feet. 'I was going to ask you to come with me anyway.'

'Why?'

'I have something to show you.'

The two of us went out through the back garden and into the field that backs on to the wood through which I had come earlier that morning. The field was not yet in shadow. Warm blocks of light lay across the unruly grass, here and there marbled by strips of light from the trees. We struck on to the narrow chalky path that brings you back to the lane about thirty yards to the west of the house. Thirty yards away from the police car, I found myself thinking.

There was one other field between us and the lane. I think it belongs to Hammerson but he has so little interest in it that it has become a place to dump things. There's a sink there, on its side, a few rubber tyres, and in the far corner, a pile of petrol cans. The objects seemed shockingly durable among the elderflowers and cow parsley of the field, rusting grimly on, oblivious of the season. What was even more shocking was the thing parked by the gate that leads into the lane.

'Thereth the bwoomthtick,' said Gwendoline, and giggled behind her hand.

It was a gigantic motorcycle and sidecar, of indeterminate age. Gwendoline and Emma rushed to the side car and dived into it head first, like frogs popping into a pond at an unexpected sound. Thomasina looked at me and raised her eyebrows, as if to say 'Kids. What can you do with them?' From the sidecar the two girls took three small helmets and one large one, which they threw at Meg. She fielded it gracefully.

'You have to wear the hatth,' said Gwendoline.

'We done good on a fairground with a snake,' said Emma. Thomasina raised her eyebrows again.

'Where did you get that thing?'

'Standard issue for all witches,' said Meg. 'We have very good contacts in the second-hand car business. There's a spare in the sidecar.' I went over the sidecar and found, on the seat, a black crash helmet, a pair of leather gauntlets and a scarf and some goggles. I put on the goggles, tugged the helmet on to my head and wound the scarf around my face. Perfect disguise.

'You look,' said Meg, grabbing the gauntlets off me, 'like Mr Toad.'

'What do you want to show me?'

'It's a surprise.'

From the way she said this, I did not feel it was liable to be a pleasant one. Juliet, perhaps, transformed into a vegetable. Juliet's *grave* perhaps, in some west London cemetery. New depredations by the poltergeist. A permanent place in Broadmoor, reserved especially for me. I decided not to ask her any more questions, not to attempt to justify my behaviour to her any more. It could not be justified.

The girls were now helmeted, goggled and scarved. The five of us looked like a party of aviators from the First World War. Meg swung one leg over the saddle and the two older girls went to join her. Emma came up to me and took my hand.

'We went to a shed,' she said, 'and we did see a punk man.'

'Good,' I said. And then I saw Ezekiel. I glanced across at Meg, but although she looked once in his direction she did not appear to see him. Perhaps Ezekiel, like most ghosts, is a product of certain emotional and climactic conditions. A cool interior, a certain lack of light, a certain degree of unhappiness, and he appears. Here, out in the late July afternoon, the only person he dared follow was me. I felt, not for the first time, angry at him. Why couldn't he leave me alone? If he hadn't written that damned pamphlet I wouldn't be in this mess, would I? I had, too, the sensation that I would never *really* know who he was or what he represented, that his appearances were some kind of tease, like a desert mirage or a phantom island that looms up out of the mist for the benefit of shipwrecked sailors. 'Piss off!' I shouted at him. Meg, who was busy trying to kick start the bike, paid me no attention. 'You're not coming with us!' I shouted again.

Ezekiel, tall and black-coated in the afternoon sun, bowed gracefully, ironically. I crossed the field towards him. As I got close to him I could see he was sweating. He smelt strongly, a damp, forgotten smell, like the odour that comes off old books in libraries. He smirked at me. There was a bead of sweat on his upper lip. 'I'm going with her,' I said. 'She's got *your* number.' He didn't reply. I raised my hand to hit him and he flinched away like a child. I dropped my hand to my side. Then I put both hands on his chest and shoved hard. My hands didn't encounter misty insubstantiality; he fell back a few paces. But still would not speak. I think I wanted him to say something, to tell me who he was and how he had lived and died. To stop all this mystery-mongering. 'Come on,' I said, 'just fucking tell me. Tell me what happened to you. I've read the pamphlet, I know about the trials, now I want the full story.'

Our past is so intractable. He, usually so forthcoming, so willing to suit my mood, kept his thin lips closed. One claw like hand went to his mouth and wiped it. I pushed him in the chest again. He fell back once more, a startled expression on his face. Over on the bike Meg was hoisting her slim frame up in the air and then, dramatically, down, only to succeed in creating a loud, dry, farting sound from the engine. The girls were watching her, absorbed. I had a sudden vision of her with some chapter of Hell's Angels, drinking the group urine in some lay-by in a Northern town. *What other people do when they go out of the door is a mystery. You better believe it.*

'Come on,' I said, pushing him again, 'who the fuck are you?

What did you do with your life? Tell me and let's go.'

He fell back again, this time collapsing on to the grass. He gasped, winded, and floundered, briefly below me, like a netted fish. Then he looked up. But his lips still did not open. I kicked him hard in the belly. My shoes went into the flesh. It folded over them. I heard him grunt with pain. But still he did not speak. They had made him talk once, I was sure of that. Put the iron boot on him, the one they used on that Scottish wizard in James I's time. Crushed the marrow bone. He talked.

'Listen,' I said, 'just tell me the truth about yourself. Tell me.' And still he did not open his lips. In fact I could see him pressing them, hard, together. I kicked him again and again and again in the the stomach and, though he groaned with each blow, he still spoke no word. I knelt down beside him, grabbed his long, elaborately curled hair and started to bang his head against the ground. There was a flinty stone just to my left. I bounced his skull along the floor and brought it into contact with that. He didn't scream. He made a noise, but not one that involved opening his lips. It was, all the time, this low aching, groan. I banged his head hard against the stone, and when I brought it up I saw there was blood on the black curls. 'Tell me,' I said, 'tell me who you are and what you did. Tell me everything.'

And still he did not reply. Crazy with rage now, I cannoned the back of his head against the flint, screaming at him. But though the patch of blood spread, though at one point his eyes closed and I saw the lower lip loosen slightly, still he did not speak. And then, behind me, I heard a sputtering roar, looked across at Meg, and saw that opposite me was the policeman I had seen earlier. He must have been watching me the whole time I had been wrestling with Ezekiel. I stopped, and let the body fall back on to the grass. The policeman (his car was just behind him, the driver at the wheel) started to say something to me, but I did not wait to hear what it was. 'Meg!' I yelled, 'Meg! Let's go . . .' The bike's engine was alive. I saw her turn her head towards me and ran for the bike. Behind me, Ezekiel got to his feet and came after me. I turned once to him and shouted something about staying where he was but he kept on coming. And the policeman, who had been shouting at me, walked

354

towards the open gate of the field. *He's going to cut us off*, I thought.

I got to the bike and climbed into the sidecar, pulling Emma on to my knee. Meg said something to me over the noise of the engine but I didn't hear, then she flicked a look down the lane and saw the policeman. '*Go!*' I yelled, '*just go!*' '*Yeahhh!*' screamed one of the girls.

But Ezekiel was gaining on us. She was gunning the engine, like a plane waiting for take-off. He was ten yards away, running, not with the easy aerobatics he had used in Dayford Square but the awkward, shambling run of a woman in high heels trying to make a bus.

'*Go-o-o-o!*'

The policeman was moving incredibly slowly. He had started to say something: 'Excuse me sir – is this your.' 'Excuse me sir – is this your.' His mouth opened and shut like a fish's mouth. I found myself amused by the way it moved, as if someone was working it for him. 'Excuse me sir. Is this your.' 'Excuse me sir.' And Meg was going to go. As she let in the clutch, Ezekiel hauled himself on to the back of the bike and stretched two enormously long arms along my two daughters and round Meg's waist. If she felt his touch she gave no sign of it. I wanted to cry out, to tell her he was on board, but she was moving shakily across the grass towards the open gate and the policeman was coming towards us with his mouth open. 'Excuse me sir is this your. Excuse me is this.' We were through the gate and past him before he realized we were not going to stop. Meg tugged the handlebars over to the right and we accelerated down the lane away from the police car. I saw the one who had come after us standing for a moment, mouth wider open than I thought possible, and then I saw him run back to the car – its passenger door was open – and hurl himself into the front seat.

'Give chase.' That was what he would say.

We sped off down the road, our speed rising – twenty, thirty, forty, fifty. And beside me, yellow teeth bared, gulping in the wind, black locks streaming out behind him, sat Ezekiel Oliphant the Witchfinder.

355

32

We bumped, swerved, bounced and rattled ahead of the police car, falling hysterically into bends, droning remorselessly up hills, and sweeping like a great, black bird across the level land that lies to the west of my parents' cottage.

Perhaps, I thought, she has been to some feminist course on dirt-track riding. Hunched over the handlebars, hair whipping out from under her crash helmet, she was like some modern dress Fury, an instrument for effecting the vengeance of her sex. I looked behind. The police car was at least a hundred yards behind us. If I had not committed an offence before, I certainly had now. But Meg, who had not spoken to me since she cleared the field, seemed to be driving for the pleasure of it. 'Let them all come,' her shoulders seemed to say, 'let them send anyone they like after me.' Had she, in her absence, fallen foul of the law? There was a time, I recalled, when we were all supposed to be outlaws. I found I was laughing hysterically. 'They won't have got the number,' I said, 'keep going, keep going.'

She accelerated again. I didn't think the bike could go any faster, or if it did, surely it would take off like a broomstick, and we would circle the fields slowly, bank left and streak up towards wherever witches go. But it did go faster, and it didn't leave the ground. It gobbled at the road greedily, gulped bends, swallowed hump-backed bridges whole, surrendered to a wind it had conjured up itself, flew past fields of rape seed, commercially yellow, lines of poplars, mile after mile of stone wall.

We were on a stretch of road shaped like an inverted switch-back. It dropped steeply to a narrow stone bridge, and then climbed away up the next hill, to the immediate skyline. As we roared down the drop to the bridge, over the brow of the hill, jerkily, its forks and rotary blades shield tremulously out in front of it like some insect's proboscis, came a gigantic yellow combine harvester. Meg continued to accelerate. 'For Christ's sake –'

The police car was somewhere behind us, out of sight.

'Meg for Christ's sake –'

The distance between us was melting. It was as if the two vehicles were in the grip of the same powerful magnetic field. And Meg seemed immobilized by the awfulness of the prospect. She reared up from the crouching position, her mouth open, as if about to voice a complaint of some kind. I had time to notice the raw colour in her cheeks, a thick, dark, clump of summer trees to my right, the sun tipping westerly, to my right, over the hill. I had time to think 'This. Jamie. Is *it*.' and then Meg had swung the handlebars to the left and we were jerking over rough grass.

'Whee!' said Emma, 'whee! 'Citing.'

'Yes,' I said, ''Citing.'

As if on tracks, the bike veered to the right and we were back on the road, the combine harvester behind us. I turned back and saw its vast rear lumbering down the hill. As we reached the next crest, I saw the police car tip over the beginnings of the descent to the bridge. I waited for the alarmingly public noise of metal colliding with metal, but it did not come. As we cleared the next hill all I felt was the wind beating against my face, like something trying to wake the dead.

'Where are we going?'

'You'll see,' called Meg.

She doesn't want me back, I thought. *There's some final proof she wants to make of my essential worthlessness, then we can all say goodnight. Fine.* I held Emma tight, craving the simplicity of children. She looked up at me. 'Where you bin?' she said, suddenly accusing. I nodded towards Ezekiel. 'I've been chasing that man,' I said.

He was holding on to Meg's waist tightly, turning his thin face to the right, his mouth ajar. He seemed to like the way the wind took up his curls and he shook his head as each gust of the breeze took them and spread them out behind him, like fuel shed from an aircraft. His arms had got longer: they seemed almost telescopic. Emma looked at him doubtfully. 'Is he the ghost?' she said.

'Yes,' I said.

'Ghosts,' she said, 'don't go on motorbikes.' And, with one

more doubtful inspection of the figure, she looked back at the road ahead of us settling herself into my lap.

And then Ezekiel started to work his scrawny hands down towards the top of Meg's jeans. He turned to me and allowed his tongue to hang out, the way it had with Anna that time in the square. *She'll push him off*, I thought. *She'll take his clammy hands and tell him where to put them.*

It pleases you to imagine your wives are faithful. They are no such thing. Turn your back and they are their own creatures. As Ezekiel undid the zipper of her jeans, she hoisted her buttocks off the seat, to give him more freedom. I could see that his fingernails, huge, curved like the talons of a bird of prey, were moving with almost ladylike neatness as they peeled away the denim of her jeans, that fell, like the petals of a flower, away from her white hindquarters. And, as he slid his hand in lower, inside her knickers (she was wearing the blue frilly ones she has had since Oxford) she obliged him by working her rump round in circles and then grinding it down on to his fingers. Up and up, then down and round, down and round. Her tongue was hanging out. All the time she worked herself up and down and up and out and down on to him, digging her genitals deeper and deeper in the bunched up claw of his hand while with the left claw he scratched and pinched at the white flesh of her buttocks and upper thighs and now her rump was in the air and her face was forward over the handlebars and her eyes had rolled up into her head and there was that flush on her cheeks and she was away up, oh much faster, faster, faster faster *putting her face first on the floor and renting her petticoats my Lord Ireton entered her from the rear as he was much excited by what? By what Anna? 'By her white arse' said Anna allowing the tip of her tongue to touch her lips and as I looked I saw that Meg's helmet was coming into flower, it was growing long red curls and the curls were Anna's curls and now her face was Anna's face, tanned and prim, lifted up to mine to be kissed.*

Sex between Meg and me went wrong after the children were born. She was tired. I seemed crude to her. I was crude, I suppose, against these tiny, delicate creatures, who sucked and wriggled and mewed and whose skin was so pure, whose eyes so bright. Gradually we stopped touching each other in the old way and somehow, although we often tried, we could not relearn the skills we had once had. They had seemed natural once and now were no longer natural. After that I gave up my teaching job and we moved to Lewes and after we moved to Lewes, the illness started. Perhaps, I thought, it is that we love each other but we can't help each other. Perhaps . . .

But Anna's face was clouding over with black metal. Her hair was black again. Meg was back. And Meg was submitting to Ezekiel, head held back, feet in the stirrups, allowing him to work her up and down and up and out and down and round and round and 'Go on Go on Go on' and 'Don't stop Don't stop' and 'Oh Oh Oh'. And up and down and round and Ezekiel was grinning wolfishly as she came to her orgasm, not with the great, shuddering, appalled sigh I had expected but with the mewing abandonment of Anna, the mild surrender of one who gave a little of herself to everyone. 'If I fancy it with Margaret,' someone was saying, 'If she fancies it with Oli-phant.' And Meg was sobbing with pleasure, but a quiet, almost ladylike cry and then the cry suddenly began to rise up the scale like a whistle, a wild spree up the chromatic scale, and now it was no longer a noise of pleasure but a noise of pain like the cries she had given when Thomasina was born, as her body was ripped in two by the minting of another, or like the cries when she failed to make it, after the babies came *for christ's sake why can't I no no no stop it Jamie they'll burn me they'll burn me Jamie please don't fuck me any more it hurts me please don't Jamie oh my god stop it can't you stop it stop it stop it my god!*

The motorbike had stopped. Meg was climbing off. She was fully clothed. Ezekiel stood, invisible to all but me, meekly by her side. My teeth were chattering.

'Are you OK?'

'No,' I said, 'I'm not OK.'

'No,' said Meg, 'you're not.' She stood by the motorbike.

'Where are we going? How far have we gone?'

We seemed to be on the outskirts of a town. Away to my right were a line of houses, a telephone kiosk and an empty sports field. No people to be seen.

'You just go away, don't you,' she said, 'and when you come back you want us there. Ready and waiting.'

359

'What have you been doing, Meg?'

'Oh,' she said, 'detective work.'

'Yes?'

The sun had gone. My limbs ached. There was no sign of traffic on the road, no players on the sports field. In the front gardens of one of the houses I saw a line hung with washing, but that, apart from us, was the only sign of life I saw.

'I got interested in your Oliphant friend,' she said. 'I wanted to know. I do still have a passion for knowledge. Don't you think that's the most interesting thing? To discover. To make sure your facts are right. To guess, but then to find two independent witnesses to confirm whether the guess is true or false. I'm fascinated by the Civil War. I want to know exactly how it was too.'

I hauled Emma up and climbed out of the sidecar. On the other side of the road beyond the trees I saw tall black railings, beyond which, at the end of about a hundred yards of parkland, was a long, two or three-storey eighteenth-century façade. It had the simplicity of something designed as an almshouse. Only the occasional carved figure suggested a more ambitious, Gothic idea. And yet there was this neatness, this regularity: window, door, window, door, carving, archway, window, door. To the right, one side stretched away, suggesting it was one of those quadrilaterals enclosing a central courtyard, a little like the Naval College at Greenwich. On the lawn that lay between us and the building two men in white coats were measuring the ground. Behind them a group of people in casual clothes, some standing, some on benches, some strolling together, talking, suggested, once again, a college or an official, charitable institution. Only the slack eyes of the one nearest to us told me where we were before I had had time to read the writing on the notice board to the right of the drive that led from formal gateway to formal, prison-like front door.

BRACKTON MENTAL HOSPITAL

PLEASE DRIVE SLOWLY.

Meg grinned. 'Bedlam,' she said. 'That's where we're going.'

She was going to turn me in. Should I run? 'Why?' I said.
She grinned again. 'To see a friend of yours,' she said 'OK?'
I looked down at the children. 'OK,' I said.

When I came to London first I was lodged at Blackfriar's, and after that, moved myself to the Western side of the City, near to Hammersmith, where, hard by the Ferry I found lodging in the howse of one Stevens. Neither did I then carry on my Trade as of old, but took such Tasks as were Offered mee, as holding this one's horse for him or carrying for the landlord of the *Eagle* tavern that was near to mee there. Neither had I anie Companie nor sought it, save for my dogge Gip that was taken from mee when the souldiers took me. For all my Companie was mine owne thoughts, which were that the vialls of the wrath of God would fall upon London & upon all the Cities of the Plain yea in all the places of this *England* that was to mee that most Pestilential of Prisons, having neither concern for LIBERTY or JUSTICE or REASON, cloaking her Vices under the Title of Laws and Great Tradition yea even of Religion which hath been, by all those who have the Ordering of it, most hellishly Abused. So it was I spake to None, but Visited in my Imagination the Scenes of my life & bethought how might I have acted the business Differently, as staied at my Father's after the flesh, synce hee that was to bee my Father (I mean Nehemiah) hath at the End abandoned mee & indeed made most Clear Proof that his Appetites and Concerns bound him to his brother's Familie more than the Path of Reason and Sweetness.

In this Manner I lived above Five Yeares, nor had Care for my Apparel or Chamber but slept beside my Dogge as wee had been two beasts in the Same Stable. And what may it bee, pray, I might have said had anie asked mee, is it Divides Imperious Man from the Beasts? I see not one Grace bestowed on us that is nott seen more Blessedlie in any Horse or Rat or Bird of the Ayre? For how do wee use *Speech* which divides us from the lower creatures, except to lie & cozen? And how do wee sett about to Emploie oure art and skill & Greater Sense but to devise Engines of Destruction & Greater Cruellties than the Savage

361

action of Claw or Mouth? *Yea this is an evill and intemperate Time and the Masters of it bee Evill and Intemperate Men & manie that say they love the Lorde have turned awaie from him – goe Out and cry it in the City that it must Fall.*

It chanced one evening, as I was walking out I saw in the crowd that gathered in the Street above the River a Face I knew. And I asked of some that were there why so manie were Gathered at this place and hee answers mee that *the Protector* rides this waie from Hampton Court to Whitehall. For Master Cromwell lodged then at the place that was his Master's Palace. 'But,' says the Fellow that told mee of this, 'hee Rides through at a great Pace and is most Closely Guarded.' At which another cuts him short, for then Fewe had anie Urge to talk openlie of *Questiouns of State* synce now, a man may ask for Plate of a Tradesman and it is cried abroad hee seek to melt it down for Armoure for the Cavalleers. So they were gone from mee and I would have Turned from that Place synce I love nott to look at the Rotten Wood on the face of Great Ones save that this Face comes toward mee in the Crowd and is calling to mee 'Master Oliphant!' and I knew him for this was that same *Sindercomb* that was late of the Armie, where hee was, I think, an Agitator in Harrison's Regiment. Whom then I liked nott overmuch for hee was of the Sect of Soul Sleepers, that hold upon oure Deathes the Soule does but fall asleep and is Lost to View but still I staied to hear Him. 'Well *Close Mouth*,' says hee, 'what Times in Babylon?' And smiles for I was known in the Armie for a Prayerful and a Sorrowful Creature. 'Not well with the World,' says I, 'as I Take it. But it may never bee Good Times in England while some Men have Governaunce over Others.' For I cared nott who heard mee. And Sindercomb looks this waie and that and puts his arm about mee and says 'Well *Close mouth*. If wee needs talk come with mee to where I lodge.' Which was I loath to do.

But at that moment comes the Protector's trayne of Horse by us that rode through London as it had been some Field of Warre in *Spain* or in the *Netherlands* & as I looked upon those Steel Helms and Swords held up and stern Visages that stared down on the Citizenry as if each and every one of us were like to Rise up agaynst them I remembered the Warres wee had fought that

362

were for Libertie and Freedom in Respect of Religion and the Right of each of us to have a Voyce as wee had had – or supposed ourselves to do so – in the Councils of the Godliest Armie that ever England saw. For then, were wee nott Englishmen that cast aside our Chaynes and *walked i'the light most gloriously lifting up our eies to the Lord and saying YE HAVE DELIVERED US OF OUR TORMENTORS AND GIVEN US BACK THE LAND THAT WAS OURES.* And what are wee now but Slaves to another Governor and it will be ever thus in England while we stand nott upon oure Rights and Separate Worths.

And so I went with him, for hee had taken Lodgings hard by there. Which when wee were safe within I noted were above the Road upon which the Lord Protector was. 'Aye,' says hee, 'I have taken the Chamber for the Express Purpose of having *Oliver* in my sights.' And hee then tells mee hee purposed to create an Infernall Engine that would Rain Balls upon the Souldiers as they passed and that, these last Yeares hee has thought of Nothing but how to Destroy *the Architect of all oure Present Miseries and Afflictions.* And hee tells mee of Divers Rash and Scarcely Considered Schemes hee has in hand for the *Execution* of this Traytour, who, says hee, hath Murdered so manie that *his Killing is No Murder.* But I knew nott whether to laugh or Cry at the Plans that hee Proposed, among them that wee should strew *Fireworks* in at the Protector's Chamber in Whitehall, or that wee should Dress his Meat with Poyson or Change his Horse for one hee could Assure mee, would *throw our Chiefest Evill & trample him to Death.* And, as hee tells mee of these Stratagems, Sindercomb laughs high, like a Woman and his eie as Bright as if hee had taken Wine, though hee had taken None. At which I had fears his Mind may bee Gone, but yet, seeing the condition of the Kingdome, could nott but feel myself to Applaud his Bravery, while having doubts as to the Substance of the Actions hee had planned. Who, indeed, could say this Sindercomb was Mad – synce the Kingdome is now so clearly Maintained and Conducted on such a Plan as would make the Brain sick to gibber and Smile their Approval of it? Where's MADNESSE nowadaies but in High Places? Synce Wit or Reason now may be said to Reside onlie in Those who have *turned their face awaie from the World that is come in upon Us.*

363

But I talked with him that Daie above two houres and when I went agayn unto my Chambere reflected this was the First Encounter I had had synce coming into the Citie where I had talked of my Concernes to anie, synce when I was with him I had said something of the matter that had passed at NORTH-AMPTON &, since hee discoursed freely & generouslie of the Nature and First Principles of the World, whether of Sensation or of Political Ordinance, I had imparted to him something of my conviction of the waies in which the Evill One goes about his Workes here in oure land of England, of how hee hath crept into Church and Altar and into Leet Court and Justices' chamber, into Parliamentary Office and Regiment at Armes. Of how hee hath dressed himself in the Guise of Prophet and Priest and said unto the Wicked *Thou art vertuous* and unto the Wise and True Man *Thou lyest like a Traytour*. Of how hee hath penetrated to the highest and most Sacred Offices of the Kingdom & laughed to see the Meek and the Gentle suffer the scorpion Torments of Cart Lashing, of Pillory and Gallowes. *Yea are wee nott all most Strangely Bewitched by this oure Rebellion? And the Sorcerie that was wrought upon us was all that when wee thought wee saw the Armie of the Kingdome of God wee saw another Matter altogether. All all is utterly changed and where there were Flowers are now but Stinking Weeds and even on the Faces of the Children are TEARS AS BIG AS Millstones. O Witchcraft that hath unmanned us and taken us from the Waie of the Lord! O Devillish Work wrought in the Lord's name! I do mourn the daie agayn and agayn when they took my Margaret from mee and when I went from my Father after the flesh and thought to rise above the Flesh which I could nott do and yet was compelled to try it. For in these Daies wee see nott the Spirit through the Flesh but talk of the Soul when wee mean naught but the Stinking Meat of Us and our oure Carcasses when wee would mean the best and most Spirituall Fragment of Oure natures. The times make us to mistake things as they are and as yett wee have nott seen them yea wee have nott looked each other in the face nott brother to brother or Father to Sonne or Husband to Wife or Friend to Friend and I have seen nothing in this my Life but Shadowes and Pretences and onlie now I face my Death do I see Plain how I have been most Cruelly Deceived & I pray for the gift of Love that may transform all yea even those that were close to mee and that I took for Devills and who were no Devills my Father and my Wife whose*

*Sinnes and Weak Confusions I do now take upon myself. For how, saith
the Lord, shall ye know your neighbour unless ye take his Hande? And
how honour they Father unless ye Remayn within his House and seek
Understanding of Him?*

So in the Daies that followed, I and this *Sindercomb* talked
often, though hee would never meet mee at the same Place
twice or Permit mee into his Lodging, synce, says hee, the
Protector's Spies are Everywhere. And hee told mee of how hee
had Fared after the Levelling Rebellion agaynst the lords of the
Armie in favour of the Agreement, when hee was took prisoner
at *Burford* and would most certayn have been shot with the other
corporalls that were taken then save that, the Night before the
Executioun hee has made his escape to Scotland where hee
joyned the Armie of the Commonwealth. But there, too, says
hee, *the Great Lordes do play being Kinges and hew down anie that will
speak their Truth to them.* And from there hee was cashiered by
Generall Monk and soe comes to London where hee has made
common Cause with Sexby, that was with us that daie at
PUTNEY. Who, says hee, is in commerce with King Charles
Abroad and may have by him, the Chance to Prosecute Designs
agaynst Cromwell. 'But I,' says hee, 'will wait no longer than
this winter when the GENERALLE (for so he often styled him)
will reside at Whitehall.'

If I am Honest, when I survey how I have purposed to live, I
could Accuse myselfe, above all else, of this. That, being Solitary, of a Quiet, Studious and Godlie Disposition and much
possessed by the Cruelties and Injustices of the World, I sought,
not to go forth and Struggle agaynst the Evill One, where I
found him, but staied my Hand and looked for a Quiet Waie to
the Lord as the *Cooperites* do teach it. And yea verily *there is no
Quiet or Safe Waie to the Lord. His Path is Hard and asks very much
Sacrifice of Us neither can ye say unto oure Father in Heaven 'Lord
Lord I am nott of the World.' For hath nott hee created thee Flesh and
Spirit, Spirit and Flesh and If ye would make a true pilgrimage here
belowe ye must go outt to Fight the Devill where ye find him, in Church
and Home and court. For lest ye do I say unto you hee will come for thee
and find thee out. This Night or the Nexte ye shall hear his Footstep on
the Stair and Sweat and Weep at the Sound of his coming as hee hath*

come for otheres that were sinners and Afrayd to do him battle.

Which as it fell out was my Case at the last. Synce Master Sindercomb, of whose Conspiracie I would nott bee a part, has taken above a Hundred Men and in the Winter of last Yeare gone up to Whitehall with a basket of fireworkes enough to Burn through stones and this Baskett is discovered. And in the Month of February MASTER Sindercomb proceeded agaynst in the High Court and condemned for Treason – though it was said his Sister gave him poyson the Night before hee was due to Die. And I have no brother and sister nor anie Wife nor Father nor anie that will deliver mee from the Torment that is prepared for mee.

If I have a purpose now it is but to tell the Unknowing World that shall come after mee, the Secret and villaynous waie agaynst which I and otheres that were privy to MASTER Sindercomb's proceedings have been dealt withal. For now, I am assured, from what was told to mee in my Confinement that the PROTECTOR'S spies knew the names of all that had had anie Commerce with Master Sindercomb, and I have seen how they were Proceeded agaynst. Some, of whom Sindercomb spoke to mee, Masters Everard, Willes and Capstick, are taken from their beds and murdered. Others, Masters Ashe and Allen and Lasckley, hanged as common criminals – but I they went agaynst more openlie, synce then it was too late when I KNEW THE Noose was all but about my Neck, I went unto this People and proclaimed what was done abroad and proclaimed the Kingdom of God clearly. Which when I was preaching near to St *Pancras* and the Howse of Sir William Devenish, was I taken by the soldiers and the Charges of Sorcery brought agaynst mee. For then I had left my lodging at Hammersmith and walked the Roads, none but my Dogge to accompanie mee, and PREACHED AND SPAKE THE Truth to all who would listen that this England is become a Prison and that Repentance must bee soon upon us and that the Devill walks and is at His Ease in High Places.

O so Corrupt and Abominable are the Times that they found some Few near there who would testify agaynst mee, One saying I HAD Bewitched her Daughter, another saying that her father had been Sick synce my coming in to that place. And though I was nott proceeded agaynst in the high Court they found *Treason enough in the Matter*. I was taken from St Pancras to the Tower and from the Tower – when they were prepared, here to St PANCRAS, WHERE THEY FOUND Witnesses enough to Cloak their Intent. Listen O listen anie who may come after – how I am proceeded agaynst. There will bee those who say I am Guilty as Charged, and those who will not Credit how Devious and Subtle are the waies of Satan when hee bee in Office. Those who say that what I Preached was but an Emptie sound to this People, that my taking by the soldiers was Meerly that I breached the Peace. But until the Circumstances of my Life bee made plaine I think none MAY Honestlie Judge of it. For how can the history of this PEOPLE and of the Late Warres bee written unless the Poorest that is among us bee allowed his voyce and Heard in the Land so that all may Judge what be Truth and what False and Perjured Testimonie in which I trust the Lord God to Assist mee for *the Lord is my Rock and my Deliverer; my God my strength in whom I trust; my buckler and the horn of my salvation and my high Tower. I will call upon the Lord who is worthy to bee praysed: so shall I bee saved from mine enemies. The sorrowes of Death compassed mee and the Floods of Ungodlie Men made mee afrayd but the Lord liveth and blessed bee my Rock for hee shall avenge mee and subdue the People under mee and give mee the Necks of mine enemies; that I might destroy them that hate mee. For now I see that to bow meeklie and to keep Plain Counsell and to Trust in Love without wee go out to do Battle for the Lord this will avail us Nothing. And so I make my Final Prayer to God.*

33

Bedlam these days is very quiet. The walls are brown or cream, there are receptionists and telephones, and the central heating is kept up high. There are windows and the windows are not always barred. Sometimes a nurse or a cleaner hurries past, and in the wards the old and the young, the sick and the mended, wait patiently for the next meal. The electric lights stay on in the wards and the corridors, in case you should suspect that, behind the smart modern lettering that tells you the way to Nightingale Ward or the Biopsy Department there are older inscriptions carved on the earlier walls, now shrouded with twentieth-century plaster, hopeless graffiti from the days when the lunatics were dragged screaming from hot bath to strait-jacket, and when doctors were cruel men in black coats and top hats, who bled their victims without mercy and broke off dry-as-dust lectures to consult huge, silver fob watches.

Nobody is screaming. Nobody is howling, or if they are howling they have been put somewhere out of sight. No one is possessed. The patients sit and wait for drugs, and count imaginary rosaries. We, the observers, dare not even show pity or wonder at them. That might wake up the now drugged spirits, set them, teeth chattering, tongues lolling, eyes rolling, to act in grim concert, as prisoners in Death Row are supposed to do when one of their number takes his last walk along the corridor to the chair or the gallows or the guillotine.

'Who,' I asked, 'is this friend of mine?'

'He's called Ronald Oliphant,' said Meg. And went ahead of me into the hospital.

Ronald was in a private room off Pasteur Ward. Pasteur was the other side of Bracksfield Ward, and to get there you had to pass along the corridor that gave you a view into Lister, Fleming and Cavell Wards. I looked though an open door at an old woman, mumbling to herself. She was wearing a red shawl, but her dress was open at the front, displaying one of her wrinkled breasts. She was arguing with somebody: '. . . oh no you don't I say you couldn't you knew you couldn't I don't know why she said that I told her . . .'

This wasn't like the place I had stayed. Or was it simply that I was getting better? Ezekiel walked some yards behind us, peering into each ward with schoolboy fascination. I saw the old lady look up and meet his eye. She saw him at once and gave him a ragged smiled. By way of answer he fluttered his fingers at her.

A plump, boyish man stood in the doorway of the next ward. A nurse passed him, tapped him on the shoulder, and, like a mechanical toy, he started to walk. An ugly girl in a blue dress whose hair seemed to have been cut at with a jagged-edged knife, walked up to us and started to say something. Her words were indistinguishable each from the other, a mere mouthful of noise – and her eyes squinted more than one way, at nothing. Being crazy does things to your body. The people here were too fat, too thin, too short, too tall. They were caught somewhere between childhood and extreme old age. Hands grasped knitting needles or tea cups as if the objects had been placed there by sculptors anxious for the figures to acquire realism. Hands were nothing to do with faces and faces stared at legs as if they had never seen them before. On one bed a man examined a row of playing cards, but too closely. Outside I could see the summer day. Meg marched on, yards ahead of me, the children clustering round her.

'How did you find out about Ron Oliphant?'

'Rick and I visited him here.'

'Why are you taking me to see him?'

'For a history lesson.'

Behind me, Ezekiel had caught some of the spirit of the place. In his full Puritan drag, full beard, wide topped boots of elegant cut, curls once more glossy, eyes alive with internal glee, he provided a welcome diversion for the patients. He bowed to them as we went past, and though some looked only briefly and then away, as if in horror, many smiled back and clapped their hands in pleasure. I could hear him muttering to himself.

'. . . I am confounding, plaguing, tormenting, nice, demure, barren Micah, with David's Unseemly Carriage, by skipping, leaping, dancing like one of the fools, Vile Base Fellowes, shamelessly basely and uncovered before Handmaids. It's a Joy to Nehemiah to come in, like a madman and pluck Folk's hair of their heads and Curse "Know I am a Madman", "Know . . ." '

They liked this. A fat man started to clap. He placed one palm next to another palm, held his hands together for a while, then drew them slowly apart, as if they had been gummed together. An elderly woman smiled, showing that she had no teeth, and then scratched herself in the crotch. We were going through the double doors that led into Pasteur. In Pasteur people seemed crazier than in Lister or Fleming or Nightingale. Not so many of them were in bed. They clung to the sides of the walls, and when they saw Ezekiel thay shuffled over to him, tried to touch his clothes. As we went through the doors at the other end of the ward, I looked back and saw that the witchfinder had climbed up on to a table and was declaiming to the company: '. . . . if Madnesse be at the Heart of every Man, then come let us be Mad together. Is this not the Island of Great Bedlam?'

Meg came back to me. 'Stop staring,' she said, 'it's rude.'

The patients were well away. They mopped and mowed as Ezekiel talked. They laughed and clapped their hands. And I went on with Meg to the small private room at the end of the next corridor. Oliphant, in pyjamas, was sitting up in bed, in front of him a pile of books and papers. He started when he saw me. There was a nurse at the door, who seemed to know Meg.

'How is he today?' said Meg.

'The same,' said the nurse.

Oliphant simpered at Meg. 'Better for seeing my pretty daughter,' he said. 'Pretty daughter pretty daughter. Pretty daughter.' He glared at me. 'I've done your family tree,' he said.

'Thanks,' I said.

'Your father was a vicar.'

'I know.'

Ron started to sort through the papers. He had lost weight. There was still the same white stubble on his chin but the pouchy cheeks were now loose, the fingers shaky and thin. The girls went to the far corner and sat on the floor. They seemed perfectly at home here. 'And his father was a schoolmaster,' Ron went on, 'and so was his father and beyond that they were

370

all Men of God har har har. It's true. All fucking curates. With the odd yeoman thrown in for good measure. There was Alan Matheson, who had the living of Marle atte Stratford, there was Thomas Matheson the 'Drunken Rector of East Hoathly', who wrote *Rare Birds of the West Sussex Coast* har har har all vicars all of them, all good solid Church of England men right the way back to the Civil War, that's how far they go.'

I didn't want to know any more about my family, suddenly. I thought of Meg and me, and the family we had made. What was the point of it? I had no way of knowing whether Thomasina and the others would grow up useful or good or brave or clever. I seemed to be none of these things. Wasn't it all just vanity, this family business? – the manufacture of images of oneself? The primal, criminal cell. Mummy and daddy and the children. When the politics had gone and the search for truth in art had gone I was left with the Family Virtues. But suppose they too were empty of promise? Suddenly my ancestors and my children were falling away from me, like unwanted ghosts. They were part of the England I had always professed to despise – narrow, safe, cautious. I was part of that. Was the only decent way left to ditch that too, along with the politics trick and the art trick, until there was nothing, no illusion, simply myself, the fact of my heartbeart, the appetites, the unanswerable questions, and then, finally, the loss of hunger or the need to know – the blessed abandonment of this sharp, ugly thing that is me?

'Way way back in the Civil War,' said Ronald, 'your great great great great great great etcetera grandfather was a vicar. A really safe little nice little vicar. He wasn't at *Bray*, though he might as well have been. He was at Essenden in Hertfordshire. He it was, would you like to know, that put up Ezekiel to prosecute his wife, but when the witch business got too dangerous he was out of it. I expect it was him who attended Ezekiel at Whipps Cross, who gave him the last rites is there anything more disgusting than a priest officiating at an execution. The witchfinder is more moral than the smug little bastards who pray for your eternal soul while stabbing you in the back that's what the safe little English had always done that was why we lost the Civil War that was why Cromwell sold out the fucking witch.'

'Sssh,' said Meg.

He lost interest in the papers in front of him. On the floor the girls were playing with their crash helmets. They were baskets and then they were broomsticks and then they were cauldrons. They made bad spells and good spells to make things better and they were bad witches and good witches then the bad witches told the good witches off and the good witches told them not to be naughty because there was the washing up to do and did they want to go to sleep now and have a hug. They did. They were tired were the bad witches. They wanted to go sleepy byes. Ron was sucking his teeth.

'It isn't true that,' he said, 'I made it up.'

'But it could be true, I suppose,' I said.

'Oh yes,' he said, 'anything can be true. There is only what you think. It's like a blank screen and we put these pictures on the screen and look at them and call them love or justice or the past or the present.'

'It's true,' I said, 'that our family have been in the church since way back.'

He grasped my arm. 'There's a psychiatrist here called Adams,' he said. 'He's one of them.'

'Really?'

'There are some of them here,' said Oliphant, 'they like the mad people. They get into the mad people when they're fucking them and then they're witches and they go out and do it to others and fuck them that girl you brought to me she was a witch she went –' here he made a convulsive motion of the thighs – 'in and out and in and out I bet she was a good fuck was she a good fuck the witches like fucking they get on top of you and fuck you dry don't they?' His face, vacant before, expressed tangible misery. Suddenly my phantoms seemed a neurotic, wished-for business. I noticed, once again, how like his long-dead ancestor he was. I looked over my shoulder, for I felt that familiar chill. No Ezekiel. But he would be here. When would he come?

'Did you read my book?' said Ron.

'Yes,' I said.

'It's good isn't it?' he said.

'I –'

He grabbed at my sleeve again. 'I read it at the College and I could see it was true, and if you read *A Cursèd Lie* that explains it and that explains why he was quartered for treason and why else? I believe it I believe it you see it's very very important that you understand it there are so many lies put about it isn't a forgery is it that paper Clarke wrote is it?'

'I can't see how it could be,' I said.

Meg yawned. 'The paper in Worcester College,' she said, 'is a forgery.'

'Oh I *faked* it did I?' said Oliphant. 'I know. People think you are family well you're not. People think his great something was a witchfinder he catches the family madness well I don't I just talk about what I see the Media the Media OLIPHANT INNO-CENT OK. I don't know I saw it I saw it with my own eyes.'

Meg sat next to him on the bed. 'You didn't fake it,' she said, 'Roger Oliphant faked it. In 1831.'

34

'The thing about historical evidence,' said Meg, 'is to find out where it comes from. Most historical theories are constructed on the deliberate suppression of sections of the evidence and, very often, built around the order in which the student approaches his or her sources. You' – she glared at me – 'committed the classic mistake of any bad historian. Instead of evaluating each piece of evidence on its own merits, or bothering to check the internal evidence of each document to see if it was or was not genuine, you allowed youself to build up a blurred picture of the whole. What was your subject? Ezekiel Oliphant. But you never went back and found out, at each stage, if you really knew who he was. The fact of the matter is, we will never know who precisely he was, or why he met his death in the way he did, or why he prosecuted his wife for witchcraft. He's a statistic, the way you or I will be when we're dead. The way millions of Cambodians or Jews are statistics. You're such a little bourgeois, Jamie, in spite of your professed opinions, such a little self-merchant. You look for biography everywhere. Just like poor Ron and poor crazy Roger, you think your family is your history. Well, yours may be. I don't know. I never felt I belonged to a family. I didn't have a *wonderful* mummy and daddy the way you did – although your mother suffered, didn't she – to make it all so *wonderful*. I had an odd, lonely woman who ended up in your wonderful basement being treated like shit by you. Being finally rather badly hurt by you, you little shit.'

Oliphant was wheezing and chuckling and grinning to himself. Shoulders hunched, he swayed this way and that in his chair. From the pile of papers on his bed, Meg produced a file and a heavy looking book. 'Who was Ezekiel Oliphant? Well, what's intriguing about him is that he is a series of unsolved questions. He crops up from time to time but it's very hard to tie the references together to make a coherent picture. He's a kind of paradigm for the hopeless and confused way we look at the

374

past. But I don't think we should make a virtue out of that. I don't believe in the abandonment of reason. Reason is all we've got. By the *very fact* of his insubstantiality, Ezekiel is the perfect subject for an elaborate antiquarian joke. Simple questions. Clarke's shorthand of the Putney Debates, how the hell did Oliphant get hold of it? Answer: don't know. Second question, not as flashy but just as relevant – how did *A Cursèd Lie* come to the *British* Library? I'll tell you. Through something called the Mansell Collection, which was bequeathed to the Museum in the same year that Clarke's papers were gone through by Worcester College. They were catalogued and indexed well before Firth got to them, but a surprisingly long time after Clarke's son had left them to the College. The student who helped in the work of sorting through both collections was Roger Oliphant.'

She was pacing the room, now, like a barrister at a summing up. Ron joined in.

'Roger was a scholar,' he said, 'he wrote a book called *Antiquarian Lore of Cornwall*. I had it but I lost it. Actually' – here he looked up at me – 'he was barking mad.' He giggled. Meg continued.

'Roger, like his ancestor, is a surprisingly well documented man. He crops up in Canon Kimble's memoirs. He's mentioned several times in Watson's *Antiquaries of the Early Nineteenth Century*. Ronald seems to have got hold of the idea that he was a soldier. He wasn't. He published a number of learned articles on out of the way subjects but was most famous for his academic jokes, which earned him the title of Mad Oliphant around Oxford. Here he is in Canon Kimble's memoirs. She passed the heavy book to me. She had opened it at a page thickly marked down one side.

'. . . Oliphant,' I read, 'used to amuse High Table with his often exquisite stories, most of which concerned what he called Forgotten Truths of Our History. One tale, I recall, concerned William the Conqueror's habit of dressing himself as a Saxon girl and visiting the hovel of a woodcutter, Alfred by name, in order to flirt, kiss and chatter with him. Another, greatly enjoyed by myself and Wedges, was his account of the devotion of Oliver Cromwell to witchcraft, an amusing extempore tale which

375

could, and often did, last for an hour at a time. I believe Oliphant even simulated 'evidence' for this jape, remarking to the Reverend Stymes-Beamish that "future ages may prove more credulous than ours".'

I looked up at Meg, miserably. She was standing by the window. Out in the garden, an old man pushed a wheelbarrow across the lawn.

'Oliphant must have found Ezekiel's pamphlet in the Mansell Collection, and been as puzzled by the quote from Sexby as you and Rick were. It sparked off the papers you and your little friend found at Worcester, probably slipped in by Roger when he was cataloguing them. It's a nice little jest, a way of tying up the loose ends of his ancestor's life in an absurd way, and also probably affording the old boy some private carnal satisfaction. I don't suppose he went in for pornography at High Table. It's for people like you, isn't it Jamie? People who live in their head, who don't think or care about others.'

I looked sulkily at her. 'Who was he then? Who was Ezekiel?'

'He was a confidant of GREAT Ones,' said Ron, 'he was a Cornish witch-hunter he was a devil's friend he was ill he was sick he was evil he was . . .' He broke off. Meg took the book from me and turned back into the room. 'That,' she said, 'is the interesting question. The one you never really addressed yourself too. Because you're so wrapped up in yourself. There's no otherness about you. Who was he? Why was he quartered? What was he doing quoting Sexby? All fascinating questions, and incapable of final answer. But there are interesting guesses to be made and they don't involve witchcraft.'

Ron didn't like this. He looked up at her, his face hurt.

'The witch hysteria of the 1640s,' said Meg, 'was not, like the American witch hunt, to do with land. It was a product of the unease of the war, the only time England has actually been invaded since 1066, or suffered any violent social change. Rick and I have gone through a number of contemporary sources but the only other reference we have been able to find seems to suggest that at some stage Oliphant was in the Army. He may well have been an Agitator who went a different way to Sexby, who took even more extreme views than his own companions. And Cromwell was quite paranoid enough by the late 1650s to see conspiracies under every bed, even if the conspirators weren't wearing black hats and flying around on broomsticks. We'll never know *who* he was, Jamie. That's an improper question. All we have is the work. The endless struggle to find out. That should be enough, shouldn't it?'

I felt heavy around the eyes. The endless struggle. Maybe that's it, I thought. Maybe I'm just too tired for any of this. All this treat all your actions as if they were subject to a universal moral law, all this only connect and love thy neighbour as thyself let's go to Moscow rubbish I am just too tired for any of it. Wake me after you've gone to Moscow and said now that the struggle naught availeth, because it avails me absolutely fuck all. Work, that's all she talks about. Our love is work and my work isn't worked enough and when do I get some time off please? I want a short leave of absence from being human. I'll be back. I promise I will. Just give me some time off.

'You think,' she was saying, 'things just fall into your lap. That nothing is quite real anyway. When Rick saw you with that tart in the car –'

'She isn't a tart.'

'Jamie, she is. That's how I know so much about her. Rick knew her. She's well known around the Library. She seems to screw around a lot. A bit of a bicycle really. The Bloomsbury bicycle. She fucked someone he knew. I wonder you haven't got herpes. I don't think it was a great love or anything so don't try and pretend it was. It was a squalid little bit of sex on the side that you are trying to dignify because you're so fucking credulous you'll believe anything my God even that Oliver Cromwell danced naked round a camp fire with a load of witches Jesus she saw you coming didn't she. And now you tell me you strangled her my God it's all so over the top, all you probably did was go back there and blub at her I can believe nothing you say you see –' But she did not get the time to finish her sentence. Ron Oliphant, before either of us could stop him, was on his feet. In his right hand was a knife, and he was plunging it into his belly and shouting something at her. Something about how this was a lie this was all a lie he knew didn't she know he knew, he *knew* he was a historian wasn't he?

377

35

I got hold of his arms from behind. He was not as strong as I had supposed. He fluttered in my arms like a trapped bird. After a few shakes and sobs, he subsided. He looked down at the knife, stupidly nodding his head. 'It's blunt,' he said.

'Yes,' I said, 'it's only a fruit knife.'

Before I could stop him he had turned the blade in on to his stomach again, pushing at the flesh with the rounded tip. It bounced off his belly, feebly.

'I want to cut my stomach open,' he said, 'and reach inside and pull out my intestines. I want to cut myself open and yank out the dirty bits. I want to put my hand up all the way to my heart and squeeze my heart like a sponge and then show it to the crowd. But I can't.'

'Not with a fruit knife you can't,' I said.

'My heart isn't working,' he said, jerking his head round so that he was looking me full in the eyes, 'it's going round but it isn't working. I want to put my hands on it and get it working.' I let him go and he sank back to his chair. 'They cut him open,' he went on, 'that's for real. They cut him open. They did do that. Why did they do that? They actually did that, didn't they?'

'Yes,' said Meg, 'they did.' She was putting the papers into neat rows. From time to time she looked up to see if I was listening. 'They hanged a lot of old women too,' she said 'they cut people open and nowadays they burn them and bomb them and shoot them in cellars.'

He looked up at her like a child that seeks reassurance. 'Isn't there any sense in any of it? Isn't there any sense? There ought to be some sense in some of it.' He was crying. Huge crocodile tears squeezed out of his wide blue stare, ran down his cheeks and on to his grey pyjamas. His face was breaking up into stiff clods of flesh. His right hand shook, and would not stop.

'Sssh,' said Meg.

And she knelt beside him. She put one hand on his knee. He

let his eyes fall to the floor. With her free hand she stroked his wild hair. After a while he stopped shaking and his eyes found hers. 'You're a kind person,' he said, 'you're good.'

'I'm wonderful,' said Meg, 'I'm really really wonderful.' She still did not take away her hand. Outside in the corridor a trolley clattered past.

'I'm the last of the Oliphants,' said Ron. 'There won't be any after me.'

'Sssh,' said Meg.

'There aren't any English people left,' said Ron, 'just Pakis and Niggers and Jews and all of those. We're running out of steam. We haven't any faith. We don't keep faith the way we did. I was OK and then . . .' His voice trailed away. He was sitting quietly when we left, his head to one side, like a bird listening for worms. And outside the bright day had faded and there were shadows across the lawns between the hospital and the road. She did go back, three days later. Like I said – she's a good person and she tries to keep her word. But the last of the Oliphants had died in the night; he was curled up like a baby, the nurse said, and, in his right hand he was clutching a crumpled copy of his family tree.

'Where to now?' I said, when we were outside.

'The police,' she said. 'Give yourself up.' She cupped her hands round her mouth in the form of a megaphone: 'This is The Police, Give Yourself Up.'

'I strangled her,' I said.

She looked at me pityingly. 'How do you think I knew where to find you?' she asked.

'I don't know.'

'Rick found you'd busted out of the hospital. He guessed you'd go to Anna's. He got there about half an hour after you. You broke into the flat, did a lot of shouting, tried to hit her, cried. That's all. No big deal. You said you were going away to the country. I knew it would be the cottage. She was worried about you, your little slag.'

'You don't like me very much do you?'

'Not a lot.'

The children walked ahead of us through the iron gates. No witchcraft, no murder, no love affair, no nothing. With Meg I

379

am nothing. She doesn't want me to be anything. I looked at her sourly as she crossed the road towards the motorcycle. Tragic gestures are for other people, I thought. At least in her mind – they are not for me. She wants me to be a comic cuts Englishman. Perhaps because she feels safe with that. But she turns me into that. The girls had put their helmets on and were prancing, in a circle, in the rough grass at the edge of the road.

'Rick seems to have been keeping tabs on me,' I said. 'Are you and he . . .'

'Oh please don't be more obvious than you have to be.'

'I know you despise me, and I know I'm not an admirable person. But you make me lonely. You make me feel hopeless and confused and lonely. And she gave me comfort. She made me feel OK. You can call her all the names you want. You make it seem as shitty and trivial as you like but the fact remains she made me feel all right.'

She bit her lip. 'Perhaps we should pack it in,' she said after a while.

'Perhaps we should,' I said.

'Perhaps you want her.'

'I don't think so, I wasn't talking about that. I was talking about you and me.'

'I don't think I want it to end,' she said slowly.

'No,' I said, 'me neither.'

'But,' said Meg, 'maybe it has. Like the good times. Maybe that's it.'

'It would be nice to hang on to love,' I said, 'wouldn't it. I mean it's the best thing about us. Growing old together. But if it isn't there.'

'No,' said Meg, thoughtfully, 'if it isn't there.'

I was crying, as suddenly as the old man in the hospital. But they were not easy tears. Great, racking sobs forced out of me as if they were devils cast out by a healer. And I was babbling things, awful, weak, appeasing things, that I knew were too late and said all wrong and not really felt or meant since I was clearly a person who didn't mean anything he said, who didn't add up, and who, like the generation that had briefly buoyed me up was going, going . . . The fact that I knew, finally, that there was nothing, that there never had been anything, that the illusion of love was not for me and never would be, just one more stunt, like the politics stunt or the art stunt, made it at once harder and easier. There was the blessed relief of certainty and not pretending, and the chill we feel in the presence of death. She came up to me and put her arms around me. *All she wants*, I thought, *is to see me cry, to see that I feel. That's all they want. They want to see that you hurt, the way they do. Is this what love is, the capacity for inflicting pain?*

'Oh, Jamie,' she said then, 'I do love you. I love you so much.' And perhaps she was crying too, but my face was in her hair and I was holding her very close to me, the way a parent might hold a child. And yet, even as I held her there, the way I had so often held her at the end of other, less serious quarrels, I felt something slipping away from us, and whether it was simply that we were so much older now and uncomfortably aware of time passing, or whether it was love that was going, gently and quietly, so as not to disturb us, I could not have said.

'And what did the policeman want?' I said.

'God knows,' said Meg, 'what do policemen ever want?'

'Is your mother OK?'

'She'll live.'

We climbed aboard the motor bike and pulled out into the road, following the setting sun. She drove quietly past the hedges and the fields of ripening corn and none of us spoke. *You could say*, I thought, *that there wasn't any love. That I didn't love Anna and never had loved Meg. Or you could say that I had love and betrayed it, or tried to revive it when I felt it slipping away. You could say there was no witchcraft involved in any of this. Or you could say the whole thing was witchcraft from start to finish.* For looking out at the peaceful English landscape, I could not recall how I had learned Anna Stafford had been hanged, how real Ezekiel had or had not been, whether I ever had or ever would love Anna or Meg or any of them. There was only the wind on my face and a few stirred memories and otherwise there was nothing. *I'm an absentee from by body. I am something a few words or stories inhabit for a while and then leave and when they leave me I'm like a statue or a tailor's dummy, an empty suit of clothes, a visitor on his way out. If you can love that, girls, then take it, it's yours for the asking.*

In my arms, Emma went to sleep, her thumb in her mouth.

Her mousy hair fell across her face and I held her as tightly as I had held Meg but asked no questions as to why I held her, or whether there would be a time when I would not or whether that time had yet arrived.

This bee my Prayer. And may all who come after hear it and Profit from it and fly nott in the Face of REASON AND Judgement as I have done but learn to trust in what the Lorde hath vouchsafed to them which is to say their Bodie and their Spirit and their Loved Ones that bee about them. And neither should wee seek after Strange or Fancied Certainties but Rest with that which the Lord hath granted to us that we can see may be Good and Vertuous and Incontestable – as, the Love of Father for Son, or Daughter for Mother or Husband for Wife or Subject for Ruler or governed for Governour. By which I do nott mean that between Parent and Child or King and Subject, there exists an Incontrovertible Contract and that therefore the King may do as hee will with this or that Subject, or that a Wife may so Honour and Love and Obey her Husband as to Ignore her own Safety and Health if hee command her to some Wicked or Foolish Course that be plainlie agaynst God's Law and Pattern. No. I rather seek to say that, given life as wee are, its Cares and Joys and Disappointments, its Light Places and its Shadowes, wee should make it ours to Struggle, each minute to each Daie to Render unto God's the things that are God's of those that are around us. And yea I say unto you that Ceasar hath no Cause to call for any Thing from us, nor are there anie of the Creatures, the Fruits, the flowers, the Grave and Solemn Institutions yea no Part of this land that may belong of Right to the Evill One. All things wee have may bee the Lorde's yett wee must struggle for them. Our Flesh itself, yea the fathers and sisters and daughters of oure Flesh and those with whom wee elect to share the Covenante of the Flesh they too are Sacred to us and wee must do Battle for them as did the Children of the Land of Israel when they were in Bondage in the Land of Egypt and manie said to them *'For there is naught here that is yours. Neither have ye fish nor Flesh nor Living thing that ye may call your own but ye may shift as ye may when wee serve ye.'* If there bee not Struggle for these Things

382

and if all bee Granted, as it was when I was with the Cooperites then Nothing is in Question and in such a world, or might I say, in such a Garden all might go merrily yet.

But wee live nott here Below in anie Garden neither are wee among the Vertuous. Wee are set aboutt with the Wicked and wee dwell in an inhospitable place and if wee think our Peace and Leisure and Proprietie should dropp like Fruit from the Tree of the Garden in the Month of September then wee do but do the Devill's work. And, as I cast back my Thoughts and Cares upon the Passage of my life it is in Labour that I see most my lack. I have nott laboured for the Kingdom where I find myself. I have nott laboured as I should in the Question of my Father and my Family, seeing myself Abused and reckoning that to be all the Question. I have nott laboured in the Matter of my Growing and Learning, except to take upon myself, without thought the Service and Assistance of my Master and so come to no Right-eous conclusion with Him. I did nott Labour either in the Defence of oure Liberties in the late Warres, being brought to the pitch of the Quarrel by Domestic Matters and by Hearth Politics more than a grave and Serious Reflection upon the State of the Kingdom. I laboured nott in Religion neither, thinking I had found mee an Easy waie to the Lord and that by singing in my voice I could recommend myself to Him. Thinking nott how the Devill may snare us who think nott on him and who are his Creatures and who yet know it nott. I laboured nott in the Armie when wee were in Battle agaynst the Enemie nor when wee were in Question of oure separate Futures at Putney. Nor Laboured I – this doth grieve mee most – to anie great effect for those that I had loved and had Concern of namely my Margaret and that Anna Stafford that was burned most cruelly at North-ampton. For – say unto the Lord – *I knew nott Thee and I knew nott thin Adversarie. I did nott see him how hee worked on mee and those that were so close unto mee and whom I would have fain loved. I saw their woe and weeping and it was as if I saw it nott. For Beelzebub hath thrown the foul Dust of Hell into mine eies and cast mee out from Light and Blessedness. And now at the Houre of my Death I travell once agayn the waie that I have taken and I resolve that I must wage a Pious Warre agaynst the Wickednesse with which I was confounded. And so I do resolve to see now my family after the Flesh and my Family after the*

Spirit to be as One. And My Kingdom as I would wish it and as indeed I find it to bee as one and to Fight, not agaynst mine owne self and how I am circumstanced, or for my Greater Vanities but for the Love which hee hath offered us and which in the End must Triumph over all.

And so I do begin my prayer to God.

Unto thee O God do I lift up my soul. O my God I trust in thee: let mee nott bee ashamed, let nott mine enemies TRIUMPH OVER MEE. Yea let none that wait on Thee bee ashamed: let them bee ashamed that transgress without cause. Shew mee thy Waies O Lord; teach mee thy paths. Lead mee in thy Truth & teach mee: for thou art the God of my Salvation; on thee do I wait all the Daie. Remember O Lord thy tender mercies and thy loving kindnesses, for they have been ever of old. O keep my soul and deliver mee: let mee not bee ashamed; for I put my trust in thee. Let integrity and uprightness preserve mee; for I WAIT ON THEE.

Redeem Israel, O God, out of all his troubles.

Yea if I die tomorrow yet but a Space and my Tormentors shall bee delivered up to the Living God and bee answerable unto him for their Transgressions the daie that followes. For wee are here nott Owners and Lordes of that wee seem to have but meer Sojourners, Travellers that look on this or that Hill or Field or Tree and pass on and are no more and yet the Hill, the Tree, the field Remayne and are changed in due season.

I will extol thee O Lord; for thou hast lifted mee up and hast nott made my foes to rejoyce over mee. O Lord my God I cried unto thee and thou hast healed me. What profit is there in my blood, when I go down into the pit? Shall the dust prayse thee? Shall it declare thy Truth? Hear O Lord and have mercy upon mee: Lord be Thou my helper. Thou has turned for mee my Mourning into Dancing; thou hast put off my sackcloth and girded mee with gladness. To the end that my glory may sing prayse to thee and nott bee silent O Lord my God, I will give thanks to thee for Ever.

I think upon McGuire that was quartered in the City these ten Yeares ago, and of how the Lieutenant would have cut him down and of how hee called but Jesus Jesus Jesus for they would have no priest unto him that would have him his prayers all my life I have observed most ceremoniouslie the Formes of Worshippe yea even in their apparent

384

absence I have observed them. *In my Plainness hath been the Decoration of the Howse of the Lord and in my silence hath been much Eloquence for Thee O my God and I ask how I shall call upon my God tomorrow. By what name shall I call upon thee O my God? In whose face shall I seek thee when they put the knife to mee and what Forme and Substance shall my PRAYERS TAKE THEN? Will it be as it was with that one – JESUS JESUS JESUS? Or will another Face look down upon mee where I suffer?*

I hear once agayn the cries shee gave and how Master Morris bade mee hear it and how hee looked upon mee as I stood in the Crowd and I seek Her Face now as surely Tomorrow I will seek it. *I will prayse the Lord at all times his prayse shall bee continuouslie in my Mouth. My soul shall make her boast in the Lord: the humble shall hear thereof and bee glad. O magnify the Lord with mee & let us exalt his name together.* Margaret I ask thee now to pray with mee to bee with mee and that ye may forgive mee my Errour and my Wicked Waies when I have given Thee to the Abominations of those that would bee the godliest and are most Abominated. *Let us seek the Lord and trust hee may hear us and deliver us from all oure Feares and may wee look upon him and bee lightened and nott ashamed. Thus may we, my Meg, wee the poor ones of the Earth, cry, and the Lord may save us out of oure Troubles.*

36

Hallowe'en. It is three months since the summer and nearly a year since I first went into the Museum and there is an armed truce between Meg and myself. The truce is broken from time to time and then, without either of us knowing quite why, hostilities resume. She works and I work and we pass each other like strangers, both frightened to admit what may be happening. Hallowe'en and still ghosts.

She is, of course, writing a book about witchcraft. It will, I imagine, have a feminist slant. There will be pictures of witches and warlocks and accounts of witch trials and it will explain and document, as other books have done, the business of witchcraft. It will be spelled away as Meg's rational mind spelled away Ezekiel and Anna and the poltergeist and me and her mother and every living thing on the planet. Meg is full of explanations these days. About where we went wrong and where we could go right. She has plans and timetables and ideas that will make us feel that way we used to feel. But, of course, she doesn't feel the way she used to feel. She isn't as crazy. Perhaps my withdrawal of love has made her harder, more determined to survive. Perhaps my gift of love was the worst thing I could have done for her, I don't *know*. All I know is that any amount of clear and rational thought won't change the way we feel, however much we want it to. Witchcraft can be explained away but the word, and the thing denoted by the word, remains, as intractable as ever. And love is still love and comes and goes as it chooses. And sometimes it goes, even when neither of you want it to go.

Meg, as I write, comes out into the garden with the three girls. She is wearing a tall black hat, a black cloak, and she is carrying a broomstick. Emma and Thomasina and Gwendoline are in similar attire. In Meg's right hand is a pumpkin and inside the pumpkin I can see a yellow flame, flaring against the crude eyes and mocking mouth, cut into the skin.

I refused to dress up as Dracula. 'I do not,' I told her, 'think that we should celebrate Hallowe'en.' My reasons were, I said, religious; if you don't believe in the devil you should not follow observances designed to cast him out. I used the same argument against our marrying in church.

'I do believe in the devil,' said Meg, 'and I believe in God.' She is becoming more religious. I even found her scurrying off to church once.

She goes to the apple tree and hangs the pumpkin from its branches. The children stand in a half circle behind her. Emma is waving her broomstick crazily. Thomasina leans over her and adjusts her hat, fusses with her cloak. I think the neighbours' children are coming in later. We have been promised four more witches, a Frankenstein, and a werewolf. But the witches are the only certain thing. It seems the little boys are sick. We are the weaker sex. This little boy is sick. And how.

Meg has piled sticks in a heap in the centre of the lawn. As I watch, the door to Juliet's flat opens and Juliet herself emerges. She too is wearing a tall black hat and a cloak, and carrying a broomstick. In her right hand she carries a can of petrol. She is limping, still, from the time I pushed her down the stairs. She sprinkles the petrol over the sticks.

I never did find out where Meg went between February and July. I ask her and sometimes she tells me, but the stories change, the way mine to her have always changed. Sometimes she was staying with friends I never knew she had. Sometimes she and the girls were sleeping rough. Once she was at Greenham, next to the barbed wire, looking out at the silos through the ugly fences, facing the obscene impersonality of phallic America. She was out there somewhere in the world beyond my story, but I will never know what she was doing or how she was changing herself. She is changed. She is stronger, quieter, stranger. And she takes her pleasure now, in sex, as she wants it, grabs me urgently and whispers, 'Come on. Now. Quickly. Quickly.'

I have abandoned the English Civil War. I have left it to the historians, who will never describe it right. I have given up soap opera too. All I write is this – what has happened to me. And when I have finished I will look for other employment. Gottlieb wants to do a series about a man with a pet snake. Gottlieb, like all of us, is a little older, a little more tired. But I admire his spirit. I saw Anna only once. I had been through Bloomsbury for some reason and I went down the street opposite the Museum, where I had made love to her and where Ezekiel had appeared to me streaked in blood.

Perhaps I went that way deliberately. I think I wanted to reassure myself that it had all happened, that her very existence was not a function of my infinite capacity for self delusion. I was half way down the street when she came up out of her flat with Derwent Mate, and before they parted (she crossed the road towards the Museum and he went south, down the street, away from me) she pushed back those red curls and kissed him. She looked like an actress from one those forties movies, where the couple part because they want to do the Decent Thing. I felt a pang as she walked away – neither of them saw me – she seemed lonely and hopeless suddenly. No one, I thought, will ever reach her. I certainly didn't. She'll be lying with some man I suppose, mewing softly, and waiting for the moment and the moment will never come.

I look down into the garden. Juliet has finished preparing the bonfire. From under her cloak she takes a taper and a large box of matches. When she sets the flame to the wood, it leaps up dramatically in the darkened garden and the girls squeal and clap. And now from the street door come yet more witches – three or four girls I do not recognize, in cloaks and hats, faces painted, fingers dark, mouths a wicked red. And the flames go up, up, up into the night. It is the real Oliphant who haunts me in this room, as I write and watch. He and Anna, who is so like a ghost herself, stand at my shoulder. And the real Ezekiel is not the obedient phantom I willed into possession of me, but a more sober, enigmatic figure. He prosecuted his wife, he may have been involved in another witch trial – though that is probably a whim of Roger Oliphant's – and he in his turn, this is certain, was quartered for treason under mysterious circumstances. Why? We'll never know any more than we will know why a century that gave us Newton and Milton and Locke should turn on innocent women in their hundreds.

The most interesting things about history are those we cannot

388

and do not know. It is those I want to explore. I want to hear him but I can't. A paragraph is all I want.

'Yea though wee are here butt a space,' says Ezekiel. He comes in from the landing. He is wearing a stovepipe hat, the breeches and the square white ruff. He fingers his goatee beard and I see once more those thick yellow nails. He does not frighten me. He's simply there – like the bonfire, the lights in the flats opposite, or the nine witches in a ring, firelight on their faces. 'And though our mortalitie vexeth and Amazeth us, yet hath not God . . . hath not God put us . . .' Go on. Go *on*. He is trying to tell me something. But I cannot hear it. What is he trying to tell me? To repent perhaps. To be sorry I turned away from Meg's misery and saw only mine. To be sorry I turned my back on so many of the things in which I and my generation believed. To be sorry I thought I could get by on cleverness. You need more than cleverness. I don't know what he wants to say to me and until I hear his voice perhaps I won't know whether Meg and I are going to make it. I want it to be the way it was before I met Anna. I want it to be like there was only me and Margaret in the world. I want us to be everything to each other. But I know that can never be because of what has happened. History is no ghost. History is an endless litany of hard, unpalatable facts. I'm frightened that there is too much history between us.

The witches below have joined hands and are dancing in a ring about the fire. They are singing something, but from up here I cannot hear the words. Their cloaks fly out behind them. Their faces red, they tumble into one another as they dance, black clothes merging, until it is impossible to tell where one witch ends and another begins. Meg and Juliet are on opposite sides of the circle, calling to each other across the flames, as the scrawled pumpkin face watches them from the tree.

I want to go down and be part of it, but I am afraid there is no place for me in the frame. She cannot forgive me, I cannot forgive myself, neither of us can face the changes implicit in what has happened. *This is the end of love*, I say to myself, and then *please don't let it be the end*. But by what sign will I know? What irrational thing will prompt me to put down my pen and go down and join them, to stand, at first, a little apart from the circle of women and girls, shrieking and screaming through All Hallows Eve? And is there something that, when the circle breaks and the fire dies, will prompt me to go with them as they go out into the dark October streets to frighten strangers? Tell me then, Ezekiel, you who led me astray so cleverly, lead me back to the light can't you? Tell me how to go down to her and join the circle with her and go into the streets with her, and, later, when the witches are no longer witches, but children laid out in innocent sleep, tell me how to take my wife in my arms once more, and love her in my own imperfect way.

Yea though wee are here but a space, and though our mortalitie Vexeth and Amazeth us, yet hath God not put us here to enjoy and Prosper and take unto Ourselves His Fruits and His Sonne and all the blessed bountie of this His Creation. And I call on anie that may come Aftere and chance to read This to have always Naught but love in Your Hearts and to Cherish and Blesse this Earthlie Familie – which the Cooperites were wont to call the Bodie Familie – just as we cherish Our Father in Heaven and Hee that Sitteth at the Right Hande of God the Father. For is not Hatred and Ignorance an Easy Commoditie and Love a very Precious Jewelle, whether it bee of Man and Wife or that of Son for Father, the which I never did enjoy and may bee in some measure the Cause of so manie of my Miseries? Forasmuch as ye will do so for each Other, so wilt Thou be admitted to the Holy Familie of Love, which is everlasting and eternall, and where, before this next day be done I hope to meet once more my Margaret and beg Forgiveness of her for my Sinnes, which I doubt not that shee will grant me. And so I commend my Soule to God and pray for the Fortitude to meet my Death with Honour and Good Heart and that anie who may read this may profitt from my Example and Stray nott from that path of Love which has been written 'Rise up my beloved and come away. For Lo – the winter is past and the rain is over and gone; the flowers appear on the earth; the time of the singing of birds is come, and the voice of the turtle is heard in our land; the fig tree putteth forth her green shoots and the vines with the tender grape give a good smell. Arise, my love, my fair one, and come away.' With which I commend my soule to God his mercie this night of Feb IV in the yeare of our Lord Sixteen Hundred and Fifty-Eight and may Christ have mercie on my Soule. Amen.